A Curse of Blood & Stone

A Curse of Blood & Stone

K.A. TUCKER

ALSO BY K.A. TUCKER

Ten Tiny Breaths

One Tiny Lie

Four Seconds to Lose

Five Ways to Fall

In Her Wake

Burying Water

Becoming Rain

Chasing River

Surviving Ice

He Will Be My Ruin

Until It Fades

Keep Her Safe

The Simple Wild

Be the Girl

Say You Still Love Me

Wild at Heart

The Player Next Door

Forever Wild

A Fate of Wrath & Flame

Running Wild

This book is a work of fiction. Any references to historical events, real people, or real places are used fictitiously. Other names, characters, places, and events are products of the author's imagination, and any resemblance to actual events or places or persons, living or dead, is entirely coincidental.

ISBN 978-1-990105-23-4

ISBN 978-1-990105-22-7 (ebook)

Edited by Jennifer Sommersby

Cover design by Hang Le

Published by K.A. Tucker

Manufactured in the United States of America

To my readers, for following me from Alaska to Islor and everywhere in between.

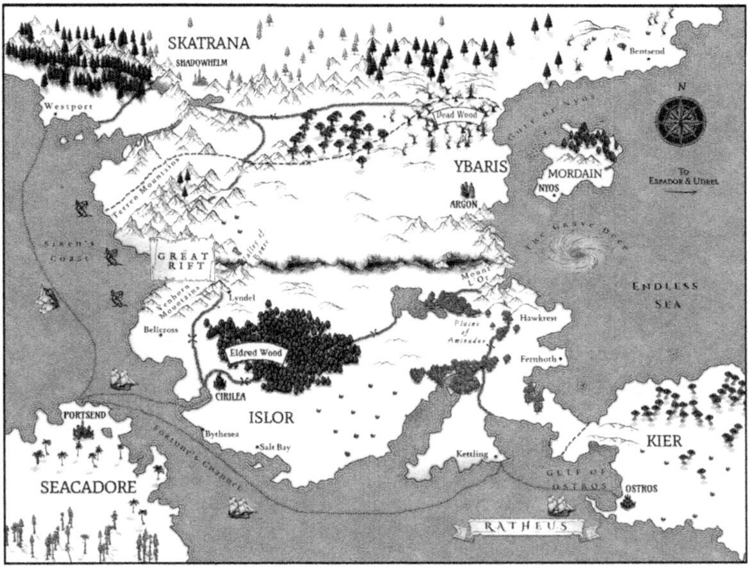
SKATRANA
SHADOWHELM
Westport
Terren Mountains
Siren's Coast
GREAT RIFT
Venhorn Mountains
Lyndel
Bellcross
Eldred Wood
CIRILEA
ISLOR
PORTSEND
Bythesea
Salt Bay
Fortune's Channel
SEACADORE
Dead Wood
YBARIS
ARGON
Gulf of Nyos
MORDAIN
NYOS
Bentsend
N
To Espador & Udrel
Mount L'Or
Hawkrest
Plains of Aminador
Fernhoth
ENDLESS SEA
KIER
Kettling
Gulf of Ostros
OSTROS
RATHEUS

PRONUNCIATIONS:

Romeria—row-mair-ee-a
Romy—row-me
Sofie—so-fee
Elijah—uh-lie-jah
Zander—zan-der
Wendeline—wen-de-line
Annika—an-i-ka
Corrin—kor-in
Elisaf—el-i-saf
Boaz—bow-az
Dagny—dag-knee
Bexley—bex-lee
Saoirse—sur-sha
Kaders—kay-ders
Malachi—ma-la-kai
Aoife—ee-fuh
Aminadav—Ami-na-dav
Vin'nyla—vin-ny-la
Ratheus—ra-tay-us
Islor—I-lor
Ybaris—yi-bar-is
Ybarisan—yi-bar-is-an
Cirilea—sir-il-ee-a
Seacadore—see-ka-dor
Skatrana—ska-tran-a
Kier—key-er
Mordain—mor-day-n
Azo'dem—az-oo-dem
Za'hala—za-ha-la
Caster—kas-ter
daaknar—day-knar
caco claws—kay-ko claws

Zorya—zor-eye-a
Jarek—yar-ek
Bodil—bow-dil
Horik—hor-ik
Sapling—sap-ling
Danthrin—dan-thrin
Ambrose Villier—Am-brose Vil-lier
Eden—ee-dun
Drakon—dray-kon
Brawley—bra-lee
Mika—mee-kuh
Iago—ee-aa-gow
Brynn—brin
Theon Rengard—thee-on ren-gard
Sheyda—shay-da
Ocher—ow-kr
Ianca— I-an-kuh
Ulysede—You-li-seed
Tyree—ty-ree
Oswald—oz-wald
Orme—aw-r-m
Fearghal—fer-gull
Golbikc—goal-bik
Isembert—I-sem-bert
Bregen—bre-gun
Eros—eh-rows

1
ROMERIA

My eyes water from the stench of sewage. If not for the endless adrenaline surging through my veins, I might have already spilled the delectable Seacadorian grapes churning in my stomach.

"I will go first—"

"No." Zander seizes Elisaf by the shoulder, stopping his loyal friend from climbing the ladder. Even in the shadows of the underground tunnel, there's no missing the stiffness in his jaw, the resolution in his stare. "If this is a trap set by Mordain, *I* am the better match for what awaits us."

Because Zander can raze a person to ash where they stand. I've seen it firsthand, as has everyone who witnessed the horrifying spectacle in the arena tonight.

I sneak a glance at Gesine. The high priestess may be bothered by Zander's blatant distrust of her people, but she hides it behind an emotionless mask, offering me a smile when she notices my attention.

I can't bring myself to return it. There won't be any comfort found tonight, not as the four of us slink through Cirilea's culvert system, running from a king's army.

"Wait for my signal and bring up the rear. Romeria, you will follow directly behind me." Zander pauses. Under different circumstances, I might have a quip for his demand, an admiring gaze for his handsome face as he awaits my answer. Now, all I have is a solemn nod.

He ascends the wooden ladder with lithe steps and disappears into the night.

And I hold my breath. Our torch flames cast ominous forms over the jagged stone walls; the foul sludge soaks into the hide of our boots. I wish I could say it's the first time I've crept through a gutter, but years of surviving the streets and then Korsakov's criminal world has exposed me to plenty of predicaments that would draw shudders and nose curls. This smell will trail us long after we've fled. But bodies can be washed, clothes can be replaced. Cleanliness is the least of our worries.

Somewhere unseen, water trickles and waves lap faintly. "Where does this end?" I ask.

"At the seawall." Elisaf's attention is hyperfocused on the exit above. "A grate fortified with merth closes it off to invaders. Nothing short of direct cannon fire or a powerful caster will break through that." His fist clutches a gleaming merth-forged dagger at his side, its blade primed for plunging into flesh. I want to think that flesh won't be mine, but nothing is guaranteed now that my secret is out.

Will there come a point when the nights Zander and I shared, our heads nestled in pillows, our words laced with heady promises, mean nothing? When the fleeing king puts his kingdom and crown before his heart and accepts the ruin a key caster—one with poison flowing through her veins—could bring to Islor is far too great?

Will I see the resolve in those beautiful hazel eyes when he makes that decision?

My chest tightens with the thought of Zander becoming my enemy again. But that needs to be a worry for another day too.

I push out *all* concerns but the most pressing one—is there any hope in hell of me escaping death tonight?

Each second that passes without any sign of Zander swells my dread.

"This must all have been so confusing for you," Gesine says. "From the moment you woke."

"I thought I was losing my mind," I admit. Just like my father had. Only now I know the truth about that too.

A whistle calls.

"Climb." Elisaf nudges me forward, urgency in his lyrical Seacadorian accent.

I don't waste a second, scaling the ladder far less gracefully than Zander, the rungs creaking beneath my weight. I wince against a splinter that slides beneath my skin as I emerge into a pitch-black space.

"Let me help you." Zander's voice is a whisper in my ear.

I can't make out anything, yet I know he can see clearly, and I sense his hand waiting inches from mine, palm up.

This is where we part ways, Romeria Watts of New York City.

His resolute words from earlier are a deafening bell toll. Zander wants to leave me. An army led by his treasonous brother is building a pyre for me, every immortal in Islor will want me dead for the poison in my veins, and the most powerful spell-casters in Mordain will hunt me down should they discover I'm a key caster …

Zander *finally* knows that I do not belong in this world, and he is searching for an excuse to abandon me to it.

I ignore his offer of help, testing the floor with my toes for clear footing before stepping off the ladder. The tunnel is supposed to lead us to the Rookery, but all I sense are walls. I occupy my hands with my cloak, praying for my eyes to adjust.

Zander sighs with resignation. "You are angry with me."

For an elven with the ability to read my mood through my pulse—to catch every jump of fear, every stir of desire, every pull of guilt—he finally has it wrong. I'm not angry. I'm *hurt*. If I allow myself a moment to absorb how much, the ache might swallow me whole.

I'm saved from responding as Gesine and her floating globe ascend from the city's bowels with the poise of a shadow, her inky hair hidden within the hood of her cloak. Elisaf is on her heels, nimbly rushing to ground level.

Between the caster's magical light and Elisaf's torch, I can finally discern the crowded, low-ceilinged room we've climbed into, cluttered with wooden crates and barrels of various sizes. Another dusty storage space that hides Cirilea's secret passageways.

Gesine flicks her wrist, and a stack of crates slides across the gaping hole in the floor, concealing its existence.

Despite our current predicament, my heart skips a beat with excitement, as it does every time I witness real magic in this world.

"A skiff awaits us at the dock. The most discreet path is along the seawall." The light of her globe fades until it vanishes. She gestures toward Elisaf's torch, its firelight glinting off the gold collar that encircles her neck. A reminder that she is still shackled by Queen Neilina, even this far from Ybaris. "There is a metal bucket of water by the door. You must leave that behind."

"This is *my* city, High Priestess, and we don't need *your* guidance on how best to move through it." Zander's voice carries a biting hatred I haven't heard since the days when I was the treacherous princess who murdered his parents.

But Zander's wrong. It's Atticus's city now. Zander practically handed his crown to his opportunistic brother when he ignored the aspirations even I could see.

Tonight, we need *all* the help we can get, including from this caster.

Gesine may be thinking along the same lines, but her expression remains stoic as she dips her head. "Of course, Your Highness."

Zander's stern gaze flickers to Elisaf, who promptly dumps his blazing torch into the bucket. The flame sizzles, throwing the tiny storage room into darkness once again.

With Elisaf's guiding hand on my shoulder, we creep out of the shack single file, Zander leading the way, his footfalls silent against the dirt path. A lean-to cluttered with scrap wood and fishing nets sits directly ahead. Beyond it and to the right are rows of one-story shanties. They're the homes in the Rookery that Zander and I visited on more than one occasion, doling out gold coins to the loitering peasants. No one lingers on the porches now, though, save for a stray cat devouring its kill.

Rhythmic waves lap against rock on my left, the only hint of the yawning expanse of sea beyond. A warm, briny breeze grazes my cheek, and it is a welcome shift from the stench of waste. If this were any other situation, I might feel the urge to sit and absorb the calm those waves carry.

But up the hill, past the stone wall that serves as a barrier between Cirilea's finer class and the humans it deems worthless, steel clangs against steel, drawing a disturbing wave of déjà vu. I've heard those sounds of battle before, upon waking in a strange world where two moons sometimes hang in the sky. That night, Princess Romeria was also at the root of the death and destruction.

Shouts soar in the streets behind us, and my panic surges. Soldiers found us at the apothecary. It's only a matter of time before they follow us here.

"We must not tarry." Gesine's voice is too serene for the situation, but I appreciate it.

"This way." Zander leads us along the narrow passage at the water's edge.

I trail closely, noting every loose stone that tumbles past the retaining wall to plunge into the black waters below, praying that I don't lose my footing and mirror their path.

With the city fair in full swing, people have flocked to Cirilea from every corner of Islor to sell and buy wares at the market and imbibe in the lively nighttime entertainment on Port Street. But it's eerily silent in the Rookery tonight. Not a soul dallies outside the dilapidated walls. No curious faces peek out from behind the grimy glass panes. The streetlights are extinguished, save for the odd lantern, its glimmer timid. Surely, these people recognize the noise of battle from above and want no part of it. Has news of Atticus's treason traveled to these hovels yet? Do these humans care which king governs when Islor's laws keep them chained in a life of servitude?

Some must care, at least. Humans like my seamstress, Dagny, who hoped for change under Zander's rule.

"Tell me, High Priestess, did your all-knowing seers foretell of Islor's king scampering through sewers and along shorelines like a rodent?" Sour humor laces Zander's words.

"Foretelling does not work like that, Your Highness—"

"Then how do they work?"

"It is as I've told you. The end of the blood curse is at the tied hands of—"

"The Ybarisan daughter of Aoife and the Islorian son of Malachi. Yes, I recall. You're speaking in riddles based on hallucinations rooted in madness," he snaps, all semblance of charm gone.

I can't fault Zander for his anger. Too late, he learned how these casters from Mordain have been spinning a web of duplicity so thick, no one can see from one side to the other. While he claims he never trusted Wendeline, I think confirming her treachery has wounded him deeply.

And her list of deceptions keeps growing. She lied about even knowing of Gesine and Ianca, let alone of their arrival in Cirilea. She knew of Ybaris's plot to kill Islor's royal family the night of the wedding, and instead of stopping that tragedy from unfolding, she altered schedules to kill Zander's parents sooner. She misled Zander about the poison, convincing him it was deliquesced merth, an odd metal vine that grows in the mountains and is toxic to immortals. Her hand was literally on the arrow when Margrethe summoned the Fate of Fire to resurrect Princess Romeria's body—unbeknownst to them, with *me* in it.

And this unparalleled key caster power that simmers within

my limbs, subdued by the ring around my finger? Wendeline discovered it the same night I arrived here, unconscious and torn apart by the daaknar. But she hid that vital truth from *everyone,* including me.

Wendeline may be more culpable for Zander's kingdom unraveling than all of Ybaris's scheming royal family put together, and she swears she did it in the best interests of Islor.

Only time will tell.

"That is better left to discussion when we are not scampering through sewers and along shorelines like rodents, do you not agree?" The faintest edge in Gesine's voice—a hairline crack in her otherwise relentless deference to a king—makes me smile. Behind all the curtsies and bows to royal protocol, she has a backbone.

And a purpose for being here that I should be wary of. According to Wendeline, the elemental caster spent years studying prophecy with the scribes. She may claim to be here to guide me, but I'd be an idiot to ignore the probability that I am a tool to serve an agenda, one that likely won't work in my favor.

"As long as you are prepared to answer it with the truth." Zander echoes my thoughts.

"I have no intention of doing otherwise."

I note it's not a promise.

The hollow thud of boat hulls as they buoy over waves tells me we're nearing the dock. I allow myself the tiniest glimmer of relief that we've almost made it to safety.

Zander stops so abruptly that I plow into his rigid body, my hands flying up to his back to brace myself. He may as well be a brick wall, immovable. "Why are there humans at the skiff?"

"They are probably the couple helping us," Gesine answers. "A woman named Cecily and her husband, Arthur. They are kind."

"They are fools. They should have made themselves scarce." His boots land with a dull clunk on a wooden surface. "Watch your step. There's a drop."

A vivid image of stumbling into the sea has me faltering. "I can't see *anything*," I remind him in a hiss. Only silhouettes and shadows.

"Experience tells me you'll refuse my hand, should I offer it."

My anger flares. "Yeah, well, experience tells *me* you'll ditch me the first chance you—"

Strong hands seize my waist, cutting off the acerbic retort. My body tenses, my palms bracing on Zander's biceps for support as he lifts me off my feet and onto the dock.

"Shouldn't I be the distrustful one?" His grip lingers for a moment before he steps back.

Another wave of hurt washes over me.

Everything between us has changed tonight.

"Perhaps we could afford a little light?" he murmurs.

Gesine's globe appears again, a dull sphere floating low to the ground, just bright enough to illuminate the gaps in wood planks.

We rush wordlessly, Zander's pace brisk enough that I'm nearly running. At the end, next to a boat maybe ten feet long, two people with mops of greasy gray hair bow.

"You should not be here. It's too dangerous," Zander says by way of greeting, surveying the nearby boats.

Echoes of "Your Highness" from them prick familiarity. I've heard those voices before. My suspicion is confirmed moments later when the couple stands. It's the woman with the liver-spotted hands and her husband, a man once hobbled by infection. But the cane is gone and when he rushes to unfasten the skiff's last rope from the dock, it's with effortless steps.

Gesine holds out a plump velvet purse for Cecily to collect. "Return to your home and say nothing of this to anyone. Your skiff was stolen while you slept."

"We seen nothin', my lady." Cecily secures the purse inside her tattered cloak before her eyes land on me. She hesitates. "We went to the sanctum like ya told us, Your Highness. Priestess fixed my Arthur up good as new. Well, he's still an old goat, but there be no magic for fixin' that."

"I'm glad to see it." Anguish twinges inside me at the mention of Wendeline. What will she face for her treason to the crown? Does she deserve it? If only I could see her again and demand she explain *why*.

"To the docks!" a soldier bellows, and my fear spikes. The army is closing in.

"We *cannot* delay another second, for all our sakes," Gesine warns, urging, "Go now!" to the couple.

Cecily grabs hold of my hand, squeezing it tightly. "May we see you again, in your *rightful* place on the throne." Collecting a small lantern, the couple huddles together and rushes toward land.

"May I see you again too," I whisper after them. Somewhere beyond the shanties, metal pounds against cobblestone. The soldiers are running.

Elisaf and Zander have already climbed into the skiff and grabbed the oars. I clamber in behind them, my entrance inelegant and noisy. Gesine uses her leg to push us off before she settles near the bow.

My pulse thrums in my throat as Zander and Elisaf propel us into the night with powerful strokes, my attention locked on the dark shoreline, the lanterns offering little light. Beyond, farther up, the castle glows orange, its imposing outline a murky shape against the sky.

"Do you think Abarrane got out?" We left the commander of the Legion and her elite warriors behind to face an entire army.

"She will meet us in Eldred Wood as agreed, or she will die trying," comes Zander's cold response.

"What about Annika?" Tonight's disaster unraveled in a blurred fury, with little time to think of anyone but myself. Elisaf handed me a dagger and told me to run, so I ran, not realizing that Zander's sister was not following.

"Annika will say and do what she needs to survive. Besides, Atticus knows her well enough to know she was blind to this."

But whose side will she be on now? I arrived in this world a sworn enemy to her and lingered in that role for weeks, even after saving her life—twice in one night. But she seemed to be warming to me, finally. Granted, our relationship is still tenuous, but I'd come to see the sharp-tongued princess as something closer to friend than foe.

"Fretting about others will not help our current situation. We will have plenty of time to dwell later," Zander adds, his tone softening.

We've gained maybe fifty feet in the water when metallic forms pour through the cracks and crevices between the buildings, armor glinting against new torchlight.

There's no sign of Cecily or Arthur. I pray they made it to safety.

"Over there! That must be them on the water!" someone shouts.

Zander curses.

My own thoughts repeat it. Damn these Islorians and their superior vision.

"Archers! Ready!" a familiar voice hollers.

"That's Boaz." The captain of the king's guard has yelled at me enough times that I recognize his booming voice. "He's commanding the soldiers to *fire on you*?" On Islor's rightful king?

"More likely on you. I'm just collateral damage." The skiff jerks forward, Zander and Elisaf's strokes increasing in both speed and strength.

But it's not enough.

A dozen flaming arrows launch into the night sky with the first volley, sailing toward us like shooting stars.

"Get down!" Zander hisses, abandoning his oars and diving forward to shield me with his body.

I cower, my stomach clenching as balls of fire illuminate the water's surface, revealing our exact location before plunging into the sea.

Zander wastes no time peeling away from me. "Is everyone okay?" The chorus of ayes pulls a sigh of relief from him.

"You don't have armor."

He still wears the ink-blue jacket he wore to the tournament, the velvet fabric useless against flying metal. "A choice I am regretting." He moves into position to row once again. "We are lambs in a meadow of wolves, and some of those arrows will be forged in merth."

Far more deadly if they land true. And he was willing to take one for me.

"Thank God they missed," I mutter, more to myself.

"I will thank the fates for *nothing* but the suffering of my people," he growls, the oar blades churning through the water with angry strokes.

Elisaf matches his pace. "I'm afraid Boaz will *not* miss again." I'm not used to hearing anxiety in my night guard's voice.

"Then we must do what we can to stop them." Gesine stands facing the shoreline.

"Are you mad, woman?" Zander scolds. "Sit down before you are dead and useless to us."

"We will *all* be dead and useless shortly." Gesine's cloaked arms reach out on either side. "Are you ready, Romeria?"

My eyes bulge with surprise. *Me*? *For what*? I shoot her a questioning look, but she's not paying attention to us, her head bent forward as if in prayer.

Whatever this powerful elemental is about to do, it involves her abilities—the three shimmering emblems marked on her forearm, hidden beneath the heavy wool, that depict her affinities to water, air, and earth.

A breeze stirs from the dead calm, like a teasing summer wind, fluttering strands of my hair, caressing my cheek.

"*Ready*!" Boaz roars from the shore as the soldiers prepare another barrage. His voice sends fresh fear coursing through me.

"Not yet …," Gesine whispers, her eyes still closed. "Romeria, you have Aoife's ring on your finger and Princess Romeria's affinity flowing through your limbs. *Use them*."

"I don't know how." I falter over my objection. I didn't know how the day of the nethertaur attack either, but somehow, I sent a water beast colliding with it.

Zander rows hard as he watches the shoreline. "We need to stop those arrows. Use the sea."

"How?" I plead for an answer because I'm drawing a blank. How do you use *water* to stop a flying steel blade?

"Fates," Elisaf hisses as more arrows shoot into the sky in unison, gliding steadily toward us. They will rain down on this wooden skiff in seconds, and Elisaf is right—Boaz won't miss twice.

My pulse drums in my head like the second hand on a clock.

Zander drops his oars and dives forward, sheltering me. Willing to take the onslaught of deadly arrows for me *again*. His arms tighten. "If only we'd met in your world instead," he whispers, his lips grazing my ear.

Then maybe we would have had a chance, I finish in my thoughts. I can't resist the urge to reach for his chest, to press my palm against the warmth and feel the steady, strong beat of a heart that is likely moments away from stopping forever.

This can't *be it,* a voice inside my head screams. *After* all *we've been through,* this *can't be how our story ends, like lame, cowering ducks before a firing squad.*

The need to protect Zander, to shield him as he shields me, surges through my body. I struggle against his grip. "Let me go."

Zander's arms only tighten their hold.

Dread, panic, and anger flare inside me as we brace for impact.

But the seconds stretch and the arrows never reach us, splashing into the water, faint sizzles as flames die. And then an eerie silence takes over.

Zander shifts away from me, and we peer toward Cirilea.

I squint into the dark, my view of the city blurred. "Is that—"

The wall of water crashes like a dropped curtain, scattering waves that rock our boat, pushing us farther out.

"That is how you use the sea." Satisfaction laces Zander's voice.

"The arrows bounced off it like useless toothpicks." Elisaf sounds equally amazed.

It dawns on me. "*I* did that." I needed to protect Zander—all of us, but he is who I was focused on—and that need channeled through this ring to create a shield. The gold band is still warm against my skin.

"It certainly was not me."

Gesine remains standing. Her eyes are open, glowing a vivid green that reminds me of the daaknar, not in color but in intensity, as if they could bore holes through any surface. She's focused on something unseen behind our skiff, her palms raised, hands trembling. The emblem of the silver butterfly on her forearm glows brighter than the other two. "Either I eliminate those soldiers trying to kill us or I take us out of range of their arrows. It is one or the other, and my hold on this element is not infinite. Your Highness."

She's asking for an order from the king.

Zander hesitates, weighing his thoughts on the shoreline where Boaz is likely scrambling to prepare another fiery assault.

"There are innocent people in the Rookery," I remind him. People who helped us escape tonight. People who don't deserve to suffer more than they already have. What exactly does *eliminating* those soldiers mean, besides the obvious? "They can't become collateral damage."

"And killing the soldiers will not end the opposition," he says, as if thinking aloud.

Boaz's commanding shouts ring out, and tension cords my neck. "What if I can't block those arrows again?" I don't understand how I did it in the first place.

"Choose now!" Gesine demands in a voice foreign to her normally calm deference.

"Get us out of here." There's resignation in Zander's tone, as if he'd prefer to select the first option.

"I suggest you hold on."

My hand has barely closed over the skiff's rail when a gust

sweeps in from behind us, strengthening by the second until my elaborate braids lash about and a relentless, high-pitched whistle drowns out all other sound.

I sense us sailing across the water. Shielding a hand against my eyes, I search the darkness, a mixture of numb terror and unbridled awe warring within. Sprays of seawater batter me from all sides, stifling my breath and soaking my clothes.

And in the midst of it, Gesine stands at the bow as if made of stone and anchored to the sea floor, her gleaming irises like demonic beacons in a turbulent storm.

A loud crack sounds, and something flies past, grazing my cheek.

"It will not hold much longer!" Elisaf's bellow reaches my ears over the deafening roar.

The skiff groans in answer. It's meant for catching meals for two peasants, notwithstanding a typhoon.

"Enough!" Zander yells.

As suddenly and ferociously as the torrent arrived, it abates, leaving us in a quiet, breezeless night, the wind's terrible howl only a memory lingering in my ear.

Blinking away the sting of the salt water, I search for Cirilea, but I can't find it. I can't find *anything*. Darkness envelops us. "How far are we from land?"

"*Too* far." Zander tosses a chunk of wood into the sea. His edge has always been his cool, calm demeanor, the way he can deliver punishing words with icy efficiency. Now, fury radiates from him. "You nearly tore us apart!"

"I am not as experienced at harnessing wind as those in the sailors' employ. It can be difficult to control. But we needed to leave quickly to avoid further attack." Unlike Zander, Gesine remains poised.

It seems to only infuriate Zander more. "And yet you brought us *here*. Which is *where*, exactly? Because surely, it is nowhere near Widow's Bend."

"I fear the area you speak of will be too congested with soldiers hunting us."

"And yet, that is where we need to go to meet the Legion."

A lyrical tune carries in the stillness then, so faint I wonder if I imagined it.

But Zander's and Elisaf's heads snap in the direction it came from, and I know it was real.

Another call sounds, like a song muffled beneath the water, impossible to decipher but pleasant. Lulling, almost. I feel an innate pull, an urge to reach for the oars and paddle out in search of the source of such enticing music. "What is that?"

Zander curses. "She's delivered us to the sirens."

Alarm bells ring in my head as I search the night for any hint of the monsters Wendeline claims have plagued the water since the tear in the Nulling that unleashed hellish beasts. They've made passage by ship impossible for any immortal, sniffing them out like bloodhounds on a scent.

"We are *not* in siren territory," Gesine counters evenly.

As if to challenge her claim, another soothing song carries, and that same pull tugs at my consciousness. If the siren fables I've read are true, that's how those creatures lure their victims.

"They will not travel this far south," Gesine amends.

"With an Islorian of royal blood and an immortal who is also a key caster, are you so sure?"

Her answering silence betrays her confidence.

"Wherever we are going, I suggest we go soon." Elisaf dumps a bucket of water over the edge and then bails more from the hull.

I gasp as I swish my feet, gauging the growing pool of water. "Oh my God, we're sinking."

"The boat's frame may have held, but not completely." He smooths a finger over a crack.

Gesine tips her head back and regards the smattering of stars that peek out between the broken cloud cover. "There is a small port called Northmost—"

"*No,*" Zander cuts her off. "I know which port you speak of, and it will be crawling with locals who would happily send word of our whereabouts to Cirilea, including that one of our companions is a woman with a gold collar around her neck. Not that my brother won't already be aware, given the display back there."

Gesine touches the shackle absently, a simple, one-inch band encircling her delicate neck that marks her as one of Queen Neilina's powerful elemental casters.

"We need to go back to Widow's Bend."

"But we have made it this far. We *must* get to the mountains, for Romeria's sake. Besides, the likelihood of your soldiers surviving this night—"

Her words cut off at the metallic ring of a dagger sliding from its sheath.

"You will take us back to the first inlet past Widow's Bend so I may reunite with my legion," Zander says crisply, an edge creeping into his voice.

Zander and Gesine lock hard gazes, and there can be no mistaking this stare down for anything other than what it is: an assessment of an opponent. The glow in Gesine's eyes has dulled, but it lingers. She still has a hold of her caster affinities. Is she considering harnessing the wind again to toss him into the sea before he can use his dagger on her?

Zander's elven affinity to Malachi's fire is useless out here, surrounded by nothing but water and no flame to draw from. Gesine knows this.

The air crackles with tension.

"Need I remind you, High Priestess, that fire is not my most formidable weapon? Neither is this blade in my hand." He smiles.

Gesine's eyes flare with understanding as she takes in the two needlelike fangs that somehow gleam in the darkness.

My heart skips a few beats. I've only ever seen them on display once, the night I discovered what Zander is. He was making a point then, just as he's making one now—or rather, a threat.

Would Gesine have a chance to defend herself before he sank

those teeth into her neck? She would be a fool to test him. But is this the moment, out here in the vast ocean, that we see the true nature of the sorceress hidden behind the serene facade?

She dips her head. "As you wish, Your Highness. Though I may need your guidance, as you are far more familiar with *your* lands."

"You seem to have navigated your way well enough so far." His fangs have already retracted. "Now do it before we sink."

I hold my breath in fearful anticipation, but rather than the previous gale force winds launching us forward, a small wave rolls beneath and carries us on its crest at a gentle clip, high enough to keep more water from leaking in. At this rate, it will take hours to make it back to shore, but at least we will make it.

I tremble within my drenched cloak as we glide through the darkness in brooding silence, moving farther away from old dangers.

And surely closer to new ones I can't fathom yet.

2
ZANDER

I knew Romeria was hiding something from me.

I study her cloaked back and her woven hair, once a regal crown atop her head, now an unkempt mess. She seems so delicate, hunched and shivering, her damp clothes clinging to her body.

All along, she reeked of deception, and I *knew*. I challenged her on it, daily.

But I never imagined *this*. How could I?

Between her poisonous blood and these supposed caster affinities, she has the power to destroy Islor. And if she does, if she causes the death of so many innocents … it will have been my fault.

I am a king without a throne, unable to make hard decisions.

She shudders, and the thought to pull her to me, to offer warmth, loiters like a regret I can't shake.

But I remain where I am.

3
ROMERIA

Dawn teases the horizon when we reach the inlet. Elisaf and Zander jump into thigh-deep water to haul the battered skiff ashore, seawater freely pouring in through a widening crack in the vessel's side. In the approaching daylight, the missing chunks from its frame are glaring. Zander's alarm wasn't exaggerated. How we *didn't* sink, even with Gesine's intervention, is no small miracle.

Ahead of us, driftwood lays scattered on a sugar-white sandy beach dappled with crops of lichen-covered boulders. A dense line of trees shelters the quiet area, the branches serving as a perch for the choir of mourning doves and robins. Aside from the birds, there are no signs of life, no witnesses to report our whereabouts to Cirilea. I see why Zander insisted on this spot.

The moment the boat's hull meets resistance, Gesine drags her limp frame over the edge, as if she can't stand being in it for one second longer. Where her dark locks were once combed neatly off her forehead, they now hang in a drenched, clingy mess. Not that the current state of my hair—or the rest of me—is much better.

Her striking pale green eyes are red-rimmed, sickly. The power she expended to carry us here has weakened her, much like Wendeline always was after healing me. But instead of finding a place to sit and gather her strength, Gesine pulls her body upright and takes several staggered steps toward me, holding out a feeble hand. "Your Highness, allow me to help you."

"I'm fine." The adrenaline that has fueled me since the square is fraying, but I've spent years in survival mode, hungry and cold and uncomfortable. I throw my legs over the side, my sodden boots landing in the sand with a dull thud. *All* my clothes are wet, right down to my underthings. "And it's Romy." Even if I'm only her in spirit now. I don't even have my face anymore, outside of the illusion Sofie bound to this ring.

"It is best we skip all formalities unless it benefits us to identify ourselves." Zander rifles through the stash bag he collected during our escape from the castle.

"As you wish." It's the first time Gesine has spoken to him since he pulled his dagger on her and flashed his fangs.

"Also, the truth about Romeria must remain among this group. If word should get out ..." He shakes his head. "No one but the four of us can know."

"Corrin knows." She was there when I was forced to divulge my secret in the mad dash to escape the castle. "And Wendeline too."

"Corrin will not answer anything unless asked, and there is no reason Atticus could *ever* suspect what you are. As for Wendeline ..." Zander's jaw clenches. "I only hope she feels the punishment is worth keeping your secret a little longer."

"What about Abarrane?" She's always been part of Zander's inner circle.

"There is only one thing the Legion despises more than Ybarisans, and that is the casters of Mordain." His head shakes. "She is loyal to me, but I fear she will have too many reservations about keeping a key caster alive."

"You really think she'd kill me?"

"I think she'll kill you when she discovers what you are. You are already so dangerous to Islor's existence as it is. News of your blood's potency will spread, stirring rebellion from the humans and panic from the elven. What we saw last night was merely a battle ahead of the coming war. But if the masses find out what you truly are, how dangerous you are not only to Islor but to Ybaris *and* Mordain ..." His voice drifts.

Is Zander having reservations? Regrets? He spent the sail back to land brooding quietly, staring out in Cirilea's direction. Does he wish, in those split seconds between Tyree's proclamation and Atticus's condemnation, that he had chosen a different path? That he had been the one to declare me an enemy?

Gesine stumbles a step and leans against the skiff's bow for support. It creaks noisily in return.

"Are you going to be okay?" I shift closer in case I need to dive in to catch her.

She waves off my worries. "I just need rest."

"There is no time for that. The trek to Eldred Wood is long. It'll take us most of the day." Zander sheds his cloak and ruined jacket, leaving him in only his black breeches and shirt, damp and clinging to his muscular frame. Beside him, Elisaf wrings the water from his tunic while his eyes comb the shadows.

"We won't need to walk," Gesine says between labored breaths. "There is a small village not five miles from here ... Shearling. A human named Saul waits with horses at the mill south of the bridge."

"Horses," Zander echoes, and there is no mistaking the shock in his voice. "But you were intent on landing in Northmost."

"I coordinated various routes for Romeria's"—she falters on my name—"departure, including passage back to Seacadore, if our route north was impeded."

"Escape routes." Just like I used to map out when I was working for Korsakov.

"Yes, to account for a myriad of scenarios." She offers a weak smile. "It took much planning. Many letters dispatched and coin purses lined. The things I've had to do to reach you ..." Her voice drifts, sadness filling her features.

"Who helped you?" Zander demands.

"Wendeline, for one. But many others. Too many to name."

"So while Queen Neilina and Princess Romeria were strategizing to murder my family and take Islor, you were scheming with *my* people to sweep in after and collect your key caster?"

"I did not know of Malachi's plan for the key caster—"

"But you knew of Neilina's plans, and you did not dispatch *any* letters or deliver *any* coin to stop that."

She sighs. "I could not—"

"You *chose* not to!" His condemnation is clear. If he were sitting on his throne, an execution in the square would likely follow.

Her throat bobs with a hard swallow. We knew Gesine had been writing letters, marked with Mordain's official scribe seal. At least she didn't lie about it.

The Princess of Ybaris must survive at all costs, by Malachi's will. That was the message Gesine sent to Margrethe. A proverbial nail in my coffin from this world, while Sofie was busy driving one into my chest from the other.

Tense silence stretches on, the rift of distrust between Zander and Gesine widening.

Finally, she clears her throat. "This inlet was not an ideal option, given its proximity to Cirilea, but I planned for it, anyway. It will take longer, but it will lead us to Bellcross just as well."

"We're going to Bellcross?" That name has been on many tongues lately, after Princess Romeria's brother Tyree and his soldiers murdered a tributary.

"Yes. That is where Ianca waits, and we must—"

"*No,* we are meeting the Legion in Eldred Wood," Zander counters evenly, cutting her off. The frazzled version from the open sea is gone, his calm, ice-cold demeanor having returned.

Gesine dips her head. "But after that, we will all head for—"

"*I* will decide where we go once I speak with my Legion commander." He looms over the sagging caster. "And before I do that, you will answer every question I ask of you about what you have been up to, about what Neilina knows, about the end to this curse, and you will do it truthfully."

Back in Cirilea, Zander was reeling from the treachery and seemed intent on two distinct paths, with his and Elisaf's having nothing to do with mine. Now, he is back to playing the domineering king, demanding people obey his will.

But he promised they would get us to the mountains where Gesine could train me. Will he renege now that he's had time to think? Now that he's seen how powerful she is? What does he want, besides reclaiming his kingdom? He ridiculed Gesine and these seers for speaking in riddles, but is Zander holding out hope that there is truth to this prophecy? That he could rid Islor of this blood curse that has plagued the lands for two thousand years?

Gesine sighs. "As you command." I can't tell if it's respect for a king or if she's simply too tired to argue.

Either way, my pity for the woman swells. Quickly behind it is my anger. "Hey, *Your Highness*"—I haven't used that patronizing tone in weeks, and it feels oddly satisfying—"in case you haven't noticed, we'd probably all be dead or in a tower by now if it weren't for Gesine's help tonight, so maybe dial it down a notch or twelve."

"I've noticed. I've noticed *everything*," he answers me, but his glare remains on her.

Gesine dismisses my defense with a raised hand. "It is all right. His anger is just."

Zander studies her another long moment, dragging his gaze over her pale face, her slouched body. When he speaks again, his tone is less hostile. "How many horses?"

"Two."

I stifle my groan. That means doubling up, and something tells me the two Islorian males won't agree to ride together.

"And you trust the human?"

"Saul's keeper is an unsavory fellow who provides little for his family, despite his thriving mill. He requires Saul's sons to work grueling hours and threatens to loan his young daughters to acquaintances for feedings any time Saul complains." She shakes her head. "The mortal holds no love for his keeper or his king."

Zander's teeth grit. This Islorian is the type of immortal he wants purged from his kingdom.

"Atticus will be dispatching riders in every direction by now," Elisaf says. "The road is not safe to travel."

"And yet to get to Gully's Pass, we need those horses and the road. Find them and bring them to us. We'll meet you as quickly as we can. Be careful."

"Wait." Gesine reaches within her cloak to fish out a small velvet coin purse. She tosses it to Elisaf, who deftly catches it. "Tell him Cordelia sent you. That is the only name he knows."

Planned escape routes and fake names. I'm feeling closer to Gesine already.

"Cordelia," Elisaf repeats and then takes off, disappearing into the tree line at a clipped pace.

She hobbles over to slump against a boulder, her complexion green.

"Do not get comfortable," Zander warns, removing an assortment of daggers from the sack.

"I wouldn't dream of it." She closes her eyes, her chest rising and falling with practiced breaths as if trying to keep the vomit at bay.

He watches her as he straps the arsenal of blades to his body. With his casual outfit and mussed hair, he reminds me less of the king I knew yesterday and more like the warrior who left camp in search of a nethertaur. Unfortunately, I fear neither is the version I face now.

"You're being an asshole," I whisper, working the countless fasteners and pins from my hair.

His attention snaps to me. "And how do you suggest I behave with a woman whose conspiracy against me has cost me my throne and put our lands in jeopardy of war? Should I bow down to her for getting us out of a predicament that she and this Ianca helped create?"

"There's a lot we don't know yet," I remind him. "I just mean that unless you feel like carrying her to the horses, you should let her rest. She is three seconds from face-planting into the sand."

"And if you believe she does not have a use for you beyond what she admits to, you are a fool."

"I know she probably does." I steal a glance to where Gesine sits perfectly still. I lower my voice. "But I *need* her. I need to understand who I am. *What* I am, what I can do. Given our current situation, don't you think that would be helpful?" While Zander brooded earlier, I spent that time mesmerized by possibilities. In just days, I've fought an underworld beast and stopped a hundred flaming arrows, and I have no clue how.

His lips purse.

"She can give us answers that no one else can."

"If she chooses to. Casters aren't known to be forthcoming, as I think you've now seen. They speak in lies and half-truths that may as well be lies."

Fair enough. "But she's powerful, Zander. Look what she did out there."

"She's reckless. That wind could have killed countless innocent people had she unleashed it against the shoreline. And do not suggest for one second she didn't intend to ignore my need for Eldred Wood and take us to Northmost."

"Maybe. But I don't think her reasons were evil. More like pragmatic." I slide my fingers through the braids Corrin so carefully spun, quietly praying my lady maid is safe at the castle after being interrogated by Atticus. Though knowing that salty woman, she would have scolded him for daring to question her. "Gesine can protect us."

His face turns grim with annoyance. "Relying on others to protect you will be the fastest way to get yourself killed. Put this on." He thrusts a strap toward me. "And remember that everyone is an enemy now."

I collect the leather piece. "Even you?"

He hesitates. "Those you least suspect." Tearing a strip off the silk jacket he cast aside, he crouches to soak the material in water.

Is he referring to his brother? Because I suspected that snake's ambitions weeks ago, only Zander wouldn't listen to me. Or maybe it's the captain of the king's guard. "I can't believe Boaz launched those arrows at us, even if he was aiming at me."

"I can. Like I said before, Boaz is loyal to the crown, and clearly, he does not believe I should be wearing it any longer. He never approved of this marriage, or of allowing the Ybarisans to set foot in Islor." Zander climbs to his feet. "Though I'm sure Lord Adley's relentless whispers have not helped. Who knows how many minds that worm has poisoned."

My anger surges at the mention of the vile nobleman's name. "You should have had the Legion assassinate him. He deserves it." Not even for the lies he's spun into treason, but for all the crimes he allows in Kettling. Humans being bred and traded in the black market, sold as babies for feeding off their sweet blood, and likely a dozen other atrocities I don't want to know about.

"*Now* you're thinking like a queen," Zander murmurs, his focus on my cheek. "A piece of debris must have hit you. Hold still."

I wince at the sting of brine as he gently dabs the soaked cloth against my skin. "How bad is it?"

"You'll live." His eyes touch mine before shifting back to his task. "So, this is not really your face?"

"Not the one I remember, no. Same dark hair, but that's it." *My* irises were a brighter blue, my face rounder, my lips fuller. That woman I saw reflected within the apothecary's mirror is striking, but she's a stranger. And yet, if what Gesine said is true, that there is no going back for me, I had better get used to this new face because without my ring on, I'll be looking at it for the foreseeable future—a reality that hasn't sunk in yet.

He mumbles something I don't catch before saying, "That must be quite unsettling."

"Not much isn't lately."

Zander tosses the rag into the sinking skiff before giving it a hard push offshore. "Your wound will heal within the day on its own, but I'm sure Gesine can mend it for you if it does not. Assuming she has abilities similar to those of ... other casters." The muscles in his jaw tense.

He can't bring himself to say Wendeline's name. Will any justification ever dull the disloyalty he feels, caused by a woman he relied upon so heavily?

"Thank you."

He grunts in answer. "How is that strap fitting?"

"I don't know." It's long and cumbersome and likely sized for a man.

Zander's deft hands take over, adjusting its position to sit a bit lower on my hips. "Did no one ever wear these where you're from?" His tone is softer, conversational, but I hear his fatigue.

"Yeah ... like, a hundred years ago." The tiny knife I used to strap to my thigh was done so with a tidy nylon band that slipped on like a garter.

He tests the belt's tautness, his palms smoothing over my hips. The simple touch stirs memories of the times he's gripped my body like that but for different—intimate—reasons.

Zander's hazel eyes meet mine. He must have caught that spike in my pulse, but unlike in the past, there's no teasing smile to go along with his awareness, no hint that he might feel the same. His expression is stony, unreadable.

This wall between us keeps growing higher; I just can't be sure which of us is faster at stacking the bricks. Part of me desperately hopes he's changed his mind about leaving me, that he'll stay by my side. But then I replay our conversation as we ambled through the castle's secret passage, when he blamed me for him being blind to what Atticus would do, for not being able to think straight. In essence, Zander blamed *me* for him losing his kingdom.

And so quickly after, he was ready to cast me aside.

I clear my throat and with it, the heady thoughts. "Now people mostly use guns."

"Guns?" He frowns. "What are those?"

"Weapons that shoot bullets."

His frown deepens.

"Tiny metal objects that fly out of a chamber and move through the air *really* fast. All you have to do is point and shoot. *Anyone* can do it." Every horrific news story of a toddler stumbling upon their careless parents' loaded pistols has proven that.

"It sounds like any idiot can be lethal in your world."

"You have no idea."

He gives the belt one last tug. "All you need is a blade."

I nod toward the karambit at his side. "I'll take that."

He reaches for it, but his hand stalls.

"I know how to use it. Abarrane trained me." For all of an hour, and not to her satisfaction. And all I want is to hear the daunting commander tell me what a useless fighter I am. I hope she survived.

"It's not that. It's just, this won't be enough." A decision skitters across his face and then his hand drops to his hip to unfasten the scabbard that holds his merth dagger. The one he had thrust into my hand in those few frantic moments after Atticus declared the throne his and me the enemy. I returned it to him as we were leaving the castle.

Zander affixes it to my hip. "This will seriously maim or kill any immortal in your path." Collecting my hand within his, he closes it over the hilt. "It is now yours. Always keep it with you."

He could have given me any of the dozen blades he just strapped to his body, yet he's given me the one I've always sensed holds value to him beyond its deadly composition. Warmth blooms in my chest at the gesture.

Whatever else he might think about me, he still cares for my safety. He wouldn't have shielded me from the arrows on the boat if he didn't. And maybe that water shield I created to protect us—him—wouldn't have been so strong if I didn't care deeply for him.

But why is he giving me this dagger now? Is it a token to ease his guilt before he abandons me?

What's going on inside that head of his?

He studies me, and I know he's trying to get a read on me too. The problem is, he's far more skilled at it than I am. I've always thrived at hiding my pained thoughts behind a veil of indifference. I can't hide them from him, though, and I hate it.

"Thanks for the dagger."

He dismisses the act with a shrug. "It suits you better, anyway."

I smooth my thumb over the black stone on the hilt. "I thought so too. That's why I tried to steal it that night in the tower."

"Yes, it certainly *wasn't* to slit my throat so you could escape," he murmurs dryly.

"Even if I had succeeded, I wouldn't have killed you. I've never killed anyone," I admit.

"By the way, what manner of larceny did Romeria Watts partake in, back in her world?"

I can't help my sly grin. "Jewel thief." My truth may be unsavory to some, but it's still *my* truth, not that of this wicked Ybarisan princess I've been forced to play.

"Why am I not surprised?" The corners of his mouth twitch. "Dare I ask how good you were?"

"*Very* good."

"I imagine you were." His gaze drifts down over my lips where it lingers a moment before he seems to catch himself. He steps back, his expression hardening. "Are you strong enough to walk, or shall I carry you?" he calls out. The set of his jaw tells me he might enjoy throwing the caster over his shoulder like a sack of flour.

Gesine lifts her head, her bleary eyes blinking several times, struggling for focus. She pulls herself off the boulder, and smoothing her palms over her damp, soiled cloak, takes wobbled steps forward.

The morning sun is a blessing. By the time we reach the road, the chill from sitting in wet clothes for hours is gone and a thin sheen of sweat builds under my collar.

Elisaf leans against the trunk of a weeping willow. Two horses graze on a lush patch of grass nearby. The second he spots us, he pulls his lean body upright. "I was beginning to think you'd taken a nap."

I can't help my genuine smile. I've always felt safer with Elisaf at my side, but also I can't fathom how Gesine is still on her feet, aside from sheer determination to avoid being tossed over Zander's shoulder.

She sways toward the brown horse closest to her, her fingers fumbling with the reins. "Would you be so kind as to help me mount?" Her request is breathless, her eyes half closed as her boot digs for the stirrup.

"Certainly." Elisaf grasps her slender waist and hoists her into the saddle.

Gesine slumps forward, her body sprawling against the horse's caramel-colored mane.

"I suppose this one is ours, then." Elisaf swings himself up and behind the exhausted caster, surveying her draped form from various angles, as if assessing how likely she is to tumble off.

Zander greets the black horse with a gentle stroke across its muscular flank. "What news from Cirilea?"

"Nothing that has reached the village yet."

"And that?" Zander gestures toward Elisaf's forearm.

I notice the hastily wrapped strip of cloth, soaked in blood. He didn't have that when he left.

"Oh yes. This." Elisaf studies it a long moment, as if deciding on his answer. "I had an interesting conversation with Saul's keeper." The dangerous gleam in his brown eyes is so contrary to the kindness I have seen. But it's a reminder that, for all the gallantry my night guard has afforded me over the weeks, he is deadly with a blade.

Zander sighs with resignation. "Come." He beckons me with a

hand. "Our pace will be hard, and I need full control. You will ride behind me."

I'm too weary to shrink from him. Hauling myself up, I edge as far back as possible, gripping the saddle.

"We're doing this again, are we?" He climbs on.

"Isn't that what you want? Distance?" I attempt an aloof tone, but resentment slips out.

"We will certainly have it when you fall off this horse, which I suspect will be within seconds of departure."

With a glower, I shift forward, molding my thighs to his, focusing on all the reasons I *don't* want to be this close to Zander.

He half turns, showing me his handsome profile. "As unappealing as holding on to me may seem, I promise you that breaking your neck will be much more so. And Gesine doesn't appear to be of any use to fix that for you at the moment."

Reluctantly, I slink my arms around his waist, entwining my hands. His body tenses against mine.

He nudges the horse's flanks, sending her off at a gallop that rattles my teeth.

4
ROMERIA

"W*hoa.*" Zander's fists tighten around the reins. The black mare slows to a canter, releasing a lengthy sigh, frothing at her mouth. We haven't stopped in hours. She's in desperate need of another break.

Same, horse, same. After galloping across the hilly terrain at a relentless pace, avoiding the road as much as possible, every muscle in my body aches, and the insides of my thighs feel raw.

"How much longer?" The dense forest of Eldred Wood is closing in around us.

"We are almost there. From this point forward, assume these woods have eyes and ears." Zander scans the trees.

I see nothing. "Friendly ones?"

"Loyal ones."

Elisaf follows as Zander steers our horse along a narrow and rocky trail. Gesine is conscious again and sitting upright, some of the color returned to her face.

The path grows more treacherous the farther we travel. "*This* is Gully's Pass?" It was one of the route options the day of the king's hunt. Atticus said it was safer for the horses. As I observe the vertical drop to our left, I fear what the other option looks like.

"Down there." He points toward the valley. "But the Legion

will have made camp on a plateau ahead. It's a defensible vantage point and one of Abarrane's favorites for hunting. She keeps supplies there." He sounds so sure that the Legion will have made it out, yet a slight waver betrays his confidence.

The trail has grown too narrow for the horses to pass. I hold my breath and cling tighter to Zander's waist, trying to ignore the loose stones skittering out from beneath the horses' hooves to plunge down the cliff, bouncing off tree trunks.

Thankfully, the trail veers away from the gorge, cutting through the densely packed trees. My ears catch the rush of moving water a moment before we break through the forest and into a small clearing where a river meanders ahead.

Zander leads us to the riverbank. Rabbits hiding in the leggy grass dash away from the horses, their white tails held high. The horses don't pay them any heed, focused on their next drink.

I struggle to dismount, gritting my teeth against the chafing of my wool pants against my skin. Where my thighs held a death grip for hours feels raw. In contrast, my backside is numb. I smooth my palms over it with a sigh that earns Elisaf's chuckle.

"It's not funny."

"It's a little funny," Zander says absently, but his attention is on the trees.

Gesine is quiet as she kneels at the river's edge and scoops shaky handfuls of water. She brings them to her mouth for a drink.

"Feeling better?" I wince as I bend down to mimic her. The cold water is refreshing, especially beneath the afternoon sun.

"Yes, much," she says through a breathy laugh. "Though I am not anxious to get back in that saddle."

"Same." Louder, I ask, "How much farther?"

Zander adjusts a harnessed blade at his ribs. "This is the meet spot."

I look around the meadow, empty save for us and the rabbits. "Shouldn't Abarrane be here by now, then?"

I'm not the only one worried. Deep lines etch Elisaf's forehead.

"They *should* be here by now, if they escaped the city when they needed to." He's answering my question, but I know he's talking to his king.

Zander scoffs at the unspoken suggestion. "There is no way any common soldier would be able to stop them. I've seen Abarrane cut through fifty men on her own."

"But five hundred? And injured by a nethertaur?" Elisaf asks gently. "I did not sense them anywhere along the path. Abarrane would have had a perimeter set."

I watch as the words settle on Zander's shoulders, their reality weighing down his posture and his hope. Did we backtrack all this way just to confirm that the Legion is dead? That we're on our own against an army that was once his to command?

"You could not sense us because you smell like a latrine," a familiar voice calls out, followed by a faint hiss a split second before an arrow grazes Elisaf's arm and spears the soft ground behind him.

Zander's body sinks with relief as Abarrane emerges from behind a boulder, her bow slung over her shoulder, her sword gripped in her palm. The warrior limps through the long grass toward us with a confidence that defies the gashes marring her sinewy body and the caked blood that has turned her wheat-colored hair dark. A tourniquet holds a ghastly wound on her thigh closed. Will it be another scar to add to her collection, the most prominent being the long, thin one that trails her hairline from her forehead to her earlobe?

I never thought I'd be happy to see the brackish Islorian.

"*That* is for doubting me." She taps the shallow cut on Elisaf's bare skin with the flat of her sword blade, smearing the bright red line of blood.

Elisaf winces. "Lesson learned."

Zander assesses her injuries with a quick head-to-toe glance. "How many of you are there?"

Her expression turns grim. "Nineteen, including myself."

I have no idea how many were in the Legion originally, but the muscle in Zander's jaw ticks, telling me there were significantly more. "Where are they?"

"We've set up camp a mile south, ready to pick off any enemy who ventures in." Sharp eyes swing to me, and I can't help but shrink at the way they harden. Abarrane has always terrified me, from the first moment I faced her in the king's war room, when she threatened torture to exact answers I didn't have. But she also didn't flinch at defending me as we ran from a charging army in the square. But that was because Zander ordered her. Where Boaz was for the crown, Abarrane and the elite guard she commands are for the man whose head it should adorn. Her unwavering loyalty to him is admirable.

But she'd also skin me alive if Zander asked it of her, and a very dark part would enjoy doing it.

Whatever reservations Abarrane may have for me, when her attention shifts to the river's edge, raw fury collects in her features. "What is one of Queen Neilina's witches doing in Islor?" she spits, her hand gripping the pommel of her sword. It's the first time I've heard anyone use that name for a caster, and it's obviously not meant as a compliment.

"This is Caster Gesine," Zander introduces. "As for what she is doing in Islor, we will learn the truth of that soon."

As we close in on the Legion's camp, I see why Abarrane prefers this area. The canopy of looming trees grants shelter while the river provides ample water for horses and warriors alike. Sheer rock walls drop along the west and south sides, limiting ambush opportunities and allowing a clear view of the valley below, so they can kill their enemy with arrows one by one.

A curt whistle sounds, and Abarrane responds with one of her own.

Movement from the corner of my eye draws my attention to

my left where a legionary stands not twenty feet away. The nocked arrow he had aimed at us is leveled toward the ground.

Aimed at *me*, I realize, as I take in that cold, predatory stare, reminding me of Sofie's henchmen, the two men who slaughtered Korsakov's entire security team on the night that started all of this. Does this legionary agree with Atticus that Islor would be better off without me?

How many of them feel the same?

In all my time in Cirilea, I've only met a few of these fierce warriors, trained by Abarrane herself. While the encounters were brief, everything inside told me that if one of them ever had reason to kill me, I was as good as dead.

The poison coursing through my veins is plenty reason to make it happen. What would they do if they knew what else thrummed in this body, waiting for release? Would the order of an exiled king be enough to stay their blades?

Zander's earlier warning—to assume everyone is an enemy—has me shifting closer to his side as we head into camp.

"Zorya," Elisaf says in soft greeting, handing off our horses' reins to a warrior with lengthy auburn hair tied off in braids and a bloody rag secured diagonally across one eye. "How bad is it?"

"Merth blade." Her voice is emotionless.

Elisaf grimaces, his pat of comfort landing on the female warrior's shoulder. "I am sorry."

"He paid for it with his life, though I wish I could have had more time taking it from him." Zorya's good eye shifts from Elisaf to Zander. She bows her head. "Your Highness." She peers at me but offers no greeting. The narrowed gaze she gives Gesine before she leads the horses away is downright menacing.

"That is unfortunate. She was one of our best fighters," Zander says somberly.

"Zorya is *still* one of our best fighters." Abarrane glares at him as if daring to suggest otherwise is a personal affront. She leads us past a bearded warrior who wipes blood and gore from his sword. Her limp grows more pronounced, the cloth bandage glistening with fresh blood despite her attempts to stifle it. That injury is far more serious than she's letting on.

The smell of roasting meat teases my nostrils, stirring the first hunger pangs I've had since yesterday. A wild boar is trussed over a firepit, manned by two warriors. A handful of simple tents —stretched leather over tent poles—are scattered throughout, the nearest sheltering a warrior who lies on the ground while another stitches a gash across his stomach. Others lounge, checking their bandages and cleaning their wounds. Those who are mobile are busy running the camp, chopping wood to stoke the cook fire, sharpening weapon blades, hauling buckets of water.

All wear leathers drenched in blood and countless scrapes and cuts.

And every one of them stops what they're doing when they notice Gesine. Zander was not exaggerating about their feelings for all things Mordain. I can practically taste the loathing and distrust in the air.

"Nineteen," he echoes, more to himself, his jaw hard.

"Are there many grave injuries among them?" Gesine surveys the warriors. There is no way she can't feel their hatred, but if she's apprehensive, she hides it behind her tranquil mask.

Abarrane watches the caster as if deciding whether to acknowledge her. "Most will heal on their own, given time—"

"I will help speed things along. I will heal as many as I can. If you will allow it," she adds, bowing her head to the war commander.

"If *they* will allow it, and I promise you, most would prefer to … stay far from your kind." Abarrane glares at the gold collar that marks Gesine for what she is. "Then again, we are without tributaries here."

Feeding off a caster might sustain an Islorian, but it's an instant death sentence for the former. I know that much.

The subtle intimidation has the desired effect. Gesine blanches.

Abarrane's responding grin is wicked.

"What happened in Cirilea?" Zander shifts the conversation from threats that are likely not idle.

Her amusement falls off. "The city was taken almost immediately as word of Princess Romeria's duplicity spread. I have never seen that many soldiers within the walls, not even on your wedding day." She scowls. "Do not tell me that was not Atticus's intention."

"I cannot be sure of anything anymore."

"He must have suspected our plans to escape because he had the north and west walls under heavy guard, and he used Kettling's men to set an effective trap at the bridge."

"Kettling's men were intentionally left outside the walls. We agreed we didn't want Adley with too much influence inside."

"Or so your brother claimed." She hesitates. "I lost Gorm."

"I am sorry, Abarrane," Zander says, his voice bleeding with sympathy.

She nods once as if to accept his condolences.

"Who will take his place as second?"

"Jarek."

Zander makes a sound that I can't pin as satisfaction or disapproval, but he doesn't say anything.

"They chased us to the border of the woods before retreating. It was the general himself who opened my leg with his merth blade."

"Adley's son? I've never known him to withdraw."

"You've never known him without his head on his shoulders." She hands her bow to a passing warrior. "It was Boaz who signaled the retreat, after we cut down half of Adley's men. I'm sure he is now busy plotting his attack here. We'll see if your treasonous brother is foolish enough to send a king's army into the pass."

Zander greets a male who sits on a tree stump, shirtless and covered in dried blood, dragging his blade across a sharpening stone with methodical strokes. I shouldn't be surprised that Zander seems to know every one of these warriors. Even as king, he learns the names and faces of those around him, from soldiers to stable hands. "My brother is many things, but foolish is not one of them. Securing Islor under his rule will be his priority. He knows how Adley schemes, and he won't risk gaining the throne only to lose it in the chaos of the aftermath. He will be busy sending letters to all corners of Islor, announcing his claim and replacing the lords and ladies who died in yesterday's royal repast with those loyal to him. But once that is done, he will come for us."

"Us, or Ybaris's poison mill?"

I don't give Abarrane the satisfaction of a reaction, shifting my attention to the river where several male and female legionaries wash the blood from their sculpted bodies. One of them I recognize as the guard from the castle dungeon that day I visited Tyree, only his blond hair is free of braids and clinging to a body carved in hard muscle. He pauses to regard us, not a hint of modesty in his nakedness, in water that only reaches mid-thigh.

I struggle to keep my expression as my cheeks flush.

"Atticus will come for *all* of us with the full might of the Islorian army." Zander's words pull my focus back.

"And we will be ready."

"We will be gone. Nineteen of you cannot hold off that army, and I will not have us sit here and wait for slaughter." His words invite no argument.

We've reached the largest tent. Abarrane wrinkles her nose. "I *should* insist you all bathe before defiling this tent."

"And I should insist you allow the caster to heal your wounds." Zander pulls aside the leather flap. "But first, she and I must discuss a few things."

I make to move forward into the tent, but Zander's free hand in the air, palm out, stops me.

"*Alone.*"

My jaw drops. "Are you kidding me? I deserve answers as much as—ow!" A sharp prick against my neck cuts off my words.

I flinch away and find Abarrane's dagger aimed at my throat, cold fury in her eyes.

"Your blood does not frighten me, Ybarisan," she hisses. "I will be happy to discuss what *you* deserve while I make you bleed."

A warm trickle slides down my throat, the slice in my skin stinging.

"Abarrane," Zander scolds in a tone more appropriate for a child throwing a tantrum as he waves her blade away.

The weapon lingers in the air for another three seconds, poised for attack, before she sheathes it.

Satisfied, he shifts his attention to Gesine. "After you."

The caster flashes me a reassuring smile before ducking into the tent.

"Elisaf." That's all Zander says before he follows her inside, dropping the flap behind him.

5
ZANDER

"Yes."

I stare at the caster, sitting primly on the tree stump in the middle of the tent—a convenient interrogation spot, likely by Abarrane's design. She's an attractive woman, her black hair close in shade to Romeria's, her pale green eyes striking as they observe with hawkish interest.

The gold collar around her neck gleams from the single torch burning within the darkening drape of the leather canvas walls. A stark reminder that Gesine is not to be trusted.

"Yes? You are freely admitting that I have been cursed to love Romeria?" I had expected her to dance around the answer.

"In a manner of speaking. The princess was created on Queen Neilina's sanctum altar, by the queen and her commander, and Aoife."

"Tiberius sired her." Tyree had alluded to King Barris not being Romeria's true father.

"Tiberius may have given his seed, but Aoife was the one who ensured what sprouted did so for the sole purpose of destroying Islor. Ianca witnessed it all."

I breathe through this revelation. "And so now what? Will I be tormented for my remaining days?" Fighting against my thoughts and the gravitational pull I feel whenever Romeria is near?

"That is entirely up to you. Now that you know the truth without a doubt, you can make your own choices. The fates may control much, but they cannot control free will—"

"I certainly didn't have control of my heart!" I roar, thankful that I demanded Gesine shield this conversation to keep our voices from carrying.

The torch flames flare to twice their size. It is so rare that I lose control of my affinity like that. In fact, I never do. Not since childhood.

Gesine's gaze never veers from mine as she gently says, "You did not know there was a choice to be made beyond the obvious. You were choosing peace between Islor and Ybaris and hope for your people. That the princess who arrived was pleasing in many ways—not the least of which was how she supported your ideology for Islor's future—was an assumed blessing, not something to be suspicious of."

"You're trying to appease me for my idiocy. I should have seen it." A king undistracted by a beautiful face *would* have seen it. "And then she murdered my parents. Tried to murder me. But it all makes sense. How else could I have fallen *back* in love with the woman after she did such unspeakable things? How could I *ever* have toyed with the idea of making her my queen unless it was never my choice to begin with?" I pace as I rant.

"Dare I say, you did not fall in love with the same woman twice, despite the physical resemblance."

"I do not see how that matters."

She purses her lips. "Your eyes are now open to Neilina's deception. Doubt no longer hangs over what she has done, and any decision you make going forward regarding your intentions for Romeria is *yours* to make."

"If only I trusted that."

"You are not the only one who fell in love despite all odds, Your Highness."

"I *also* fail to see how that matters." Regardless, those odds are no longer in our favor.

Romeria has been trying to close herself off since last night. The moment I suggested we part ways, I felt her slamming the door shut on her emotions. She can't hide the hollow ache in her heart that swells every time our gazes touch, though. Not from me.

But what do I feel for this woman who has lied and deceived me in one form or another, first as Princess Romeria, and then as Romy Watts from New York City? Nothing that's untainted by Aoife and Neilina's designs, and nothing that can continue now that I know what's at stake. There isn't room for these emotions between us anymore.

"And now I am to ally with this *supposed* key caster—"

"It is very real, Your Highness. *She* is very real. Do not doubt that. The power that courses through her body is like nothing I have ever felt before. It will be like *nothing* you have ever seen before."

"Really? Because I've stood at the edge of the Great Rift and watched Ybaris's casters level an entire battalion with their affinities." A wall of them, attacking with an arsenal of elements, honed for war. They failed at invading our lands, but our army suffered catastrophic losses. "Are you saying she will be stronger than that?"

In Gesine's eyes is a spark of hope, but also something I haven't seen from her yet—fear. "Yes. Possibly."

"Fates," I mutter. "How does she not realize what is inside her?"

"I suspect it will not remain hidden for much longer." She smiles softly. "This Romeria, she is a curious creature by nature."

"Yes, a jewel thief who thrills in secret tunnels." I continue my pacing around the sparse furnishings inside the tent. Had Abarrane had time to collect supplies, she still would not have. She prefers to curl up on the ground like a wild animal rather than sleep in a proper bed. "And how exactly are Romeria and I supposed to end the blood curse together?"

"It is not clear. Perhaps it will become so."

"That sounds like more of Mordain's lies." My footfalls are measured as I circle her dignified form, her shoulders pulled back, her chin held high. "After what Wendeline has orchestrated, do you honestly believe I will accept such an ambiguous answer? Do you think I do not know you work to one goal?"

"*I* am not Mordain—"

"Perhaps we should discuss what the Legion will do to you if I grant them access?" The cloying aggression that rippled through the camp when we entered was enough to choke a horse, and only some of that was intended for the Ybarisan princess.

Gesine's throat bobs with a hard swallow. "If such taunts bring you solace, you are welcome to continue, but there is no need to threaten me for information. I will freely tell you all that I know. If you will listen."

"Why would you do that?"

"Because if I do not, you will fail in whichever direction you choose. Of that, I am certain."

Her unwavering confidence gives me pause. Wendeline convinced me of much, but there was always a hint of nervousness swirling about her. I came to believe it was just her nature. Gesine, on the other hand, has been steady since the moment we walked into the apothecary.

"Continue."

"It is imperative we get to Ianca soon, and then to Venhorn."

"The seer."

"Yes. They see things we cannot. Traces of affinities woven and summonings answered, connections to talismans. There could be hints in that ring that offer answers. Being near Romeria may spark visions that help us understand more about Malachi's plans."

"I will not lie. This seer piques my interest. I have always wanted to meet one."

"Ianca is not an exotic animal to gawk at." Gesine's face tightens. "And I fear she is fading fast. We will not have long with her."

"Fine. We will travel to Bellcross." There are benefits to that plan. Namely, to learn if I have any allies left. "Though we have nineteen bloodied and maimed warriors, including a commander who grows weaker by the hour."

"I can help her. I can help all of them if they will allow it."

"I've seen legionaries suffer for weeks rather than accept a healing hand from a caster."

"They will accept aid if you order it."

"Their commander complying would surely help." I shake my head at Abarrane's stubbornness. Something else pricks at my thoughts. Gesine behaved as if Venhorn was one option for escape, but I'm sensing it's the *only* route that has ever interested her. "Why do you push so hard for the mountains? There is nothing there for us but caves, saplings, and whatever Nulling creatures have survived the centuries." Elisaf and I know the area well, having spent months there when I turned him all those years ago. And every legionary is required to live—and survive—there for a year during their training, so they are even more familiar with its challenges.

"That is not true. There *is* a place where we will find assistance. I believe you may know it. It's called Stonekeep—"

I bark with laughter. "Is that what Mordain has taught you? Stonekeep is *not* a place. It is a sheer rock wall surrounded by deadlands." A vast, flat expanse of parched soil where nothing thrives. It gained its name because of the peaks along the wall's face—like that of a castle.

"But there are carvings on its face, much like those in the nymphaeum, are there not?" She tilts her head. "Have you *never* wondered what it might mean for you and your people?"

"No one can decipher that script." I pause. "What do *you* know of it?"

"For certain? Not much. It existed long before the rift tore

Ybaris in two. We assume the nymphs created it, but we have never understood why. If there is a message within that design, the casters do not recognize it, but the nymphs' methods of communication were not always as simple as the spoken word."

"Then why would you suspect there is assistance for us there?"

"Because the seers have seen it in their visions."

I snort. More talk of prophecy. "And what have they seen? Let me guess, you cannot say."

"As I have explained already, foretelling does not work like that. But the seers have seen a token of the nymphs' loyalty waiting for Islor when it needs it most. I would venture that day is now."

"A *token*?"

"Yes."

"What kind of token?"

"One of great value but beyond that, I am not certain."

Or will not share. I can't deny that Stonekeep's existence has been a source of many unanswered questions over the centuries for Islor. "And you are certain the nymphaeum door has nothing to do with this prophecy?"

She falters in her answer.

"Around and around we go." My smile must look menacing through my gritted teeth. "Wendeline was more proficient at misleading me than you are."

She sighs. "I am not trying to mislead or deceive you. Where the nymphaeum door is concerned, *all* paths may lead to opening it. I cannot say anything for certain."

"Explain," I press.

"The power of the nymphs may grant Malachi what he wants, but it also might give you what *you* want. It is hard to say. Much of what we know about the nymphs is understood through vague foretelling and a few ancient texts that have survived the ages. We know for certain that the nymphs existed long before the casters, and for whatever reason, the fates felt the need to quell that power by locking it up within its own little box of sorts, never to be unleashed again. All four agreed to this, and they agree on so *very* little, which tells us they had a compelling reason. And there is only one reason I can think compelling enough. One thing that the fates hold above all else."

Power. "The nymphs were too powerful."

"Even now, locked behind that door, their ties to this world are potent enough to give life to so many of you. Have you never pondered that?"

Too often. "Are you saying the end of this blood curse may require that Romeria open the nymphaeum door?"

She pauses. "Will you allow me to share conjecture, knowing it is based on nothing more than hallucinations rooted in madness?" A tiny smile curls her lips. She's echoing my bitter words from last night, and she's enjoying it.

With a heavy sigh, I fold my arms across my chest. "Proceed."

"Some scribes believe the fates banished the nymphs because their connection to this world allowed them to unravel the fates' meddling and return existence to its original shape at conception. With the age of the casters, this became a glaring problem."

"Return it to before a summons is answered." I see where she's going with this. "You think the nymphs can reverse Malachi's blood curse."

"It is possible. If they chose to. As I've said, it is only conjecture, but it would explain much. The fates see themselves as the highest of judges in the highest of courts. They do not appreciate *anyone* interfering. To have these nymphs roaming freely, causing chaos by negating their powers, overruling their schemes ..."

It would explain *everything*. "And how does one open the door?" Farren tried and failed.

"There is a way we are almost certain was Malachi's intent." She gives me a knowing look.

"A key caster taking the stone on Hudem."

"With an elven as powerful as you are, yes."

The stone that is deep within Cirilea and now inaccessible to us. We couldn't reach it on a normal day, forget on the holiest of days. Atticus will have guards next to every secret passage in and out of there. He knows them all as well as I do. All except for the one deep below the castle, meant only for the king.

But even if we could get to the nymphaeum on Hudem, I can't expect Romeria would willingly go along with this option, and I would never force her. "Is there no other way?"

"There *may* be. We would need to find it. I don't know that it matters *how* the door is opened. What matters is that it *is* opened. And once that happens, Malachi will get what he wants as well. To reign over these lands."

Another king vying for power. "Would it be so terrible?" It's a glib question, without much thought.

"History would suggest yes."

Her words stop me in my tracks. "*What* history? I have a full library of texts, and I have read them *all*." Some, multiple times. "None hold mention of the fates ever ruling these lands."

"As there was no mention of it in Mordain's vast archives either. Not until twelve hundred years ago, when the ruler of Shadowhelm, Queen Bodil, sent word to Mordain, requesting an emissary. They had found scripture deep within a tomb. They could not read it, or access it. It had been preserved, it seemed, by elemental power."

"I thought Skatrana had no love for your kind."

"It comes and goes with each new ruler. Mostly goes." A faint smile touches Gesine's lips. "Fortunately, Queen Bodil was pragmatic. She could see that whatever had been hidden within her realm had to be important. As mortals, they would never have the means to interpret or even touch it. So she asked for our help, and we gave it. And we learned much from these preserved accounts.

"Aoife and Malachi once reigned these lands, long ago, assuming the forms of a king and queen who held the throne. It resulted in war and famine as the two fates could not coexist, each demanding that the other relent and for all to bow. More than once, both the humans and the elven dared rise against the thrones, only to be crushed. Malachi used his daaknar to punish any who challenged him while Aoife turned rivers red with the blood for all those who did not kneel before her. Crops rotted under the scorching sun and froze in the frigid air as Vin'nyla and Aminadav expressed displeasure with their fellow fates' antics. It was a dark time. Merely uttering the names of the fates inspired fear, and tearing down sanctums previously erected in their honor became a cornerstone of rebellion. The suffering and destruction went on for centuries."

"And how did it end?"

"That, we do not know for certain. The author of the texts gave us an account of what had come to pass, not the future beyond their words. Nothing else exists from that time. It is as if the record of these dark days was deliberately purged. Perhaps more scrolls are hidden within Shadowhelm, but we have not been made aware of them, and our access is limited by the ruler at the time and their desire for knowledge of our ancestors."

But twelve hundred years ago ... "This tale of yours does not ring true. We have had casters escape to Islor during that time, and none have ever breathed a word of this history." My voice drips with skepticism. "Even Wendeline, for all her duplicity, would have enlightened us."

"It is not discussed in Mordain, Your Highness. It has not been taught. There are those in the guild who would prefer that scripture showing the glaring failings of our creators not be dwelled upon. Some have called for their destruction. The scribes have protected the knowledge thus far. But very few are aware, and I can assure you Wendeline is not one of them."

"How is it that you, an elemental caster who has been locked up within Argon's towers for years, *are* aware?"

She smiles. "Before Argon, I spent my life running through those dark corridors beneath Mordain's great hall, hiding from instructors and falling asleep with my face in dusty books. I was far more interested in hearing stories than wielding my affinities. The scribes could not keep me out, so eventually they stopped trying and chose to teach me instead. I value their knowledge like nothing else."

She has an answer for everything. Either she's telling the truth, or she has prepared her lies well. "Hopefully, you also value candor, because I will not tolerate another priestess misleading me for her own gain."

She dips her head. "I can appreciate that. Especially after all you have faced thus far."

The scenario she has painted so far is grim. "And what of the Nulling? Would it be open to Malachi again?"

"I would suspect so, yes. The Nulling is a space that exists between time and place, where the fates relegate creatures of various dimensions without need for their deaths, as transition to Azo'dem or Za'hala requires. If the ancient scripture from Shadowhelm is any indication, they use it to build a waiting army that will unleash when anyone dares tamper with the nymphaeum."

"Successful or not."

"Precisely."

Something pricks my memory. "Romeria thinks the husband of the caster who sent her is trapped in there. This woman—Sofie—her whole purpose is to free him."

"Into *this* world?"

"Possibly."

She frowns as she considers this. "What are you up to, Malachi?"

Nothing good. "If all this speculation is true, it could mean we would not only face Malachi as a ruthless ruler, but whatever crawls out of the Nulling *and* the wrath of the fates."

"And the chaos the nymphs can stir up. Yes. All that to put an end to the blood curse. *If* the nymphs could be compelled to do your bidding."

"What would compel them? Have the scribes ever speculated on that?"

"Based on what the seers have seen"—she meets my gaze—"they barter in lives."

A sour taste fills my mouth. "Whose?"

"It is difficult to say whose would suffice. Yours. Romeria's. Both."

"'At the tied hands of the Ybarisan daughter of Aoife and the Islorian son of Malachi.' Can you truly *not* predict?"

"Perhaps. Would you not sacrifice yourself to bring peace to your lands?"

"A hundred times over. But what you have described does not sound like peace. It sounds very much like war and suffering." Which we are heading toward, regardless. My gaze drifts toward the tent flap. Beyond it, surrounded by bruised and battered warriors, Romeria sits quietly, none the wiser about how formidable she is. "Could Romeria defeat a fate who is in mortal form?"

"Some say yes, she would be powerful enough. And others say that opening the door will destroy her as the attempt did Farren."

My heart clenches. "She would be sacrificing herself for Islor, and it may not make a difference in the end."

Gesine sits silently while I pace around her, my mind desperately searching for the right path forward. Walking into this camp today, counting the remaining legionaries, the sense of defeat was a dark shadow trailing me. Nineteen of them against Atticus and an entire army has no chance of surviving.

But could a key caster change our odds?

Would it not behoove me to find out?

"The more we speak, the more I am certain the door should remain closed. Romeria's immense power should be used for means beneficial to Islor without the added risk."

"Beneficial, as in reclaiming your throne."

"So I can change the course of our future. Yes." That is what a good king who can make hard decisions would do.

A glimmer of something sparks in Gesine's eyes. "You will work together, your hands still tied."

"I suppose so."

"As you see, there can be more than one path to prophecy." She pauses. "Though I would be remiss if I did not tell you that the seers have seen the door opened in the age of the casters."

"Not by my will." Or the will of anyone else who might try to use the key caster for their own benefit. I harden my resolve. "You are not to tell Romeria of what we have discussed."

She frowns. "If you are requesting that I deceive her—"

"I'm asking that you not tell her more than she needs to know." Not until I've had a chance to consider what telling her might mean.

"She will have many questions. If she is to trust me and accept my tutelage, I must answer them."

"Then answer them. But not with speculation like the kind we just walked through. Not yet. It would be distracting for her."

Gesine considers that a moment. "Such knowledge might divert her from her focus with training, and we need her learning as quickly as possible so she can protect herself."

"Exactly." Atticus may not be on our heels right now, but it won't be long before he's hunting us—her. "I will enlighten her when it makes sense." *If* it makes sense. It means we're back to keeping secrets from each other, but that has always been the case. "I am willing to lead us to Venhorn for shelter within the caves and because I want to root out the Ybarisans. We will pass Stonekeep on our journey, and you can see for yourself that no tokens are waiting for us. But you will not speak of this to *anyone*. If the Legion thinks we are following one of Mordain's schemes, I will lose their loyalty, and that is far more important to me than anything these nymphs could offer. Is that clear?"

Gesine bows her head. "As you wish, Your Highness. Is there anything else?"

I pull back the edge of the tent, effectively breaking the sound barrier Gesine constructed. Noise erupts instantly, with shouts carrying and blades ringing. I seize the flame, intent on laying waste to any enemy, only there doesn't seem to be one. The legionaries hang back as Abarrane marches toward Romeria and

Elisaf, her dagger gripped within her palm, water dripping from her braids.

Clearly, Romeria has done something to irritate the commander. Again.

I sigh. "Yes. Train her well."

6
ROMERIA

"He wouldn't have found Gesine if it weren't for me." I yank a plump green berry off the vine Zorya tossed at me on her way past. They may look like grapes, but grapes they are not, their sourness bordering on unbearable.

"Many things would not have happened, if not for you," Elisaf reminds me, adjusting his position against the tree we're both using for back support as we watch the camp's activities.

The Islorian guard who used to pace outside my wallpapered prison, ten steps to the left, ten to the right, hasn't left my side since Zander's abrupt dismissal at the tent. Not even when I had to squat behind a bush to relieve myself. I'm not sure whether he's stuck to my side as my friend, my guardian, or my captor. Was that simple call-out earlier Zander's order for Elisaf to watch me? He can't think I'd run, not without Gesine. And if any of these legionaries decided to go against his order and sacrifice their lives and their honor for the greater good of Islor … I've seen Elisaf go toe-to-toe with Zander in the sparring square, and he knows his way around a blade, but could he stand long against these hardened warriors?

My mouth puckers around the tart berry.

Elisaf chuckles. "I will wager Corrin's stew does not seem so bland anymore."

"Is this really the only edible thing that grows around here?"

"What do you think?" He smirks, telling me my suspicions are accurate and this was Zorya's way of telling the Ybarisan princess to go fuck herself. "But at least your stomach has taken a break from growling. I'm sure they could hear it across the camp."

The gathering around the boar grows as warriors finish their tasks and venture over to carve off a hunk of meat. How much sustenance will they get from that animal?

Abarrane's earlier threat to Gesine has me questioning it. "What will they do when, you know … they need to feed?" No humans live in Eldred Woods. How long can they last before they grow weak?

Elisaf seems to consider his answer. "These warriors have built up a tolerance and can go several weeks between taking a vein if needed. It is a requirement as a legionary, and as you can see in present circumstance, an important one. But mortal blood also speeds up the healing process."

And *so many* of them are injured.

"Regardless, we will all have to seek tributaries, eventually."

I don't miss the *we* in that statement. The legionaries, Elisaf.

Zander.

He says he only uses tributaries when necessary, but it will become necessary soon enough. It's been weeks since I spied him feeding off that woman. How long will he be able to hold out before he disappears into a room or tent with a human?

"Where will you find them?"

"In the towns and villages that we move through once we leave here. We will request the use of them from their keepers."

"And if the keeper refuses?" They own these humans. They feed, clothe, and shelter them, the cuffs on their ears branding them.

A faint, amused look crosses Elisaf's face. "Refuse a request from the king or his right arm?"

"It isn't much of a request, then." These tributaries will

undoubtedly be young and willing and eager to impress the king —exiled or not. My jealousy flares with the thought of Zander that close to another woman, despite the act. Despite the reality that we are all but estranged now.

My attention drifts to the large tent in the back, my fingertip skating over the tiny cut against my neck. It feels like forever since Zander shut that flap door in my face and sent me away. "What do you think they're talking about?"

Elisaf lifts an eyebrow. "I think you have a *very good idea* what they're talking about."

Me.

Princess Romeria.

This curse.

But what will happen when Zander gets the answers he wants? What will he decide?

The legionary from the castle dungeon strolls toward us, a hunk of cooked meat speared on the end of his dagger. He's dressed in leathers and strapped with weapons, his hair pulled back with three fresh braids that Zorya plaited with swift hands earlier. From my angle huddled on the ground, the brawny warrior may as well be a giant.

He stops a foot away from us and holds out the meat for Elisaf, who collects it with a murmur of thanks.

My mouth waters as I watch Elisaf sink his teeth in, the juice dripping down his chin. What I would do for a taste of that right now.

"I've never understood Ybarisans, living off twigs and berries. It only weakens you," the warrior says, his voice deep and gravelly and laced with ridicule.

Reminding me that, as far as anyone here is concerned, I'm still Princess Romeria, a Ybarisan who doesn't consume "animal flesh," as Corrin put it.

I force my head back to meet soot-colored eyes. He's attractive, his jawline square and prominent, his lips full, despite their sour pucker. But I learned long ago not to let good looks distract me.

My irritation—or maybe my hunger—flares. "I've never understood Islorians, living off innocent humans. Then again, it's because your craving makes you weak."

His gaze narrows, a challenge within it. I doubt most people are stupid enough to taunt him.

Elisaf clears his throat. "Romy, this is Jarek."

I make the connection. "Abarrane's new second."

"So I've been told." The warrior's lips twist as if tasting something unpleasant.

"Not happy with the promotion?" Interesting.

"I'd be much happier with the simple task of killing Ybarisans." His attention grazes my neck, and I can't be sure if he's noting the cut Abarrane gifted me or imagining his fangs sinking into my jugular.

"I'm sure you'll get your chance, eventually."

"I plan on it."

I struggle not to shrink from his steely stare as he seems to dissect me under it.

"You want more of that boar, come and get it yourself." He turns and saunters away, his steps slow and leisurely, dripping with the confidence of someone who knows his skill and doesn't fear any opponent.

My unease stirs. "Do seconds-in-command normally deliver food?" Maybe things work differently in the Legion.

Elisaf watches Jarek's back. "They do when they're coming to take a measure of someone."

That someone being me, obviously. "What do you know about him?" I didn't see so much as a scratch on him—and I saw *most* of him earlier—which means none of the blood he washed off that sculpted body was his.

"He is a fierce warrior, as brutal with his blade as Abarrane. His lineage comes from Skatrana. Ancestors who happened to be in these lands when the blood curse ran rampant and the Great Rift tore Ybaris in two. He hails from Lyndel, born to an army officer."

"His affinity?"

"I've heard it is to Vin'nyla."

"The goddess of air." I picture the stone statue in the sanctum, the curvy woman with butterfly wings. "How strong?"

"I hazard it's as ineffective as most affinities granted under the blood moon."

Parlor tricks, as Annika once called the Islorians' affinities. Except for Zander, it seems. He could engulf half this camp in flames with just a spark from that cook fire.

"Regardless, he would never use it. None of these warriors use their affinities. They consider relying on the fates a weakness in battle."

Another warrior watching me says something to Jarek. The second-in-command tips his head back and laughs. It's a boisterous and yet vicious sound, and it makes my cheeks flame, knowing I'm at the butt of their joke.

"I think it's safe to say he doesn't like me."

"Jarek's father died in the Valley of Bones, battling Ybaris and Mordain in the last great war when Jarek was just a boy. He holds a passionate hatred for both. Be careful of that one."

"You think he'd go against Abarrane's order?" Assuming Abarrane has told them I'm off-limits, and *if* she refrains from killing me herself.

"No." Elisaf's headshake is firm. "He will follow her orders to his death, even before the king's, as will all legionaries. But he is second-in-command now, which means he will replace Abarrane should she fall, and I fear his loyalty to Zander isn't as infallible." Elisaf tears another strip of meat off with his teeth.

"Does Zander know this?"

"There is very little Zander doesn't know. Though, that seems to be changing lately." When Elisaf notes how I'm eyeing him, his chewing slows, realization dawning. He swallows. "I don't suppose Romeria Watts from New York City lived off twigs and berries."

"No, she lived off Quarter Pounders and street meat, and she would *kill* for a bite of that right now."

"I will not pretend to understand what you just said, but you devouring wild boar would certainly stir unwanted questions."

"But I'm *so* hungry." I lean in and inhale.

He chuckles and shakes his head. "If you *really* want some, I will bring you a piece once we are in the privacy of a tent," he promises, adding, "though I doubt Princess Romeria's body will appreciate it later."

"Yeah, well, she better learn to adjust because I'm tired of living her life."

"And yet Zander is right. She is the best cover for you right now, given recent revelations. Unless you'd like Abarrane to test her dagger on your skin again."

My focus veers to where the commander stands at the river's edge, her back to it, her head swiveling between the camp and her tent. A sentry on guard, ready to spring at any second, despite a still-oozing wound. There is one other person in this camp she might trust less than me, and that's Queen Neilina's elemental caster.

As if sensing my attention, her sharp eyes dart to me and narrow, assessing.

Whatever ground I gained with her that day of the royal hunt is lost, leaving us at odds again. I doubt she'll be willing to train me to fight, something I'm in desperate need of learning if I'm to survive in this world.

I need to remind her of that day we fought together against the nethertaur. She needs to remember that I'm *not* the enemy, that I can be a powerful ally. How powerful, she has no idea, but neither do I. I *need* to—

The surge of adrenaline floods my body a second before a wave rises from the river's surface and sweeps over Abarrane, drenching her from head to toe.

"Oh hell." My gold ring is warm against my skin, my stomach twisting in knots.

Warriors shout and draw their weapons, moving into a defensive stance, searching the trees for the unseen enemy.

"You did not," Elisaf chides.

"I didn't mean to!" *Why* did I just do that? It's not going to help my cause.

A look of cold shock stalls Abarrane for one … two … three seconds before her hate-filled gaze swings to me. She marches toward us, her dagger suddenly in hand. Even with her heavy limp, she's menacing.

Elisaf curses, scrambling to his feet, drawing his sword.

"I didn't mean to!" I echo myself, though I doubt she hears me. I doubt she cares. But if she harms so much as a single skin cell on Elisaf …

"Abarrane!" Zander's deep voice cuts into my panic, pulling the camp's attention from the coming massacre to the tent. He fills the doorway, his hand pulling the flap open. "Come. *Now.*"

I can practically hear her teeth gnashing as she reluctantly pivots toward the tent, water dripping from her clothes and braids.

I sag against the tree trunk.

Zander searches the camp, quickly finding me. His chest lifts with a deep breath, the seriousness of his expression only stirring more anxiety. What has Gesine told him?

He jerks his head, beckoning us to come, before vanishing inside.

I pull myself to my feet, longing for a hot bath, clean clothes, and some of Wendeline's salve for my chafed thighs. All things I suspect I am a long way from ever seeing again.

"While I am sure we will one day laugh at that, perhaps you can refrain from doing it again." A hint of annoyance laces Elisaf's tone, his sword still in hand as we head for the tent.

My nerves churn. Plenty of hostile eyes are on me, but the ones I feel most acutely are soot colored and paired with a smirk. What amused Jarek, I can't guess—was it dousing Abarrane, or that I've managed to make her hate me more?

I do my best to ignore the warrior as I duck into the tent.

Inside is absent of luxuries. No couches to lounge on or rugs to tread upon like those from tents at the king's hunt. There's nothing but a single skin off to one side. But I guess that's to be expected. This is the tent of a military commander who ran from battle with nothing but the weapons on her body. She doesn't seem the type to demand comforts.

But, for as vacant as it is, the way Zander paces around the space, his hands clasped at his back, his face stony, it doesn't feel sparse or empty at all. The moment his eyes touch mine and I see the indifference that hides the man I've come to know behind the shield of a king, it's clear something monumental has shifted.

Hovering near him is Gesine, unharmed by all appearances.

Zander gestures toward the tree stump centered in the tent, his voice calm. "Abarrane, take a seat. We will discuss plans while Gesine heals your leg—"

"I will heal on my own," she spits.

"You can barely stand. And that was not a suggestion." He doesn't raise his voice. He doesn't have to. The icy command is enough.

And he's right. The obstinate warrior sways slightly, her complexion sickly.

Abarrane eases herself onto the stump, sparing a warning glare at Gesine as the caster kneels before her.

But Gesine's attention is on Zander, waiting.

He nods once, and she settles her hands on Abarrane's wounded thigh, her eyes closing.

Abarrane's chest heaves with a sigh, as if even a second of unwanted magic is already providing much-needed relief from her silent agony.

"We will go to Venhorn," Zander announces. "All of us."

All of us, meaning Zander is keeping his promise to get us there. Despite everything, my heart skips a beat. He's not abandoning me … yet.

Abarrane's mouth opens, but she falters on her words. Clearly she wasn't expecting these plans, and by the way her face pinches, she isn't impressed by them. "You mean to scurry away and hide from your brother?"

A muscle in Zander's jaw ticks. "When have you *ever* known me to scurry and hide?"

Technically, we just did, but I bite my tongue. Now is not the time to poke holes in his claims.

Abarrane smooths her expression. When she speaks again, it is more conciliatory. "Why Venhorn?"

Zander paces again. "Because we know the terrain well, and the caves can provide us suitable protection from any army hunting. And, according to Prince Tyree, Ybarisan soldiers have concealed themselves somewhere in those mountains with their vials of poison to distribute across Islor. We need to find them."

Her laugh is mirthless. "I spent hours familiarizing him to my blade, and I obtained nothing but blatant lies. You trust that lech to tell you the truth?"

"He did not tell *me* anything. He told Romeria the day she went to him in the dungeon."

"When he shattered her face against the bars?" Cold eyes flash to me, and I'm sure she's picturing herself doing the same. And enjoying it. "You told me that visit was fruitless."

"I lied," he says without hesitation. "I did not know who to trust with the information, so I trusted no one. But those lies end now. You are my loyal advisor, and if you are to follow me down this path, you deserve to know what cause you are fighting for. You deserve to know what Romeria truly is."

My stomach sinks with cold realization. He said to keep that secret to ourselves, that telling Abarrane would be too risky. Based on her reception of me so far, I'd argue he was right.

But something has changed.

Zander turns to face me, firm resolution in his jaw. "The woman who stands before you is not from Islor or Ybaris or any other realm we have ever heard of, and she was sent here to wreak havoc on our world."

7
ROMERIA

Abarrane gawks at Zander as if he just slapped her across the face. "That is not possible."

My heart drums in my chest. Where is he going with this? Is Zander *trying* to get me killed? Does he want mutiny among the warriors we raced here to find?

Or is what I feared most unfolding before my eyes? Is Zander back to wishing me dead?

"You speak as if you understand these things. None of us do. Not even those in Mordain." Zander watches her.

"You're right. I do not understand," Abarrane says slowly. "Are you suggesting that Princess Romeria is not born of this world?"

"I'm not *suggesting* anything. I'm *telling* you that the person who stands before you now is not the princess of Ybaris at all."

Abarrane's gaze swings to me, dragging over my frame. "Who *is* she, then?"

I struggle to hide the tremble in my limbs, but this feels very much like the night I was in front of Korsakov after I stole his daughter's diamond ring, a multitude of blades laid out, any of them sharp enough to cut off my hands—or more—with a single swing.

"That is a good question." Zander resumes pacing. "Princess Romeria did exist. She is who traveled here from Argon and plotted to kill me and my family. And she died by Boaz's arrow the night we were to marry."

"And yet she stands before me now."

"Because Malachi made it so." Zander's lips purse. "Many years ago, in rebellion against King Barris's wish for peace between Ybaris and Islor, Queen Neilina bade one of her casters to summon Aoife to create a weapon that would destroy Islor's immortals. Aoife granted her request with the birth of Princess Romeria, an elven whose tainted blood was designed to rid the world of our kind"—his jaw tenses—"and whose appeal was intended to ensnare my heart."

"So it is true, then," Abarrane hisses. "You *are* spellbound to her."

Bewitched, everyone has been whispering, unable to see Princess Romeria for her evil because he was too busy trying to get under her skirts. It's not just a rumor …

"It *was* true," Zander grits out. "Now that I know with full certainty, it is true no longer. The spell is broken."

His words wash over me in a cold wave. They sound like a promise—a definitive end.

What did Gesine say to him? I frown at her back, but she is intent on nothing but her task.

"Malachi must have discovered Aoife's goals to rid the world of us, and so he made plans of his own. When Margrethe summoned him to resurrect the princess, at the behest of Gesine"—he regards the kneeling caster—"Princess Romeria returned in physical form only."

"That is impossible," Abarrane whispers, her words a growing theme in this conversation.

I would have agreed with her if I weren't living the reality.

"*This* Romeria was not faking her bout of amnesia, per se. She knew nothing of the fates, our lands and our people, or of elemental affinities. She's never seen Argon's castle or met her queen mother. In her former life, she was a jewel thief who until recently believed herself to be human."

Abarrane's eyes narrow. "If she is not human, then what is she?"

"*Zander*." I finally find my ability to speak. What is he doing?

But he's watching the commander closely. "A key caster."

"That is …" Abarrane's eyes flare, and for the first time, there is something other than courage. I see a hint of wariness. Of panic. Of fear. "What purpose would Malachi have for sending a key caster here?" She asks it, but the answer is undoubtedly forming in her mind.

"We believe he wants her to open the nymphaeum door."

My apprehension spikes as I watch the pieces clicking in Abarrane's expression.

I am Aoife's weapon, sent to eliminate her race.

The king's judgment can no longer be trusted.

I'm here to unleash the Nulling's monsters at the behest of Malachi, the fate who has cursed this world many times over.

Abarrane's nostrils flare with adrenaline the moment she makes her grim decision. "Then she must die." The declaration is followed by wide-eyed panic and Abarrane's glare shifting from me to Gesine. "Why can't I move?" She grits her teeth, her head jerking as if trying to propel her body with it. "What have you done, witch?"

Gesine doesn't so much as flinch at the commander's shrieks.

"When you release me, I will tear the flesh from your bones—"

"She is doing what *I* ordered her to do." Zander's commanding voice ricochets off the leather walls. "I decided to tell you the truth, but do not think me naive enough to believe you would accept it peacefully."

Abarrane's breathing is ragged, her rage a palpable tension churning around the tent.

"You will sit and you will listen, and when I am finished, you will realize that killing Romeria would be a graver mistake than keeping her alive."

It sounds like he's already weighed those two options.

Elisaf's hand has settled on his sword pommel, as if worried that whatever force Gesine is using to bind Abarrane might lose its grip.

I sneak a glance through the tiny slit in the flaps. So far, the legionaries remain where they are.

"They would not dare," Zander says, as if reading my mind. "Let me know when you are ready to listen to reason, Commander."

Uncomfortable silence drags in the commander's tent as Gesine toils away with her magic and the rest of us wait for Abarrane to stop seething.

Finally, she huffs out a breath. "Have you forgotten that the last time Malachi used a key caster in this way, the *only* door he opened was to the Nulling?"

"I'm not opening *any* doors for *anyone*." I shake my head in emphasis.

But Zander doesn't look at me. "As of right now, Romeria would have no idea how to. She has no skill with wielding her affinities, either elven or caster."

"Is that so?" Abarrane's eyebrow arches, her sodden braids and clothes saying otherwise.

"I told you that was an accident," I mumble.

She studies me. "What good is a key caster who cannot wield her affinities? Why keep her alive?"

"Because she will be able to in time," Zander answers. "Gesine will train her."

The warrior sneers at the woman kneeling before her. "And what is the witch's role in all this? Why would she want the princess resurrected in the first place?"

"The high priestess is guided by prophecy. She believes the seers have seen the end of the blood curse and peace between our people, and it requires this reincarnated version of Romeria to achieve it."

"Fools and their prophecy," Abarrane spits out, but the slight no longer holds the same noxious anger.

"If Gesine chooses to allow such folly to drive her purpose, that is her choice, as long as it does not hinder my path forward. What I do know is that we now have a key caster, and I intend to use her to regain my throne."

I flinch at his choice of words. Of course, that's why he's changed his mind about going our separate ways. Now that the initial shock is over, he's realized how stupid he would have to be to let Gesine and me take off.

I've become a weapon for his cause and nothing more.

A hollowness blooms inside my chest.

Gesine's eyes open then. She stands and eases back from Abarrane. "The wound was deep, but the flesh knitted together nicely."

"I wouldn't know. I can't move," Abarrane mutters.

"Can you blame us?" Zander chuckles, and it sounds so out of place in this tension.

After a moment, she smirks. "No."

"Is the Legion still with the rightful king of Islor, Commander?" Zander watches her closely.

"Aye. Always." There's no waver in her voice. "Though this secret, we shall keep between us for as long as possible. I will enlighten them to *Her Highness*'s terrible bout of amnesia"—she cuts a glare my way—"but as far as anything else, Jarek and the rest must not know."

Which means she doesn't completely trust her second-in-command either.

That's reassuring.

Zander nods, seemingly appeased by her answer. "You can release her now, Gesine. I think she has seen reason."

Another beat passes, and then Abarrane pulls herself up from the stump.

Beside me, Elisaf shifts his weight as if expecting her to pounce.

But she only stretches her leg out in front of her, testing it. "That was much faster than Wendeline."

"Wendeline knows how to heal, but she is not a healer. I am one such, and I am far more powerful." It's a simple statement and likely true, given that Wendeline would be hunched over with that one repair. Yet within those words, I sense a subtle warning to Abarrane, maybe to Zander. Do not underestimate her.

Abarrane unfastens the tourniquet and tosses it to a corner with a sigh. "When do you wish to leave, Your Highness?"

"At first light," Zander confirms. "Before Atticus has time to create obstacles for us."

"That might be a challenge. As you have seen, many of my warriors are grievously injured."

"Gesine will heal the worst of them tonight."

Abarrane opens her mouth—to object, likely.

"In that, we need your help to convince them it is in the best interests of Islor." Zander holds an arm toward the tent door, palm upturned. A signal.

Gesine glances at me once before moving swiftly out of the tent.

I know stomach slashes and gouged eyes take priority over my questions about my future, and yet my frustration surges all the same.

With one last lingering look my way, Abarrane marches for the door. She stalls at Zander's side and quietly—but not quietly enough—says, "Please tell me it isn't your heart that continues to stay your blade."

"My heart is no longer a hostage in Aoife's scheme. We cannot win this war without the key caster. She is too useful to us alive."

He's not even using my name now.

He might as well have driven a dagger into my chest.

I meet Zander's gaze. He holds it for mere seconds before shifting his focus to the ground. Can he feel this yawning emptiness he's just created in me? Does he care? "Elisaf will show you to your tent. You can bathe in the river if you wish."

I grit my teeth, willing my heart to harden and my words to sound unbothered. "With an audience of warriors? I think I'll pass."

"Suit yourself. Gesine will come to you when she is finished. Rest while you can. The next few days will be long." He speaks to me now as if we're strangers, as if we haven't spent many nights entangled in each other's bodies over the last weeks.

I watch his back as he strolls away, a sting burning my eyes.

"Come." Elisaf gives my shoulder a gentle squeeze.

8
ROMERIA

Deep shadows still linger as I kneel at the river's edge, splashing cool water against my face and neck. Legion warriors move swiftly and with purpose, disassembling the camp, collecting only what won't weigh us down on the journey. The most gravely wounded of the lot now have only bloodstained leathers to hint at the battle they endured. Not all, though, I note, watching Zorya stalk past with a black leather eye patch. But she looks better after Gesine's help, the scar that stretches from her eyebrow to her cheek nothing more than a tidy silver line.

Feeling slightly more refreshed, I aim for the horses and Elisaf.

Gesine sits on a log at the smoldering firepit, studying the black-and-blue rib cage of a warrior who towers over her, his enormous frame layered with muscle.

She spares a second for me, offering a brief smile before refocusing. I fell asleep before she came to bed in our shared tent last night, and she was gone when I woke, the only evidence she was ever there the rumpled skins where she slept. How she is still going now astounds me.

Elisaf is adjusting the strap on his saddle when I reach him. "You certainly *look* better, Your Highness. How do you feel?"

"Like I should have stuck to those stupid sour berries." As

promised, Elisaf brought me a sliver of wild boar. A test, he claimed, insisting I chew slowly.

But instead, I shoved the entire piece into my mouth, hoping it might somehow fill the empty pit inside, and then I demanded more.

An hour later, I felt the first stomach cramps, and a half hour after that, Elisaf found me curled in the fetal position, groaning in agony. He fetched Gesine to settle my mutinous digestive system for me. It didn't take long for her to do so, but it left me weak. The silver lining was that I drifted off to sleep on a night where I might otherwise have tossed and turned until dawn. Though I suspect that might also have been the work of the caster.

"I *did* warn you."

"Yeah, I know, but I thought I'd be fine. This girl in my art class, Rebecca, was a vegetarian who suddenly started eating meat, and *she* was fine." I sat across from her as she devoured it on more than one occasion.

"Was Rebecca elven?"

"No. I mean, *maybe*." I snort. "The hell if I know. I thought *I* was human, didn't I?"

Elisaf scans around us, checking for ears. There aren't any, but he lowers his voice, anyway. "Do not forget that our Ybarisan cousins have distinct differences, beyond the obvious."

"Yes, I got this lecture last night from Gesine."

"Legion, prepare to move out!" Jarek calls out in his deep, raspy voice, his stride sleek as he rallies the warriors for their horses.

Zander strolls across the abandoned camp, Abarrane at his side, her hand resting on her sword's pommel. The king's expression is stony, his jaw set with determination as he speaks to her.

Just looking at him pricks at my chest. Now what? Am I going to have to spend the next however many days with my arms wrapped around his waist?

"What are the chances I'll get my own horse?"

"Given there aren't enough, and you haven't proven yourself

proficient at steering one, I would say slim to none." Elisaf frowns in thought. "Actually … definitely none."

Great. "Can I ride with you?"

He opens his mouth but falters.

"*Please.* I can't go with him. I just … I can't." My voice cracks. "I'd rather ride with Jarek at this point."

His eyes flitter in the direction of his king, his friend. With a heavy sigh, he holds out his hand.

And a lifeline.

From the castle balcony, Islor's countryside seemed nothing more than lush green bumps that rolled into the horizon, interspersed with crops of trees. Seeing it from this angle, though, the horses cantering toward Bellcross, I realize how high Cirilea sits above its lands, how craggy this terrain is, how vast the forests.

Somehow, in this steady procession of warriors, I feel alone.

We emerged from Eldred Wood to a gloomy sky and a fine mist, and have been riding along the king's road that borders it at a steady pace for hours, breaking once at a small stream to water the horses. But the clouds have since scattered, we've veered off the main road, and the air grows muggier. I'm baking in this wool cloak. Finally having enough, I tug at the clasp around my collar and shove the heavy material between us to keep from losing it.

Elisaf checks over his shoulder.

"I'm hot." I unbutton my tunic to widen its collar around my neck and shoulders.

"That is not a surprise." He smiles. "But you are not usually this quiet."

"Not much to say, I guess." My eyes drift ahead to the front of the line where Abarrane and Zander ride, side by side. He didn't say a word when he saw me perched behind Elisaf, his face unyielding as he swiftly climbed onto his horse. I couldn't tell if he was bothered or relieved.

Directly behind them is Gesine, her cloak drawn and firmly fastened despite the heat, likely to hide her gold collar. She's sharing a saddle with the mountain of a man whose ribs she fused earlier, a warrior named Horik, I've learned. His hulking frame makes her willowy one look childish by comparison.

I desperately need to talk to her, but it seems Zander is doing his best to keep us apart. Not that we could have a real conversation about anything with all these ears around.

"How much longer until our next break?" I can't seem to get my bearings. I thought Bellcross was northeast, yet I would bet money we're traveling south. Then again, there are sometimes two moons in the sky in this world, a truth that makes me doubt all I know.

"There is a town beyond that ridge ahead. We should reach it before daybreak. That is where we will stop for supplies."

"You mean, for blood."

His shoulders lift with a sigh. "For *all* necessities."

And mortal blood is a necessity for every single one of these fierce warriors. They may appear relaxed, but I've seen their hands reaching for the pommels of their blades too many times to be misled. Everyone is on edge, as if expecting to crest a hill and find an army waiting, despite the scouts sent ahead to sound alarms should they need to.

But how will these townsfolk respond to a line of warriors strolling through, demanding their veins?

Even with my worries, my curiosity is piqued. Aside from Eldred Wood, I haven't seen beyond Cirilea. The Islorians I've been exposed to so far have left much to be desired. Pompous lords and ladies angling for power, clueless nobility who come to the castle for the parties and the royal grounds, humans enslaved to work the market for their greedy and cruel keepers.

Hooves pound against the road behind us, announcing a rider advancing quickly.

My stomach clenches as Jarek sidles up next to us on a white horse painted in swirls of dried blood, the pattern too specific to be accidental. I dread to think who unwittingly provided the art supplies.

The sides of his freshly shaved scalp show off a silver scar that runs horizontally along his hairline. I assume a merth blade did that. The three thick braids that gather the hair at his crown, he's fastened into a ponytail with leather bands.

"Tell me, what is waiting for us in Venhorn, besides saplings?" His attention is on Elisaf, not sparing me so much as a glance. I'm fine with that.

Sapling. That's what they called the man who tried to drown Annika the night I arrived.

"Perhaps a demon or two?" Elisaf's tone is flippant. He doesn't seem bothered by the second-in-command's menacing presence.

"Or perhaps more of the princess's co-conspirators?" His sooty eyes shift to me, skimming my neck.

My shoulder, I realize, as they flare with recognition. The gruesome claw marks earned from the daaknar are visible. I fight the urge to adjust my shirt collar. There's no point hiding them beneath Dagny's capelets anymore, not that I have any. "Why don't you ask your commander? She's up there." Abarrane *must* have told him that the Ybarisan soldiers are hiding in the mountains with vials of my toxic blood, so what's the point of these questions?

"I hope you're not expecting to find any allies. Even your brother has turned on you." Jarek studies my jaw in an assessing manner, the corners of his mouth curling.

"I'll bet you two thought my face getting smashed against those bars was funny." If that's the case, they're no better than the likes of Tony.

"We both thought it deserved."

My anger is a stinging prick at my throat. "You *both* can go fuck yourselves."

His amusement drops from his face. "Asha is dead because of

you. And you are a traitor to all." Jarek nudges his horse, and it speeds toward the front of the line.

"That's one way to get rid of him." Elisaf checks over his shoulder, his big brown eyes tinged with sympathy. Or maybe pity.

I release a shaky breath. That won't be the last time Jarek confronts me, I'm sure. "What's a sapling?"

"The worst of our kind."

I wait a few beats for more information. "Care to elaborate?"

"Not especially." He scans around us, but the warriors have given us ample space, whether by coincidence or design. More likely the latter. They want nothing to do with me. "They are Islorian immortals who feed off their own kind."

My eyes widen. "By own kind, you mean …"

"Other Islorian immortals."

"I didn't know you could do that."

"Not without dreadful results. They become dwellers of darkness, the sun scorching their flesh in daylight."

More like the fictional vampires I've heard of. Though maybe not so fictional after all. That these creatures might have lurked in my world … "They live in the mountains?"

"In caves deep within the range. It is the perfect place for them to survive."

"The caves. Where *we're* going?"

"The mountains are a vast place. There is plenty of room for all of us."

That doesn't make me feel better. "The Ybarisans are hiding somewhere in there too. Won't the saplings feed off them?"

"We do not know precisely where the Ybarisans are. There is a settlement called Woodswich, where humans live without keepers and shun the rule of Islor's king. It is a hard life, given the terrain and the climate, but they do it to escape the tributary system, surviving on their own. Immortals won't settle there for fear of the saplings pulling them from their feathered beds while they sleep. Our armies have not bothered with them for the better part of a century. It might be where the Ybarisans have holed up.

"But no, it is not likely the saplings would feed off them. At least, not for sustenance. They lose their taste for everything else. Mortal blood no longer sustains them, and their venom becomes impotent. They cannot turn anyone as a means to create their blood supply, and so they must hunt for other immortal Islorians."

"He was going to enjoy Annika later. That's what the one at the bridge meant."

"Yes, they abduct Islorians and imprison them. Shackle them, I have heard."

"Seems a bit karmic, if you ask me." The mortals may not be shackled in a cage, but they wear the cuffs of imprisonment all the same.

"Perhaps, though the rare few who have escaped over the years share stories the likes of which I have never seen a mortal experience." His brow furrows. "The more they feed on us, the more strength they gain, the weaker we become. They sap the strength from their immortal victims, hence the name."

"Can they kill you?"

"If they take too much. But their feeder stock cannot survive long anyway. Not without mortal blood for themselves. One cave exit on the east side of Venhorn allows the saplings access to Lyndel. The city spends its nights guarding the walls against any who might venture in. They kill them on sight."

"How can they tell someone is a sapling?"

"There is no mistaking them up close. Fortunately for us, they are limited to traveling in the cover of darkness, which makes it a challenge to reach great distances."

"The one who tried to take Annika made it to Cirilea." *You have failed, Romeria.* He thought he knew me. "Princess Romeria was working with him."

"Yes, that is a curious alliance, one we have not been able to understand. Regardless, he would have relied on caves and cellars and covered wagons. Perhaps he never made it back at all."

"And now we're going *to* them." All these legionaries are following Zander's order to march to a lair of cannibals.

"As I've said, the cave system is vast and mostly unoccupied. There's even an old mine. It fell to the Nulling's creatures when the seam tore and no one has ventured to reclaim it since, given its proximity to the rift and whatever may still lurk there."

"Things still *lurk*? What things?"

"Nothing we can't kill."

I picture the nethertaur and shudder. Now I see why Elisaf was not excited about this.

We fall into silence for the rest of the ride.

The sun dips toward the horizon as our company crests a hill and the first rooftops appear. Soon the town's wooden outer wall is visible. Four guards at the open gate shift as they observe us.

"Do you know where we are?"

"I do. It's a name I believe you will remember well." Elisaf steers our horse out of line and coaxes it forward with his heels. "Freywich."

9
ROMERIA

"Freywich?" I hiss as we gallop forward. "Isn't that *closer* to Cirilea?"

"It is. But we need supplies and information, and this is the best location to acquire both. It is a distance from the king's road and not prominent, having struggled over the years. Atticus will not have sent a messenger here." Elisaf moves us beside Gesine and Horik. The line of warriors slows as we approach.

"But Lord Danthrin was *in* Cirilea. He would know what happened. Wouldn't he have come back by now?"

"We will see soon enough."

I shake my head. Elisaf is far too calm.

The entry gate is nothing more than two halves of an oversized wooden door, held together by iron straps and propped open with chains. Several men in armor guard it. On the ramparts above, more guards wait, arrows nocked. They seem to be multiplying by the minute.

"What if they don't let us in?" I whisper.

"That would be foolish," comes Elisaf's smooth response.

Surveying the hardened bodies and harder faces traveling with me, I would have to agree. Each of these Legion warriors has at least five weapons on display—and far more hidden beneath their leather.

"What if they shoot arrows at us?" I amend.

"Also foolish, but we are shielded by our caster, just in case. And you must relax. Even if they have heard what has transpired in Cirilea, they would not dare refuse someone of royal blood."

Our caster. Whatever was shared between Zander and Gesine in that tent, they seem to have come to an understanding. An alliance.

"But I doubt anyone here knows what has happened. It will take weeks for word to spread. Months. There are villages in Islor that believe Zander's father is still alive and king of Islor. Granted, Freywich will hear the latest sooner than most, given its proximity to Cirilea."

"Here, eat this." Gesine reaches between us, thrusting an object into my hand.

"What is it?" Besides something shriveled and brown.

"A special mushroom."

I give her a flat look. "I've taken those before, and they did *not* relax me." I spent hours hiding behind trees in Central Park, believing a man on a bike was chasing me.

"These are morels grow on the islands off the Gulf of Nyos. They can disguise the scent of Ybarisan blood."

"The orange blossoms." Or rather, neroli oil from the blossoms, Zander had said. An appealing scent for the Islorians and unmistakable. It's why I can't move freely among them without stirring notice.

"Exactly. And until we can confirm what these people know, you shouldn't parade through the gate as Princess Romeria. Just in case. With these morels, they will assume you are an Islorian." She studies the guards ahead. There's a slight shimmer in her green eyes to hint of her channeling, and through the material of her dress, I see the outline of the glowing doe emblem. She's using the air to shield us. "Chew it well before you swallow and it will work faster."

The mushroom tastes like wood and sunflower shells. I'm forcing it down my throat just as we reach the entrance.

"Halt and identify yourselves!" the guard on the left hollers.

"Are you saying you do not recognize your king?" Abarrane's voice is crisp and mocking.

The guard falters, his eyes shifting between his partner at the gate and then Zander, to his filthy tunic and breeches that are far from regal. "We were not aware that the king would be paying a visit to Freywich." Has he ever seen Zander? Maybe they heard the news, and he now assumes this is Atticus?

"Well, he has, so you should beg forgiveness appropriately."

"I apologize, Your Highness." His face reddens. "Lower your weapons!" He dips his head toward Abarrane. "My lady—"

Abarrane is out of her saddle and holding a dagger against the guard's neck faster than I can blink. "I command the King's Legion, and I will split you in two if you *ever* call me that again."

Soft chuckles carry from behind me, the warriors amused.

"Yes, my—" He winces as the tip of her blade digs into his skin. "Yes, Commander."

I catch the subtle shake of Zander's head. "We require the lord's manor for the night."

The guard bows. "Yes, Your Highness. We will notify the lady of the house so she may prepare suitable accommodations for you." He snaps his fingers at the other guard, who takes off running, his hefty armor hampering his stride.

Zander's gaze skates over the parapets. "The Legion needs tributaries and supplies. I would hope that Freywich's keepers will be generous in this regard."

That earns a second bow, and a third. "Yes, Your Highness. We will make sure of it."

Zander urges his horse through the gate, and we trail behind.

Freywich is a small but bustling town, the buildings situated around the square. Most have thatched roofs and are simple in design, some neglected. Here and there are more elaborate stone cottages. The keepers' homes, no doubt.

"You said this place has struggled?" Scrawny children run in the streets, their faces streaked with dirt. Equally malnourished parents chase them in unkempt clothing. The sour stench of unbathed bodies surrounds us. Even the stray animals are gaunt.

"For years." Elisaf smiles at a little girl. "Given their location away from the king's road, they do not benefit from travelers' coin, and their proximity to Eldred Wood limits their hunting grounds. Lord Danthrin beseeched King Eachann to excuse them a portion of their levies on more than one occasion. If I recall correctly, the last issue was a horrendous blight upon their crops."

Townfolk pause in streets and shop windows to watch the legionaries peel off in various directions with their horses. To scout for enemies, or maybe for a vein. I wonder if these people have ever seen one of the king's elite warriors before.

"Abarrane, seek out the supplies we need. And have Zorya collect a change of clothing for us." Zander's gaze stalls on a barefoot little boy strolling through the street, his pants torn. "Pay the people adequately for all that we procure. And stop intimidating them."

"Your Highness." She holds a hand in the air, palm up, and Elisaf tosses a hefty change purse he produced from his pocket. With a curt bow, she takes off.

"Elisaf, take five legionaries and escort Gesine and Romeria to the manor before you leave on your task. I will follow shortly."

But worry gnaws at my stomach. "Zander, this is Lord Danthrin's place. Do you remember? The asshole from the market? The one who burns children for eating wormy apples?"

His eyes shift to me, veiled of all emotion. "Yes, I recall. The one you wanted my guards to castrate."

Horik clears his throat.

"He would have been at the square, and he knows my face. We can't stay in his house with him. He'll slit my throat while I'm sleeping—"

"He's not here, and do you honestly think I would allow him in the same room as you?" Zander says with forced patience.

I swallow. I'm used to the aloof version of the king, but right now, I hate it. "How do you know he's not here?"

"Because Danthrin would not leave the city when there is a new king buying loyalty with lands and titles. Lowly noblemen like him will force their way in for an audience. He's probably in the castle, on his knees, groveling as we speak."

An alarm swells inside me. "Gracen and her children are in the castle." What if I rescued them only to have them land back in that monster's hands—

"Atticus will not release that family to him," he assures me. "Not if he knows the truth, and I promise you Corrin will inform him."

"You can't be sure of that." Atticus hates me. Why wouldn't he send them back as a punishment?

"I think I know my brother."

"Given current circumstances, I beg to differ."

Zander's lips twist with distaste. "You are right. Perhaps not as well as *you* got to know him during all those late-night games of draughts on your journey south." He sets his horse in motion, cantering down a side street.

That was not me, I want to scream.

A soft hand settles on my shoulder. "Let him be." Gesine's expression is full of sympathy.

I grit my teeth as we pass through town.

Where most homes within Freywich are built using everything from twigs to pine boards to plaster, Lord Danthrin's manor is solid stone, five times the size of anything else in the village and surrounded by its own wall.

If he's a lowly nobleman in an impoverished town, I'd hate to see how more prosperous noblemen live.

The guard who rushed ahead to announce the king is waiting at the open gate with another. A woman in a flowing white gown approaches us along a path that cuts through a rose garden. Elven, surely, by the way she carries herself, much like the ones who spent their days gossiping in the royal gardens. Behind her, a young woman follows. If her simple gray linen dress doesn't mark her as a servant, the golden ear cuff does.

"Lady Danthrin?" Elisaf asks.

"That is correct." Her blond hair is collected at her nape in a tidy chignon.

This is that pompous snake's wife? And his child, I presume, taking in how her palms settle on her swollen belly. Which means they requested access to the nymphaeum on Hudem, and Zander's father granted it. Does she know the terrible things her husband does to the mortal servants in their household?

Her piercing blue eyes skitter over our faces, lingering on mine a moment before dismissing me. She assumes I'm just another Islorian elven. Gesine's shriveled morels must be working because she doesn't seem to suspect she has the Ybarisan princess at her doorstep. "Will the king be arriving shortly?" Her voice is smooth with an air of snootiness.

"Indeed, he will. He had matters to attend to."

"My lady." She glares at Elisaf. "You will address me appropriately for my station, soldier."

Elisaf dips his head in acknowledgment. "Yes, of course, *my lady*."

I gnash my teeth. Sometimes I wish Elisaf was capable of being an asshole.

She sizes up Gesine. "You are one of the king's priestesses?"

Gesine nods.

"I would request that you attend to me later. I would like to know how my child is faring."

"It would be a pleasure, my lady." Gesine's smile is warm and genuine, and I wish she would also be less so.

"My people are preparing two rooms as we speak. That is all I can spare. The stables are to the left. Your soldiers will be crowded, but I should expect they find suitable respite there for the night." Displeasure mars Lady Danthrin's features as she regards the legionaries with us.

Suddenly, I regret Zander sending Abarrane off on an errand. She wouldn't tolerate this.

Lady Danthrin's cold stare settles on me—on my stinking, dusty clothes and boots—and I tense with anticipation of what might come out of that sour mouth.

"I will have my servants fill one of the horse's troughs so those traveling with the king may cleanse."

Those traveling with the king. She couldn't say "common whore" louder.

With everything I've been through and all that I know of her despicable husband, my anger reaches its boiling point. Yeah, she knows damn well the kind of monster she married. "Your Highness," I hiss.

Confusion mars her tight face.

"You will address me as Your Highness, as is appropriate for someone of *my* station. And I can't wait to tell the king what you think is suitable for his future queen." I may as well throw that title around while I still can.

All color drains from her face, her gaze flittering among faces as if searching for the truth to my claim. "I … I did not realize—"

"I will take my bath in the room you have prepared for me." My voice is cold and hard. I nudge Elisaf with my hand on his back.

"My lady." He leads us along the drive. Only when we're halfway to the stables does he whisper, "You do choose odd times to wield that title, *Your Highness*."

The sheer curtain at the window provides ample cover for spying on the warriors as I drag a comb through my freshly washed hair. Lady Danthrin transformed into an exemplary host after her humiliating introduction. By the time a servant led us here—a large guest bedroom with an enormous four-poster bed draped in velvet—warm towels and robes had been laid out and a copper tub was already half full, a steady line of gangly mortals rushing up the stairs with buckets of water. They've returned twice, delivering platters of food and pitchers of wine.

Most legionaries have made their way back to the stables and are either cleaning up in the water trough or settling on hay bales to rest, their laughter carrying into the otherwise quiet evening. Three tributaries huddle in a corner behind an elven man, the torchlight glinting off their gold ear cuffs. I assume the Islorian is their keeper, his clothing fashioned from fine cloth that doesn't hint of the poverty I saw entering town, his hair pulled into a ponytail to highlight the severe cut of his cheekbones. His scowl says he's complying with Zander's demand, but he's not happy. Or maybe it's about being made to wait, given how he keeps tapping his foot and looking around. No one seems in a rush to take advantage of his donations.

What of these tributaries, though? What do they think of being passed over to a group of fierce warriors?

"Do you think any of those vials have made it here yet?"

"I think not, but I will test the tributaries before they feed, just to be sure."

"You can do that?" I can't help but steal a glance at the priestess, submerged in her freshly drawn bath, scrubbing a dried patch of dirt from her elbow. A simple beige linen dress hangs by the door for her, delivered by Zorya, along with riding pants and a fresh tunic for me. Danthrin's servants are busy scrubbing the smell of sewage from our other clothes. A futile effort, I'm afraid.

"I can because I know what to look for. I will go to the stables as soon as I'm finished here. There are still those with less critical injuries to tend to."

"What about me?"

"You have injuries you need tending, Your Highness?"

"No, I'm fine." My hand smooths over the knife prick from Abarrane. It'll be gone within a day. The scratch on my cheek has already healed. "But I have a million questions." And I haven't had a chance to ask one. "What did you tell Zander yesterday?"

"The truth." Water sluices off her arm. "That the two of you together can bring an end to the blood curse."

"How?"

"That remains to be seen."

"So you have no idea how."

"Prophecies do not come with instructions. It is not how they work."

"What else did you tell him?"

She considers that a moment. "He asked about the summons Ianca made, if it was true that Princess Romeria could have clouded his judgment as so many have suggested."

"And you said it was."

"The queen felt the most effective weapon against the Islorians would be one that could get exceptionally close to him."

Into his bed and his heart. "And now Zander doesn't believe that *anything* he feels for me is real. Or *felt* for me. That it's all fake." My chest burns. What I felt for him was *very* real. It still is, no matter how much I might wish it weren't. And this ache settled within, that's also painfully real.

"He has reservations, yes." She wipes the washcloth across her brow. "But now that his eyes are open, Aoife's manipulations have far less power over him. She cannot force him to love the princess."

"Just like Malachi can't force me to take the stone." Because the fates can't create will. Wendeline said that. And now that I know Malachi's plans, I'll never do it.

"The king will make his decisions for himself."

I peer out the window as Gesine climbs from the tub and towels off. "I think he already has."

"Do not assume Zander does not care for you. But it is often easier to wield anger than to drown in sorrow. He is in a difficult position. The idea of a key caster roaming these lands has been feared for two millennia. That fear—and the risk—will not dissolve simply because of your good intentions. And any choice he makes will have consequences. He cannot make those decisions based solely on his heart. That is not the way of a good king."

"He's committed to getting his throne back." Even if he admitted he doesn't want it. And I am now a tool for him to accomplish that, a reality that stings more than his previous plan to leave me behind.

"You cannot find fault with him for that. It is commendable. They are his people and his responsibility."

"Why are you defending him? Since we met you he's been nothing but an asshole, but you keep deferring to him *every time*." I think back to the formidable wind she unleashed to push us across the water. Something tells me Gesine could strike all of us dead if she wanted to, but she's too busy bowing.

"There will be a time to make a stand. This is not it."

I watch from the window as another group of young women arrives with a keeper. Horik has ventured closer, bending his massive frame to stroke a stable dog's ears while he sizes up his options.

They're all the same, these Islorian immortals—tall and lithe, their movements graceful. Dressed well, finely polished. And all the tributaries seem the same—wide-eyed and shrinking away from the Legion, afraid of them.

Maybe rightfully so. I think back to how those savage nobility attacked the Ybarisans at the royal repast. Will these warriors treat their tributaries much differently?

"I should get out there before they get impatient and take needless risks." Gesine peers out from beside me, dressed, her lengthy black hair still wet. She's tied a silk scarf around her neck to hide the gold collar. "While I'm gone, practice removing the token from your finger and breathing through the discomfort. You must learn to compartmentalize your caster affinities first before you can wield them."

I fumble with my ring. "How long will it take for me to get a handle on all this?"

"That, I cannot say. Some manage it within days, others take months. Years. But you must practice. The sooner you have a hold on it, the sooner I can teach you how to channel the immense gifts bestowed upon you." She collects an apple, tossing it into the air once before pocketing it. From Danthrin's prized orchard, I'll bet. I saw the tops of trees behind the stables before it grew too dark. It must be somewhere out there.

"I will be back as soon as I can." With a bow and a murmured "Your Highness"—because she can't seem to help herself—she ducks out.

I watch from my hiding place as Gesine emerges from the house a few minutes later and strolls across the grounds toward the tributaries. She turns the heads of warriors on her way past. They don't seem as openly hostile toward the caster as they were yesterday, a few tipping their heads in a subtle greeting when their eyes meet. I suppose taking away agonizing pain can forge relationships.

Jarek has joined Horik by the tributaries. Judging by his stern expression, he's saying something to the newly arrived keeper that the immortal does not appear to like.

I ease open the window.

"… are you calling us savages?" Jarek's tone is casual, amused, but his hand is resting on his dagger handle, as if primed to draw and drive it into the other male at any moment.

The keeper swallows but then pulls his shoulders back. "We have honored the king's request for the use of our tributaries as a matter of *need* for his soldiers, but we will not have our property defiled by their *wants*." His nasally voice grates.

He's agreed to let the Legion feed, but he's drawing the line at fucking. Fair enough. And good for him for standing up for them. Maybe the keepers aren't *all* scum like Danthrin.

Jarek takes a step forward. Even his stance, his feet squared off with his shoulders, is menacing. "The Legion is bound by honor and duty to the king, and it does not take things that are not offered."

The keeper's hands go up in a sign of surrender, a tight smile pulling at his lips. "Then we will have no issues because my mortals will not be offering anything beyond their vein. Where is the king, by the way?" He peers around, searching. "I should very much like to meet him."

"He doesn't care to meet with commoners." Jarek's smile drips with challenge and stinks of arrogance. He's trying to provoke a fight.

The keeper's eyes flare.

"If I may …" Gesine slips in between the two males, forcing both to step back. It's a distraction from the growing tension, and, if I'm beginning to understand Gesine at all, her way of defusing an explosive situation. Maybe she has armed herself with an invisible shield.

Or maybe either of them could kill her in an instant.

Without any explanation, she reaches out for the closest tributary, a blond who can't be much over eighteen.

The young woman presents her hand tentatively, and Gesine collects it, bowing her head a moment. "She is ready."

Jarek juts his chin at Horik. "Feed now. You're on watch next." He beckons others over with a snap of his fingers.

The woman's eyes grow wide as she takes in the giant, and I hold my breath, half expecting the enormous warrior to collect her by the scruff and drag her away.

But Horik only takes a step back to give her space.

Gesine shifts to the next tributary, following the same process.

The keeper scowls. "Who are you and what are you doing?"

It dawns on me that the people of Freywich may not know about the poison working its way through Islor.

Gesine's smile is soft as she guides the tributary to another waiting warrior. "I am the king's caster, and I'm granting them the fates' blessings so they may give the warriors strength."

Damn, she lies so smoothly. I would be wise to remember that.

The keeper grunts as if weighing that answer, but he's distracted as Horik and the other warrior lead the tributaries into the stables. "Where are they going? I did not give permission to take them anywhere. No, they will feed right *here* where I can see them."

"The Legion will feed *where* they want, *when* they want"—Jarek steps in closer, his looming size making the other male look fragile and small, though he is neither—"and *how* they want."

Three tense seconds pass and then the keeper moves several steps back, shrinking from Jarek. He notices his last tributary stalled, and wrenching her arm, he shoves her forward. "Go." He glowers as she leaves with Zorya.

He's not a kind keeper. He doesn't care about their well-being, or the warriors taking things too far. He just doesn't like sharing his toys, and he'll probably unleash his irritation on them later.

My anger flares, the need to lash out overpowering my senses. This prick needs a good slap.

I can't help myself. Adrenaline floods my veins, the gold around my finger heating. I focus on the trough and watch with satisfaction as the water comes alive at my will, twirling into the air, taking the shape of a woman's hand—delicate, long fingers—to smack the keeper from behind.

Only the blow is harder than I intended. My stomach drops as the keeper sails across the space and lands in a mound of dirt.

Time stands still as everyone watches, some with gaping mouths, others with smirks.

He pulls himself up, spitting out bits of hay while surveying his sodden and filthy clothes.

Not dirt, I realize. The day's collection from the horse stalls.

A bubble of laughter bursts from my mouth before I can stop it, drawing all eyes to my window. I fight the urge to duck behind the curtains when the keeper finds me there, a mixture of shock and rage filling his expression.

More stuffy immortals herd their tributaries through the stable gate, some waving at them like cattle.

"This must be the Ybarisan princess we've heard about," the horseshit-covered keeper pushes through gritted teeth. "To what do I owe this treatment?" He doesn't cap it with any address—even for show, as Danthrin did—and I immediately know what he thinks of himself and of me.

I glower at him, forcing ice into my tone. "They are human beings, not your possessions."

"If you are to be the queen of Islor, I suggest you familiarize yourself with Islor's customs." His chuckle is condescending as he looks to the other keepers gathered.

"And *I* suggest you start treating those who keep you alive better before they rise against you." *You have no idea what's coming, you arrogant fuck.* A part of me hopes one of these young women is handed a vial and decides she's had enough.

He cocks his head. "What you're suggesting would be tantamount to treason against the crown."

"And what is being suggested?" comes a deep voice.

My heart was already pounding, but now it skips entire beats as Zander strolls past the tributaries who drop with deep curtsies, their keepers following quickly. His mane of golden-brown hair looks freshly washed. He's replaced his ragged outfit with fitted and finely made black leathers similar to the Legion's clothing, with as many weapons strapped to his solid frame. He appears just as deadly.

Abarrane is close on his heels with two other warriors—one the size of Horik, his arms laden with a wooden keg, another carrying an enormous metal platter stacked with roasted meat.

"What is happening here?" Zander's focus shifts from the keeper to the puddle of water at his boots and the clumps of horseshit and straw clinging to his fine coat, to the trough of water, and then lastly to the window where I stand.

I offer a mock innocent shrug. Gesine *did* say to practice.

"Never mind, I think I have an idea." He sighs heavily. "I appreciate your generosity. The Legion will ensure a safe escort for your tributaries back to your home once they've provided their service." He raises his voice to address the other keepers. "*All* of your tributaries."

My teeth grit. Their service. Will I ever get used to this?

Several keepers move for the gate, grasping the dismissal. But the horseshit one hasn't. "Your Highness, I am Ambrose Villier, a dear friend of Lord Danthrin's. I must say, I am surprised to see you *here* on the last days of Cirilea's fair—"

"No one cares what surprises you." Steel rings in the court as Abarrane draws her sword. From this view, she appears a full head shorter than Villier, but she doesn't so much as flinch while peering up at him. "Leave now, or I'll ensure you leave in parts, beginning with your slippery tongue, *Ambrose Villier*."

The keeper rushes away.

My gaze settles on Zander.

"Your people skills are improving," he teases her, smoothing a hand over the back of his neck, a tell for the tension building.

She slides her sword back in place. "Do not pretend you keep me at your side for *those* skills."

"No, I do not. But you should go and feed. You have been in an exceptionally foul mood lately. More than usual."

She moves for the line of tributaries that Gesine has cleared but stops abruptly, her eyes skimming my window. "And what about His Highness? Should I bring one for you, or would you prefer to choose?"

But of course, Zander will take a vein tonight. It's been weeks, and he needs all the strength he can gather, now more than ever.

I know this, and yet the question lands like a blade, piercing my chest.

As I'm sure Abarrane intended.

Zander studies the group, and I hold my breath, waiting for him to glance my way. He knows I'm watching. He always does.

"That one." His jaw is tense. "The one on the end."

I swallow the growing lump as I search out the tributary he means. A brunette with rosy cheeks and full curves steps forward, curtsying deeply. When she rises, she's smiling.

Maybe she doesn't mind being fed on, or maybe it's the king she doesn't mind.

His return smile, albeit small—nothing more than a slight twitch at the corners of his mouth—twists my stomach with dread.

I move away from the window before anyone can see my misery.

10
ROMERIA

"Who were you?" I examine the stranger's reflection staring back at me in the small vanity mirror. Her blue eyes are as pale as an early-morning sky, her cheekbones high and jutting, her lips plump, the top curved like a heart. She appeared the moment I removed my ring and has watched quietly as the uncomfortable pins-and-needles buzz of these caster affinities vibrates along every limb of her body.

Learn to compartmentalize? It's taking every ounce of my determination just to tolerate it, and several breaks in between.

Slipping my ring back on, I breathe a sigh of relief as the unpleasantness dissolves into silence and the familiar face appears again. This face—*mine*—is a welcomed illusion in a world where I feel more alone than I did as Korsakov's thief.

The sun set many hours ago, and Gesine hasn't yet returned. I venture over to the window to search for her. The warriors have quieted, many settling down wherever they can find a snug space, sated by ale and meat and mortal blood. The ones on watch lurk in shadows somewhere unseen. Elisaf hasn't returned. He must still be on that task Zander mentioned.

Where Zander is … I have no idea. My chest tightens, thinking about what he might be doing with that tributary right now.

The other window in my room shows a different angle of the stables.

I spot Gesine right away and slap a hand over my mouth to stifle my giggle. She's perched on a wooden barrel in front of a red-haired warrior whose pants are pushed down to his thighs, her delicate hands hovering over his bare ass.

I remember that one griping on the way here about taking an arrow. His injury hadn't been deemed severe last night, but I guess a day in the saddle must have changed that.

A soft feminine moan pulls my attention away from Gesine and the injured warrior. There's no mistaking that sound for what it is.

Oh God, please no. My blood rushes to my ears as dread builds, coaxing me farther out my window, desperate to know whether Zander will finish breaking my heart tonight.

A couple sits in an empty wagon. I can only see the tops of their heads from here, but the nearby lantern casts enough light to show Jarek's telltale braids as he buries his face in the crook of the woman's neck.

The wave of relief that hits almost buckles my knees. Wherever Zander is and whatever he's doing, at least he isn't doing it right below my room.

I should move away, but my curiosity keeps me anchored. I've seen these Islorians feed on numerous occasions now—Zander, the night I discovered what he was, at the Goat's Knoll when we rushed past cubbies and corners of various salacious acts, at the horrifying royal repast where they demonstrated the savagery they are capable of.

In truth, I expected something akin to the last with these legionaries, who seem so cold and abrasive. But Jarek is surprisingly tender, one hand collecting the tributary's lengthy hair, the other splayed across her lower back, holding her in place as she straddles his lap. Everything about his demeanor is calm and gentle.

The bodice of her dress is unfastened and sits low, exposing her chest. She sighs, her hands wandering over his broad shoulders, along his cut arms, around his lengthy braids.

Much like the tributary that night with Zander.

Jarek shifts away from her neck with feathered kisses along her exposed shoulder. I can't see the bite marks from here, but I know they'll be nothing more than pinpricks, these Islorian fangs so much more delicate and needlelike than the daaknar's. Unintelligible whispers carry, along with her soft giggle and his—a sensual, deep chuckle that, for once, carries no derision—and then their lips find each other's in an intimate kiss that is almost … sweet.

Her hands disappear between them where they fumble—with buttons, material, and body parts—before their forms double over into the wagon, shifting and wriggling. They both release deep groans.

My cheeks flush as they rock against each other, Jarek's hands seizing her hips to guide her movements.

The Legion won't take what isn't offered, but if it *is* offered …

I'm on the verge of ducking away from the window when the tributary sits up, leaving Jarek lying below her as she rides him with enthusiasm. But Jarek's eyes are not on her. They're locked on me, leaning out my window. He shows no hint of surprise. It's as if he knew I was here all along.

I jump out of view.

A deep, mocking chuckle curls into my room.

It's well after midnight when I give up on sleep and venture downstairs to find Gesine.

The interior of Lord and Lady Danthrin's manor presents hospitality that its owners do not. The stone walls are lined with heavy velvet drapery, flickering candle sconces that cast a romantic light, and a gallery of colorful oil-painted canvasses.

Most are of landscapes, but a few offer portraits in surreal likeness, including two sizable images of the manor's owners.

I glower at Lord Danthrin's beady eyes as they watch me descend the stairs into the foyer.

The young woman who escorted Lady Danthrin sits in a chair knitting at the bottom of the stairs. She scrambles out of her seat when she sees me, setting the needles and wool on a side table. "Your Highness." She curtsies. "Is there a problem? Were you calling for me?" Panic fills her face as she glances at the panel of bells.

"There's no problem." Not that she can help me with, anyway. I hesitate. "Has the king come in?" Maybe he's asleep in the bedroom next door, and I somehow missed the creaky wooden floor announcing his approach?

"Not since I've settled here, and I've been here for hours. He would have passed had he come in."

I regard the bells, a system in place so the servants can be at the Danthrins' every beck and call. "So, you just sit here?"

"Yes, Your Highness. In case Lady Danthrin needs me." She tucks a strand of corn silk–blond hair behind her ear. The move shows off puckered skin on her wrist.

I've seen burn marks like that before, on a little boy in a market, for daring to eat a rotten apple off the ground.

"Can I get you something? A drink? A late meal, perhaps?" She takes a step toward, I assume, the kitchen. "I believe there are fruit tarts fresh from the oven and cooling overnight."

As much as I would love something sweet … "No, thanks. I'm just in need of fresh air."

Her eyes widen at the door. "You mean, outside? *Now*? Your Highness, it wouldn't be wise. It isn't safe."

I smile despite my heavy mood, thinking of all I've escaped. "We have nineteen warriors out there. Anyone who tries anything with one of them around would have to be an idiot." I pause. "Though I did meet Ambrose Villier earlier, and I think we can agree he *is* an idiot."

She hesitates, biting her lip before a slow smile escapes. "Yes, Your Highness."

I decide I like her. "What's your name?"

"Eden, Your Highness." Her thin frame is still rigid, as if ready to bolt at my first request.

I lean against the wall, trying to soften the mood. "You just sit here *all* night? In case Lady Danthrin needs something?" How exhausting that would be.

"That is one of my duties, yes."

How many duties does Eden have? The heavy bags under the young girl's blue eyes suggest too many. "Does she call you a lot?"

"Rarely. Lady Danthrin is a deep sleeper." She shrugs. "But it allows me time to knit. One of the other servants in the household is having a baby. I want to surprise her with a sweater when she returns from Cirilea. I should have it ready in time." Eden holds up the woven scrap that looks nothing like a sweater yet, the move drawing my attention to her angry scar again.

She must be talking about Gracen.

"What happened to your hand?" I ask as gently as I can.

"Oh. Nothing, I just … I was silly." She tugs at her sleeve to hide the mottled skin.

She's covering for Danthrin, which boils my blood. But that's what she feels she needs to do to survive. I know what that's like.

What will happen when Danthrin returns without Gracen and the children? Is this poor girl primed to follow in her footsteps?

"Why don't you come for a walk with me? I need a guide to the stables."

Eden glances at the wall of bells.

"She's a deep sleeper, right? And if she does wake up, you can blame me."

With hunched shoulders, Eden collects a lantern from a table and leads me out a different door from the one we entered.

The night air is cool, almost enough to require the cloak I left hanging on a hook upstairs. I don't recognize this side of the house; the torches casting a dim light over a small but manicured garden.

"Lady Danthrin has quite the green thumb. She spends much time out here." Eden moves along the narrow path through the floral landscape. Wafts of jasmine and mint stir my senses, and crickets sing in my ears.

"It's beautiful." So contrary to the noble who nurtures it.

A shift in the shadows pulls my eyes left where a legionary leans against a tree, watching us.

Eden notices him a second after I do and jumps.

He doesn't so much as flinch, or smile, or try to appease her in any way.

"Don't worry, they won't hurt you."

Her laugh is breathy, nervous. "My father once told me stories of the Legion warriors, and none of them were particularly comforting. This way to the stables, Your Highness." She guides me along a garden path and beneath a vine-covered trellis. As we round corners and move farther away from the garden, the floral scent gives way to horses and hay, the crickets to whinnies and soft, rhythmic snores.

We pass the wagon where Jarek was occupied with his tributary, but it's vacant now. Still, my cheeks burn with embarrassment, knowing I'll likely hear about my spying later from the abrasive warrior.

Gesine is where I saw her last, sitting on the barrel, her slim body slumped, her hands trembling as they hover over Zorya's damaged eye.

"Is that the king's healer?" Eden whispers.

"A high priestess. Yes." A lie, but maybe also the truth now because she's as valuable a tool to Zander as I will be when I know what the hell I'm doing.

"I've never seen one before."

"Yeah? Well, now you'll see an exhausted one who's about to collapse." I shake my head as I march toward her.

Zorya sits on a stack of wooden crates, watching us with a

severe gleam as we approach. She cradles her leather eye patch in her hands.

"Gesine, you've done enough for the day," I say.

Of course, Gesine doesn't answer, her focus undeterred.

I sigh, shifting to the warrior. "She'll be no good to the Legion like this. She needs to rest now."

The warrior's jaw clenches. "We are done for the day, witch."

Another few beats pass and Gesine's hands drop.

A strangled sound escapes Eden's throat at Zorya's damaged eye staring back at us. The enemy blade cut right through the center, splitting her iris. Now it's nothing more than a cloudy gray mass with a line through it.

"They need to be at their strongest for what is to come." Gesine's lids are heavy.

"But you already know you can't fix that."

"It was worth a try."

I shake my head at the stubborn caster. Is she doing this to win the Legion's trust? Or maybe Zander's? Regardless, she'll be lucky if she can climb the steps. She's barely staying on the barrel. "Can you help her to our room?"

When Zorya doesn't move, I push, "*Please*?"

Zorya slips on her leather patch with a grim smirk and stands. Grabbing hold of Gesine's arm, she throws it over her shoulder and hauls the caster to her feet, her treatment not gentle.

But Gesine doesn't seem to care. "I am not the only one who should be sleeping now, Your Highness."

I survey the quiet stables and the peaceful warriors. Even the horses are asleep. No sign of Zander anywhere. "I'll be up soon." I point toward the house, mouthing my thanks to Zorya.

Her brow pulls tight, but she says nothing, towing Gesine back along the path we took.

"I want to see the orchard. Take me there, please?"

Eden hesitates but leads me across the dirt grounds, past the manure pile I launched Villier into earlier, and through another gate.

A clear night sky and moon allow for some natural light as we walk deeper in, but all I can see are dark forms.

Beneath my boot, something hard gives way with my weight. A fallen apple, left to rot.

"It would be more impressive seen in the daylight, Your Highness." Eden holds up the lantern, casting light on the ripe red bulbs hanging from branches.

"So this is Lord Danthrin's prized apple orchard?"

"There are pear and plum trees too. Cherries and peaches in the back."

"How many?"

"Too many to count, Your Highness. My lord and lady pride themselves on their produce."

Something pricks at my conscience. Elisaf called Danthrin a minor lord of an impoverished area, but this manor and the way Lady Danthrin regards herself would suggest otherwise.

I knew a guy once. Sneaky Pete, they called him. He was this skinny twenty-year-old kid, a small-time dealer, carving out a tiny corner of Staten Island for himself. Korsakov found out, but instead of ending his little operation, he decided to let the kid keep going in his territory, as long as he moved his product. He said he liked Sneaky Pete's gusto.

Until he discovered that Sneaky Pete was also getting his drugs from three other suppliers and selling four times what he admitted to Korsakov, beyond his original borders. Sneaky Pete was raking in money.

I overheard Tony joking about how they buried a wad of his cash with him so he could spend it in hell.

I'll bet if anyone looked at Danthrin's books, so to speak, they might not call him impoverished, despite how the townsfolk live.

"Do you like living here, Eden?"

She falters. "I … Lord and Lady Danthrin are …"

I collect the lantern from her grasp and hold it up to her face. Fear is splayed there. "The burn on your wrist reminds me of one I recently saw on a little boy from Freywich. He was at the market in Cirilea. His keeper punished him for eating a wormy apple off the ground."

Recognition streaks across her face. She swallows hard. "I broke one of the lady's dishes. I was washing, and it slipped from my grasp."

"*She* did that to you?"

"It was one of her favorites. Passed down through generations." The way Eden says it, it's as if it's excusable.

How nostalgic. So torturing their servants isn't only the lord's pastime of choice. "Is that the only time they've punished you for something?"

She hesitates before offering an almost imperceptible head shake.

My ire flares. Eden doesn't deserve this. None of them do. "Gracen and her children are now part of the royal household, living in the castle in Cirilea."

Her eyes widen with shock. "My lord allowed them to leave?"

"He wasn't given a choice."

She blinks, processing this. "So ... they're never coming back?"

"Not if I can help it. They'll be treated well there." *I hope.* I pray Zander is right about Atticus in that regard.

"That is good. They will be happier there." Her words are hopeful, yet her shoulders sink as if weighed down.

"Do you have family here?"

"No. I grew up in a small village near the Plains of Aminadav, with my mother, father, and younger brother." She smiles. "It wasn't so bad. Our keeper was much kinder."

"And then you were forced to leave with Danthrin on Presenting Day?" Corrin spoke of the day when young mortal men and women who'd reached eighteen years were lined up in town squares to be bid on.

She shakes her head. "I wasn't of age yet. My keeper had a gambling problem and owed Lord Danthrin considerable money, so he paid off his debt with me."

The curse slips out. I know I shouldn't be doing this—I'm in no position to, yet, I can't help myself. Who knows how much longer I'll be able to wield this fake title around? "I gave Gracen a choice that I'm now going to give you. We are leaving here tomorrow morning, and you can leave with us."

Her mouth gapes. "To Cirilea? To the castle?"

I hesitate. I don't want to lie, but I can't tell her the truth. "Eventually, I hope so. There are some complications we need to sort out. But for now, where we're going is not safe. You'll be with me and a powerful caster, and probably the scariest warriors in all of Islor, but it won't be safe. It's your choice. You can stay here if you want. I'm not forcing you."

She peers back toward the house. "There's nothing left for me here."

"But it might be safer—"

"It's not. What they do to us ... All of us." She flinches. "All the keepers in Freywich are alike."

I wish that water slap I'd given Villier had been harder. Hard enough that he never got back up.

From the house, a faint ringing carries.

Eden gasps, panic twisting her face. "That is my lady. If I don't answer her—"

"Go ahead." I wave her off with my free hand.

She makes to move, but then freezes. "Your Highness, I can't leave you out here alone."

"I'm not alone, don't worry." I know there is a legionary somewhere close, watching. I can feel their eyes on me. "Go on. And blame me."

She tears off into the darkness, leaving the lantern in my grasp. I hold it up as high as possible to cast light on her path to the gate.

I'm not ready to head inside. Nearby, a stack of baskets sits in a pile. So Danthrin's servants can collect—but not dare eat—the fruit. On impulse, I grab one, and balancing it against my hip, I guide the lantern light upward in search of ripe apples.

Zander leans against the trunk of the tree.

I let out a surprised yelp. "Do you have *any* idea how creepy that is?"

He smirks. "I always forget how weak your vision is in the dark."

"I don't think you do." Swallowing against my racing heart, I shift back to my task. "How long have you been standing there?"

"Long enough to know you have a habit of collecting strays."

I shoot him a dirty look. "They're not *strays*. They'd probably be better off if they were."

"A young mortal woman like that would not last long without a house to run to." He hauls himself off the tree and approaches, pulling an apple off a branch and setting it in the basket, his hazel eyes holding mine steadily. They're brighter than when I saw him last, the tired lining beneath them gone.

Much like they appeared the morning after he last fed.

I look away first, pushing out dark thoughts as my stomach roils. "Did you hear, then, that some other asshole keeper traded her to pay off his gambling debt? And not even on Presenting Day. They don't follow Islor's rules. Danthrin doesn't take care of his people." Not his household. Not the town.

"Yes, I am seeing evidence that points to that. Abarrane said little food and supplies were found until she knocked on the doors of the more prominent households. It has become clear that Freywich's struggles have more to do with bad keepers than bad crops." Zander's tone is bleak.

"You have to stop him."

"How do I do that, Romeria? Danthrin isn't here to collect a punishment, and I do not have a kingdom anymore technically, a truth the people will learn soon enough."

I don't bother correcting him when he uses my full name. I've always liked the way it sounds rolling off his tongue.

We quietly pluck apples off branches, Zander's impeccable vision and height allowing him three for every one I find. The basket grows heavy, forcing me to shift it against my hip.

"Are you collecting for the road?"

"Just collecting." Though having a few to snack on might be wise. Knowing it would piss off Danthrin if he were aware makes it more appealing. "I'd strip these trees of every last piece of fruit and give them to those hungry people. "

"You always have had a soft spot for these humans. At least now I understand why."

"You don't know anything about me." All Zander knows is that I was a jewel thief. He doesn't know what I've been through, what I've seen. But information is power, and the less I give him, the better off I'll be. Still, I admit, "We used to do this when I was young."

"Pick apples?"

"Every fall."

"I can't imagine Queen Neilina in an orchard."

My lantern light catches the warning in his stare. A legionary must be nearby and listening. That, or he's reminding me to keep up all pretenses.

Zander reaches over to take the basket from me, his hand sweeping across my rib cage, sending a warm shiver through my body.

Until I look up and note the drop of blood on his bottom lip. An ice-cold bucket of reality douses the warmth. "You missed a spot."

Understanding skims across his face, and his tongue darts out, erasing the evidence.

I may have been looking for Zander earlier, but now that I've found him, I regret it.

Reaching for another basket from the pile, I move to the other side of the tree in search of more apples but really to put space between us.

"I had no choice."

I swallow the lump swelling in my throat. "You don't have to explain yourself to me." It's clear in every way that we're no longer together. But what choice did he make? Was it just her blood, or did he also satisfy himself in other ways?

"You're right, I don't."

The lantern light shines through the branches, allowing me to meet his gaze.

"I am what I am, and you are what you are, and we can't change any of it. There is no point dwelling on what we shared in the past because it is just that—in the past."

It's official. The king of Islor is breaking up with me. I knew it was coming, yet I feel no relief hearing the words now. "You think I haven't figured that out already? It's been over since Cirilea." I set my jaw. "You abandoned me when I was standing right in front of you!"

"And have I left your side?" he asks calmly.

Every night. "No, but only because you need me."

He picks an apple off the stem. "I have the people of Islor to think of, and I must do what's best for them, no matter the cost."

"And what exactly is this costing you?"

His chuckle is derisive. "What *hasn't* it cost me?"

His family.

His crown.

His heart.

Another darker thought stirs, and my chest tightens as the pieces click together. Little comments he's made, things Gesine has alluded to. I level him with a hard look. "You want to use me to get your throne back and then what? What happens to me after that?"

He's the first to look away. "I cannot see into the future."

Neither can I, but I can guess. "Everyone's an enemy now, right?"

"I must prepare for *all* outcomes for the sake of Islor." His voice is wooden as he focuses on the fruit in his grasp.

I push aside this nauseating sensation, knowing the kinds of choices Zander must be weighing about me. "Don't worry. I'm used to being a pawn." I spent years playing Korsakov's game, knowing he would have me killed the second I outlived my purpose.

The difference is, I wasn't in love with him.

Zander flinches, but then his body stiffens with his resolve. "We cannot take that girl with us. Venhorn is no place for her. It'll be dangerous enough as it is."

Switching topics. More proof of a guilty conscience. But I let it go because the truth is, I don't think I can hear him say those other words out loud without it breaking me. "It's Eden's choice."

"And if you told her the truth, do you think she would make the same one?"

"Fine. We can find a better keeper for her in Bellcross."

"We do not have time to evaluate suitable keepers."

I try another angle. "What about Woodswich? Elisaf told me the mortals who live there are free."

His chuckle is dark. "The girl wouldn't last the winter there with *those* people."

"Well then, I don't have an answer, but at least I'm doing *something* to try to stop this abuse. What have *you* done, besides talk about it?" My voice cracks as my emotions spill over and my frustration swells. "You're too busy playing king to fill the role."

His eyes blaze with anger.

But I don't relent. "And you think *you*'re the only one who's lost something? I've lost *everything*!" I drop the basket of apples, scattering them over the ground, and rush away, unwilling to let him see me cry.

By the time I shove through the gate, the tears are streaming down my cheeks.

11
ZANDER

Romeria storms away, her back rigid as she crashes through the gate, likely waking half the Legion—though they're never fully asleep, ready to spring into action at a second's notice.

Moments later, my ears catch the first sob as it escapes from her throat.

My molars grind. Pacifying others with lies has never been my strength, but it wouldn't have mattered, anyway. She is weighing the same sorts of decisions I must. She just doesn't have all the necessary information.

Standing in that arena, facing Atticus's accusations, I chose Romeria over my crown. There is no other way to explain it. And if I had to do it again, I would choose the same. But how can I choose a key caster, regardless of what I feel for the woman who wields that power, when I know the cost could be catastrophic?

I am a king. I do not have that luxury.

Tonight, with her staring up at me through those alluring blue eyes, I wanted to dismiss every doubt, every fear, every worry, just to feel her warm body and soft lips again. I wanted to tell her that I abhorred my time with that tributary, that I didn't take a drop more of her blood than needed, and nothing else.

I wanted to tell her that my feelings for her are still very much in the present.

But is that by my will, or Aoife's?

It's infuriating to not trust my own heart.

And the day may come where I'm forced to ask her to open the nymphaeum door, knowing she may die. Ask her to trust these nymphs, knowing they may demand her life. If I had to risk her like that today, I wouldn't have it in me.

For all that Gesine laid before me, I cannot be sure of any path forward.

And what if the day comes when it is not me but Romeria making the impossible decision? Would she be willing to sacrifice me to see peace restored? Would her gentle and welcoming heart allow her to do that? To put Islor ahead of me? Of us?

I fear I already know that answer.

This is why I should keep my distance and allow her feelings to harden toward me. I know where her thoughts were going just now. Maybe it's best they remain there to rot until hatred breeds.

The crunch of an apple beneath a boot warns me of Abarrane's approach, though I sensed her there, lurking in the shadows. "What have you learned?"

"That she's too emotional."

I roll my eyes. "About Freywich."

"It is as you suspected. Many keepers have cellars full of food and wine and stables full of hungry servants."

A vast expanse of trees stretches into the darkness. Lord Danthrin has spent years nurturing the idea of a simple, struggling domain. Given Freywich's location off the king's road, it is removed from common travel and therefore not visited. No one would have suspected he's been cultivating far more than lies with the lands given to him by my father, being this close to Cirilea.

"She's right. All I've done so far is talk," I murmur, more to myself. Talk and strategize and arm myself with information about the atrocities Islorians commit every day.

Talk, but no action.

"What do you know of *this* Romeria?" Abarrane asks quietly to avoid nearby ears. Though, they wouldn't be foolish enough to eavesdrop on their king and commander.

"She was a jewel thief." One with a relentless—and endearing—need to help those less fortunate.

Abarrane snorts. "A thief who cannot wield a weapon?"

Who cannot even seem to figure out how to affix one to her hip. "That is why you will train her how to fight."

"Not *this* again."

"Yes, Commander. *This* again. She must be able to stand up for herself in every way, in every situation."

"So she can be more dangerous to us than she already is?"

"As long as we can keep her reined in, she will be an asset to us."

"And what of after? Once you are back on your throne?" Abarrane doesn't waver in that goal, does not doubt the outcome. Her resolve is admirable.

But I know what she's asking. It's the exact thing Romeria just implied. "I will make the right choice for the future of Islor." I study the scattered fruit on the ground and the full basket nearby. It's time I spoke in the only language these keepers seem to understand.

"Wake the Legion."

12
ROMERIA

The stables are bustling when Gesine and I emerge in the morning, the legionaries affixing animal skins to their saddles for the next leg of our journey. Zander hovers near the orchard gate with Abarrane and Elisaf, a rolled parchment in his grasp. Whatever they're discussing, Zander's glower is dark, his lips moving fast and furious.

My heart pangs with sorrow at the sight of him. Did he sleep last night? The floor in our hall is full of creaks, and yet, as I lay in bed for hours, struggling to stifle my sobs, I didn't hear a single sound.

As if sensing me, Zander turns and meets my gaze, revealing nothing in his. I would do *anything* for a pair of heavy sunglasses to hide my puffy eyes.

He looks away, his conversation continuing, as if I'm nothing more than a minor distraction.

Gesine is wrong. If he felt any sadness for me, he is over it.

"We need to leave," I whisper, the second time I've said those words to her this morning.

She gives me a sympathetic smile. "You know why we can't."

Because we wouldn't survive long out there, just the two of us. And because Zander won't ever allow us out of his sight, not when he has a powerful elemental and a key caster at his disposal to win back his throne.

But mostly because of this stupid prophecy Gesine clings to, that Margrethe gave her life for.

Gesine may not be willing to run, but I am. I decided last night, staring at the velvet canopy of the bed, absorbing the cold shock of my encounter with Zander. Now that I know where he stands, and what's likely in store for me once he's back on his throne in Cirilea, I have no other choice.

One day, after I've learned what I can from Gesine, I will run where no one will ever find me.

Where no one can use me ever again.

I scan the stables for Eden. She wasn't in her chair when I returned last night. It was a relief at the time, not wanting her to see my tears. But the servant who brought plates of food and water for cleaning up this morning seemed cagey when I asked of Eden's whereabouts.

We pass a group of warriors perched on their horses, Jarek among them. I avoid meeting his stare.

"My arse feels fantastic today, thanks to you, witch," the burly redheaded warrior announces, stirring a round of chuckles.

Gesine dips her head. "I am *so* relieved for you *and* your arse, Drakon."

He grins. But his humor evaporates when Jarek bites into a red apple beside him. "If I have to see one more of those fucking things …"

"This one's sweet, though," Jarek mumbles between chews. "And I do like them sweet. Isn't that right, Your Highness?" He caps off his words with a wink.

"No idea." I race away before he can see my flushed cheeks, ignoring the roar of laughter that follows.

Gesine rushes to catch up. "What did he mean by that?"

"Nothing. He's a pig." I dismiss Jarek from my thoughts as I make my way toward Elisaf, who has left Zander's side. "Where have you been?"

"I missed you too." He strokes his horse's muzzle with one hand while cupping a palmful of feed with his other. "I was on an errand for the king."

"Where?"

"Cirilea."

My jaw drops with shock. "He sent you back there?"

"As close to it as I could get, yes. Atticus is dispatching riders to every corner of Islor. I intercepted one such message."

The parchment. It was a letter. "What did it say?"

His brown eyes flitter around our surroundings. "That Atticus has claimed the crown. That Zander is conspiring with the princess of Ybaris to eliminate the world of Islor's immortals and is considered an enemy to the realm, along with anyone who harbors him. He is working with one of Queen Neilina's collared casters, who she sent to Islor to provide aid for his plans."

I curse. He knows Gesine is with us. That could be through Corrin or Wendeline. Or maybe Bexley, the owner of the Goat's Knoll, who deals in valuable information and likely feels slighted by me. "Will people believe it?"

"It has the royal seal. They have no reason not to. It also tells of the poison running through your veins, and how one drop of it in a mortal's blood will kill anyone who feeds off them. He has instructed lords to kill any mortal found with a vial on their person or with poison in their veins, without trial, and he has set a bounty on your head. He wants you alive, though."

"Do I want to know how much?"

"A lordship and a large parcel of fertile land in the plains, and gold. It is quite generous." Elisaf pauses. "I've always fancied myself a title."

I snort. "How about I call you Lord Elisaf from now on?"

"I suppose that will do."

A door from the house opens, and Lady Danthrin breezes through in a sky-blue silk dress that looks more suited to a ball than an early-morning farewell in the stables. The girl who brought our breakfast trails her. Eden is still nowhere in sight.

While I'd like to think it's because Lady Danthrin gave her the morning off to sleep, my gut tells me I'm right to worry. "Do you think she knows yet?"

"No, but she will soon. We have stayed too long. Freywich is not high on Atticus's priority list, but we intercepted two messengers yesterday—one with a letter from Danthrin to his wife, condemning Zander as the gutless king they always believed him to be and hoping your head finds its way to a stake. Another with a letter from an Ambrose Villier to Danthrin, notifying him of the king's arrival at his house." Elisaf smirks. "He mentioned the future Ybarisan queen's distasteful attitude, something I wish I'd been here to witness."

"How did Zander take it?"

"How do you think he took it?" He flashes me a knowing look.

If I know him at all, Zander will consider it a challenge.

We watch as Lady Danthrin reaches her destination and curtsies. "Your Highness. At last, we meet. I was afraid I would miss you before you left on your travels. I hope you and your company have found your lodging satisfactory?" Her voice is at least two octaves higher.

"All sugar and spice and everything nice for her dear king," I mutter, earning Elisaf's chuckle.

Zander doesn't acknowledge her at first, handing Abarrane the rolled parchment.

"Prepare to move out!" she bellows, and the last of the Legion mount their horses with ease, radiating fresh energy. They needed the rest—and as much as I hate to admit it, the feedings.

With that done, Zander turns his attention to the pregnant elven. "Lady Danthrin, we appreciate your hospitality." His tone is calm, emotionless, his expression bored.

She beams. "You probably do not recall our first meeting in the throne room, when your father blessed us with the gift of Hudem." She smooths her hand over her belly, drawing his attention to it. "A terrible thing to happen to a great leader, but we are fortunate to have another fierce king to govern Islor."

Zander glares at her while she lies to his face.

"Still, my heart hurts for such a tragic and *avoidable* loss."

Was that a dig at me? If it is, she doesn't dare glance my way.

"As does mine." He peers at the young woman standing behind, her head bowed. "I'd like you to invite your servants out to the stable. *All* of them, including the young female who was working overnight."

He means Eden.

I frown. What is Zander up to?

"Your Highness?" Confusion fills Lady Danthrin's face. "I do not understand—"

"I should think my request is clear."

She falters a moment, flustered, before she waves a hand at the girl who hurries off toward the door. "Of course, my king is welcome to request anything he wishes of me, and I will comply eagerly ..." She falters, as if searching for the right words. "But might His Highness allow me the opportunity to ask his purpose?"

"My purpose will be clear soon enough."

She takes in her surroundings. Where yesterday she had haughty looks for the warriors, now she watches them like someone might watch a pack of stray dogs primed to attack.

Zander begins to pace. "The level of poverty I've witnessed in Freywich alarms me."

"The town and its people have faced many difficult years." Lady Danthrin's smile is uneasy. "Unfortunately, this side of Islor isn't blessed with the same fortunes as those lands in the Plains of Aminadav."

"Yes, your husband has sung that song once or twice before. I remember you bowing before my father the king, using the excuse of rotted trees as your compelling reason for access to the nymphaeum, so you may give the people of Freywich hope for the future in the form of a noble-born child."

"Yes, that is correct," she says slowly. She's wondering where he's going with this, as am I.

"And yet your vast orchard is overflowing with produce, not even a year later. Enough to feed the entire town for a winter, if needed, I would suspect. But instead, your lord is at the Cirilean fair this week, selling barrels of mead and baked delicacies."

She laughs nervously. "But Your Highness, the law permits him to, does it not?"

"I am glad you would like to discuss laws." Zander's smile is outright wicked. "The law permits him to, yes. The law *also* requires that tributaries and servants are given adequate food, shelter, and clothing, and are cared for to the best of their keepers' abilities."

"We provide for our servants with the utmost care." She snaps her fingers at the nearby stable boy, beckoning him. "Don't we, Brawley?" Her smile for him is full of teeth and empty of sincerity.

"Yes, my lady," he mumbles, hanging his head to cover the lie.

"Does that care include burning a small boy's hand?"

She blinks, unable to hide her surprise that the king would be aware of Mika. "He stole from us."

"A wormy apple off the ground because he was hungry. And what, pray tell, will your excuses be for using a pregnant woman as tributary? Or for collecting girls as payment for gambling debts, and outside of Presenting Day?"

Lady Danthrin's mouth gapes like a fish out of water.

Her servant returns with a line of others following. Eleven in total—six women and five men, ranging in age from late teens to thirties, all with varying degrees of wariness to fear marring their expressions.

Eden trails at the end, her complexion paler than yesterday. Still, relief swarms me to see her.

"Is that all of you?" Zander asks the servant who fetched everyone.

"Yes, Your Highness." She curtsies. "All those who didn't travel to Cirilea with my lord."

"Good." Zander smooths a palm over his horse's snout. "Lady

Danthrin, you will relinquish all servants and tributaries to me and enough horses for their travel. We've taken the liberty of preparing them."

Her face pales. "But, Your Highness! You can't—"

"You have proven you cannot adequately care for them, so I will find them new keepers, ones who treat them with the respect they deserve."

The servants' eyes widen as they glance at one another.

Mine must match. Only last night, Zander insisted we didn't have time to find a new keeper for Eden, and now we'll be looking for keepers for eleven of them?

"Come!" He beckons them forward with a hand. "Choose your horse. Two riders to each."

Lady Danthrin watches with shock as her servants rush away from her, diving in twos to clamber onto a horse.

Except for Eden, the odd number and last in line. But she's moving too slow, as if each step causes her pain.

I hurry toward her. "What happened?"

Eden's timid gaze darts to Lady Danthrin, but she says nothing.

I swing my attention to the noblewoman. "What did you do to her?"

"Nothing outside the law." Lady Danthrin lifts her chin. "Eden was not performing her duties and required a reprimand."

I've seen a person walk like this before. A man who Korsakov punished for trying to force himself on me. I check Eden's back—telltale blood spots seep through her linen dress, proving my fears sound.

My rage ignites. "You whipped her because she didn't answer your bell *fast enough* in the middle of the night?" My words are nearly a growl, coupled with blooming guilt. I'm to blame for Eden's suffering. It's my fault she wasn't there in the first place.

Adrenaline buzzes and heat builds against my finger as I decide how hard I can water-slap this vile Islorian without harming her baby.

A cool hand clamps around my forearm, stalling me.

"Do not do it," Gesine whispers. "I will heal the girl so she is fit to ride, but do not do what you and I would *both* like to. Allow the king his day of judgment." With another pause, as if to make sure I've heard her, she releases me and leads Eden away with a gentle smile.

The legionaries and servants file out of the manor's stables, two by two, the latter wearing bewildered looks. They're terrified, but the more I learn about this wretched place, the more I think they'd be safer in Venhorn with the saplings than staying here.

Soon, only a handful of warriors remains beside Elisaf.

"I can see why you would have to keep such a large household." Zander draws open the gate that leads into the orchard. It relents with a loud creak, revealing what I didn't grasp in the darkness last night. Fruit trees stretch as far as I can see. There must be hundreds of them. "It would require many hands to produce all the goods you sell at the fair, all the barrels of mead and wine you trade." Zander props open the gate door with a hook. "All the farmers you sell rotten fruit to for their soil and animals. *So much* produced for the town of Freywich and its prominent keepers, who also all have full households. I imagine those servants work here?"

"We need many hands to manage an orchard this size." Lady Danthrin's voice is strained. "Our town's keepers are generous with their labor."

"But not the fruits of that labor, from what I can see. Tell me, Lady Danthrin, do you feel you've paid the kingdom a suitable tithe?"

I see where he's going with this now. It's where my head was going with memories of Sneaky Pete last night.

Lady Danthrin fumbles with a silk ribbon on her dress. "My husband manages such matters, of course, so it would be best to discuss them with him."

"I do not have to discuss anything with Lord Danthrin. I've confirmed it on my own. You have been painting yourselves a struggling lordship for years, yet you and a handful of unscrupulous keepers now thrive on trade that you've built on the backs and suffering of Freywich's mortals. All while lying to the king to avoid paying appropriate taxes."

She swallows. "I will speak to my lord at once and ensure reparations are made if what you claim is indeed true."

Zander's eyebrow arches. "Are you suggesting I do not know what I speak of?"

Her head shakes furtively. "No, Your Highness. Of course not."

His gaze lingers on her before shifting to Gesine, whose focus is on Eden's back, the dress unfastened to expose whatever atrocities hide beneath. It then flips to Abarrane.

To the flaming torch suddenly in her grasp.

With an eerie calm, Zander turns to face the orchard, his tall and powerful body framed within the two sides of the wall.

As one, the trees burst into flame, blazing with the intensity of a lit match against a gasoline-soaked woodpile. Only the fire doesn't die down. It burns and burns and burns, hundreds of fiery orange balls, black smoke billowing into the sky, a beacon of warning for anyone within miles.

We stand, speechless, as Zander razes the entire orchard, expressions ranging from open horror on Lady Danthrin's face to grim satisfaction on the warriors.

And Gesine? I can only describe that look as pure, unbridled joy, either at his actions or at this display of raw power, or both, a story that will undoubtedly spread through all of Islor. She knew. The moment Zander walked into the apothecary, she saw the strength of his affinity to Malachi.

As quickly as they erupted, the flames vanish, leaving nothing but charred trunks.

I'm torn between ugly pleasure—Danthrin will feel Zander's wrath for years—and despair, for all the people that produce could have fed. But I can see Zander's rationale without him needing to explain it to me. Ordering Danthrin to distribute this food to the hungry townspeople would have been pointless. He knows Zander is no longer king.

Elsewhere in the town, shouts carry as people panic, not realizing the black smoke leads to nothing but ash.

Within the Danthrin manor, stripped of servants and horses, the only sound is Zander's footfalls on the dirt ground as he approaches the noblewoman, until he towers over her trembling frame.

"Tell me, Lady Danthrin, do you still think me gutless?"

I didn't think she could pale more.

"You owe your life to Hudem's blessing in your womb. Without it, you would already be dead. But make no mistake, I will return one day, and if I do not discover a vast improvement in the treatment of the mortals of Freywich, you will not survive a second time. You may go."

She falters a step and then rushes for her empty house, nearly tripping twice.

"Does the princess find the actions I've taken satisfactory?" Zander's voice is light and airy, a hint of mocking in his tone, his eyes, blank.

Yes, I want to say.

No, I want to scream, because it makes it impossible for me to hate him when he does things like this.

I shrug. "It's a start."

The corner of his mouth twitches. "We must leave immediately. That smoke will surely draw attention from the south. How is the girl?"

"Healed enough for now." Gesine fastens the buttons on Eden's dress.

He climbs into his saddle. "Jarek."

"Your Highness." The second-in-command drops from his horse and holds out a hand.

Eden gapes at the warrior. There's nothing soft about him—not his voice, not his eyes, not the way he looms. He's all hard edges and sharp blades.

I realize what's happening. "She can't ride with him," I blurt.

Zander's stare is flat. "With the Legion's second-in-command? Why not?"

Because it'd be like escaping a snake's fangs only to land in a lion's maw. I don't want him *anywhere* near her. "Can't she ride with Drakon, or Zorya, or …"

"*Anyone* but me." Jarek smirks, amused.

"I don't have time for this nonsense," Zander snaps. "Move out." He takes off, Abarrane following closely.

Gesine climbs into Horik's saddle, leaving only Elisaf and Jarek.

I curse, knowing what I have to do. "Eden, go with Elisaf."

She follows my gesture, and the tension releases from her shoulders as the kindly guard smiles at her.

With that taken care of, I climb into Jarek's saddle.

"I don't think so. You ride in front."

"*Why?*"

"Because I don't trust having you at my back."

"Honestly, what do you think I'm going to do to you?" With a huff, I shift forward, stiffening when he fits himself behind me, his thighs bracketing mine, his arms reaching around my waist to grab the reins.

"What are *you* upset about? I've seen how you ride. This will be a much longer day for me." He urges the horse forward.

I grit my teeth, the urge to tell him to go fuck himself—again—overwhelming. We join the group as they pass through Freywich toward the main gate. People line the streets, watching us pass as the thick smoke plumes dissipate in the sky behind us. An odd mood hangs over the crowd that I can't place. Many wear cautious smiles. Several curtsy and bow. A few shout their thanks. How much longer before they trade those for curses and blades once they hear the lies Atticus is spreading?

"Why can't I smell your Ybarisan blood anymore?" Jarek asks suddenly, reminding me how close he is.

"I have no idea," I lie, and then tip my head to the side on impulse. "Why don't you see if my blood still tastes Ybarisan?"

His deep, grating chuckle skates across my exposed neck. "I think I'll pass on that generous offer."

Zander leads the charge through town. He glances over his shoulder once, searching. As soon as his eyes touch mine, he returns his focus ahead.

Checking to make sure his weapon to regain his throne is still here.

My anger bubbles with that thought. But it's good—I need to let that fester. Gesine was right: it is easier to stew in anger than drown in sorrow.

A blond woman waves frantically at us, beaming. "Thank you," she mouths, pressing her fingers against her lips.

"Why are they thanking us?"

"That is the tributary from last night, and we both know why she's thanking *me*."

I roll my eyes. "She's not the only one, though. Are you saying you serviced more than one mortal?"

"It was an eventful night." Behind me, Jarek bites into a fresh apple.

"Where do you keep getting those?"

He pats a pouch by his leg.

"Whoring yourself *and* apple picking. Gosh, you have been busy," I taunt.

"It's not like I had a choice. The king ordered us to fill as many baskets as we could and deliver them to Freywich's mortals. Dragged us out of slumber to do it," he mutters.

Suddenly, Drakon's comment about not wanting to see another apple makes sense. Zander must have had plans to raze that entire orchard last night. Did he already have them when I accused him of doing nothing for these people? Regardless, I smile with an overwhelming sense of relief—all that food did not turn to ash for the sake of punishing Danthrin.

We round the bend in the street, leading into Freywich's main square, the gates ahead.

My smile falls off with a gasp.

A man is tied to a hastily erected wooden post, his wrists bound above his head, his throat slashed wide, blood spilled over his naked body.

An apple jammed in his mouth.

It's Ambrose Villier.

Nine others are lined up alongside him in a similar predicament, in various states of dress—some in nightgowns, others wearing nothing—as if they were yanked from their beds. I recognize the men. "They're the keepers who brought the tributaries last night." And their wives, likely. They ran Freywich alongside Danthrin. Those prominent and unscrupulous ones who Zander accused of having houses full of hungry servants.

And now they're all dead, waiting to greet Lord Danthrin when he returns.

Several guards lay in heaps where they fell to the Legion's blades.

My mouth hangs as I take in the gruesome stage.

"As I said, it was an eventful night," Jarek purrs in my ear.

When I demanded Zander do *something*, I wasn't thinking *this*. *This* is … My heart pounds as I try to wrap my mind around such brutality.

This is precisely how an Islorian king sends a message that will spread through the lands. A warning to those who abuse their servants, and a promise to mortals that they still have a king who will fight for them.

I watch Zander's stiff form, hoping to catch his gaze again, as we pass through the gates and speed up to a steady canter.

He never glances back.

13
ROMERIA

The day is as long as Jarek promised it would be. It's dark when we reach camp—a field five miles off the king's road, next to a small lake and sheltered by trees. Others are already unloading their bedrolls and meager supplies. A cook fire blazes, and the first of several tents stands on its own.

The servants Zander rescued from Freywich huddle by their horses, sharing whispers and wary glances at the warriors who pay them no attention, until Abarrane barks at them. They jump to action. What will their roles be here? It's naive to think more than one warrior hasn't considered who they'll feed off tonight.

There is one who is *not* on the menu.

I search out faces and quickly find Eden's, pale and streaked with tears. Sitting in a saddle all day at our pace is painful enough, but doing it with a back scored with whipping wounds?

Jarek's boots haven't hit the ground when I'm wriggling out of the saddle and rushing for her, my body stiff and aching. Before I can reach her across the campground, Gesine whisks her away, both of them disappearing inside the tent.

Elisaf steps into my path, handing me a metal cup. "The caster has talents like nothing I've ever seen before. The girl will be healed soon, as if it never happened."

Physically, sure. I swallow my lingering guilt with a gulp of cold water. Only then do I appreciate how thirsty I am. "That was a long day."

"And how was the ride?"

"Fine. Jarek didn't talk to me." A strange dynamic, to ride for hours on a horse with a stranger, his body against mine, and *not* acknowledge him. But I was more than happy to match his silence, occupying myself by slipping my ring into my pocket and attempting to compartmentalize my affinities, to no avail.

"They set up camp fast." I scan our surroundings, pretending my focus is on the Legion when really I'm searching for Zander. I don't know what to say about the brutal judgment he passed today, but he's nowhere to be seen.

"We will not stay long. Expect to be woken well before dawn."

"And we *are* going to Bellcross this time, right?"

"Yes. We have another two and a half days of travel. We must assume Atticus's messages have reached Lord and Lady Rengard and that the reception may not be as warm."

"So, you're saying we won't be invited to stay at the manor?"

Elisaf chuckles. "More likely their dungeon, though it is hard to say. Scouts will travel ahead to gauge the temperature." He motions toward the tent. "Gesine asked that you join them. You'll be sleeping in there tonight."

"And what about the other servants?" I seek them out. Brawley the stable hand is helping Zorya with the horses. Several others carry buckets of water.

"They will find meals and rest, and safety. Go. I'll bring you something to eat."

I guess that's all I can hope for. With my murmur of thanks, I head for the tent.

Inside is cozier than I expected, a layer of animal skins smothering the grass and a lantern burning in the corner. Eden lies on her stomach, her dress pulled down to her waist. Thanks to Gesine's skilled healing, most of the lashes Lady Danthrin delivered are nothing more than red welts. But one gaping split remains across her backbone, and that is where the caster's intent focus rests now.

Eden's eyes stay closed.

"Is she asleep?" I whisper.

Gesine nods but doesn't answer otherwise.

The girl looks so peaceful in slumber, not a hint of the anxiety that seems to absorb her every waking moment. She appears so much younger than her eighteen years. And yet, she's seen *so much*. In that way, she reminds me of myself. But she's gentle, kind, and meek, and she's been broken by this world and her circumstances. Maybe that's why I'm so protective of her.

Raised white lines mar the pale skin on her shoulder blades, old scars that magic can't heal.

A dark, vicious side of me wishes Lady Danthrin hadn't been pregnant.

I settle onto the ground, cross-legged, and slide off my ring. The buzz arrives almost instantly and doesn't relent until I slip the ring back on again. I sigh, my frustration mounting.

"Close your mouth and breathe in through your nose, count to three, and then release it through your nose. Over and over again," Gesine instructs, her back still to me. "You *must* find your center. Focus on that, and your affinities will follow."

Her instruction echoes that of Hessa, the yoga instructor who works in the studio two doors over from my old apartment.

My old apartment. Has someone else moved in there already? Did they bag and toss my things? What about all my sketches? My art supplies?

I guess it doesn't matter. That life no longer exists.

Slipping off the ring again, I follow Gesine's directions, counting in my head over and over again as I pull air deep through my nose, my lips pressed together.

Gradually, with each new breath, the buzz dissipates.

I open my eyes to find Gesine watching me expectantly. "What does it feel like?"

I search for a way to describe it. "Like a tiny ball right *here*." I press my palm against my chest. It's still very present, but not uncomfortable.

She smiles. "Which is where it should remain, as long as you focus on your breathing and do your best to maintain your equilibrium."

"Is that why you're always so calm?" *And Wendeline too?* "Because you're so focused on your breathing?"

She seems to consider my questions. "Perhaps. I was a rather hyper child. A caster's affinity does not make itself known until they begin to mature into adulthood. The simple casters, ones with a link to one fate, often can't feel it until Mordain's instructors coax it out. Elemental casters are usually afflicted with this discomfort you've been feeling, and the more powerful their links, the more focus they must give to centering them."

"I never felt it *at all* before."

"It is a strange situation, indeed, given how powerful you are. But now that you can, you must remember to keep it centered."

"If you'd just told me to do yoga breathing, I'd have had it days ago." I wouldn't have wasted so many hours, struggling.

"I will have to remember that." She smooths a palm over her forearm, drawing my attention to the emblems that glow through her threadbare sleeve.

"Were you born with those?"

"These?" Gesine pulls up her sleeve and holds out her arm for me. "No. These, I was given in Mordain when I mastered each of my affinities. All casters are marked as such. Even Wendeline has one."

"I never saw hers."

"It is much smaller. They reflect the caster's strength."

I only briefly saw the emblems, the night we met. Now, I'm able to study them in more detail. The gilded doe—Gesine's affinity to the god of water—is twice the size of the other two. I think back to that tremendous wind she drew the night we escaped. If her connection to Vin'nyla, the god of air, is only half of what she has to Aoife ...

"I still remember the days I received each as if they just happened. It is an occasion for celebration among the casters. I earned this last one"—she taps the butterfly—"much later than most, but I didn't mind because it allowed me more time studying in the library with the scribes." Her laughter is musical. "I spent *all* my hours in those dank, dark halls, surrounded by dusty scrolls and immersed in prophecy, absorbing all I could while making friends. Since I was a little girl, I've always found what the seers see fascinating. I had wished that only one affinity would develop, so I could scribe for the remainder of my years. But the law required that I enter service for Queen Neilina, so I did. You were twelve when I arrived. Princess Romeria was twelve," she corrects, her eyes flittering to Eden.

The girl is fast asleep, her breathing slow and rhythmic.

"Did Romeria know about her blood?" That a god designed her to kill an entire race?

"When I arrived? No. She knew of her father's efforts to tender your hand in marriage to Islor's heir and bring about peace, and she knew of her mother's vigorous opposition to the idea. But she did not learn what Neilina had done with Aoife's aid until several years later, and by that point, her mother had thoroughly poisoned her thoughts to all things Islor. When Princess Romeria mounted her horse to cross the rift, she had but one goal: to destroy the kingdom and claim it for her own."

"And when did *you* get involved in all this?"

"Not for years. When I arrived in Argon, I hoped that the union King Barris was attempting to broker between his daughter and King Eachann's son would lead to realizing the prophecy. It was not until years later, after Ianca and I had formed a close bond, that I would learn what Queen Neilina had made her do." She smiles sadly. "Ianca was so young and naive when she arrived there, nineteen and eager to please the dreaded queen, and without any love for Malachi's demons. That's how we were raised, to fear them. Even I was apprehensive upon first arriving here," she admits sheepishly. "When the queen demanded that Ianca summon Aoife, Ianca didn't think she had any other choice.

"As the years passed, Ianca grew wiser, and when it became apparent that the Islorian kingdom would accept Romeria in this peace treaty and that the queen's plans might come to fruition, she began to worry. She knew Neilina's ambitions were not that of her husband's, and Ianca could not see how the poison running through Romeria's veins would ever inspire peace between the two realms. The only future she could see was war and death, and the suffering of many. One night, she divulged her secret to me.

"Others may not have seen it for more than the obvious—a violation of a sacred oath that, in any other circumstance, would've resulted in Ianca's execution. But because I had spent so many years immersed in the seers' foretelling, because I have seen much, I knew immediately that what Neilina had done would have greater consequences than Ianca feared." She pauses, as if deciding how much she wants to share. "Many do not value the seers' visions, nor do they see purpose in the scribes' work. It has been that way for thousands of years, but especially since Neilina became queen. And many of the guild's leaders concern themselves far more with politics and power than Mordain's true purpose. They are happy to relegate the returning seer casters to dwell in the undercarriage of Mordain's halls, spewing their nonsense until they expire." Gesine's jaw grows taut, her anger visible.

Eventually, she will be one of those seers, as all elemental casters are.

As I would have become had I stayed in my world, in my own mortal body.

"I have told you about the prophecy, the one widely accepted. It has been spoken by three different seers, almost word for word. But it is not the *only* prophecy about the daughter of Aoife and the son of Malachi. There are others, studied by the most scholarly of the scribes. On their own, they may seem nothing more than confused prattling, but when pieced together, they paint an ominous picture of what may come to pass."

My scalp prickles with unease. Zander warned me of how these casters only share what they feel necessary at any given time.

"There was once a seer who foretold of a day when the fates would meddle in the joining of the daughter of Aoife and son of Malachi, and a great reckoning would follow. This was spoken before the Great Rift, and to this day, most tie that prophecy to Queen Isla and King Ailill."

Because Malachi did meddle. He gave Ailill immortality—and what this world has come to know as the blood curse. "But you don't think it had to do with them?"

"I have never felt certain, especially because King Ailill was not *only* a son to Malachi but also to Aoife."

"And Zander's affinity is only to fire."

"Yes. And it is powerful, leagues beyond any other Islorian gifted on Hudem. Princess Romeria is not only a daughter to Aoife by the affinity she was born with, but also by the summons Aoife answered."

"Which was how she meddled."

"Exactly."

I shake my head. "And now there are vials of my poisonous blood floating around. Atticus is writing letters to all corners of Islor, giving them carte blanche to lock up their humans in cages." I think back to the square, to the children tied to posts, awaiting their execution. "Or slaughter them." This may not be what the seer meant by a reckoning, but it's certainly going to make life worse for the humans. "If you know all this, why didn't you kill Princess Romeria before she got to Islor?"

"And would you so easily drive a knife through someone's heart? Is that who *Romy* is?"

I falter. Years on the street taught me how to defend myself, but I've never done more than strike hard enough to get away.

Even the knife I kept strapped to my thigh for protection was designed to deliver a meager flesh wound.

"Our purpose has never been to collect prophecy so we may change the course of its unfolding. The scribes believe that prophecy must unfurl as intended to maintain a balance set by the fates themselves. We did not see the elimination of Romeria as a simple solution. As I said, other prophecies exist. One such, delivered almost three hundred years ago by a seer named Caster Delphine, foretold of a day when Malachi would be summoned to save the daughter of Aoife, and when she rose again as a daughter of many and queen for all, only then could there be hope for peace among the peoples. Again, most would not link this to Princess Romeria because they have been purging any elemental caster with affinities to Malachi since the days of Farren. But we knew of an elemental caster with an affinity to Malachi who lived in Cirilea."

"Margrethe."

She dips her head in answer.

"How did Mordain learn that?" Wendeline said she couldn't figure it out. Unless that was a lie.

"Only the scribes know of her. They value knowledge above all else, and there is a source within Cirilea who deals in information. She has been helpful for decades."

Oh my God. It clicks. "Bexley." Of course. How did I not put that together? Bexley knew Wendeline was receiving regular letters from Mordain.

"I immediately notified my scribe sisters of what Ianca had done for Neilina, knowing this was not something I could keep to myself. There was much discussion on what it might all mean. Involving the guild was pointless. They are not likely to speak out against the queen. Many among them vie for power and would be as happy to rid the world of the Islorians as Neilina. If anything, they would have put Ianca to death for it.

"We briefly discussed removing the problem of the princess," Gesine admits, "but we feared that obstruction would cause cataclysmic repercussions. If Princess Romeria's survival is the way to achieve peace, then her demise could eliminate the possibility of an end to the blood curse. We agreed to do what we do best—wait and watch and learn all we could, and when the time arrived, ensure prophecy comes to pass. With Ianca and I in Argon, we pieced together elements of Neilina's plans. The scribes made contact with Cirilea's casters."

"Mordain's official scribe seal. You used that to send letters to Margrethe." And Wendeline, according to Bexley. "They could have told the king all of this, and Neilina's entire plan would have folded."

"It was a risk, yes, but Caster Wendeline was known to be a supporter of prophecy and a pragmatic ally. Regardless, we didn't have much choice. The prophecy spoke of Romeria's rising again with the aid of Malachi, so we could only assume she would be somehow struck down."

"By a merth arrow to the chest."

"In that case, Margrethe needed to be ready to summon. The royal family trusted Wendeline, and she was able to get close. The scribes tasked her to watch and collect what information she could, and when the time came, to ensure Margrethe completed her part in the prophecy. *That* was to be her role."

I think back to what I know of that night. "And make sure the king and queen were poisoned before the wedding?"

"No. That was *not* part of the plan, but a direct interference with the prophecy. On the day of the attack, Wendeline made her own choice. She knew through us of the Ybarisan plan to dose the royal tributaries and of Princess Romeria's toxic blood. With the newlywed couple taking the stone in the nymphaeum, it would mean certain death for the future king.

"Much like Ianca, Wendeline could not see how that would *ever* bring peace between the Ybarisans and the Islorians, especially if the Ybarisans killed them all. She saw a different path, one where she could reveal the Ybarisans' deceit while protecting Zander and any involvement by Mordain. Beyond that, she would let the fates decide how it should unfold." Gesine pauses. "I think now, knowing what we know, perhaps she may have been right. 'When she rises again as a daughter of many and queen for all, only then could there be hope for peace.'" Gesine studies my features. "That was the part we could *never* understand, not until Wendeline's letter arrived after the attack, when she confirmed the Romeria who Malachi returned to us was not the same who left us. A daughter of many, or four, to be more specific. But a queen for all. For the elven of Ybaris and Islor, for the casters of Mordain." She brushes a strand of hair off Eden's forehead. "And for the humans who seem to suffer most with this never-ending plague."

My ears catch the sound of boots crunching against grass outside the tent a few seconds before the tent flaps open and Elisaf ducks in.

"Something to eat, from what was scrounged in Freywich." He holds out half a loaf of bread, some butter, and not surprisingly, apples.

"I'm beginning to understand what Drakon was complaining about." While Jarek never attempted to strike up a conversation with me, every time my stomach growled, he wordlessly fished into his pouch and thrust the fruit into my hand.

"Unless you would prefer some of the fowl roasting on the fire—"

"Apples are fine. Thanks."

"I thought so." Elisaf hesitates, but then, seeing that Eden is asleep, surveys her back. "She looks much better."

Gesine covers the girl with a skin. "She will get a good night's rest and be hungry in the morning."

"As should you both. We will be breaking camp before dawn." Elisaf ducks back out with a bow, fixing the flaps behind him.

Gesine's gaze lingers on the now-empty space. "He is fiercely loyal to you."

"No, he's loyal to Zander. He can't help it. It's how he was made."

"*Oh.*" Her eyes widen. "You mean to say the king is his maker? I didn't think that was allowed."

"It's not, and it's a long story. And a secret I'm not supposed to share," I mock whisper. A part of me regrets saying anything, but keeping it no longer seems necessary in the grand scheme of things. Zander's father isn't here to punish him.

"Hmm. Well, maker or not, he is also loyal to you. There may be a day when he has to choose. I cannot say which way his compass will point, but regardless, in a world of enemies, you will need as many allies as you can find." She sets to fixing herself a slice of buttered bread and devouring it.

But my mind is still too busy to allow myself a moment to eat. I study the ring that sits in my palm. I've had these affinities all along, and I had no idea. "Do I need to wear this anymore, now that I have a handle on it?"

She laughs through a mouthful, and it's a pleasant sound. "You have not begun to understand the destruction you can cause if you are not careful. Uncontrolled affinities mixed with surges of emotion often prove detrimental, and right now, given all that has transpired with the king?" She gives me a knowing look.

"You're not wrong," I admit. Will I ever have that same aura of calm as Gesine and Wendeline? I don't see it happening anytime soon.

Her thoughts seem to drift as she chews. "Consider it a gift from the caster who sent you here, a way for you to protect yourself and others, and also a way for you to adjust to this new body."

"I wish I had my old body," I say around a bit of buttered bread.

"May I see it for a moment?"

I slip the ring into her waiting palm and watch her study it intently for long minutes.

"Interesting." She hands it back. "It is as I thought. The ring holds a powerful illusion spell to trick you into believing you are still *you*, a human with no feel for her affinities. But this elven version of you is not human. I think you may come to find your stronger senses an asset once you have the time to explore them. They aren't as strong as these Islorian cousins of yours, but stronger than humans, nonetheless. Until then, wear it. It helps you channel your elven affinity."

"But I'll be able to do that without the ring, too?"

"Yes. Sooner than your caster affinities. It is far easier to draw from what already exists than to create something wholly new." She holds out her hand and a bubble of water appears on her palm, like a perfectly formed marble.

My mouth hangs with amazement.

"There are *so many* things you will be able to do, *eventually*, Romeria." She smiles. "You will be limited only by the boundaries of your imagination."

"Will I be able to heal people?"

"With your affinity to Aoife, yes, you should be capable of that one day. It requires much practice, though. I will, however, commend you. You are already growing in skill. Only yesterday, you threw that vile keeper into the pile of horse dung."

"*Slapped* him into horse dung." I purse my lips. It feels wrong to laugh, given how we left him in the square.

"With water shaped in *your* hand." She points toward my clasped palms. "You pictured slapping him and made it so, did you not? That shows controlled intention, which is the cornerstone for wielding any affinity."

I smile, her compliment bolstering my confidence.

"Tomorrow, we can practice more. But for now, we must rest. Fates know how many arses I'll need to mend before the day is through." Dusting the crumbs off her lap, she reaches for a skin. Balling it up, she lies down and tucks it beneath her head.

I blow out the lantern and lie down, expecting to watch the tent's ceiling for hours.

I drift off in peaceful sleep.

14
ZANDER

A single wave rolls across the water's glassy surface.

Romeria's lips stretch with a childlike, prideful smile.

And I can't help but smile along with her from my vantage spot on the far side of the lake.

Abarrane roused the camp twenty minutes ago, when the sky was clinging to its last moments of night. Our stay here has been brief. We would have forgone it if not for the mortals and the horses.

While the Legion folded tents and strapped skins and supplies to their horses, Romeria stumbled over to crouch at the lake's edge. She didn't notice me sitting here on the opposite side, and I didn't make myself known, content to watch her splash the sleep from her face. She's never been a quick riser, preferring to burrow into blankets and warm bodies. I learned that once we began sharing a bed. Each morning I left her like a caterpillar within its cocoon, wishing I could stay with her all day.

When Gesine emerged, I expected Romeria to rejoin the caster, but instead, she slipped off her ring—the one I once slipped on a different woman's finger—and tucked it into her pocket, her focus intent on the water, as still and smooth as a mirror.

And I watched.

It was five minutes before a small wave formed at the edge closest to her, crawling across the lake's surface, and I realized what she was attempting to do: channel with her elven affinity to Aoife, without the aid of her ring. Since then, she has sent several more waves across. This last one—the one that stretched her lips with such pride—reached the bulrushes and sent several resting ducks to flight.

I can't imagine this innocence ever morphing into anything I should fear. That has always been the crux of the issue with key casters, regardless of how history has painted them as villains. They're too powerful to remain unleashed. Far too powerful to exist in a world where kings and queens rule.

What about in a world where Malachi ruled?

Romeria is so concentrated on practicing her newfound skills, she doesn't seem to hear the approaching footfalls of the warrior behind her.

I can't hear their conversation, but I doubt it's pleasant. Jarek has never been one to show deference to Ybaris, despite the crown's recent position. I wonder if that would have changed had she become queen. It certainly won't with all that has transpired.

Romeria rises and slips on her ring, her stiff posture confirming her distrust is mutual. Though, I already knew that based on yesterday's exchange in Freywich.

Jarek holds out Romeria's sheathed dagger.

My jaw tenses. I told her to *never* let that out of her sight.

She snatches it from his grasp and affixes it to her belt.

He says something and then strolls away, carrying himself with that pompous air. But she charges after him, grabbing hold of his gauntlet. Jarek's posture changes instantly, like a coiled snake ready to strike as he peers down at where she grips him. Even from this distance, I can sense the air around him morph from mocking to ominous.

I'm on my feet, fist curled around a blade at my hip, ready to launch it across the expanse of water.

"You cannot make that throw." Abarrane is suddenly beside

me. She's the only one who has ever been able to surprise me like this. "And your interference will not help her earn their respect."

"And if he should slice open her throat before she can earn that?"

"It's a good thing you have a powerful caster to put her back together."

"Reassuring." A warning shout waits at the tip of my tongue. Whether it will do anything, I can't be sure. My blade driven into Jarek's skull certainly would, but again, it will be too late. The cook fire still glows with embers. I seize my affinity, just in case, as we watch the scene unfold.

Romeria releases her grip on Jarek and steps back, but she doesn't concede, her chin high as she responds to him with words that are no doubt acerbic. I've come to enjoy that about her.

Jarek's attention strays to our side of the lake. He knows we're watching. Worse, he knows he is indispensable, more so now than ever before. Perhaps that is why he keeps testing boundaries.

Romeria follows his direction, and squints. Now that the sky is lightening with the dawn, surely she can make out the two figures standing here.

With a mutter of something, Jarek marches away.

After a pause, Romeria follows, veering toward her tent.

I wish I could have heard that exchange. "Is he going to be a problem?"

Abarrane observes Jarek's path through the camp. "I have vouched for her amnesia and pushed him to see her as an ally rather than an enemy, but honestly, I do not know."

"And yet you've made him your second."

"He was the natural choice. Yes, he is arrogant, but the others listen to him without question. He is the only one among them who will ever test me, but he does it with intelligence. For that, I value him. All leaders need to be challenged occasionally."

"Or daily, as seems to be the case with us."

Romeria ducks into her tent, disappearing from view.

"She needs to find her way with him—with *all* of them—otherwise, they will never trust her."

And if they don't trust the key caster, I will not regain my throne.

How long will we be able to hide what she is, once we're deep into Venhorn, and Gesine unlocks this vast power that lies within?

I sigh. "To what do I owe you creeping up on me?"

"I would hardly call this creeping. If you weren't mooning over her—"

"What do you want?" I snap. It's bad enough that I must hide and watch Romeria from afar so I can keep her at a firm distance. That Abarrane mocks me for it …

Romeria has become my own personal curse.

Abarrane's lip quirks. "Two of Danthrin's servants ran in the night. The couple."

"As I expected they would." Their furtive whispers and glances didn't leave much to the imagination about their plans.

"The idiots walked within five feet of Iago without realizing he was there."

"But he let them pass without issue?"

"Begrudgingly."

"What direction did they go?"

"South."

Likely toward Cirilea. Maybe to the Rookery. "They won't last long, but that is their choice." Surely, they've heard the stories of what lurks among these hills—immortals without honor, cast out by their communities. The marauders cower within the trees until a caravan passes and then attack, usually at night, to steal the humans away from their keepers. They've never learned how to practice restraint, though, and the humans don't survive long.

I'd heard rumors that the attacks were growing bolder. We sensed several spying on us yesterday. If we weren't pressed for time, the Legion would have hunted them down and ended their plague upon Islor.

"I will say, for the record—again—that I do not think it wise to release these mortals we've procured. The Legion needs tributaries, especially in the mountains."

"They can stay if they agree to it willingly. I did not remove them from that shameful situation solely for our benefit. They've been through much." And my guilty conscience reminds me that I could have rescued them sooner. *Should* have rescued them sooner.

We've known of the growing atrocities across Islor for years but had grown too focused on politics and civility. As the prince, I could have taken a more active role in bringing the Islorians responsible to justice, instead of simply talking about it. In that, Romeria was right.

Did she agree with the brand of justice I delivered, though? Romeria has never had the stomach for that sort of punishment. But in this world, it is the only message that will carry far, the only warning that might be heeded. She will learn that soon, and she will need to strengthen her resolve if she is to survive, with or without my protection.

Still, I've been avoiding her since, afraid to see the judgment in her eyes.

"What happens if *she* decides she wishes to leave?" Abarrane asks, nodding toward where Romeria stood moments ago. "If she is no longer willing to remain with you?"

"Think of what she has endured thus far with me."

"Blind luck."

"You call it luck. I call it intelligence and a desire to survive. Romeria will not leave, because she is not a fool. She does not have the luxury of choice."

In that, our fates are the same.

15
ROMERIA

I grin at the rush of ducks flapping out of the reeds, their quacks stirring the early-morning quiet. I hadn't expected the wave to reach that far, but it did, and it happened without the ring on my finger. I'll bet kids feel this rush the first time they pedal their bikes down the sidewalk without the training wheels.

"Your Highness." Jarek's voice from behind pulls me from my focus, his tone raspy and mocking as usual. "Your guard might wait on you, but the Legion isn't going to give you special treatment. Come and collect your shit. We're leaving soon."

I rise and slip my ring back on with a heavy sigh of annoyance before turning to face the arrogant warrior. Even within the dim shadows of the predawn light, I can make out the sharp angles of his jaw, the long, ropelike braids of hair, the hard gleam in his eye. "And which *shit* would that be? I don't own anything."

He smirks. "Your skins, for one. Unless you feel like sleeping in wet grass tonight. And this." He holds up my sheathed dagger, the one Zander gave me. It was digging into my hip while I slept, so I unfastened it and set it next to my makeshift pillow.

I yank it from his grasp. "Is there someone *else* I can ride with today?"

"The king. Otherwise, I'll bear that burden so the others do not have to."

"How gallant of you." I fumble with the dagger, trying to affix it to my belt. Something so simple, and yet I'll need more practice to master it.

"Abarrane told me a fascinating tale last night, about how you do not remember your life before the night you killed King Eachann and Queen Esma. How did you convince anyone of that?"

"Because it's the truth? I don't remember the princess who came from Ybaris, or anything about that life. She's a completely different person."

"And the king fell for that? You must have a compelling method of persuasion." His gaze flitters over the length of my body.

It's too early to deal with him. "What were you doing in my tent, anyway?"

"*Not* looking for *you*." His chuckle is dark as he walks away.

If that's the case, then there is only one person he *would* be looking for in there. My anger flares. I charge after him, grabbing hold of the first thing I can reach—the gauntlet covering his wrist. "Eden is *not* here for you, do you understand? None of you are feeding off her or using her in *any* way. She's been through enough."

The muscles in Jarek's arm flex, his glare settling on where I grip him.

"Brynn took an arrow in her shoulder yesterday while dealing with the guards in Freywich, and it's not healing as fast as I would like," he says with icy calm. "I was looking for the caster."

"Oh." I release him and take a step back. It's likely unwise to grab a lethal warrior like that, especially one who's made it clear he hates me. I have no idea who Brynn is, but I assume she's one of the few female warriors I haven't met. Is she someone special to Jarek? Is *anyone* special to Jarek?

His attention veers to somewhere across the lake. I follow it and spot the two forms on the far shore. My heart stirs. How long has Zander been standing there, watching me?

When Jarek meets my eyes again, I struggle to not shrink. "Do not grab me again, unless you'd like that favor returned." With that, he stalks off.

I release a shaky sigh and aim for my tent.

It's midday when we crest the tallest hill. In the distance sits the vast stone wall of a city. Between is forest and low-lying farmland dotted with villages.

"Is that Bellcross?" After two long and tedious days of nothing but rolling landscape and dismal company riding at the back of the line with Jarek, today we're in a three-deep row next to Elisaf and Horik a few horses behind Zander. I can't tell if this is by Jarek's own choice or if he's been ordered. Regardless, I'm happy for the chance to ask questions of someone who will answer.

"It is," Elisaf confirms. "It is the third-largest city in all of Islor, next to Cirilea and Kettling, and well fortified. There is a deep gully with a river surrounding two sides, impossible to attack from."

"It's beautiful." In the sunlight, the stone is a pale gray. Several towers loom in the center. The lord's castle, I assume, and likely a sanctum.

"Second only to Cirilea, most would say as Kettling's aesthetic is more that of a port city, adopting its flavor from Kier. When the Great Rift struck and Islor became its own realm, there was talk of making Bellcross the capitol. But then the Nulling spilled into our world, and its beasts made homes in the mountains, and the king and queen had no interest in living closer to them."

"And now we're heading there willingly why?" Jarek grumbles behind me.

I ignore him, though I said something similar the other day.

"Your Highness." Eden clears her throat, her nervous eyes flipping around as if checking to see if anyone else pays attention to her. "Is it true that your castle in Argon is made completely of rubies and emeralds?"

The hell if I know. "That may be a slight exaggeration?" Zander said Princess Romeria lived in a jeweled castle, but I don't know what that means. I steal a covert glance at Gesine.

She smiles, catching my call for help. "The spires on the king and queen's towers each hold enough precious stones to wink ten thousand times with each ray of sun that hits them. And at noon on a clear day, the gleam is a beacon seen clear across the land. Some believe, all the way to Shadowhelm in Skatrana."

Jarek snorts. "Only an idiot would believe that."

I resist the urge to elbow him. "Why don't we put you on a boat in Northmost so you can go to Shadowhelm and confirm it for us?"

"You want to send me to my death with the sirens now?" Amusement laces his voice.

"I'm not worried. They'd spend two minutes with you and send you right back." Of Gesine, I ask, "Have you been to Shadowhelm?"

"I have not. Queen Neilina does not allow her casters to go … well, anywhere."

"But she allowed you to come to Islor to ally with the king and future queen." Eden smiles first at her and then at me.

Eden's continued ignorance about the current state of the throne, and the fact that we're running, is both a relief and a concern. She needs to be more aware to survive in this world. Enough comments have been made that she should have picked up on *something* by now. Then again, I can see that she trusts me, and I've lied to her. The longer I keep up this charade, the more deceived Eden will feel. I'll have to explain things soon, though I have no idea where to begin.

"To get to Islor, I traveled west along the mountain corridor that separates Westport from the rest of Skatrana, so I did not have the opportunity to visit Shadowhelm," Gesine says, smoothly diverting the conversation. "But one of the elderly scribes traveled there on an information-gathering expedition once, and she had much to say on the city."

"What was it like there?"

"Very different from the lush green islands of Mordain and the bustle of Argon. The city is built high in the mountains, with only one road leading in or out. Perhaps that is why the snow seldom leaves the ground." Gesine smiles fondly. "Agatha said she spent most of her time wrapped in furs and warming by the fire."

"I wouldn't mind that mountain air right now." Or at least the cooler morning air. I unfasten my cloak and drape it around my lap. "What about the people?"

She frowns in thought, as if choosing her words. "Simple in their priorities, abrasive in their communication."

"Oh, well, Jarek! Something you have in common with your ancestors," I say dryly, not bothering to look over my shoulder.

"I see you've been gathering information for your next attack. Tell me, do you have all my routines down yet?"

"I'm sure it won't take me long. You have simple priorities, after all."

He grunts. "And please tell us, witch, is *all* of Ybarisan royalty a pain in the arse?"

Eden's eyes widen.

In a burst of spite, I collect my hair at my nape and flip it back, knowing it'll feather across his face and—hopefully—irritate him.

"There it is."

"There *what* is?"

Jarek inhales. "Neroli oil. It's faint, but it's there."

A shiver runs down my spine as it always does when one of these bloodsucking Islorians comments on the intoxicating scent of my Ybarisan blood. That means Gesine's morels are losing their potency. It's been days. Impressive for such a tiny piece of mushroom to work so well.

I push aside my aversion. He's trying to get a rise out of me. "Too tempting to resist yet?" I tip my head to the side, exposing my neck as I mock him. There's an odd comfort in knowing we each hate the other and we're not going through the pretense of hiding it.

Jarek's chuckle is deep. "You would like that, wouldn't you?"

"I'd have my own horse." A riderless one lingers ahead, tethered to a legionary. Apparently, the servant couple who left Danthrin's manor on it ran from camp the first night. When I asked if I could ride it, Zander's answer was a resounding no, not until I learn how to control one. The risk of an attack is just *too great*.

Abarrane raises her sinewy arm in the air and shouts a command I don't catch. Suddenly, hooves pound on either side of us as the Legion splits into three groups, the bulk of them veering off the main road, their galloping horses vanishing down a steep hill to our left.

"What's happening? Where are they going?" I ask.

"Cutting across a more rugged countryside to get to camp. Bellcross is known for its lookout glasses. They watch all who approach their city." Elisaf watches Abarrane as she falls back behind us to join Zorya, the only warrior left besides Horik and Jarek. "The closer we get, the more likely they are to notice us. If they should see a band of legionaries, they will know who we are long before we reach their gates."

"And we *don't* want them knowing that we're coming?" Eden asks curiously.

"Not until we're sure of where Lord Rengard stands with the current … political landscape."

"Right. *Of course.*" Eden nods, as if she grasps what's happening.

I've been in her shoes—so many times.

Elisaf smiles at the back of her blond head, but it isn't condescending—not like Jarek. "But traveling in *this* manner, they are less likely to pay us heed."

I survey the group that's left—nine servants, Gesine, and me, who wouldn't appear to be a threat to the casual observer. Only three single riders. I see what he means—not exactly a threat. "When will we see the Legion again?"

"We will rejoin them closer to Bellcross, where we can set up camp away from view."

They obviously came up with this plan when I wasn't around. Resentment stirs inside. Not too long ago, Zander divulged everything to me. I miss those days.

As if privy to my thoughts, Zander half turns, gazing into the distance. But I know him well enough to know he can likely sense my emotions from there. Thanks to my inability to shield my feelings from him as the previous Romeria could, we've always had a peculiar connection. I only hope that changes when I learn how to hide them as Wendeline can. It's high on my list of priorities.

Until then ... I slip my ring from my finger and welcome that uncomfortable buzz, pouring all my focus into centering myself for the next several hours.

The trek away from the king's road to our camp for the night takes us past fields of wheat and corn and along a stream the horses welcome. When we reach the crop of tents, a fresh kill is roasting over a campfire—a goat, from the looks of it.

"Whose farm is this?" I take in the wooden barn and the small stone cottage nearby. On the other side is a small pond.

"Someone willing to accept a bag of coin and stay out of our way." Jarek steers our horse toward the rest.

Zander and Abarrane have galloped off to meet two cloaked warriors. They push back their hoods in greeting. It's Drakon and another I haven't met but I recognize.

Both wear somber expressions.

I wait for Jarek to dismount before I ease off, my body aching. "What's that about?" It's far too hot to be wearing cloaks, which tells me they must have been using them to hide their identities.

"The commander sent two scouts ahead to Bellcross to learn what they could about the current situation in the city."

"And they're back already?" The entry gate to Bellcross is still an hour's ride away, according to Elisaf.

"They never stopped riding ahead, our first night at camp." Jarek hands the reins to Brawley, who has eagerly assumed his previous role of stable boy.

Jarek's right. I haven't seen the burly and loud Drakon in some time. "What do you think is going on in the city?" By the dour look taking over Zander's face, nothing good.

"If I knew, we wouldn't need to send scouts, would we?" Jarek strolls toward them.

I'm tired of standing on the sidelines, especially if Zander thinks I'm going to help him regain his throne.

I rush to pace myself at the warrior's side, my chin held high.

Jarek cuts a sideways glance. "What do you think you're doing?"

"Same as you. Finding out what's happening in Bellcross."

"Yes, but *I'm* second-in-command of the Legion. And *you* are …"

A key caster who Zander needs. "Just an heir to a throne?" I finish with a saccharine smile before speeding up to pass him.

"… several of the seedier taverns. The whispers are endless, but we could not confirm them as truth, Your Highness." Drakon's voice is far more serious than the last time we crossed paths.

"And the mood in the city?" Zander's back is to me, but I can practically see his body stiffen as I approach.

"Most do not care who calls himself king," the other legionary, a wiry man with rich, russet-brown skin, says. "Their focus is on which of their mortals shouldn't be trusted."

I can't help myself. "Maybe their focus should be on how they treat those mortals to earn their resentment."

Zander sighs heavily. "Thank you both. That will be all for now."

Drakon and the other warrior bow and then charge off toward their comrades.

"So glad you could join us." Abarrane smiles at me through gritted teeth. "We were just talking about how much havoc your little *gift* is causing Islor."

I ignore her, focusing on Zander as he turns to face me. My heart skips a beat the second his eyes touch me. "What's happening in Bellcross?"

He opens his mouth, but stalls.

"Are they hurting the humans?" I press.

"Not yet, but it will surely come. The reason behind the death of Lord Rengard's tributary is now broadly known, as is the culprit behind the act. Beyond that, rumors run wild. Several immortals have supposedly fallen prey to tributary schemes, but the two names Drakon checked in on were of keepers very much alive. Still, it is only a matter of time before the fear takes hold of common decency."

Elisaf joins our little group. "And what of Lord Rengard? What is his position?"

"He has not made it known. He hides within the walls of his manor, not allowing anyone in or out. I suppose I cannot blame him. The only reason he didn't face the same fate as my parents is because Tyree made the mistake of assuming all mortals would wish their keepers dead." Zander's lips twist with distaste. "He did not travel to Cirilea for the fair, but we must assume he has received word from Atticus by now. If he hasn't made any bold declaration yet, perhaps I have not completely lost his support. I will not know until I speak to him."

"Wait, you're going *into* the city?" I glare at him.

Zander peers up at the sun. "I should have enough time to get inside the gates before dark."

"I will ready the horses." Abarrane marches off, Jarek on her heels.

Zander makes to move away.

I grab hold of his forearm. "You can't just walk in through the gate." I'm sure at least some of the guards will recognize him.

"Of course I can. I'm the rightful king of Islor, which includes Bellcross." Tension cords his muscles beneath my fingertips.

"Except Atticus has declared himself the king and you an enemy to the throne. What will happen if Rengard isn't your supporter anymore?"

Zander's eyes snap to Elisaf. "Is there *nothing* you don't tell her?"

"Thankfully, *someone* around here does."

After another lingering glare at his friend, Zander says, "There are other ways to get into Bellcross."

I should have known he was planning to sneak in. He's spent years slinking in the shadows of Cirilea, first as a prince and then as king. "I'm going with you."

"No, you are not—"

"I *am*." I set my jaw stubbornly.

"If your guard has informed you of the details of Atticus's edict, then you know how perilous it would be for you if you were caught."

"Except I won't get caught." I'm no stranger to lurking, remaining unseen and unnoticed.

"This is not your world. You are not merely a thief here."

"I have Gesine's morels, so I don't have to worry about any scent outing me for who I am. How many people from Bellcross have ever actually seen me? And would recognize me like *this*?" I wave a hand over my breeches and tunic. "I look like any other traveler. I definitely smell like one after sitting on a horse for days."

"Lord Rengard has seen you, for one. He and his wife were in Cirilea for our wedding."

"I won't go with you to the castle."

He gives me an exasperated look. "Then why go to Bellcross in the first place?"

"She can come with me to find Ianca," Gesine says, approaching us, unnoticed.

"Yes, exactly." I silently thank the caster for the excuse. "I'm going with Gesine to find Ianca."

Zander squeezes the bridge of his nose, as if dealing with both of us simultaneously is too much. "Where is the seer?"

"Somewhere safe."

His gaze narrows. "You're keeping her location a secret from me? For what reason?"

"For her protection, as well as mine. And I have given you no cause to doubt my purpose here."

"But you expect me to *allow* you to take Romeria into the city—"

"*Allow*?" I snap, my anger flaring. "You're not my keeper!"

Neither of them are listening to me, though.

"I will share the location when I am within those walls and on my way to her." Gesine's voice remains serene as they stare each other down.

"And have *I* given *you* any reason to not trust me?" Zander says calmly.

Her lips press together, but she doesn't answer. She isn't going to acquiesce, not about this. I see it, and Zander is beginning to as well.

He shakes his head. "What use to us is a seer who cannot wield affinities or grasp reality anymore?"

Rage flares in Gesine's emerald eyes—the first time I've ever seen her reveal so much as a hint of it. "She is of utmost importance to our cause." A touch softer, she adds, "And she is important to *me*. I will *not* be leaving Bellcross without her."

I fold my arms across my chest. "And *I'm* not leaving Bellcross without Gesine."

Zander's gaze drifts between us—likely evaluating his options, or how worthy this fight is. "Fine. You two can come into the city with me and get her out, but only if you take Zorya and Jarek."

"What about Horik or Drakon or—"

"Jarek is the most skilled and respected warrior next to Abarrane."

"He *hates* me." I drop my voice, scanning for ears. "You don't think he'll be a major issue when he finds out?" I don't have to elaborate.

But Zander isn't to be swayed. "You're with Jarek, or you remain here. I will *not* bend on that."

Gesine dips her head. "That is a wise decision, Your Highness."

I groan, knowing I've lost this battle.

Zander's eyes drift over me. "We'll soon find out how wise."

Somewhere deep within the city, a clock tower gongs six times.

"I have to say, I didn't expect you to be so eager to get back in a saddle." Jarek steers our horse behind Elisaf's along the crumbling fieldstone wall—a divide in someone's farm field, suitably shielded from view of the looming city wall by lush, overgrown trees. We've been following it for miles, in single file along the worn path.

"Did I *look* eager?" I think I swore as I threw my sore leg over. "I've had enough of saddles for the rest of my life." All those car rides sitting behind that buffoon Tony don't seem so bad anymore.

"And thank you for volunteering me for this run."

"It wasn't my choice."

"Either way, there are plenty of taverns off the main square. I needed an excuse to visit one, and you gave it to me."

Mention of taverns reminds me of that night on Port Street and Bexley's bar. "Because you want to feed."

"Why wouldn't I, if the opportunity presents itself?"

"And does it usually?" It's been days since his night with that pretty blond in the wagon.

"What do you think?" He chuckles softly.

Feed and fuck. He seems like the type who might end up in a back alley. As much as I despise Jarek, I can see how others might find him physically appealing. "I think you might be in luck as long as you don't speak." I doubt he'll have time for taverns once we find Ianca, but he's in an oddly upbeat mood, so I'm not about to burst that bubble.

The path ahead has closed in with undergrowth. Abarrane, who leads our line—eight of us in total, on six horses—hops out of her saddle. "We must continue on foot. Loth, you will remain here to safeguard the horses and our weapons."

The legionary collects reins from each of us as we dismount and follow the path leading into dense forest.

To our right, beyond the trees, the main entrance gate to the city of Bellcross sits open. Distant shouts, clomping hooves, and squeaking wagon wheels suggest a bustling city. But within this thicket, only the twigs snapping beneath my boots and the leaves brushing against our cloaks make a sound. No one seems in the mood to talk, too focused on dodging branches.

Eventually, I find myself trailing Zander. We've avoided each other—or rather, he's been avoiding me—for days. Despite the tension between us, I itch for conversation. "So, how do you know about this *other* entrance into Bellcross? And don't tell me it's because you're the king and therefore you know *everything*."

"Have I become that predictable?" He glances over his shoulder, and to my surprise, flashes a smirk. "As boys, Theon and I spent our days sneaking around the city. He's the one who showed me this." Suddenly, we've reached a dead end, the trees and bramble butting against the city's exterior wall. Zander yanks away vines that clamber up the stone, intently focused on the blocks beneath.

"Looks like this escape route hasn't been used in some time." He ducks beneath tree limbs, smoothing his palm along the stone as he searches for something. "Every large city has at least one secret entrance. I've heard Kettling has many, though my spies haven't been able to find them yet. That information should always be guarded. Foolish to reveal such secrets, but I suppose Theon assumed it was okay to reveal this to his friend and future king."

He stalls on one stone in particular—a square stone in a sea of rectangles. Bracing his feet against the ground and his other hand on the wall beside it, he gives it a shove. A cascade of clicks sounds, followed by a deep scraping, until a narrow doorway opens.

A curse slips from my lips, laced with awe.

"I thought you'd like this little trick." Zander's hazel eyes twinkle. It feels like eons since I've seen any hint of playfulness in them, not since everything between us fell apart.

"This is the work of a talented stone caster." Gesine edges past the others to peer inside. "They are rare and fascinating intellectuals. It requires a certain aptitude for architecture and construction *and* a strong affinity to Aminadav. I could not begin to wrap my brain around the complexity of this puzzle work."

"You mean, you couldn't do this?" She has an affinity to Aminadav too.

She laughs. "No, there is training, and then there is capacity. Some skills can be taught, like mending flesh and bone or sparking a flame, but the way a caster's mind works allows them to bend the affinity to their will in certain ways. This must have been created before the Great Rift, when Islor still had casters in these lands. Where does it lead?"

"The last I used it, to a small courtyard garden," Zander says. "I assume not much has changed in that regard, but I could be wrong. We will find out shortly. Is everyone ready?"

Quiet grunts answer the king.

"Behind me, Romeria." Zander steps into the darkness.

A glowing orb appears above his head, casting light in an otherwise pitch-black space. "Thank you," I whisper, knowing Gesine has done that for herself and me more than anyone else.

The stone wall is far thicker than I imagined, and the path

through is not linear, weaving first left and then right. In single file, we move along quietly, the space narrow and low, forcing Zander to bend his head in some spots.

"Any chance this maze will shut on us while we're in here?" I whisper.

"Not unless someone triggers it to close." Zander pauses. "Then again, Theon once told me a story of a thief who somehow discovered this passage, and after stealing jewels from the queen's bedchamber, tried to escape through here. Only he must have gotten trapped inside. They found his skeleton years later, still clutching a handful of gems. I assumed it was a tall tale, a way to deter us from using this route too often, but I would not linger long enough to test its truth."

"That's encouraging," Jarek mutters, tension in his voice.

I can't help but smile. Finally, something the fierce warrior is unsettled by. "So you and Rengard are *good* friends, then." Maybe I don't have to be so worried about his plan to march right through the lord's gate with an enemy-to-the-crown banner hanging over his head.

"Bellcross has always been a staunch supporter of Cirilea and my family. Whether that extends to Atticus, we shall soon see. But Theon has, on many occasions, expressed admiration for my vision of Islor. I do not know how he feels about Atticus's latest edict, especially after being targeted by Tyree."

Zander's vision is one where mortals have freedom and choice, their blood a commodity they own. But not one where the mortals rise up and scheme murder.

We've reached a part in the wall where the stone blocks haven't fully parted, jutting out in a zigzag pattern. Zander turns sideways to shimmy between. "I do not recall it being this way before. But I was much younger and smaller back then."

"It's as if the mechanics failed here." Gesine sends the globe floating above him. "It's been thousands of years since the caster constructed this tunnel. Some of the logic within it could be deteriorating."

I mimic Zander, holding my breath as I edge through. On the other side, the path bends into a cramped corner that meets a dead end. There's barely enough room for us, our bodies nudging each other.

"I should go back …" I make to rejoin the others, to give Zander more space, but his hand lands on my hip, stalling me.

"Stay there, Gesine. There isn't enough room."

I tip my head and find a towering Zander peering down at me, his entrancing face only inches away, his eyes raking over my features. We haven't been this close since he shielded me from the oncoming arrows in the boat. Before Gesine told him about how Neilina and Aoife plotted to ensnare him.

Zander shifts his attention to the wall, smoothing his hands over the stones, his palms coming away dusty. "The lever to the outside is here, somewhere."

I'm standing still, doing nothing. I may as well help. "What does it look like?"

"Much like the other one, only smaller."

We're all knees and elbows, bumping into each other as we search along the walls. It's laughable, almost, given the kinds of things we've done beneath sheets and candlelight.

I spot the perfectly square block behind him, at shoulder level. "Is this it?" I tap the surface with my finger.

"That is definitely it." He shifts, reaching for it.

"Wait!"

Gesine's sudden outburst freezes us both in place, our hands over the same stone.

"Do not trigger anything until I say so. I may not be able to construct one of these passageways, but I can keep it from closing on us, should something else in the mechanics fail. Give me a moment."

Zorya and Abarrane echo twin curses.

The light orb dims and then vanishes, throwing us into complete darkness as Gesine focuses all her attention on her task.

The seconds drag on.

"Those morels of hers work wonders." Zander's soft breaths skate against my cheek, reminding me how close we are positioned. It doesn't help that our hands are still hovering over the stone. I pull mine away in a pathetic effort to put space between us.

I feel his eyes tracing the lines of my face in the darkness. Meanwhile, I can't see a hint of his, no matter how hard I search.

"You can still turn back. Wait with Loth in the safety of the forest."

"I won't learn how to survive in this world by hiding from it."

I sense him leaning closer, a moment before he whispers in my ear, "What is causing you so much distress? Is it simply being this close to me?"

His lips so close to me stirs a shiver. "No. I don't like not knowing what we're heading into."

"That's why I told you to stay behind."

"I'm not worried about myself." I can move anonymously. But what if Rengard is no longer the trusted visionary Zander hopes he is?

"I see." The tip of his nose grazes my ear, stirring my blood. "Do you regret it?"

"Regret what?"

"Everything."

I falter on my answer. What is he asking? Do I regret going along with Sofie's request? I was never given a choice.

Playing Princess Romeria in order to survive? Also, no flexibility in that decision.

But I know he's not talking about either of those things.

"Do you?"

"I *should*."

I revel in this brief closeness. I can *almost* pretend we're still together. "That's not an answer."

"Isn't it?"

The tension in our little alcove swirls, my fingers itching to reach for him. If I leaned forward, let my mouth graze his, could it fix everything that's gone wrong between us?

"Any time now, witch," Abarrane's strained voice on the other side of the narrowed corridor cuts into the moment.

A beat passes, and then Gesine announces, "You may proceed."

Zander's body strains against mine as he pushes against the stone. Instantly and without a sound, the wall slides into itself, allowing filtered daylight through. A tall hedge obscures the opening from the city beyond, and the muted sound of voices carries.

Whatever moment passed between us is gone, back to business as usual. Zander puts his finger to his lips and leads us out. The others follow, their backs against the wall behind the shrubbery, daggers clutched.

Zander presses on a stone, and the passage slides shut again. "You cannot stroll through Bellcross with blades out. You know this."

With seeming reluctance, the daggers vanish, Zorya's one-eyed pout especially fervent. They already have only a quarter of their usual weapons on them, an attempt to blend in.

"Once we leave this courtyard, we will part ways. Abarrane and I will make for Rengard's home. The rest of you will go with Romeria and Gesine." He looks to the caster expectantly.

"Ianca is seeking shelter in the sanctum."

"I should have suspected as much," he mutters, more to himself. "It is on the east side of the main square. Guard your words, spread out, and do not reveal who you are to anyone."

We edge out from behind the shrubs and step into a park. Thankfully, the benches are empty, the paths meandering through flower gardens free of people. On the far side, past a narrow street, sits a row of small shops with signs advertising everything from confections to leather goods to books. The last of them is closing, a hunched older man closing his door. If he noticed us emerging from behind the bushes, he isn't paying us any heed.

"The market square is that way. We meet here when the hour passes eight," Zander commands, pointing to the right.

That gives us nearly two hours to navigate this city unnoticed, find Ianca, and bring her back. My gut says it's either far too much time or not nearly enough.

He turns to Jarek, Zorya, and Elisaf. "Protect them at *all* costs. Do I make myself clear?"

A chorus of somber ayes follows. There won't be any *Your Highnesses* within these walls.

"What if we're not back in time?" I ask.

"Be back in time."

I roll my eyes. "What if *you're* not back in time?" What if he's chained up in a cell, or worse?

A myriad of emotions I can't read flash across Zander's face. "Rengard will either allow me to leave by then or not at all. If I'm not back, you go without me." He and Abarrane take off to the left at a brisk pace.

As if I will leave without you, I want to scream.

A nearby fish-shaped fountain spurts water. On impulse, I focus my attention on the steady stream shooting into the air, willing its angle to shift seventy degrees. A spray of water catches Zander in the side of the face as he passes.

I bite my lip to stop laughing as he spins around, continuing his pace but moving backward. I'm sure there is a hint of a smile hidden behind that stern expression.

"Are you finished playing yet?" Elisaf asks mildly, and I realize the others have ventured out to the street.

"For now."

"Is it *always* like this here?" People move in every direction, their arms laden with boxes of produce and meats or bundles of fabric.

"Not always, but today is market day." Elisaf stays close,

herding Gesine and me through the crowd, his hand hidden within his cloak, covertly on the pommel of his dagger.

Jarek and Zorya have spread out on either side, within quick reach but not noticeably associated with us. A good thing, given the latter seems to be garnering interest. I can't tell if it's her eye patch or her ferocious scowl that's stirring wary gazes.

"It wasn't this busy at the Cirilean market." And that is supposed to be the biggest fair in all of Islor.

"Traders coming into port often visit Bellcross at this time of year to sell their wares. There are *many* villages in the surrounding lands, and people would prefer to come here than travel all the way to Cirilea. Also, as we get closer to the mountains, those living in the villages are preparing for the change of seasons so they may be stocked for the cold months. You will see, in the square."

Elisaf's claims are proven right a few minutes later when we enter a vast space lined by four-story buildings. In the center is a circular pool with a water fountain, and all around it, men and women stand on platforms affixed to their colorful wagons, hollering to announce their merchandise. The aroma of cured meats and baked bread wafts, and banjo chords play from somewhere unseen.

On this side, onlookers clap and laugh as two lithe men duel with wooden sticks, volleying exaggerated stabs.

"There are mimes here?"

"The painted faces? Yes, they are popular performers. More so in the east. It is said you can't walk a block along Kettling's streets without running into someone busking."

The late-day sun gleams off their ear cuffs. "They're mortals."

"And their keeper is right there." Elisaf looks pointedly at the distinguished man in the suit, strolling around the circle with his top hat to collect money in its crown.

"Will they see any of that?"

"Hopefully in the form of a warm bed and hearty meal."

"We must keep going." Gesine clutches her cloak close to her neck to cover the telling gold collar that will earn attention we don't want. Still, several leering men—immortals, by their dress and confidence—ogle her. Two begin keeping pace behind us. They remind me of Korsakov's men with their smarmy smiles. If I didn't know better, I'd assume it was because she is strikingly beautiful.

"She's not wearing a cuff," Elisaf says.

"You read my mind." And to any of these immortals, she is just like any other human. One who isn't currently owned by a keeper and is therefore free for the taking. "We should have given her a fake one."

"We will be out of this throng soon enough." Elisaf shifts closer to her side, his normally soft brown eyes hard with warning as he turns to face our pursuers.

But it's Jarek and Zorya closing in to bank either side of the two men, their hands resting on their daggers, their wicked smiles begging for an excuse to use them, that steers the men in another direction.

The remainder of our passage through the square is uneventful, and soon we are on a quiet, cobblestone street, our two Legion warriors fanned out on either sidewalk.

"That is the sanctum, up ahead." Elisaf points to a tall church. It's nowhere near the grand spectacle of the one in Cirilea and only half the size, but it is elaborate nonetheless, its walls a pristine white stone, the clock tower gilded.

"I didn't think there were casters anywhere except Cirilea."

"There aren't. These are false priestesses. Unremarkable humans who devote their lives to the fates in prayer. Almost none have even met a real caster, but they study Mordain's belief system as if raised within it."

Gracen's words spring to mind. She'd said she had never seen a "real" priestess before. This must be what she meant. "You don't sound particularly fond of them."

Elisaf chuckles. "My feelings are mixed. Some are pious and

gracious. Others develop rather grandiose and self-righteous illusions of their value to society."

"Are there sanctums with false priestesses everywhere in Islor?"

"Even in the villages. There was one in Freywich. I'm sure Lady Danthrin is in there at this very moment, seeking salvation for her sins."

"Some of these priestesses do have skills as healers. Not with affinities, but with knowledge of herbs, tonics, and a delicate hand. The woman who runs the apothecary where we met had such a gift." Gesine picks up her pace, her keen focus flipping between the iron doors ahead and a small laneway to the side that leads into a well-tended garden and stable. A covered wagon and horse sit idle. "I think that was her wagon."

"When did you last see Ianca?"

"The night we arrived. Wendeline was worried that word of a seer would spread, so we paid a man to bring her here and not ask questions."

"And you know she made it?"

"I do not. We left Cirilea before I received word. I gave him half his payment up-front and promised the other half when I arrived here to collect her, and I hoped Wendeline's trust in him was well placed." Her brow furrows. "But I have heard the legionaries talk about raiders in the hills. I fear what may have happened during her travels."

"I'm sure she's fine."

Gesine offers an appreciative smile before pausing at the bottom of the steps. "Sanctums are a place for prayer and reflection. Warriors and their weapons normally wait outside—"

"Except in this case." Jarek strolls up the steps and yanks open the door. "After you."

Gesine walks through the doorway, offering a cold look to Jarek—which earns her a stony glare.

He trusts her as much as I trust him—not at all.

Inside smells of incense, lavender, and cedar. I inhale, the scent oddly soothing. Perhaps because it reminds me of Wendeline, and she was my sole comfort for many weeks after I first arrived.

Rows upon rows of gleaming pews sit empty, not a person in sight.

Gesine leads us down the aisle toward the altar.

"Do all sanctums have those?" I examine the four looming statues. They're like the ones in Cirilea, but they seem larger. That could be on account of the smaller building.

"The pillars? Yes. Of course, they do not have to be *that* grand, but in the days when summoning was permitted, many believed the larger and more elaborate the pillars, the more likely one would gain the fates' attention. They serve as a gate for a fate to visit the caster calling on them and must all be present and positioned in that way, encircling the altar. Within the boundaries of those pillars is the only way a fate can assume a corporeal form within our world."

"So, if an elemental caster summoned the fates, one of them could stand within those statues, right up there?"

"Yes. Exactly."

Sofie had pillars in that dungeon-like vault under her castle. And an altar.

That must be where she summoned Malachi.

But it's not the only place I've seen these. "The nymphaeum has pillars around the stone altar too."

"I'm not surprised. The nymphs' affinity is an ancient and especially potent connection to the elements, but it is still rooted in the fates."

We're nearly at the dais when a woman in gold-trimmed, white garb matching that of the Cirilean priestesses appears. "I sense great wariness in you today, visitors." The woman dips her head in greeting. "I am Sheyda. How may the sisters of Bellcross and I be of service to …" Her words trail, her eyes growing wide as Gesine unfastens her cloak to reveal her gold collar.

"I am looking for a friend who was brought here for safekeeping until I could reach her."

Sheyda's mouth gapes. "Yes, indeed. She arrived several days ago. We have done our best to make her comfortable during her transition."

Gesine heaves a sigh of relief. "Thank the fates."

Silence hangs, the false priestess staring at Gesine in utter shock. What must it be like, to devote your entire life to playing a character only to find yourself standing in front of the real person? Does she feel foolish?

"Can we see her?" Gesine presses.

"Oh!" Sheyda throws her hands in the air as if startled out of her stupor. "Yes, of course!"

We trail her as she rambles nonstop—about the night Ianca arrived in a wagon, driven by Ocher, the sanctum's groundskeeper; about Ianca's long days of sleeping and nights of prattling to no one, about her lackluster appetite and her declining health—along a long hallway. The air of calm she exuded during her greeting is gone, replaced by an almost frantic quality.

We turn down a set of winding stairs illuminated with lanterns. The deeper we go, the more concerned I get. "Is this where you have your dungeons?" Is that where they're keeping her?

"Oh, no!" Sheyda laughs nervously. "We don't have dungeons in the sanctum. Many of our priestesses live in modest rooms down here. Sometimes guests from out of town too. We had your friend upstairs in one of the spires, a lovely room with a view out to the garden, but that became problematic. The change is progressing swiftly in her. One morning she woke up and wouldn't stop shouting out the window. With that gold collar … well, Ocher said you were *very* specific about her remaining hidden."

"That is correct." Gesine's voice is tinged with worry.

"It seemed a safer place for her down here, and I think it's helped. She seems more … at ease."

What is she like when she *isn't* at ease? My father stood on park benches and wooden crates, shouting about demons when he was especially agitated.

We finally reach the bottom. One long, low-ceilinged, windowless hall stretches in front of us. Solid wood arched doors line either side. While Sheyda's explanation of these rooms seemed sound, in my mind, this screams prison.

"She is in the last one on the left." Sheyda fishes for a ring with countless dangling keys from within her cloak. "We don't normally use these, but it seemed imperative for her safety." She unlocks the door and raises her fist to knock.

"A moment. Please." Gesine holds a hand in the air, and then turns to us, pausing as if to gather her thoughts. Or maybe her composure. Her complexion has paled a few shades. "Receiving so many strangers when Ianca is this fragile may be a poor choice."

"The room is quite small," Sheyda confirms. "Even two or three will find it cramped."

"And I do not know what Ianca might say." Gesine gives Elisaf a knowing look.

What she might say about the many secrets she knows, the biggest one being what I am.

Elisaf picks up on the unspoken meaning and turns to face the warriors. "You two will wait out here."

Jarek snorts. "You don't order us around, *guard*. I am second-in-command to the King's Legion, and I outrank you. I go where *she* goes." He jerks his head toward me.

Elisaf huffs. Everything these Islorians do involves a pecking order. I guess being the king's friend doesn't elevate him high enough.

Unfortunately for Jarek, I can play this game too. I meet his hard gaze and say with a saccharine voice, "And I am pretty sure *I* outrank *you, warrior*. You two will stay out here."

His molars grind. I'm right, and we both know it.

Behind him, Zorya smiles. I can't tell if she's impressed by my mettle or imagining how she might like to kill me when all is said and done.

Another beat passes and then Jarek pivots on his heels and takes up position, his broad back against the wall. "As you command." He leaves off *Your Highness* for Sheyda's benefit, or maybe because he can't stomach the words.

Gesine releases a shaky breath and whispers a soft "thank you" to me as the false priestess raps her knuckles against the door.

Silence answers.

"As I said, she has been sleeping a lot, especially with the calming tonics we've been giving her."

They've been sedating her.

After another moment's pause, Sheyda pushes open the door. A loud, eerie creak carries as she steps back to allow us through. Inside is a narrow, windowless room with stone walls. In the corner by the door, a wooden desk holds a single lantern and a vase with freshly picked wildflowers. The tray of food someone left has been upturned, the sliced apples and berries scattered, thick stew splattered over the wall as if the bowl had been thrown.

"Who's there?" a thin voice calls out, pulling my attention to the far end, to the small pallet bed and the frail old woman with chalk-white hair seated upon it, the gold collar hanging off her skeletal neck. A cloudy gaze roams the space, not focused on anything. "Is that you?"

The simple question tugs at my memory. My father asked the very same thing the last time I saw him, on the streets of New York, squinting against the drizzle in search of his daughter's face.

A sob wretches from Gesine, her face morphed with shock as she takes in her friend. The change between when she saw her last and now must be drastic. But she gives her head a shake and wipes her tears with quick strokes, gathering her composure. "It is me, dear Ianca." She moves in to sit next to the old woman. They appear generations apart.

"My eyes, they are lost to me." Ianca's voice is sad.

Gesine collects Ianca's shaky hands in hers. "I will be your eyes for you."

There's not much to see in here. It's barely more than a furnished cell. My cage in the tower overlooking the execution square was bigger and brighter.

"And my mind. It comes and it goes, and it spins in circles, and it …" The end of the sentence ends in a garble I don't catch.

"Is there anything I can get for you?" Sheyda stands in the open doorway, watching curiously.

"No, thank you, priestess." Elisaf shuts the door, pulling it tight.

"A man … a man … there was a man on a horse …" Ianca frowns as if trying to pull memories. "Do I hear this man now?"

I can already see similarities between my father and Ianca—both elemental casters whose minds have fractured, as Sofie called it. The muttering, the repetition, the air of confusion that swirls around them. And yet there are stark differences. My father "broke" a decade ago. This woman, only a few weeks ago, and yet her body seems to be failing far more quickly.

"You are thinking about Ocher, the kind gentleman who brought you here. The man you hear now is named Elisaf. He is King Zander's guard, and he is going to help me get you out of Bellcross." Gesine strokes a wispy strand of hair off Ianca's face with a tender touch. "We will not be separated again. Where I go, you go."

"We will spend my last days in Mordain?" There's no missing the hopefulness in Ianca's voice.

Gesine's composure cracks, her expression buckling with sorrow before she smooths it again. "We cannot go back, remember?"

"Yes, yes, yes. My mistakes, my mistakes." Ianca hangs her head. "I can feel her in the room. So very powerful."

Gesine's eyes flicker to me. "That's right. Princess Romeria is right here."

"The princess who is not the princess. One left and another one came. She is not the same."

"We know. We remember."

"Hello," I croak.

Ianca releases a long, slow sigh. "Aoife *knows*. She *knows* what he has done, and there will be retribution."

Gesine falters. "You've seen something, then?"

The seer's head bobs, and her frail body bobs with it. "When the second moon falls asleep and the sun awakes, all will suffer for what they have done."

The hairs on the back of my neck lift with her ominous words. "What *who* has done?" Is she talking about Aoife and Malachi? Malachi and Sofie? Zander and me?

"The gilded doe has *seen* you, girl!" she shrieks, the sudden outburst startling me enough that I jump backward into Elisaf. "She has seen the ruin you will bring!" Her cloudy irises seem to bore into me as surely as if she can see me standing here. She peels her hands away from Gesine's grip. "She will do whatever it takes! Whatever it takes! Whatever it takes!"

Who is she talking about? Who will do whatever it takes? Aoife, or me?

Ianca stabs the empty air in front of her with an accusing finger, her agitation growing by the second, until her words garble and her shoulders slump.

Gesine guides her frail body down to lie in bed. "That will soothe her for a few hours, at least." She may be feigning calm, but her hands tremble.

"Are you okay?" I ask. I know I'm not.

She offers a tight smile. "I have experienced the mind of a seer before, but I have never watched someone I love unravel in such a way. It is unnerving."

"Yeah, I know what you mean."

"Your father." She nods slowly. "Yes, I imagine you do."

I study the brittle seer on the bed. "How are we going to get her out of Bellcross? She can't walk through the streets like that without drawing attention. And getting her through that secret passage in the wall? Not a chance."

"She would not fare well in there, if she could manage the trek," Gesine agrees.

Elisaf's lips purse. "Then we will have to come back for her tomorrow—"

"I am not leaving her again. You heard what she said. She has seen something."

"Something that makes little sense."

"I do not pretend to understand what it means, but we must try to decipher it. Seeing her now, like this … I fear every day may be her last. We *must* take her tonight."

Elisaf paces the tiny room.

"What about that wagon?" I say suddenly. "That's how they brought her here, right?"

Elisaf shakes his head. "That will not work. They close the gates at dusk for safety. No one travels in or out without intense scrutiny, and I assure you, two collared women will draw that."

"Then we must leave before dark," Gesine announces. "We must leave immediately."

"We cannot. We are to meet Zander in the courtyard."

But Gesine's right, and my mind spins on the solution. "So then we split up. Jarek can go with Gesine and Ianca—"

"The only way Jarek will leave without you is if he is sent to Azo'dem with a blade through his heart. And before you suggest it, neither will I." Elisaf's tone carries that rare edge—still polite, but unyielding.

"And I won't leave the city without knowing Zander hasn't been chained up by Rengard."

"Then we are at an impasse."

"No, we're not. Zorya can get Gesine and Ianca outside the wall. We'll wait inside for Zander and Abarrane and then meet them after."

Elisaf bites his bottom lip in thought.

"We don't have a choice. Whether today or tomorrow, Ianca

needs to leave in a wagon out that gate. Tomorrow, all the guards may know that Zander was in the city, which means they could be looking for Gesine. And me."

Elisaf rubs a hand through his hair. "You are right, but for the record, Zander will not appreciate us going against his command."

"We're not going against them. We're modifying them, given changing circumstances."

"Remind him of that when he's holding a blade to my throat," he mutters.

16
ZANDER

"I did tell you what I thought of this plan, did I not?"

I sidestep a mortal hauling a bag of grain over his shoulder. The upward climb from the market is steep and sweat pours from the man's forehead. "That you do not approve, that I am an idiot, and we will both likely get ourselves killed, in which case you will haunt me in Azo'dem for all eternity."

"Oh, good." Abarrane nods with satisfaction. "I wanted to be certain you heard me."

I smirk at the warrior. She has commanded the Legion for nearly a century, after the last commander fell during the war at the rift. My father always warned me that my gravest mistake as king would be losing her counsel, loyalty, or sword. It's probably why I never acted on the brazen suggestions she's made over the years, the Legion commander attempting to bed the prince. A joke, perhaps, or a test to see what kind of leader I would be. Either way, I'm happy I abstained. I value my friends too greatly, especially now.

Which is why I am banking on my friendship with Theon standing against Atticus's preposterous claims that I want to see Islor fall.

It's been decades since I visited Bellcross. Not much has changed, though the streets seem busier than when Theon and I were mere children running around, causing mischief. The lord's castle ahead looks much the same, save for the vines growing along the wall, the mature trees that fill out the private garden, and the red clay tiles on roofs that were once thatched.

Behind us, a clock tower gongs seven times, drawing my focus down over the city. Time is moving quickly, and Romeria is somewhere out there. A key caster with no clue how to wield her power, in the poisonous body of Ybaris's heir to the throne, weaving around the clueless folk of Bellcross.

I can still feel her slight body pressed against mine from earlier. Despite my best efforts to keep my distance, for those brief moments, enclosed in that tiny space within the wall, I lost my resolve. I was ready to ignore all our problems. I didn't want to let her go.

"You fret worse than Corrin," Abarrane scolds. "She has two legionaries, Elisaf, and a caster with her. *She* will be fine. Worry about keeping your own skin for the meantime." She jerks her chin ahead, toward the guards at the main gate—three Islorians with shiny suits of armor that have likely never seen a day of battle.

I fear their day is coming, and soon.

"Halt. Come no closer!" the middle one barks, his hand shifting to the pommel of his sword. "State your business or be gone."

"I am here to see Lord Rengard."

The one on the left sneers. "My lord does not answer requests from drifters who walk up to his gate."

"*Drifters.*" I peer down at my leathers. They may not be kingly, but they are far from impoverished.

"You always did say you preferred traveling incognito. How do you enjoy it now?" Abarrane mocks, sizing up the speaker. "Permission to gut him like the animal we roasted on our spit last night, Your Highness?"

The three share a wary glance. She could have them disarmed and disemboweled before they had the chance to raise an alarm. But I imagine it's the *Highness* that has them more perplexed.

I sigh. "Please inform your lord that the king of Islor and commander of the Legion are standing outside his gate *like drifters*, and we wish to speak with him."

"My sincerest apologies, Your Highness." The guard bows a third time before rushing out of Theon's private solar. We didn't have to wait long before the gate swung open, and Theon's guards clambered over themselves to lead us here.

"Happy now?"

Abarrane paces around the settee. "I am never happy."

"I am certain he soiled himself."

The corners of her mouth twitch. "Maybe a *little* happy."

I pause to study the tapestry on the wall, a colorful, floor-to-ceiling depiction of the fates smiting the lands for Ailill and Isla's folly. Impressive artistry, if not a tad morbid, the plentiful corpses piled at the bottom. In all our years of friendship, I have never been in the lord's private chambers. When we were young, these were his father's rooms, off-limits to children.

I haven't been to see Theon here since he became lord. "I suppose it bodes well that he didn't lead us straight to the great hall." A formal and impersonal gathering spot, reserved for announcements and punishments where witnesses are needed.

"Too many ears collecting valuable information in that drafty old room," comes Theon's voice from another doorway. "As it is, I'm sure there is a bird taking flight to Cirilea with a message about this audience, as I speak."

As long as you're not the one who sent it.

Despite my worries, I smile at one of my oldest friends as he strolls into the long room, dressed in a simple but elegant suit. I haven't seen him since the day I was to marry Romeria. He hasn't changed, right down to that odd stripe of gray through his black hair that appeared at six years of age when the blood curse took hold.

But so much else has changed since that day. "Thank you for allowing us a chance to speak."

"I did not think I had much choice." We meet halfway and clasp hands. A rather unorthodox move between royalty and subject, but welcome nonetheless. "I will admit that this visit is a surprise yet not entirely unexpected." He hesitates. "Your Highness."

"Is that an empty platitude or declaration of continued fealty?"

"That is me trying to keep my head out of the way of two feuding brother-kings' swords."

"There is only one king!" Abarrane snaps.

Theon dips his head in deference. "You are correct, Commander. There is only one king, though two claim the title, and both have come to me, demanding Bellcross's support."

"So you have heard from Atticus?"

"Of course, I have heard from him. I did not believe what I was reading, even with the king's seal on the letter, not until my contacts from Cirilea followed up by messenger on horseback two days later to confirm."

"Yes, I have seen the lies he is spreading."

"It is not true, then? The Ybarisan princess's own blood is not behind this new poison that threatens to ruin us?"

I sigh. There is no point denying it. "That part is true."

"And yet still you protect her?"

"I do."

His lips purse. "Please grant me permission to speak freely."

"You do not need to ask that, Theon. Especially not while we are in private." Given our history of visiting establishments far less savory than the Goat's Knoll, I'm surprised he would. But I suppose a crown and an army change things. Right now, though, I have neither, and I need his honesty.

"I've known you long enough to know you always see reason. Why would you keep this Ybarisan alive and lose *everything*? Unless what Atticus claims is true, and you are no longer in your right mind?"

"My mind has never been more right."

Theon raises his hands in surrender, his tone softer. "You are truly in love, then? With the woman who wants to destroy Islor."

"I ...," I falter, feeling Abarrane's steely gaze on me. "I am *not* in love with Princess Romeria of Ybaris." Perhaps with Romy Watts of New York, but that is neither here nor there.

"Then please, my friend, explain why you had to flee your city and your throne in the night to save this Ybarisan?"

"There are circumstances at play that I cannot reveal at this time, but she must survive at all costs." I couldn't begin to wrap my head around how to explain them, even if I wanted to.

Theon takes his time filling three crystal tumblers with amber liquor from a nearby crystal decanter. I wave the offer away, as does Abarrane. He shrugs and collects a glass for himself. "How did a Ybarisan princess's blood become toxic to our people?"

"I think you can figure that one out."

"I'd like to hear you say it."

"Queen Neilina disagreed with King Barris's call for peace. She wanted a different outcome, so she had one of her elemental casters summon Aoife. Princess Romeria was born this way."

"I worried that King Eachann's aspirations would be his downfall." He finishes half his drink in a single gulp before topping it up again. "And is the elemental caster who broke that cardinal rule the one who travels with you now?"

"No. The one you are referring to came here to help." *The other one is already in your city.*

"Help whom? Neilina?"

"She escaped Neilina. Of that, trust me, I am sure." Tyree confirmed it.

"So, Mordain?"

"In a manner of speaking, perhaps. But also maybe us. The

scribes believe there is a prophecy to end the blood curse, and it requires that Romeria and I work together."

"The scribes." Theon shakes his head. "Do they still dedicate their lives to deciphering meaning from delusion?"

"Apparently so."

"In what way will you and the Ybarisan princess end the blood curse?"

"That remains to be seen. And while I have never subscribed to the prattling of seers, now that we know the fates' designs are at play, it bodes well to heed their words. I would do anything to end this curse for all, you know that."

Theon smooths a hand over his goatee. "And yet with each day come new reports of poisonings."

"From what I've heard, the ones in Bellcross have all been false."

"Aye. But people grow more fearful, waiting for the day they are not false."

"And yet you haven't announced support of Atticus's decree." I watch him closely.

"I haven't. Not yet." His brow furrows with worry.

"Because you know you can't. Theon, it abolishes all laws that protect the mortals. You can imagine the abuse of power that will follow."

"More than the abuse I've heard about? Do you think we are blind to what is happening in Kettling?" He sets his half-finished glass down. "Adley is still in Cirilea, maneuvering. He has all but declared his daughter Saoirse future queen."

I snort. "Atticus would not be so stupid."

"Was that a rhetorical question, Your Highness?" Abarrane asks.

Theon's grim chuckles says he is thinking along the same lines as she is—yes, Atticus is, in fact, stupid enough to solidify his position by marrying that conniving creature. "I do not want to go down this dark path, but I do not see what other choice I have.

Atticus sits on the Cirilean throne. It is his rule, not yours, that I must obey if I am to keep my lordship. And it's not only Cirilea. Hordes of keepers are coming to my gate, demanding I address these distressing rumors. It won't be long before they take matters into their own hands, and then what am I, except an impotent noble, unable to control his people?"

"You are in a difficult position. I appreciate that."

"I know firsthand what it feels like to be targeted. Our tributaries haven't left these walls in weeks. They're afraid to eat or drink." He swallows. "Did you know? About her blood?"

I could lie. Maybe I should. "I discovered it was toxic the night the daaknar attacked her, but I did not realize it was her blood that had poisoned my parents. Foolish in hindsight, but the priestess misled me to believe it to be deliquesced merth."

"And yet you entrust another of these casters?" In his eyes, I see reproach.

"Not without reservations. But she is powerful, and I need her, so I will keep her close, for now."

"And where is the princess?"

I hesitate. "Safe and out of sight, and not causing anyone harm. She has no intention of allowing her blood to be used as a weapon against Islor."

"How can you be so certain? Come now, Zander." He gives me a pitiful smile. "Do not tell me she didn't realize what her blood could do when she crossed our borders. And we all know she was complicit in the attack that killed King Eachann and Queen Esma, despite that theater production in your court to convince us otherwise."

"Also a necessity at the time." I knew Theon would press me on this. "I will say this only once, and I say it because our long-standing friendship deserves the truth. The princess who left Ybaris had ill intentions. She deserved to die for her crimes and die she did."

Theon's eyebrows pop.

"The princess who travels with me now does so with a kind heart and no ill will toward Islor." If only I could convince others to see what I see.

"And yet it may not matter. Atticus's letter says there are countless vials of this poison in the hands of those who bear enough ill will to wreak havoc."

"That is why we are heading for Venhorn. We believe they might still be there, and we're hoping to stop them before too many vials reach the realm."

He bites his lip as he seems to absorb that. "What do you ask of me?"

"Your support and your friendship."

"Is that all?" He chuckles. "My friendship, you need never fear losing. My support will not be helpful to you when I lose Bellcross to Atticus's wrath upon him learning you were here and I did not apprehend you. He has made it clear that any who aid you will be considered enemies of Islor." He studies the tapestry on the wall for a long moment. "If you are going to Venhorn, you will need supplies that I imagine you do not have."

His eyes graze over the clothing I procured in Freywich. "I will gather what I can and have men I trust escort wagons to your camp in the morn. Beyond that … my support will have to be my faith that you are acting in the best interests of Islor, and that you will prevail. And I do hope you prevail, my dear friend, because I fear what awaits us if you do not."

A knock sounds on the door.

"Enter," Theon commands.

A guard pokes his head in. "My lord, there is a ruckus in the square."

"*Why* am I being interrupted during this important private meeting for something that happens *every* market day?"

The guard wavers, suddenly unsure of his choice. Theon isn't known to be this dismissive, but much weighs on his shoulders. "My lord, you wanted to know about any new claims of poisoning."

Suddenly, Theon's apathy is gone. "Is it valid?"

The guard scratches his chin. "That's the thing. We're not sure."

17
ROMERIA

The square is still lively when Elisaf, Jarek, and I weave through. The dueling mimes are gone, replaced by a man painted bronze imitating a statue, and a woman drawing a bow over her fiddle, playing a spirited tune. Some merchants have sold out of their wares and are closing their wagons, but many remain, perched on their platforms, trying to persuade passersby to part with their coin.

I glance back the way we came, but the wagon is long gone. Ocher, a kindly older gentleman, steered it toward the quiet back streets rather than deal with the hassle of this crowd. "Do you think they'll have any issues getting through the gate?" Gesine borrowed a gown from one of the priestesses, but Zorya refused to part with her leathers.

"Guards generally don't give issue to those traveling from the sanctum," Elisaf assures me. "They fear their standing with the fates will diminish, and they will land in Azo'dem. Besides, I'm certain Gesine could convince just about anyone to do her bidding."

"And if not, Zorya will kill them all," Jarek adds.

"Comforting."

"That's what I'm here for. To comfort you." His gaze roams a nearby tavern on the east side of the square. The last dribs of sun shine a spotlight on several women loitering on the second-floor balcony, scantily clad and strutting before the crowd.

"They're selling their blood?" Among other things, I'm sure. And they have caught his interest.

"Their keeper is selling their blood," Jarek corrects.

"I prefer the former." At least then they are in control.

"And yet what you prefer bears no weight on *anything* in Islor. Funny how that works."

"You're in a delightful mood." I dismiss him, my attention shifting to the food wagons ahead. A single doughy pretzel hangs off a hook at one. My stomach growls, reminding me that I haven't eaten since before we reached camp. Now the shadows are long, the sun almost spent.

As if reading my mind—or maybe hearing my stomach—Elisaf produces a coin. "Quick, before he feeds it to the birds."

I grin as I snatch it from his grip and trot over to exchange money for my meal. The vendor begins closing shop immediately, only too happy to be done for the day.

Elisaf smiles as I stroll back. "Well? How does it taste?"

"Like it's been hanging on a hook all day. I hope I don't break a tooth," I say through my chews. "Where'd Jarek go?"

Elisaf waves toward a tavern.

"He couldn't resist, could he?" The women are all attractive, curvy figures dolled up in dresses with revealing necklines.

"Don't worry. He won't take long."

A memory hits, of Jarek and that tributary in the wagon in Freywich. "Can't last, huh? I'll have to bug him about that."

"And I am sure he will find it amusing."

I hesitate. "Don't you need to … you know, too?" I nod toward the women.

"I would not leave you, not for a second." Elisaf checks the clock tower and then points to a nearby bench by the water fountain where two mermaids entwined in each other's bodies play the showpiece. "Come, we may as well sit. We still have an hour before we meet Zander."

From the comfort of our seats, I work on my stale pretzel while Elisaf scrutinizes anyone who comes within twenty feet. But they're all families and couples, and no one is paying us any attention.

"Bellcross seems like a nice place to live."

He watches a toddler who crouches low to the ground, coaxing a nearby pigeon over with a piece of bread. His mother lingers not far behind, allowing him this experiment. "It is one of the most civilized cities in Islor. Much of that is on account of its governance. Lord Rengard is considered a noble man and an ally to the mortals."

"It's why his tributary wouldn't take the vial from Tyree."

"Yes. Because he treats his servants with dignity."

"Zander treats his well too." I think often he's kinder to the mortals than he is to the nobility.

Two young children tear across the cobblestone, chasing a flock of birds. A woman in a simple gray dress chases after them, scolding, while a prim and finely dressed woman trails behind, her face pinched with an odd mixture of irritation and amusement.

"Those two there? That is a mortal and an immortal child. They're being raised together. That is not a common occurrence anywhere but perhaps here."

Before I can ask more about the dynamics of that, a shout pulls my attention to the other side of the water fountain. A small crowd gathers where a man stands on the edge of the fountain pool wall, his grip on the collar of a gangly boy.

"What's going on there?"

Elisaf frowns. "It doesn't look promising for the mortal."

I assume the man is a keeper, given his leathers.

I focus my ears to catch any words over the trickling water and buzz of people.

"... saw him toss it into the river outside the wall!"

"It was a coin! I was tossing a coin into the river in memory of my ma!" The boy's voice cracks. He sounds older than his form would suggest.

The denial earns him a rough jostle.

"His face looks sweet, don't it? But don't buy the lies. It's all an act! He's been a lazy lout since the day I took his family in, always arguin' about chores, sleepin' in piles of hay when he should be stokin' the fire pot at my forge. Still, I've tolerated his behavior, for his mother's sake. But now she's gone, and he's taken the Ybarisan poison to get rid of me, the ingrate!"

"I haven't!" the boy shouts. If he says anything else, it's drowned out by the spectators and the growing chant, "Punish him!"

The keeper draws a dagger from his hip and holds it up for all to see.

I clamber to my feet.

Elisaf is a second behind me, grabbing my arm. "What are you doing, Romeria?" he hisses.

"*Not* just sitting here while they murder that kid. Are you going to help me do something?"

Elisaf curses under his breath but releases me.

I stroll around the water fountain, doing my best to ignore its presence before I accidentally will it to attack. That would only exacerbate the issue.

"The king of Islor has demanded we rid ourselves of this scourge before it can take hold of our lands!"

No, he did not, I want to yell. Do they know Zander no longer sits on the throne? I weave through the growing crowd, getting closer to the speaker as he projects his deep, booming voice over the square.

"His Highness has empowered the keepers of Islor to act now and act swiftly! And if Lord Rengard is not willing to take a stand, we will need to do it ourselves at the king's command."

A cheer of support explodes, and the brawny man beams, encouraged.

The boy's face pales as he looks out over the people demanding his execution. He's older than I thought, "sweet-looking" as his accuser suggested, with a button nose, expressive, chestnut-colored eyes, and mousy-brown curls across his forehead. He reminds me of Mika. Just as wiry, more noticeable next to this beast with forearms the size of my thighs. The man mentioned a forge. A blacksmith, likely.

Elisaf is on my heels as I reach the front, formulating a plan. Before I can give it too much thought—or any at all—I hop onto the pool's stone wall.

The keeper stalls in his sermon, his bushy eyebrows pinching together as he studies me. "Yes, miss?"

I shrug nonchalantly and take a bite of my pretzel, more to stall while deciding on my angle. I pretend to ignore the countless gazes now on me. I'm banking on the hope that none of these people traveled to Cirilea to see Princess Romeria. If one of them recognizes me, this will all blow up.

Meanwhile, Elisaf bores holes into my face with his eyes, but I keep my focus on the blacksmith as I chew.

The sudden interruption seems to be working, though, some of his bluster fading as he waits for me to speak. "Can I help you with something?" he prompts.

"I don't know. Can you?" My flippant answers always drove Tony nuts, but it worked to hide the fear stirring inside me.

"Who are you?"

"Lady Diana. Of Cornwall," I blurt. It's the first name that came to mind. Still, playing a role on the fly feels like slipping into an old, comfortable coat. I used to do this all the time. Except now I'm doing it with an audience, something I don't enjoy.

The crowd hums with curiosity.

"Cornwall. Never heard of it." He eyes my outfit with doubt. That I'm gnawing on this pretzel probably doesn't scream nobility either. Perhaps I should temper that.

"It's near Hawkrest. And it's safer to travel like this in these parts, with those marauders in the hills. Even with my skilled guard"—I gesture at Elisaf, whose expression is the flattest I've ever seen—"you can never be too careful."

The keeper's eyes narrow on Elisaf's polished breastplate. "Yes … well, *Lady* Diana of Cornwall, I don't see what business it is of an *easterner* what a keeper in the west does with those tryin' to kill him."

"Oh, no business of mine at all, really. I just missed the first part of your big reveal. How did he"—I lean forward, closer to the boy—"sorry, I didn't catch your name?"

"Pan, my lady. My name's Pan." His voice trembles.

"Nice to meet you, Pan." I smile. "How did Pan try to murder you?"

The blacksmith gives me an exasperated look. "He took *the poison*."

I gasp, pressing my free hand to my chest. "Oh my goodness, I heard rumor of that. I wasn't sure it was true. How does it work? How do they take it?"

"They ingest it."

"But how? Do they swallow it? Put it in their drinks? How much do they need to take?"

"You'd have to ask Pan. He didn't take it in front of me."

"No?"

"Of course not. He's no fool, but I know he did. I watched him throw the vial into the river—"

"And what did the vial look like?"

The blacksmith falters on the question. "Like a vial."

"But we should know what to look out for. Was it black, white, clear—"

"I didn't get a look at it." He's losing patience with me.

"So, it *could* have been a coin, like Pan says."

His eyes narrow. "Except it wasn't."

"*Or* it *was*, and you're ready to put an innocent boy to death."

"Except he ain't innocent!" the blacksmith roars, finally seeing through my act.

"Except you have *no proof*!" I raise my voice to match.

Pan watches us lob retorts back and forth, his eyes wide.

Steel rings in the air. Elisaf has drawn his sword.

I raise my hand to stall him. This blacksmith can't be foolish enough to stab Lady Diana of Cornwall with his dagger, especially not with an entire square of witnesses. Even the fiddler has stopped her recital.

"And how do you suggest I obtain that proof?"

"You could feed off Pan."

"You wish me to prove my claim with my corpse?" He bellows with hollow laughter and gestures toward Pan. "Please, be my guest. As his keeper, I will grant you access to his vein so you can get the proof yourself."

I hold up my half-eaten pretzel. "I'm still digesting. Thanks."

"A convenient excuse." He addresses the crowd as he continues, "I can only assume she knows my fears are well founded."

Clever bugger. I try a different strategy. "Why would Pan want to poison you? Unless you haven't been a good keeper—"

"I'm an excellent keeper!" the blacksmith boasts as Pan shakes his head furtively.

I can't help but snort.

"You shut up, boy." He releases Pan's collar long enough to slap the back of his head, making him wince.

I struggle to control my flare of anger, my ring hot against my hand, my power thrumming, waiting for release. "Yes, I can see your exemplary behavior."

The blacksmith's nostrils flare. Tony's used to do that, too, right before he threatened me. I've likely pushed my luck as far as I can with this one, but he's still holding Pan in one hand and the dagger in the other.

Startled sounds pull my attention to where the crowd parts, people jumping out of the way to make room for Jarek as he charges in. The glare he gives Elisaf has me stifling a curse, but the storm brewing in those gray eyes when he peers up at me has me genuinely worried about whether he'll help.

"Oh, look! There's another one of my guards. As *Lady Diana of*

Cornwall"—I emphasize for Jarek's benefit—"I always travel with several."

Where the blacksmith gave Elisaf a glance, he stalls on Jarek's stony face, then sizes up the weapons strapped to his hip. Anyone with half a brain would be wary.

"My lady was just questioning this keeper's claims that the mortal has ingested poison." Elisaf gestures at Pan.

One … two … three beats pass before Jarek says in a wooden voice, "*My lady,* is there some way that I can provide you with aid?"

"Maybe?" While Jarek might punish me later for this, he's sworn to protect me now. "I was just pointing out the obvious—that this keeper is ready to kill a mortal without *any* proof to back up his claims."

Jarek's eyes flip to the blacksmith. "Is that so?"

The blacksmith swallows. "I do not need to prove my claim to some easterner or her guards."

"Maybe not, but I would think you need to prove it to Lord Rengard," I retort.

A rush of approaching hooves draws attention to the left. From a side street, guards on horseback emerge, charging this way.

"Oh, perfect timing! I'm sure they'll take you right to him." I hop off the wall and edge in closer to Jarek and Elisaf, swarmed by both relief and trepidation. "Maybe we should leave."

"Maybe we shouldn't have been here in the first place, Lady Diana of Cornwall," Elisaf chastises. "It's too late now. That is Lord Rengard himself, and he is already here."

Sure enough, the riders have closed the distance in an instant. A regal-looking man with a trimmed goatee and a single stripe of gray through his otherwise black hair leads the pack when they reach us.

Next to him are Zander and Abarrane.

Shit.

Zander's dark gaze finds us almost immediately.

Jarek's smirk is grim. "After Abarrane is done whipping me, remind me to define 'inconspicuous' to you."

Thankfully, Lord Rengard is focused on the blacksmith. "What is the meaning of this, Oswald?"

"My lord." The blacksmith—Oswald—releases Pan's collar and bows.

That Zander and Abarrane are free and seemingly well is no small joy, but I don't know what story they fed Rengard about me. I shift behind Jarek as covertly as possible, thankful for his size. I can just barely see over his shoulder.

"Why are you making a spectacle of your servant in the town square?" Rengard asks smoothly. "And why do you have a weapon drawn in the presence of nobility?"

"Oh yes, my lord. I mean, I'm sorry, my lord." Oswald's bravado is gone. He sheathes his dagger. "I believe Pan has ingested some of that poison."

"Really. And why do you believe that?" Rengard's tone is flat, revealing nothing. "Do you have proof? Has someone fed on him and died?"

"Well, no—"

"Where is the vial you found on his person?"

"I didn't, but I saw him throw something—"

"You have no legitimate reason to suspect this, then, do you, Oswald?"

I like this nobleman.

There's a long pause, and then, "No, my lord."

Rengard shifts his focus to Pan. "Are you eighteen yet, boy?"

"Just turned, my lord. A week ago," Pan says.

"So you will be included in the next Presenting Day."

"Yes, my lord."

"And are you the only servant in Oswald's household?"

"Yes, my lord. My ma passed the day before my birthday."

"I'm sorry to hear that." Rengard maneuvers off his horse, his boots hitting the cobblestone. "I'll tell you what *I* think, Oswald." He approaches slowly.

I edge in closer to Jarek's back.

He peers over his shoulder and whispers, "Subtle," but at least he doesn't shoo me away.

"I think you are without extra coin and down to one servant—a gangly boy who you feel might not fetch much for you come auction time—to live off until next spring. Our law states that should any upstanding keeper find themselves without a tributary due to untimely death, they can plead for compassion in my great hall and be awarded a new one outside of Presenting Day at a fraction of the cost. You, Oswald, saw an opportunity."

"My lord, I did not—"

"Did you honestly think my court clerk wouldn't tell me when someone has been lurking around his office, asking about available female tributaries of childbearing age available in the case of special recompense?"

"Yes, my lord. I mean, no, I did not think he would tell you, my lord," Oswald stammers.

With a heavy sigh, Rengard climbs up beside Pan on the wall, turning to address the crowd.

I shrink farther behind Jarek, until my face is practically buried within his back.

"Seeing as I have half of Bellcross here now, and I know most of you have heard about the poison that travels in evil hands through Islor, let me be *very* clear. The king of Islor has declared *any* mortal found with the poison on their person or who has ingested said poison and caused death shall face swift and severe punishment." He pauses. "I support this mandate. What I *will not* support, under *any* circumstances, are keepers taking matters into their own hands without legitimate proof of said crimes. Boy … what is your name?"

"Pan, my lord."

"Pan, have you ingested poison to kill your keeper?"

"No, my lord." He punctuates that with a head shake.

"And you would allow me to take your vein to prove your keeper wrong?"

"*You*, my lord?"

"I would not sacrifice another of my people if you are lying."

There's a pause. "Of course, my lord. If that's what you'd like to do, I mean, I can't stop ya." He's fumbling over his words, his nervousness increasing tenfold. "It's like I told Lady Diana, who was trying to stop Oswald from killin' me, I was only throwing a coin in the river for my ma's memory."

"I'm sorry, who?"

"Lady Diana from Cornwall, my lord. She's right over there. Behind that guard."

Jarek's body stiffens as Rengard's eyes land on me.

Shit.

"Come forward, please, my lady." Rengard beckons with a hand.

I ease out from behind my barrier.

Rengard's eyes widen before darting to Zander. He takes a few seconds to gather his composure. "It's a pleasure to meet you, *Lady Diana*."

I give him an esteemed noblewoman's nod—Corrin trained me well. "And you, my lord."

"You'll have to forgive me. You look *so much* like someone else I know."

"I've heard that, once or twice."

"I'm sure you have." He opens his mouth to say more but decides against it, shifting his attention back to the mortal. "Well, Pan? Should we get on with this?"

Pan's scrawny throat bobs with a hard swallow. "Right here? In front of everyone?"

"What better way to prove your innocence?"

"My lord." Zander urges his horse forward, its hooves clicking against the stone. "I have other means for ascertaining the answer to your question, and my gut tells me it would bode well to use them in this situation. Do not risk yourself needlessly."

He means Gesine, which says he is suspicious of this shaking human. Then again, Zander has always been suspicious of *everyone*.

Rengard considers his veiled warning. "I have always trusted your gut, *my friend*. Very well. I will leave Pan in your care and expect that you handle the situation accordingly."

"If he is infected, I will swiftly deliver his judgment."

"And if he's innocent, he is free to find a new keeper. Oswald will have no use for him in the dungeon while he pays out his penance."

The blacksmith's face pales. "But my lord—"

"Everyone, go home! The excitement is over," Rengard commands, hopping off the wall.

The guards move in, collect the burly blacksmith at sword point, and whisk him away. Pan's eyes dart around the dispersing crowd. I'd be looking for an escape route in the shuffle if I were him.

Unfortunately for him, Abarrane is already off her horse and closing in. She flashes a toothy grin. "I have eyes on the back of my head, boy. If you try to run, I will sink an arrow into your arse, and I will not let you remove it. For *weeks*." With that threat delivered, she spins to face us. "You were given a direct order to guard her with your life and keep attention off her, yet there she was, standing on this very wall, flaunting herself in front of everyone. Are you incompetent or a fool?" she hisses at Jarek.

A muscle in his jaw ticks. Abarrane is probably the only person who can get away with speaking to him like this.

"How did you let that happen?" she presses.

Something tells me admitting he ducked into a blood brothel will only make things worse, and that the whipping comment was not frivolous. As much as I don't like Jarek, I can't have him punished because of me. I step in between them. "I pulled rank on him."

"*Rank*?" Abarrane's face twists. "You have *no* rank!"

Before she can argue further, Zander joins us, Rengard beside him. "Where are Gesine and Zorya?" No mention of Ianca, I note. A secret from his dear friend, perhaps?

"They left, through the gate," Elisaf explains. "We agreed to meet after the first bridge."

Zander blinks, as if trying to process what possible reason we may have for going against his orders. "It is time for us to leave now, too."

"*All* of you. I doubt anyone in the crowd would recognize you"—Rengard's eyes are on me—"but someone will know the king's face. What that means for me once Atticus hears ..." He shakes his head. "I will provide you with two more horses. Go through the gate. None will question you."

"And the supplies?"

"They will arrive at dawn as promised."

"Thank you." Zander clasps hands with Rengard. "You are on the right side of this."

"Time will tell. Hopefully, I am not on the *dead* side of it, and that you know what you are doing." Rengard's gaze flitters over mine again before he turns. A quick order to his guards frees two more horses for us.

I move for one, assuming I'm relegated to Jarek's care again, but a firm hand seizes my biceps. Zander steers me toward his horse. "In the front" is all he says and then waits, his face steely. A sure sign that he is furious.

"I didn't have a choice. He was going to kill the kid." I mount.

"And now we have another stray. One who may be intent on killing us." Zander is behind me in the saddle in the next second. Despite the tension radiating from his body, it feels comforting to have my body enclosed in his arms as he reaches for the reins.

"He's just a terrified mortal. I don't think you have to worry about him."

"And I do not believe you think *at all* sometimes." He mutters something under his breath that I don't catch. "A noblewoman from Cornwall?"

"What? It's not like anyone here would know her." I smile. "They call her the people's princess."

"Is that who you're pretending to be now?"

My smile sours. "I did what I thought was right. I don't want more people to die because of what Princess Romeria did."

"Many people will die for what she did. Innocent people. You need to accept that and not risk yourself unnecessarily for one when you can save so many."

"Gee, thanks for the pep talk," I snap.

"I am trying to keep you alive."

"Oh, I know. So you can use me. Don't worry, I haven't forgotten." I turn in the saddle to meet his gaze. "By the way, what the hell was that earlier, back in the wall?"

His jaw tenses. "A moment of weakness. It will not happen again."

"Good."

He steers our horse forward. We say no more as we move through the square at a steady clip, Pan paired with Abarrane, while Elisaf and Jarek ride solo.

As promised, the guards wave us through without question.

"Jarek, get Loth and meet us at the bridge." Abarrane's eyes narrow on the horizon where the sun has dipped. "And make haste. I do not care how powerful that witch is. These hills are not safe for a wagon after dark."

Jarek takes off to the right, his horse galloping.

"Does *no one* heed my commands anymore?" Zander roars into the emptiness, turning our horse three hundred and sixty degrees to survey the area around the covered bridge that traverses a narrow river. Lanterns burn on either side of it, tiny beacons to mark the path in the dark.

"Perhaps something happened with the seer," Elisaf suggests.

"Or Zorya may have sensed a threat and decided to keep going. It is a solid hour's ride by horse. Longer with a wagon."

"Or she was arrogant enough to assume she could handle a few raiders."

"I will ride ahead and find them," Abarrane declares. "They couldn't have gotten far."

"And divide us more? No. We will wait here until Jarek and Loth arrive with the horses. It shouldn't be too much longer."

"Your Highness," comes her curt response, laced with disagreement, though she doesn't voice it. It's followed by a hiss of, "Stop squirming."

"I don't ride horses much, my lady—"

"Commander!"

"I'm sorry, Commander." Pan pauses. "Hey, why'd you call him Your Highness?"

"Because he is the king of Islor, you imbecile."

I watch Pan's mouth gape in the lantern light as he stares at Zander. "If that's the king, why is he—"

"No more questions," she snaps, turning to Zander. "I do not think we need to worry about this one having ingested the poison. He is too stupid to be cunning. Allow me to release him."

"He cannot go back to Bellcross, and he would not last an hour in these hills."

"Precisely."

Zander sighs heavily.

I dismiss their bickering, my attention drifting into the darkness. We took a different route here to avoid Bellcross's notice, but I know basically what the landscape looks like—hills and forests and farm fields and tiny villages with high walls for protection.

An orange glow radiates in the darkness, growing by the second.

"What is that? Over there." I point toward it.

Zander follows my direction. And curses. "Come." He sets our horse charging toward it.

"Fates," Elisaf whispers.

The moment we crest the ridge and spot the attack in the shallow valley below, it's clear Gesine and the others are in trouble. Their wagon is surrounded by men closing in from all sides, held back by Zorya's skilled sword and Gesine's gusts of wind that send them flying backward like scattering bowling pins. Nearby, a great oak tree blazes, the beacon that drew us in.

"I count two dozen. Their horses are down. They cannot get away." Elisaf draws his sword, and without waiting for Zander's order, charges down the hill and into the violent fray.

My heart pounds in my ears, watching my loyal guard rush into battle alone against twenty-four armed men. "Help him!" My voice cracks with desperation.

"Get off," Abarrane demands.

Pan scrambles down, tumbling in the process, but he's on his lithe feet again quickly.

"You *cannot* bring her into battle." With that, she's gone, her sword held high.

"She's right, Zander. Let me off. We'll be fine here."

A cry of pain rings in the air. Zorya crumples to her knees, an arrow protruding from her rib cage.

Zander curses, and with impossibly quick movements, is out of his saddle and pulling me down by the waist. "It is dark, and they are all focused. You two, hide *here*." He points to a crop of boulders. "You have your dagger."

I pat my hip. "Go!"

He hesitates, a frantic look in his eyes. For a few seconds, I think he's going to kiss me, and I can't breathe with the anticipation. But then he pulls away, leaps onto his horse, and gallops off.

Steel clangs against steel as I watch first Elisaf join the fight, then Abarrane, her blade strokes vicious and sweeping. My pulse hammers in my throat. It's a moment before I remember I'm not alone. I give Pan a gentle push toward the boulders. He crouches down beside me, and we observe the battle unfold from our hidden perch.

The blazing tree flares to three times its size, earning shouts as the attackers back away, not understanding the cause of its surge. A suitable distraction as Zander cuts down three of them from behind before they realize he's there. He soars off his horse, his sword blade curving in a deep arc, to cut down a fourth.

I watch, mesmerized, as the tide of the battle shifts, our side sorely unmatched and yet incomparable in skill. Even Zorya, barely standing, blocks blow after blow, and Gesine, crouching in her white caster's garb, stops every flaming arrow with her air shield before they can embed in the wagon's canvas cover.

Abarrane vaults over the wagon and fells two men on the other side, landing on her feet only to stab a third with her dagger.

"Wow." Awe laces Pan's voice.

"She wasn't kidding about hunting you down, so don't get any ideas about running."

"Right beside you seems like a smart place to stay, huh?"

I smile. It's refreshing to hear Pan speak to me like anyone else I might have known in my previous life, not capping off his words with *Your Highness* or *my lady*.

"So, that's *really* the king?"

"Yeah, that's him." An odd swell warms my chest as Zander fights against two assailants, even as trepidation ensnares my breathing. I've seen him in the sparring square but never in a life-or-death situation such as this. He moves with the grace of a seasoned warrior, anticipating every assault as if it's choreographed. I shouldn't worry about him. His opponents should worry—whether it's one or ten.

Except the ball in my stomach says I *am* worried.

All it takes is one misstep, one bad parry … No matter how much he's hurt me, no matter how much he infuriates me with the things he says and does, my heart still skips a beat every time

I see him and aches with longing every time I think of what we had.

Maybe I'm an idiot, but if he were to come to me tonight and ask for a second chance, I'd give it to him without hesitation.

"What's he doing out here, without his army?"

"It's a long story—"

A tree branch snaps behind us, a split second before something hard strikes the back of my skull.

18
ZANDER

"I need to see. Please, allow me." Gesine kneels before the warrior where we laid her in the grass, the burning oak providing plenty of light for the caster.

Zorya grits her teeth and snaps the shaft protruding from her body. "Stop talking and do it, then."

Gesine unfastens Zorya's vest with gentle fingers.

Nearby, Elisaf drags the bodies of the attackers into a heap.

"You were supposed to meet us at the bridge. What happened?" Abarrane's face is streaked in blood—none of it hers.

"Three men were prowling. I figured I'd lure them here and kill them out of sight of the guards on the wall, to avoid drawing attention to us." Zorya pants through the pain, struggling to speak.

"But an axle broke," Gesine continues. "We started the fire to give Ocher enough light so he could try to fix it. That must have been what drew them in."

My gaze veers to the fallen man, lying in a heap. "I'm surprised they didn't take him alive."

"I guess they were more interested in the two women in the wagon."

"They didn't realize one was a batty old seer and the other, a witch with a nasty temper." Zorya cackles, but it quickly dissolves into a grimace of pain.

"How is the seer?" I glance at the back of the wagon. There's been no sign of her.

"She sleeps." Gesine's face is worried as she holds open the leathers to expose the wound beneath. "The arrow is lodged in her lung."

"Merth." Zorya's teeth grit. "It burns."

"Riding will only cause more damage. I need to treat this immediately."

Zorya's one good eye searches the caster's features in the firelight. "What are you waiting for, then?"

Gesine looks at me.

"Start now. We need to wait until Loth and Jarek get here with the horses."

"Your Highness." Settling into a cross-legged pose on the ground, the caster closes her eyes and begins her work.

I ride back up the hill, desperate to feel Romeria's body tucked against mine again, where it's safe. She infuriated me with that stunt in Bellcross, putting herself in danger like that. So many things could have gone wrong. She *must* learn to surrender a few for the many. In that, she would be flawed as a leader.

Yet I cannot fault her motivation. It's who she is. It's part of what I fell in love with.

When she does things like that … it reminds me that I love her still, Aoife's curse or not.

And that is a problem.

All is quiet at the crest. "You can come out now. It is done."

No one responds.

I dismount and move for the boulders, only to find the space empty. "Romeria?" She wouldn't have run at her first chance, not without the caster to guide her. Not unless she's foolish enough to think she can figure it out on her own.

Or desperate enough to get away from me.

A sinking feeling hits the pit of my stomach.

I've been too cold toward her.

I've hurt her too much.

I should have explained everything Gesine said so maybe she'd understand what weighs on my thoughts.

Maybe she'd—

My nose catches the trace of blood in the air. Blood that isn't smeared over my blade or soaked into my clothes.

I inhale deeply.

Her blood. Even masked by whatever fungi Gesine gave her, I recognize it.

Would this scrawny kid—Pan—have had the opportunity to overpower her? I can't see it. But someone did.

Zorya mentioned three marauders trailing them. Were they part of the attack or a different group of bandits who hung back? The mortal would be a prize for them, and Romeria a burden to dispatch. That they didn't kill her here, though ...

A fresh wave of fear engulfs me. If anyone discovers who she is, they'll drag her back to Cirilea, and I can only imagine what Atticus and Boaz have in store for her.

I scan the hills around us but see no movement in any direction. Whoever they were, they moved quickly. I look to the forests on either side. They could be anywhere in there.

They could be doing countless things to her.

Dread seizes my insides.

"Romeria!" My roar carries into the night.

19
ROMERIA

I regain consciousness lying next to a campfire, its blaze warming my back, its crackle snapping in my ears. My thoughts are dizzy, my head aching as if split open.

But the most concerning issue is the electric energy buzzing inside me.

Someone has taken my ring.

"Let her go, and you can have me." The tremble in Pan's voice betrays his brave words.

"We already have you." Male laughter follows, a low and throaty and wicked sound. "Who is she, anyway?"

"Nobody. Just my keeper."

"Why is she riding with those warriors?" someone else asks.

"Just coincidence. They were leaving Bellcross same time as us."

"And they offered you both a ride? Is that it?"

"Yeah. That's right."

"What's your keeper's name?" a third male asks, his words tinged with a strange and harsh accent.

"Diana." Pan doesn't miss a beat. "We were on our way home to our village and got caught up at the market later than expected. She runs a bakery and needs to be back before the morning to open up." He's quick on his feet with the lies—and convincing, I'll give him that. Also, he could have outed me as a noblewoman to gain favor with these bandits, but he hasn't … yet.

"A keeper who runs a bakery but wears a ring like *this*."

I wish I could see these immortals who are speaking, but I don't dare move until I can get more information.

Pan falters. "I don't know where she got that."

I struggle to calm my breathing and center myself, but it's impossible under these conditions.

"Please, just let her go. *I'm* the mortal. She's no good to you."

"I wouldn't say that." Heavy footfalls sound, and suddenly I'm flipped over. My head spins. "Oh good, you're awake."

It takes me a moment to focus on the dark, hateful eyes watching me with intense interest. The male surely lives on the fringes of society, his clothing tattered and marked with old blood and dirt, several days' worth of stubble covering his jaw. "You see this face?" A grimy, strong hand grips my cheeks, squeezing. "I'll bet the rest of her is pretty nice too." His gaze drops down, sizing up my body.

I grimace.

"Oh, that doesn't appeal to you?" He releases me.

I work the ache from my jaw. "Not particularly."

He grins, exposing yellowed teeth. "Too bad, but don't worry, I'll enjoy it enough for the both of us."

"I doubt that." We're in a stony enclave, surrounded by an overhang on three sides, with dense trees at the opening. It's secluded. The fire won't be visible if anyone's looking for us.

A lanky, long-haired male sits next to Pan, keeping him in place with a dagger. The third male is perched on a rotten log opposite the fire, watching. He's small and wiry, a sword strapped to his side. When our eyes meet, my gut tells me he's the most dangerous one.

On instinct, I fumble for the sheath at my hip.

"Lookin' for this?" The one who threatened me holds up my dagger, the brilliant silver blade gleaming in the firelight.

I stifle my curse. Of course, they would take my dagger along with my ring.

"A valuable weapon for a baker. Where'd you get it?"

"At the market. They had a 'buy one and get a free pretzel' deal."

He smirks. "I must have missed that sale."

"You ever use a merth blade on someone, Orme?" the small one asks.

"Can't say I've ever had the good fortune to."

"Cuts like butter." His beady eyes settle on me. "Go on. Try it."

Orme drags the tip of the blade along my collarbone.

I hiss as it slices into my skin.

"That's gonna leave a mark."

Another scar to add to my collection. It won't matter if I don't survive this, though.

He tosses the dagger aside as if it's trash. It lands five feet away—too far to reach, but close enough that I feel the urge to dive for it. "Go on, then. Get it," he taunts.

I'm not stupid. He wants me to try so he can pounce, pin me down, and have his way. I remain where I am, frantically searching around us for any source of water I might be able to draw from. There's nothing, not a river or stream that I can see or sense. But I doubt I could do anything with this distracting buzz inside me.

And he just sliced me with a merth blade.

That will stifle my elven affinity. Damn it, I'd forgotten about that.

I school my breathing as best I can, needing my wits and my focus.

"I don't normally bother with the males." The male grips Pan's chin in his palm, keeping him from moving as he studies Pan's skinny neck. "But you're dainty."

"Let's just get this over with." Pan's cautious eyes meet mine.

"Fine with me." He opens his mouth, and the two needlelike incisors extend.

I stifle my shudder. On him, it's an utterly repulsive feature.

Pan winces as the Islorian yanks him closer and bites down without any of the gentleness I've seen from Zander or Jarek.

"He's not having *all* the fun tonight, is he?" My attacker moves in, intent shining in his eyes.

For once, I wish my blood wasn't laced with these morels. If he knew I was Ybarisan, he'd feed off me and then we'd be evenly numbered. His fangs in my neck seem far less disgusting than what he has planned.

It's now or never.

I bolt for my dagger, my fist clamping over the handle a second before strong hands seize my hips. I swing my leg out as hard as I can, and my heel connects with his shin, earning a grunt.

His fingers dip into my hip bone. "You're a feisty one. *Good.* I like the ones who put up a good fight before I—"

An ear-piercing scream cuts into the night, instantly chilling my blood.

I've heard that agony before.

The night of the royal repast.

The male who bit Pan convulses on the ground, his fangs still distended, his back bowed as the poison tears through his insides.

And Pan? Beyond the perpetual terror that seems to hang in his expression is a grim smile of satisfaction.

Oswald the blacksmith may have been guessing, but he was right.

It doesn't matter at this moment. Right now, all that matters is that the horrific spectacle has drawn our other attackers' attention away momentarily.

I seize the opportunity to swing my dagger, aiming the tip at the nearest immortal's neck. It lands true, the razor-sharp blade slicing into flesh without resistance, embedding deep.

Blood sprays everywhere as the male topples, his hefty body trapping me as he takes his last breaths. In the background, the poisoned attacker's screams don't abate, a gut-wrenching sound to behold, no matter who is suffering. Zander once said it took fifteen minutes for his parents to succumb.

I struggle to free myself from beneath this dead weight. Pan sees and scrambles to help me onto my feet. With my boot on the corpse's shoulder, I grimace and yank my dagger from his neck, my hand slick with his blood.

The agonizing screams cut off abruptly, courtesy of the third male and his sword. Now he turns to us. "Who are you?"

I reach for Pan. "He told you already. Just a baker and her servant."

"I don't think so. I heard you two talking." The male moves cautiously, forcing us into a dance around the fire. "That's the king you're traveling with, the traitor they exiled from Cirilea, isn't it?"

"I've never met any kings, exiled or otherwise." My bloody dagger is out in front of me, my free hand gripping Pan's forearm as we shift away together. "Why? What have *you* heard about what's going on?"

He pauses, as if deciding whether to play this game. "That King Zander tried to surrender Islor to Ybaris and make feeding off mortals illegal, but his younger brother stopped him with an army."

Is *that* what's floating around? It's probably what Atticus is telling the public. He's trying to win their fealty after he's stolen the throne. How many versions of misinformation will make their way through Islor before this is all over?

"That doesn't make any sense. None of you can survive without mortal blood, including the king."

A knowing glimmer sparks in his eye. "Don't you mean none of *us* can survive?"

I grit my teeth against the curse that wants to slip out, but it's too late. I've made my mistake, and it seems he was hoping for it.

"I was in Cirilea a few months ago. I left the city before the Ybarisans arrived, so I didn't see this princess, but I've heard she's a real beauty. Hair that's black as night, eyes as light as a morning sky." His gaze narrows. "A drop of her blood as toxic as ten thousand viper bites."

I've watched enough sparring sessions from the castle balcony to know this guy moves with the precision of a trained soldier. We have no chance of outmaneuvering him. I can only hope to outsmart him, and he doesn't seem as stupid as the other two. He's a raider who keeps his ear to the ground.

"This is Queen Isla's ring, isn't it?" He holds up his hand. My ring sits on his pinkie. "The prince gave it to you when he proposed."

"A scumbag who knows his history. How charming."

"What's he talking about, my lady?" Pan whispers.

"Nothing." I squeeze his forearm, meeting his eyes. "When I tell you to, run."

"What? I can't—"

"If you know who I am, then you know what I'm worth," I say loudly, drowning out Pan's protests. I release my grip on him and edge in close to the fire. "Land, gold, a lordship."

The male's step falters.

I smile. "Oh, you hadn't heard that part yet, huh? But you'll only get it if you bring me back alive."

"And why would the king care one way or another if you're alive?"

"Because we have unfinished business. You know, with me killing his parents, and nearly killing him. I guess Atticus wants to make a spectacle of my execution."

"That would make sense." I see the wheels churning in his eyes.

That's when I strike, kicking the stack of burning logs toward him. "Run!" I scream, giving Pan a shove. "Run, or you're dead!"

With a wild look in his eyes, he sprints off.

The time I hoped I'd bought is not enough, and when I turn back, the male is already charging toward me. But his balance is off as he beats down the flames that grip his pants, threatening to spread, and I use that to my advantage, lunging as Abarrane taught me.

I aim for his chest, but he shifts at the last moment, and my dagger catches his sword arm, slicing deep across his biceps.

He howls in protest but keeps coming. His body slams into mine, sending me sprawling onto my back, the wind knocked out of me, my dagger flying from my grip.

A stabbing pain explodes in my thigh.

"You think you've saved him? That dumb kid won't last a night out here alone," he hisses.

"He might surprise you," I push out through my agony. He surprised me, how convincingly he stood up there and lied to a crowd, to Lord Rengard, to me.

Not to Zander, though.

"I don't care one way or another, now that I have you." The male inhales. "Your Ybarisan blood doesn't smell different."

"There must be something wrong with you then. You should have that checked out by a doctor."

His responding laugh is wicked. "You have a smart-mouthed answer for everything, don't you?" He hauls himself up. "Let's see how smart that mouth is when you're on your knees in front of the king, begging for your—"

I see movement a second before a thump sounds and the male slumps to the ground beside me, unconscious. Pan hovers behind him, his chest heaving with adrenaline, his eyes wide, the wooden log gripped within his hands like a baseball bat.

"You were supposed to run." But I'm so glad he didn't.

"I told you, not without you." He tosses his makeshift weapon away.

I try to pull myself up, but the pain in my thigh is unbearable.

"Oh." Pan grimaces at where a branch on a fallen log has impaled my leg.

Our attacker won't be unconscious forever, and we can't get away with me anchored here.

"Okay, this is … not as bad as the daaknar's claws," I remind myself. Gritting my teeth, I yank my leg free. The resulting shot of pain has me leaning over and spilling the pretzel from my stomach onto the forest floor. Where previously plugged by the branch, blood now pours freely from the wound.

"Here." Pan tears a strip of material from the poisoned man's shirt and binds my leg. "That should work for now." He hauls me to my feet. For a scrawny guy several inches shorter than me, he's surprisingly strong.

The male lets out a feeble moan.

"Go, Pan. You can still get away."

"So I can have that arrow in my arse? I told you, near you is the safest place." He slips my arm over his shoulder. Together, we hobble into the trees.

Until I remember.

"My ring!"

"Is it really that important?"

"Yes! And my dagger. I can't leave without them." The unpleasant buzz has been drowned out by pain and panic, but it'll return soon enough.

"Where are they?"

"The dagger is somewhere near where I fell. The ring is on his finger."

Pan swallows, studying the body lying still by the fire. "You stay here. I'll get them." He guides me down to the ground and then sprints back, nimbly leaping over bushes and fallen logs.

He hunts for the dagger first, holding it up in the air as proof once he's found it.

I wave for him to hurry.

He rushes over to the still form, priming the weapon for use if needed while he gingerly slips the ring off the male's finger. The light from the bonfire catches the impish grin on his face.

I breathe a sigh of relief when he rushes this way. It only gets caught in my throat as a hand shoots out to grab hold of Pan's ankle, sending him flying forward, sprawling onto his stomach.

My pulse races as the male drags himself upright, fumbling for his sword on his rise.

Pan tries to scramble to his feet, but he's not fast enough, and I see this all play out in my mind seconds before it unfolds in reality before my eyes.

With a ferocious smile, the male swings his sword over his head.

"No!" I scream as a surge of horror and fear and anger erupts inside my chest, the need to stop this from happening bursting from deep within. I throw my hand up as if the simple act might stop Pan's slaughter.

The next few heartbeats happen with painstakingly slow and precise clarity.

One beat ... the male sails backward through the air as if hit with a mighty, invisible force and slams into the alcove. Somehow, I can feel every bone in his body snap as if beneath the weight of my boot.

Another beat ... a second surge of power rises, and the forest floor rumbles, the trees swaying.

A third beat ... a mighty crack sounds and the stone enclave crumbles, boulders crashing down over the male, the fire, the entire area.

My mouth hangs at the destruction that now hides in darkness. Only a faint glow from the buried fire remains.

"Pan?" I wait. "Pan?"

Silence answers.

Oh my God. "Pan!" My voice splinters over his name, as I realize what must have happened.

I only wanted to save him.

"Romeria!" Zander's voice echoes through the forest.

"Here!" I call out, hot tears flowing down my cheeks.

Footfalls pound and branches snap, and then suddenly Zander is there, dropping to his knees when he reaches me. His palms cup my face. "You are hurt."

I don't care about myself right now. "Can you please help Pan? Or find him? You *need* to—"

"Okay, shh." He brushes the tears from my cheeks. "Where is he?"

"It all came down," I stammer. "And I think he's buried in there."

Zander ignites a nearby tree using the embers, providing a glow over the area. "Fates," he whispers as we take in the pile of rubble together. "I do not think anyone would have survived that, especially not a mortal."

"He should have run." A sob tears from my chest. "I told him to run, but he wouldn't leave me."

"Then it was destiny to bring him with us, and he was far braver than he seemed." Zander's bloodstained fingers are gentle as he strokes a hair from my forehead. "How did this happen?"

"I don't know." But I do. *I* did that.

When Zander meets my eyes, I see that he knows too.

"They took my ring, and then the man was going to kill Pan, and … I stopped him." My emotions spiraled, and I somehow pulled down an entire cave with my caster affinities, just like Gesine said could happen. Now, an empty calm replaces the constant buzzing, as if whatever power was waiting idly has fizzled with the destruction.

Zander's eyes lock on the trees, his hand going for his sword.

A second later, Jarek and Loth appear.

"We heard the screams and ran as fast as we could, Your Highness." Jarek's breathing is a touch ragged. His eyes widen as he takes in the mound of debris. "Where are the others?"

"With the wagon, a league southwest of here. They were under attack when we came upon them."

Jarek's shoulders sink. With relief, I realize. He was afraid they were buried in that stone too.

"Gesine?" I ask.

"Trying to heal Zorya. She took an arrow." Zander grimaces at the cut across my chest. "They used your blade on you."

By sheer luck, or to intentionally disarm me. That last assailant seemed suspicious. Unfortunately for him, the slice did nothing to stifle my caster affinities.

"If you don't need us here, we will bring the horses to the wagon—" Jarek pauses midsentence, listening. "Do you hear that?" He frowns. "Is there someone buried in there?"

My hope surges. "Help him!"

The three Islorians rush toward the pile of rock.

"Over there!" Zander points to an enormous boulder, and as one, they heave, their powerful bodies straining from the effort. Finally, it rolls.

And out pops Pan, crawling through a tunnel on all fours. He clambers to his feet with a bewildered expression. Aside from a scrape across his forehead, he appears unharmed.

I struggle to stand, using a nearby tree for support. "*How* are you okay?"

He takes in the debris with wide eyes before shrugging. "The boulders formed a little tunnel where I could crawl through." He lifts my ring and dagger.

"I hear thanks are in order for your heroism." Zander holds out his hand. "I will take those."

"Yes, right. Here you go. I mean, Your Highness." Pan gives my belongings to Zander and then bobs and bows awkwardly, reminding me of a duck.

Zander presses his lips together to keep from laughing as he strolls toward me. "What did I say about keeping this on you at all times?" He wipes the bloody blade against his pants before tucking the dagger into my holster. "And this." Collecting my hand in his, he slips the ring on my finger. "Try not to lose this again."

Flutters stir in my chest as his thumb strokes my palm, but I tell myself it was an accident. It meant nothing. "I didn't think you'd be able to find us."

"I wasn't sure I would. Not until I heard the screams. But before that, I will admit, I was panicking."

Because he thought he'd lost his key caster, that little voice reminds me. *You two are nothing more now.* My disappointment flares with the reminder. But I mustn't be blinded by my lingering feelings and his gentleness, that I know my worth to him.

"What happened here, boy?" Jarek asks.

"I don't know, exactly." Pan scratches his curly brown mop. "One minute, my lady was screaming, and the next, the ground was moving and the whole gosh darn thing was coming down."

Jarek's expression is calculating as his attention flips from me to the mountain of rock, back to me and the ring. As if he's piecing together things he shouldn't be. Couldn't be.

"Get the horses to Abarrane," Zander commands.

Another beat passes and then Jarek mutters, "Aye," and takes off.

"Zander, he—"

"Do not worry about Jarek. Let's get you to Gesine."

I reach for his shoulder, intent on using him as a prop, but he gathers me in his arms instead, much like he did the day Tyree smashed my face against the bars.

"Ready?" he asks softly.

Despite my better judgment, I settle my cheek against his shoulder, reveling in this tender moment, however fleeting it may be.

Behind us, Pan hangs back, his furtive glance on the trees in the opposite direction. Now that I'm safe, he's remembering that he's not.

"No one's going to hurt you," I assure him.

His big brown eyes flip to Zander, full of doubt.

Zander surveys my neck. "That first scream I heard, it wasn't you, was it."

My instinct is to lie—to protect Pan—but the truth will come out, anyway, and very soon. "We don't need Gesine's testing method."

He sighs heavily.

"Pan protected me tonight. He tried to convince them to release me, he lied about who I am—"

"He doesn't know who you are."

"That's beside the point. He wouldn't leave when he had his chance. He even went back for my ring and my dagger, which is how he got trapped."

"But I gave Rengard my word—"

"I don't care! You told him you'd pass swift judgment, not necessarily swift *execution*. We can mark him like Wendeline marked the others."

"That didn't work out well for them. Atticus ordered their deaths immediately after."

I wince, the memory of those terrified children still in my mind. But I can't help them anymore. I can, however, help Pan. "No one is laying a hand or a blade or an arrow or *anything* on Pan unless I say it's okay. I mean it, Zander."

The corner of his mouth twitches. "Is that an order, *Your Highness*?"

I roll my eyes at his mocking. "I'm serious."

"I can see that." A pensive look flickers across his face. "Pan, you will not be harmed while you remain with us, as long as you promise me two things. One, you will *never* allow anyone to take your vein."

Pan's head bobs before changing his mind and shaking it furtively. "I won't. I promise. I only took it because Oswald is a mean bugger who sold off my sister to a horrible keeper. Broke my ma's heart. And then she died, and a peddler was sellin' this stuff, and he told me it would make my blood taste bad—"

"We'll get those details later," Zander cuts off his rambling. "That's the first thing. The second"—he considers the crumbled cave—"you *never* repeat what you saw happen here. To *anyone*. And if someone should ask, you inform me."

"Yes, Your Highness. I mean, no, I won't say a word. I didn't really see nothing. I was facedown."

"Let's get out of here." Zander jerks his head in the direction

Jarek and Loth disappeared, waiting for Pan to catch up. Perhaps thinking he might still bolt.

But Pan trudges along. "What about the guy in there? Should we make sure—"

"He's dead." I flex my hand, the feel of crushing bones haunting me.

"Oh. Okay." But his forehead is still furrowed.

"What is the matter now?" Zander asks.

"No, it's just, I had some time to think while I was stuck under there, and ... you're not really Lady Diana from Cornwall, are you?"

I chuckle. "You can call me Romy."

20
ROMERIA

"Careful, or you will undo all my hard work tonight," Gesine scolds as she helps Zorya out of the wagon. "Rest now, and I will finish in the morning, as soon as I have more strength."

"Aye, witch." Her one good eye meets the caster's before she hobbles away. The camp is quiet tonight, with only a few warriors awake and on watch. The windows within the farmhouse are dark, curtains drawn, its residents keeping their distance.

I wriggle down, testing my leg before I put full weight on it. Gesine cauterized the gash during the ride back to camp, but didn't fully knit the muscle together, the last dredges of her power needed elsewhere. "Will she be okay?"

"I believe the worst is over." Gesine watches the warrior cross the campground toward a tent. She's hunched over, favoring the side where the arrow hit, her vest hanging open to reveal a taut female torso, no concern for modesty.

Gesine isn't in much better shape, leaning on the wagon for support, her once-pristine white caster garb streaked in everyone else's blood.

"You saved her life tonight. She knows that. Eventually, she's going to trust you completely. They all will."

"Trust is easy enough to lose even after it is gained. I will continue to help them in every way I can, regardless." Her drawn and red eyes survey me. "Can you manage until tomorrow for your other injuries?"

"Yeah, I think so." I smooth my fingers over the back of my skull. She also sealed that wound, leaving nothing but a headache. That, along with the throbbing in my shoulder from the collision with that male, can wait. "Get some sleep." I'm dying to tell her what happened, to ask her questions, but there will be plenty of time over the coming days as we head north to the mountains.

"I will stay in the wagon with Ianca tonight, to ensure she remains comfortable." She peers into the darkness where the seer rests on skins. The old woman hasn't stirred once, not even during the attack. I don't know if that's from what Gesine did to her or her affliction. Maybe both. At one point, I almost suggested checking to make sure she was still breathing.

"How old is she?"

"We celebrated her forty-fifth year halfway to Westport. The change began two days after. That is no small feat, for a caster to avoid it for that long." Gesine's smile is sad. "I suspect her age is also why she declines so rapidly."

This change from caster to seer usually happens between their third and fourth decade, Wendeline once told me. I hesitate. "And how old are you?"

"I've passed my thirty-sixth year."

Thirty-six. Which means Gesine could technically go through this same change any day now. It could happen before she's been able to train me. What must this be like for her, to watch her friend fade, knowing she may be following her soon?

"My lady? I mean, Highness! ... Romy!" Pan's desperate shouts pull my attention to the horses.

"I will make it swift," Abarrane promises, drawing her sword. It seems she's learned his secret already.

"For crying out loud." I charge forward as fast as my injured leg will carry me, searching for Zander. Since setting me in the wagon, I haven't seen or heard from him. Now, I find him by the barn with Jarek, the two of them alone and facing off in conversation.

I can guess the topic, but it will have to wait.

"Zander!" I holler. "Some *help*, please?"

Pan scurries over to hide behind me as Abarrane stalks forward, her bloodied blade glinting in the torchlight.

"She cannot help you. This is the king's decision, and he has declared it."

"Put it away." Zander marches in, Elisaf closing in quickly behind him. "He has earned his place here. We are going to mark him instead."

"Mark him? With that useless symbol?" Her expression sours. "You cannot be serious—"

"I *am*." He glares at her. "Go and clean up. You look like you bathed in blood tonight."

"I did. And I enjoyed it *immensely*." With one last scowl at Pan, she stalks off, her back rigid with anger.

Zander rubs the back of his neck. "Pan, why don't you go find the other mortals. They're likely asleep in the barn. Tomorrow, you will be given your daily tasks."

Pan looks to me, waiting expectantly.

I smile. "Go on. They're really nice. Especially Eden. You'll like her."

He trots off, eying the direction Abarrane left as if she might charge out again, blade swinging.

"The king gives him an order, and he checks with *you* to see if he should carry it out," Zander mutters.

I shrug. "What can I say? We *do* have a special blood bond."

Zander's flat look says that joke doesn't amuse him.

"I fear that blacksmith wasn't wrong when he called him cunning. He had me convinced." Elisaf shakes his head. "Are you truly going to keep him alive?"

"Romeria insisted. And as long as he does not give me a reason to change my mind, I will honor her request."

"I appreciate that."

Zander opens his mouth but stalls, whatever he wants to say held back.

"Your Highness?" Eden treks across the dewy grass, the hem of her dress damp and stained with mud.

"Hey, why are you still up?"

"I was waiting for you."

"You shouldn't have." I didn't take her from that hellhole so she could stay up all hours of the night to serve *me*. "Go sleep."

"I will." Her wide blue eyes take in my blood-smeared form. "I prepared a bath if you'd like to clean up before you rest. It should be the perfect temperature."

She must have been tending to it for hours, awaiting my arrival.

I sigh. "Thank you, Eden. I would love that."

She beams and then with a bow, offers, "I can show you where the bathhouse is?"

"I know where it is." I saw the little stone shack in the trees earlier, the farm's servants hauling in buckets of water. "I'll be there in a minute."

With another curtsy and a murmured "Your Highness," she hurries back the way she came.

"You should take advantage," Zander says. "Who knows when we'll have such accommodations again."

"I'm going to. I just … can I talk to you for a minute?" Alone, preferably. I'm not sure what I want to say.

Thank you for running to my rescue, even if your motivation is selfish.

Thank you for supporting me with Pan, even if you disagree.

Thank you for not being the cold king tonight, even if I'm sure he'll be back tomorrow.

He opens his mouth, and I hold my breath, waiting to see if he'll continue this routine of avoiding me—

"Highness!" Horik marches over and hands Zander a parchment. "News from Cirilea."

With a frown, Zander unfolds and begins reading. His teeth grit together.

"What is it?" Something terrible, likely. "Zander?"

"You should get to that bath before it turns cold." He spins and heads toward Abarrane's tent.

"Good night," I whisper, though I doubt he heard it, the dismissal clear. There was a time when he would stall others, steal a few moments, just to hear what I needed to say. But those days are gone.

"Sleep well." Elisaf offers a sympathetic smile before following his king.

I never thought I'd say this, but I miss my time in the castle.

I miss my rooms and the panoramic view from the balcony.

I miss Corrin's daily scolding as she delivered a repetitive menu of vegetarian stew and freshly baked bread.

I miss Dagny's prattling as she pinned silks and linens to my body to match the designs I'd sketched.

But right now, what I miss most is the bath in my queen's chamber—a large copper tub that seemed constructed for my body and my body alone, cocooning me in warmth.

Not that this stone hut doesn't have charm—a small hovel surrounded by weeping trees, with uneven ledges built into the walls where tapered candles blink, a hearth where a fire burns beneath a cauldron, a floor covered in silky animal skins soft against bare feet. It's a far cry better than the frigid lakes and streams the Legion use to bathe.

My hair is still matted with dried blood and mud, and my attempt to wash it proves painful. I thought the water might soothe my aching shoulder while this elven body works its healing magic, but now I can barely lift my arm. I'd think it was dislocated from my fall, if I didn't know better.

I sink deeper into the round, barrel-like wooden tub, absorbing the last hints of warmth from the tepid water before it officially turns too cold. I shouldn't have sent Eden to bed after she cleaned and hung my clothes to dry, but I wanted to be alone to wallow in my conflicting emotions.

My ring sits heavy on my finger tonight. It has ever since Zander slid it back on with all the tenderness of a man who still cares deeply for me. That's just wishful thinking, though. That, or the depth of his feelings for me can never compete with his love for Islor.

Can I fault him for that? Isn't that what makes him a good king? A king the mortals of Islor need?

Still, it hurts.

Through the small rectangular opening in the wall, branches stir. A moment later, the door creaks open behind me.

"I told you to go to bed."

"If you mean Eden, she did. I watched her go."

My stomach flips as Zander's voice fills the room. "What are you doing here?"

"You said you needed to talk." The door shuts with a click.

"Yeah, and then that letter came, and I figured you were busy doing king things."

"King things?" His footfalls are slow and measured as he crosses the little room to the simmering cauldron. He stoops to place another log beneath. The flames engulf it instantly, aided by his affinity. "That water cannot be comfortable anymore."

"It's not." I fight the urge to curl my arms across my bare chest, just an inch beneath the water's surface. He's the one who decided to intrude. "But I don't want to get out yet."

"Good, because you are still filthy." He sheds his cloak and weapons on the floor, the gory evidence of the earlier battle smeared on the blades.

"You're one to talk." His forearm is covered in dried blood.

"I am not the one sitting in a tub."

And unfortunately, he wouldn't fit in here with me, no matter how creative the positioning.

He sets to filling the pitcher with hot water.

"What did the letter say?" I wait expectantly, my pulse thrumming, as he saunters over to add the steaming water.

But he keeps his eyes downcast. "Atticus has announced his betrothal to Saoirse."

The news derails my lewd thoughts. I groan. "What an *idiot*!"

He smirks as he returns to the cauldron and refills the pitcher.

"That horrible snake is going to be queen of Islor. These poor people will be under her rule." She's going to sleep in my bed and sit on the throne I once sat in. *My* throne. While it was never truly mine to begin with, I feel an odd claim to it now, and a surge of disappointment at its loss. "Why are you not upset?"

"Because stewing in my feelings will not change anything."

I sigh. "When?"

"The next Hudem."

That was supposed to be our wedding day. Our second one. A sham to buy us time to uncover the traitors working against Zander. But then things changed between us and … I don't know what would have happened if we had gone through it.

"Do you think he's told Saoirse about me?" All my secrets?

"Atticus is not marrying Saoirse for love or companionship. It is merely a move on a chessboard to further entrench himself on the throne, so that I may not take it back." Zander pours another pitcher of hot water into my bath. "He does not trust her or her father. He will guard all vital information."

"Will it work? This marriage?"

"He'll have Kettling and the east standing behind him." His eyes settle on mine. "But I will have you."

I swallow under their weight. "Water shields and crumbling caves will not beat an army. I think you put way too much faith in me."

"And I do not think you put enough in yourself." Finally, his attention drifts over my waiting body, his gaze rousing a delicious heat along my limbs, through my core. "How is the temperature now?"

"Better." I hardly feel it one way or the other, far too focused on Zander, on the way he makes my heart pound, my blood race, and this ache stir deep inside. And I know he can sense it. That muscle ticking in his jaw tells me so.

"You haven't washed your hair."

"I tried, but my shoulder is killing."

Zander collects a stool from nearby and settles next to the tub. "Relax for me," he coaxes, cupping my nape.

I admire his mouth as I settle into his grip, allowing him to shift my body until the back of my head is immersed. His other hand works against my scalp, his fingers weaving through my hair. He grazes the spot on my skull that was bashed when they knocked me out. "Does that still sting?"

"No. Gesine fixed it." And the dull ache that's plagued me since melts away beneath his touch.

"And your leg?"

"Didn't you just get a good look at it?" I tease. The room is dimly lit, but with those Islorian eyes of his, I can't be sure what he can see.

"I did not come here for that." When his eyes drop to meet mine, the hazel in them is molten. He may not have come for *that*, but I can see that he wants it.

My throat goes dry. "It doesn't hurt."

"Good." A quiet moment passes where the candles flicker, and Zander collects a lather from the bar of soap on the ledge. I inhale the delicious scent of rose petals as his skilled hands work it through my hair.

"How was your meeting with Rengard?"

"He's protecting his interests and those of his people, and I cannot fault him for that."

"Will he help you?"

"With supplies, yes. With information, perhaps. He has also agreed to take any of the Freywich mortals who wish to go—"

"Eden will go with him."

Zander scoops water in his hand to rinse the soap from my

hair. "She seems to have taken a liking to you. I suspect she will not be willing to leave your side."

"She'll be safer here, in Bellcross."

"Probably, yes. Theon says the villages in the north grow restless. The rebellions have been brewing for years, but each day brings new stories of mortals defying their keepers and the crown. If there was ever a part of Islor to turn against us first, it is where we are going. Perhaps Tyree's choice to send the vials to that area was not a coincidence. As for Eden, I thought you were an advocate of these mortals having a choice."

"I *am*, but she still thinks we're going back to Cirilea after this. She has no idea what's going on."

"Then perhaps you should tell her the truth and allow her to decide for herself." Zander frowns, then shakes his head.

"What?"

"Nothing. I just ... Your hair should be clean now."

I collect the cloth I'd been using, and gripping his wrist, I wash the blood and dirt from his skin, remembering the cords of muscle in these forearms as they braced his weight over me, these skilled hands on my body, not long ago. In his bath, in our beds, brazen as they searched for my every hidden spot. Now they remain motionless, uninterested, as I clean them.

"I thought I lost you tonight."

I look up to meet his steady gaze on my face. "You can't get rid of me that easily. And I should know because everyone keeps trying. Shot with an arrow, skewered by a demon, attacked by my brother, chased by an army. Then there were *more* arrows, flaming arrows—"

"I thought you *left* me. That you ran." There's a desperate ring to his words.

"And you're afraid you won't get your throne back without your weapon?"

He flinches as if my words are an accusation. "Yes, I need what you are, for Islor's sake. I need it to have any chance of regaining my throne and stopping what is about to happen to my people.

But do not assume that is all you are. Do not assume this is easy for me." He pulls away from my grip, hands me the folded linen towel Eden set out, and then spins on the stool to give me privacy.

"I don't know, you wrote me off pretty quickly."

"I will not pretend to understand what that means. But there are things *you* do not understand, too."

"I understand being used." Water sluices off my body as I climb out and towel off. "My old boss used me to get rich. Sofie is using me to get her husband back. Even your god of fire is using me like some sort of key. And for what? So he can play king to a court?"

I wait for Zander to argue, but he says nothing, and we're left lingering in silence with nothing but the rustling of leaves against the wind and the odd hoot of an owl to fill the void.

"I wanted to run," I admit. "I asked Gesine to leave with me."

"When?"

"After Freywich."

"Because of what happened there? My actions?" His voice holds a rare tinge of insecurity.

"No. I know why you did what you did. Jarek could have enjoyed it a bit less, but you had no choice." In this world, it was the only way to punish those guilty of decades of abuse. Had he not, the mortals of Freywich would only have suffered more.

"We should have done something years ago. We should have traveled to all these towns and villages and made examples of their kind. But I suppose I got too comfortable in my towers of gold, playing politics and trying to win favor in idealistic ways. Now I fear it is too late."

The chilled evening air flows through the gaping window, stirring gooseflesh over my bare thighs and arms.

The flames flare from the hearth, the waft of heat warming my skin. He didn't even need to look at me to sense my discomfort, so acutely in tune with my body.

"Thank you."

"You are welcome." He studies his hands, his head bowed in

solemn thought. "Isn't this nice? Talking without throwing barbed words at each other?"

"Maybe. It doesn't mean you'll like what I have to say."

"And what is it you have to say?"

I hesitate. "I wanted to run because of all the people who have used me in my life, having you do it hurts the most."

He stares at the ground. "Our entire scheme in Cirilea was born of my need for you, but you took no issue with it then."

"You're right, I didn't. Maybe because there were so many secrets between us, and I was using you too." Until I wasn't. "But now it's all out in the open. We're sitting here in a room full of truths, and you're *still* using me."

The muscle in his jaw ticks.

I wring the water from my hair using my good arm. "I'm not going to run. I'm not stupid. Where would I go without Gesine? I wouldn't last a night."

"Something tells me you will survive much longer than you think."

"Maybe you're right. That's all I've been doing since I opened my eyes here, though. Surviving. And for years before that too." Not that Zander knows the first thing about my previous life. "I want to do more than just survive. And for that, I can't run."

Zander half turns, his gaze on my bare legs. "And what is it you want to do?"

My instinct is always to protect my underbelly, but I've been vulnerable with Zander since the beginning. "I need Gesine to teach me all she knows about affinities before she can't. And I need Elisaf to be the loyal friend by my side he's always been. I need Abarrane to show me how to save myself with a knife when it's the only way. If she doesn't kill me with it first."

Zander snorts.

"I need people like Eden and Pan to remind me why I shouldn't run. Why I should stay and help you." What I would've faced had I been born in this world.

He swallows. "What do you need from me?"

Everything. "I need you to remember that I didn't ask to be here. I didn't ask to be a puppet or to curse you. I don't want you to feel trapped by your feelings for me. It's the *last* thing I would ever want. And I didn't ask for you to give up your throne."

"You would be dead if I had not."

"Then maybe I'm supposed to be dead, prophecy or not. Wouldn't it have solved *all* your problems?"

He shakes his head. "You do not want that."

"No, what I didn't want is to have fallen in love with you." It feels like I'm confessing, only instead of my sins, it's my weaknesses. "You asked me if I regretted it—I don't. But I also haven't made a smart decision since." And if I stay in this little stone hut, wrapped in a towel and professing my feelings to a man who has made it clear he doesn't want them, I'm sure my streak will continue.

I rush to collect my clothes, hugging them to my chest. I'll have to dress in my tent. "Enjoy the bath. The water will be cleaner than nothing."

I've reached the door when Zander is suddenly there, his hand flat against its surface, barricading me in. "I can feel what you are feeling. You know this by now." He moves in behind me, his looming body pressed against my back.

I inhale his scent—that intoxicating, sweet, woodsy fragrance. "Good. I hope it hurts."

"Every day." The rawness in his voice tugs at my heartstrings. He sighs, his breath skating across my bare shoulder. He's leaning close. "You were testing me tonight. Is it to see if I still desire you, or to watch me break?"

"Both," I admit, realizing the latter is true. I did want him to respond. "But it doesn't matter, does it? What we had is over, just like you said."

His deep, derisive chuckle fills the tiny room. "I promise you, those were just words, meant to convince myself as much as you." With a hand on my shoulder, he gently guides me around to face him.

"Words can be more effective than any one of *those*." I nod to the heap of weapons he left on the floor. "More harmful."

"In this case, they were entirely useless. These are still damp." He collects my bundle of clothes from my grasp and tosses them near the fire, leaving me huddled in my towel. He falters over his next words, shaking his head as if unsure how to say what he wants or unsure whether he should say anything. "Gesine says my feelings for you are now my own, the veil pulled back, Aoife's influence ineffectual. But after today, after what happened tonight"—he slides his index finger over the faint scar along my collarbone, still visible but far less than a usual merth wound—"I do not see myself as having a choice."

"Choice about what? What are you trying to tell me?"

That same finger slips beneath my chin, lifting it until I've met his eyes. They roam over my features as if drinking them in. "That I am still very much in love with you, despite my best efforts not to be, despite all I've said and done."

My heart thrums in my chest. "You don't act like it."

He leans in, pressing his forehead to mine, his slender nose grazing my cheek. "Because I do not know how to love you *and* be a good king to my people, and that is a relentless war I have been fighting daily, without ever touching a sword." His voice bleeds with the turmoil of his words. "But I realize now that I will *never* be him if it means losing you."

His blunt admission stalls my tongue. I'm a nuclear bomb, primed to wreak havoc in the wrong hands. Maybe Atticus is making the right decision for Islor. Maybe my death would solve all their problems.

And then what? Would they squash this threat of poison and go back to the way things were, enslaving the mortals and living in wealth? No, that doesn't seem to be the solution either. I don't know what is, but that's a problem for another day.

"Then love me tonight and be the king you need to be tomorrow."

He leans in to brush his tongue against the seam of my lips, drawing my deep moan. Suddenly, my towel is gone, tugged off and cast aside by his eager hands. With firm fingers gripping my hips, he steers me into the middle of the room and down to the pile of animal skins.

The flames in the hearth blaze by his silent command, warming my body as I lie on my back and watch him undress. He tosses his shirt dangerously close to a burning candle before kicking off his boots and unfastening his pants.

It feels like an eternity since I've been able to admire his naked form. Now I take all of him in as he drops to his knees in front of me, parting my legs to fit his muscular body between them.

"Which shoulder is sore? Is it this one?" He leans in to trace my skin with his mouth, his tongue, while his hand busies itself in one fell swoop, memorizing the shape of my breasts, smoothing over the tautness of my belly, testing my readiness at the apex of my thighs.

"Neither." Because right now, I don't feel anything except this overwhelming need for Zander to fill me again. On other nights, I've happily laid back and allowed him his exploration, but tonight, I grip the back of his golden-brown hair with my fist, dragging his face to mine so I can feel the intimacy of his lips. With my other hand, I reach down between us, wrapping my hand around his hard length, directing it.

He inhales sharply but doesn't waste another moment, sinking into me with a single push.

Surely, my guttural cry carries through the still forest, perking ears of the owls and whichever legionaries guard against dangers. But right now, the world is only Zander and me. No one and nothing else matters as our bodies writhe and grind against each other, the impressive span of muscle across his back tensing beneath my fingertips with each thrust.

Over and over, he moves inside me, his breathing ragged as my skin grows slick, our cries unchecked in the night.

With a swift maneuver, I find myself straddling Zander, his eyes blazing as he grips my hips. I roll them, and the smile he gives me is slow and satisfied. He's never been able to last long in this position once I begin to move, his glazed focus struggling between my swaying breasts and where we're joined.

He seems to remember that quickly. The padded muscle across his stomach flexes as he sits up, our chests meeting in the middle. "Not yet." His mouth lands on mine, his fingers collecting a fistful of hair as he pushes my lips wide open in a deep kiss, our bodies rocking in a sensual, well-timed dance.

I hold his gaze as my hands crawl over his shoulders, his arms, his chest, until they settle flared against his back, pulling his body flat against mine.

"You wanted to see me break," he whispers, his breathing uneven.

"No, I wanted to see you love." My focus shifts to where we're joined, the feel of him filling my welcoming body … My release hits me in a sudden and unexpected rush, stealing my control. I cry out Zander's name as my muscles spasm around him. He follows immediately after, his arms flexing around my body as he pulsates inside me.

I remain straddling his lap afterward, our chests heaving from exertion, our lips sneaking gentle kisses along jawlines and necks. The only sound to compete with us is the occasional snap of roasting wood.

I could stay like this all night.

But when Zander's body tenses, I know this reprieve is over, and his worries have begun to consume him again.

"Those warriors out there have pledged their loyalty and their lives to me. They must have faith that I remain focused on a way out of this mess."

"And not chasing to get under my skirts?" I mock, as Corrin loved to say.

"Abarrane will worry that I'm under your influence again." He smooths his palm over my bare thigh. "I suppose I am. But I need her every step of the way. She cannot think my judgment is compromised."

I know what he's saying. "It's fine. I won't take it personally." I kiss the tip of his nose. "Just don't be a fucking asshole again."

He sighs heavily. "Would the people's princess use that foul language?"

My head falls back with a bellow of laughter that reminds me where he's still deeply seated.

21
ROMERIA

I sense a figure standing over me a second before a toe digs into my calf.

"Wake up," Abarrane snaps.

I grimace into the shadows of my tent. Zander walked me back last night and laid beside me but must have left when I fell asleep because I'm alone now, aside from this brackish warrior kicking me. "What's going on?"

"Scouts have seen the supply wagons approaching. They'll be here soon."

I pause to rub the sleep from my eyes. "And?"

"*And* Rengard is with them. Do you not think he will ask about your poisonous little pet?"

"Oh, shit."

"Yes. Exactly. Zander can answer for his decision, but you need to get the witch to mark that imbecile so it appears we're taking the issue seriously."

"We *are* taking it seriously."

"Seriously would be my blade across his jugular."

Low voices and rustling carries outside my tent. "Where's Zander?"

"Too busy for you."

I scowl as I haul my body up. While my thigh feels mostly fine, my shoulder still aches. "I think I'd rather deal with Jarek in the mornings."

"I will be sure to send him in next. I'll tell him you did not get enough in the bathhouse last night." She throws the tent flap open, allowing me a glimpse of the dawn light and the bustling camp. My cheeks burn. I suppose there was no keeping Zander's and my reconciliation from her.

I quickly dress and roll up my bed before venturing out. Dense fog veils the farm, hiding the barn from where I stand. It must have rained after I went to bed; the long grass weeps under the weight of moisture.

One of the Freywich mortals sees me emerge and rushes over. With a bow and *Your Highness*, which I don't bother to correct, he begins taking down my tent.

I head in the direction of the wagon while scanning for Zander and Pan, but I find neither within the mist.

Gesine is already awake and working on Zorya's wound again. She's changed out of the caster's ruined white gown and back to the beige linen dress from Freywich.

The warrior stands with her vest hiked halfway up her torso, a cautious glower marring her face as she studies Ianca, seated in the wagon, guiding spoonfuls of cold porridge to her mouth with surprising precision. The seer's sparse white hair seems thinner today, if that's possible, exposing patches of her scalp.

Zorya isn't the only one wary. I doubt anyone here has ever seen a seer before, and many nervous glances drift this way. I understand that. I used to watch my father from a distance. People would change course when they noticed him sitting on the sidewalk, as if he might lash out at a passerby without warning, like his enraged rants would lead to ambiguous violence.

Thankfully, Ianca is quiet this morning.

"Nice scar," I say by way of greeting. All that's left is a jagged silver mark on her ribcage.

"I am collecting."

I draw the collar of my tunic aside, where the faint, thin line from my dagger crosses over my collarbone. "Me too."

"Not bad, but not lethal."

"I'll try harder next time."

She smirks. "Good."

"There. You should be fully healed now." Gesine gently pats Zorya's scar before shifting away.

The warrior yanks her vest down and turns to leave, but then falters. "Thank you, witch." She meets Gesine's gaze as if to silently convey her gratitude.

Gesine dips her head with her usual deference. "It is my pleasure. As always."

"A strong warrior. A protector. She will make a good lover, and not hesitate to end your suffering when the time comes." Ianca gulps another spoonful of oatmeal, her defective eyes on her bowl.

Gesine's jaw drops and a nervous laugh escapes, her cheeks flushing. "Do let me know if there's any more pain or difficulty drawing breath."

With one last glance at the seer, Zorya strolls away, readjusting the daggers at her sides.

"Ianca! Do not say such things!" Gesine chastises, sounding less like the serene caster and more like an appalled friend. Or *more* than a friend. I'm beginning to see a deeper connection than simply two powerful casters who were trapped in a jeweled castle together.

Ianca shrugs, unbothered. "I can feel her. The other Romeria."

"Yes, she is right here."

I hesitate. The last time I spoke to Ianca, she started screaming. "Good morning?"

"Morning, dear." She shovels in another spoonful.

Shaking her head, Gesine turns back to me. "You're protecting your shoulder."

"Yeah, I must have torn something. It kept me up half the night." With the help of someone else.

"Allow me to look while you fill me in on all that happened yesterday after we parted ways." She reaches for me.

I take a quick step back. "I will, but first, I need you to mark the mortal from Bellcross before the supply wagons get here."

"You brought a mortal from Bellcross? Why?"

I explain as quickly as I can.

"I see." She frowns. "What kind of symbol?"

"The day of the royal repast, Wendeline put an emblem on the hands of the tainted humans. It glowed like the marks you have on your arm, except it was—"

"The mark of Ulysede," Ianca cuts in. She tosses her spoon, and dipping her hand into her porridge, she coats her fingers with the slop and finger-paints on the wagon wall. While the medium isn't the most effective, the intersecting crescent moons are unmistakable.

"Yes. That's it. How did she know?"

Gesine studies not the drawing but the seer for a moment, a quizzical look on her face, before she hops off the wagon. "I'll be back soon, Ianca. You'll stay here?"

Ianca doesn't answer, focused on drawing swirling patterns on the wagon wall.

The grass tangles at our ankles as I lead us toward the horses and the barn. "Is that normal?"

"Nothing is normal anymore. But seers will often illustrate what they see with surprising clarity. It is why the scribes give them paper and graphite. Unfortunately, we don't have either, so Ianca improvised." A small smile curls her lips. "She always was clever like that."

"So she has seen that symbol?"

"All of us in Mordain have. It has appeared in seers' illustrations for millennia, without any explanation from the seers themselves as to what it means. Some assume it represents the two moons of Hudem, but those are full moons, and these are crescents. Others have called it the mark of two worlds, because the moons intersect. That Wendeline chose this symbol for the mortals

… I wish I could speak with her and understand if it was mere coincidence or something more." She glances back at Ianca. "But I have never heard this term *Ulysede* before."

I hesitate, looking around us to make sure no one's near. "I've seen the symbol too. In *my* world." I explain the People's Sentinel.

"Was their blood poisoned? Does the blood curse plague your world?" Gesine asks, intrigue in her tone.

"I don't know. Definitely not like here. Sure, we've *heard* of vampires, but it's all fiction." At least, I thought it was.

"Vampire," she echoes, as if the word is as foreign as Ulysede.

"What do you think this all means?"

"The symbol itself could represent something entirely different in your world. It is not uncommon for words and ideas to lose their original purpose as they're passed down through generations and appropriated by other cultures." She shakes her head slowly. "But it means you have much to reveal during our travel north."

A shout rings out, pulling our attention to the fence line, where wagons and soldiers on horseback appear like apparitions through the mist. Rengard is at the front, his plum-purple cloak marking him among silver armor.

I curse, scouring the camp until I spot the curly brown mop among the horses. "Pan!" I holler, waving him over.

"*That* is the mortal? He looks so young," Gesine notes as he jogs toward us.

"He's eighteen, though he seems a lot younger sometimes."

"Hey, Romy," he says, panting. "You were right about Eden. She's great. Helped me get set up with a bed and a meal, and now I'm helping—"

"I'm happy to hear it, Pan. But right now, I need you to give us your hand so Gesine can mark it like we talked about last night."

"Mark it?" He squirms as he looks at her.

She bows, shifting into her usual serene demeanor. "Hello, Pan. I am Caster Gesine, and I'm here—"

"You're a caster? Like a *real* one?" His eyes widen. "I heard people talkin' about you, but—"

"Pan!" I cut him off. I'm learning the guy blathers when he's nervous. "We need to do this *now*."

"Okay." His head bobs. "Is it gonna hurt?"

"Not as much as what Abarrane will do to you if we don't get you marked before Rengard arrives."

Pan's arm shoots out.

"So, this is what's left of the Legion." Lord Rengard's gaze swings over the trampled grounds and the warriors readying their horses. His face is a portrait of noble elven tranquility, his skin smooth across high cheekbones. He seems older than Zander, though by Zander's words, they grew up together. Maybe it's the gray hair that ages him.

Is it surprise or concern that laces his tone?

"Each of them is worth fifty soldiers," Zander says coolly. He appeared as the company pulled in, his tall, powerful form a portrait of confidence strolling across the foggy camp.

But I now know it's all an illusion to hide the weight of the turmoil that tortures him.

My chest aches as I watch him close in on the nobleman.

Rengard drops from his saddle, his boots hitting the ground with barely a sound. "Can I assume the smoldering bodies we passed on the road here are thanks to you?"

The two leaders clasp each other's wrists. Anyone watching can see they're more than court acquaintances, more than a king and his nobleman.

They are friends.

"Raiders attacked us on our return last night."

"They did not realize who they were challenging, Your Highness."

"They learned. Thank you for this." Zander waves a hand

toward the four wagons, each one twice the size of the sanctum's rickety cart and constructed with solid wooden walls painted in deep burgundies and forest greens rather than simple stretched leather canvas.

"You will find plenty of provisions inside for your travels north. Grains and cured meats, warm skins, new leathers, and weapons, including a few from my collection. And enough tributaries to satisfy this lot, hopefully."

Zander's brow pinches. "We've discussed this already. It is not safe for mortals where we are going, and the trip will be grueling."

"I would wager it is not safe for any of you. And it will be far less so if you are too weakened to fight. But fear not, I asked rather than ordered, and they agreed to aid their king. They are skilled in various tasks, whether it be cooking or mending or hunting, so they will prove valuable in more ways than one."

"It is more likely their loyalty to their lord that sees them here. Still … thank you." Zander dips his head. "In return, we have seven mortals from Freywich who want to find homes in Bellcross. Good homes with decent keepers."

"I will make it so, my king."

Zander has already talked to the Freywich mortals. Seven want to stay in Bellcross, meaning two want to leave with us. As I search the faces standing quietly by the barn, I don't have to guess one of them, at least. Eden beams at me, her excitement unmistakable.

That illusion has to be doused. Or at least, a frank conversation has to happen. I won't let her follow me blindly into what sounds like hell.

"Your Highness." Rengard's voice draws me back. I find his shrewd eyes on me. "Glad to see you were not harmed in the skirmish with the marauders."

I can't tell if his words are genuine. "Nothing Gesine couldn't fix."

He shifts his attention to her, to her gold collar. "If only all of Islor had access to such gifts."

Gesine bows graciously. "If only it were up to me, my lord."

"Maybe one day we will be blessed again." He returns his focus to Zander. "Might we walk a moment?"

Zander gestures toward a groomed path around the pond. To Elisaf, he instructs, "Have the Freywich mortals board the sanctum's wagon so that we may return it to them. Send enough coin for repairs and compensation for their driver. And we will need to make room in one of the wagons for those better suited to privacy."

He means Ianca. I guess he's still keeping her presence a secret, even from his friend. Sometimes it's difficult to understand why Zander keeps things close to his chest. It could be habit, or maybe he has good reason.

The two males fall into step beside each other and stroll away, leaving his guards behind, their circumspect eyes flittering over the legionaries.

"What do you think that's about?" I ask.

"I am sure you will hear soon enough, if it is something meant for your ears." Gesine gives my arm a gentle tug. "Come, we must retrieve Ianca before someone disturbs her and she causes a scene."

22
ZANDER

"Lady Saoirse." Theon shakes his head. "Did we not have this conversation yesterday?"

"We did." And though I denied it at the time, I feared it all the same.

"Seems your brother *is* that stupid, after all."

"I wish that were the case, but it is likely the opposite. With Saoirse, he will have Kettling. A lukewarm alliance at best, but it will hold. And with Adley's son gone, Atticus will ensure he commands that army. Perhaps Abarrane did me no favors by removing his head."

"That warrior of yours …." Theon grunts. "Still, I would rather offer my cock to a daaknar than Saoirse."

"I felt the same when I thought I would be forced to marry her." And then Romeria came along, and everything changed.

For the worse.

For the better.

A smile tugs at the corners of my mouth as memories of last night consume my thoughts—of her warm body, hard in all the right places, except where she is *so* soft. It was a special kind of torture, having to leave her in that tent when all I wanted was to lie next to her.

In hindsight, it seems unfathomable that I ever fell for that other version—Princess Romeria—and all her acquiescing and mollifying and batting of eyelashes. *This* Romeria … so fiery and temperamental, sharp-witted, and yet brimming with a genuine empathy that elven are incapable of. If last night taught me anything, it's that I will not risk her, not for all the crowns and all the kingdoms. There *must* be another way.

"And what of Adley?" Theon brings me back to the dour conversation. "Do you have any idea how Atticus will deal with him?"

"I do." I've thought about it plenty, and I know what *I* would do. "He will neutralize him as best he can and send his men in to infiltrate Kettling, but Adley will see through that and sabotage his efforts. Atticus will grow angry and lose patience, and once his heir is born, he will rid himself of the problem. An accident, or an attack. Perhaps I will be the one accused of his assassination. His hands will remain clean in the view of the court. Whether Saoirse believes it is another story. She is as conniving and distrustful as her father. There are those in the east well-stocked with gold and power by Adley's hand who will wish to remain so, and that will only happen with Saoirse's support."

"So Cirilea and Kettling will remain divided, and war will likely follow."

"Yes. Though our more pressing issue is not war with the east but the uprising in the west."

"Yes, something I wanted to discuss." Theon's face is bleak. "I received a message late last night. The reports of poisonings are growing in many villages around the mouth of Venhorn. The mortals are being brought to Norcaster, where Isembert is ordering their executions."

"Already?" The minor lord who governs the gateway town into the mountain range has been known to be harsh, as many who live in the area are, but this is unexpected. "How could Atticus's edict have reached him so quickly?"

"Isembert is no fool and surely receives word from the south. But he would not wait for permission. He has planted himself as the ruler of Norcaster and all the surrounding villages. We have not helped matters by allowing that arrangement to continue all these years." He doesn't have to add that it was at my father's request that Bellcross leave these villages alone rather than start a civil war that could prove bloody. I remember that well. Father figured that if these Islorians preferred the threat of saplings and the harsh mountain climate over his crown's rule, he would leave them to it, as long as the trade goods—furs and lumber, mainly—continued flowing south to the markets each year. He claimed these people were too isolated in their valley to cause harm to Islor.

"Did the note say how the poison is moving? If there are Ybarisans there?"

"They did not mention Ybarisans, though they did say Isembert is suspicious of any southern traveler passing through his gates. More than one has gone missing, so I would be careful if I were you, thinking of venturing in there, whether under your banner or not."

"I appreciate the warning." The farther north we go, the less my banner will mean to these people, anyway. "If *you* are hearing this news, I have to assume pigeons have carried similar messages to Cirilea." To my brother, to Adley, to anyone searching for an opportunity. And Atticus, with his war-centered mind, has never agreed with our father's stance on leaving the Venhorn villages alone. This gives him his excuse to act, if he feels the need to look for one. "Has my brother sent an army from Lyndel yet?"

"I received word that they'll be leaving within the day."

"How many soldiers? I'll wager it will be substantial to deal with the likes of these people." The northerners are hardy and strong, elven and mortal alike, and they're fighters.

"A thousand. They will take the mountain pass rather than go around the range, so you must move fast to avoid crossing their path." He hesitates. "Forgive me for questioning your plans, but where in those mountains can you go that the armies can't follow, can't surround you? How long can you defend yourself in those caves with nineteen legionaries and a single caster?"

I force a smile and hope he can't read my trepidation when I say, "Do not worry, friend. There is plenty of higher ground to establish a solid defense, and no one knows those caves better than we do." Save for the saplings.

And, despite my doubts, I haven't been able to shake Gesine's claim that answers await us in Stonekeep. But I can never share that with Theon. He would think Mordain and prophecy are guiding me, two things no king in their right mind should ever trust.

"And what of the boy? Were your methods able to deduce anything?"

I knew this would come up. "Whether your blacksmith saw what he saw, I cannot say, but he was not lying about the mortal's blood being tainted."

Theon curses. "I sensed there was something deceptive in him. It has become so difficult to read these mortals, though, all of them perpetually full of fear. And to think I nearly made such a foolish mistake. Thank the fates for you, my friend."

"Thank my mother. She always did say I was gifted with a highly suspicious mind." A gift for a king faced with too many enemies.

"Still, I do feel empathy for the boy. What was his name … Pan?" Theon shakes his head. "Oswald proved a terrible keeper, and yet it was the mortal who suffered the most."

I hesitate, but only for a second. The days of trying to run this realm with truths only when they suit me are over. "He has not gone anywhere yet."

Theon's mouth falls open. "You've kept him alive?"

"He has proven useful, and I think he will prove useful still. He is utterly loyal to Romeria. And smitten, it seems." The scrawny mortal's pulse races every time she is near. "The caster has marked him, and I have put the fear of the fates' judgment into him should he ever allow anyone on his vein. Though in truth, a look from Abarrane is just as effective. His intentions no longer concern me." I have far bigger things to worry myself with.

"I hope you are right, friend." But worry etches Theon's forehead as we round the pond.

23
ROMERIA

Ianca sits in the corner of the sanctum's wagon, her shoulders hunched.

"She's calm today," I whisper. "That's good, right?"

"Yes, I think being near me has helped. She doesn't feel so lost."

What would that have been like, to step off a boat after a long journey, hustled into a wagon and led away by a stranger, then locked up in a church with more strangers? All while losing her eyesight and her bearings on reality? No wonder she was agitated. "How long do you think she has?"

Gesine shakes her head. "Some seers can live years, others only weeks, which is why we must gain whatever knowledge we can from her now. For that, you must travel with us."

"Of course." Gladly. It'll be a break from dealing with Jarek and stiff, chafed thighs.

Gesine climbs in. "Ianca, we are moving to more comfortable accommodations for the journey north, and I must get you ready."

Ianca's eyelids crack open. "I am tired," she complains.

Gesine's gentle hands pull Ianca's hood over her scant hair, hiding her. "I know. We will move you, and then you can rest." Her palms stroke the old woman's face.

I turn away to give them privacy.

And find myself staring at a wall of leather and weapons, the scent of clean sweat and male muskiness filling my nostrils. At least Jarek bathes regularly. Even his hair looks freshly washed and braided.

His expression is as harsh as always. "Feeling better today?"

I sense he has an ulterior motive for checking on my welfare, and I hope it has nothing to do with the collapsed cave. I play into his game, plastering on a wide smile. "I am. Thank you so much for asking. And how are *you* feeling? You know, after that little visit to your blood brothel—"

"I didn't need you to defend me to my commander."

"But I did it, anyway. You're welcome." I pause. "Unless you're here to ask Gesine to heal whatever Abarrane did to punish you?" She didn't touch him, and we both know it.

He grits his teeth, his gaze raking over my face as if searching for hidden truth. "This story of amnesia. Is it genuine?"

The quick change of subject distracts me, but I recover quickly. "I'm sorry, what's your name again?"

He snorts at my flippant answer. "I'm expected to protect you at all costs, including my own life, and yet it is obvious you are keeping rather significant secrets. You and the king. Abarrane, too, likely." His steely eyes wander to where she barks orders. "I am her second-in-command. I should be in their confidence."

"Maybe you need to prove that you're loyal."

"Do not *ever* question my loyalty to Islor, to my Legion, or to my king," he snaps.

"Fine. Maybe it's not your loyalty. Maybe it's your prejudices."

"My *prejudices* … I'd say I've been more than open-minded, literally saddled for days with a Ybarisan from whom a single drop of blood would tear me apart, tasked to give my life for hers." He steps in closer. "I would like to know why she is *so very important* to Islor's future."

Is that what Zander told him last night during their little private conversation?

"Some help, if you will?" Gesine calls out, guiding a hunched Ianca to the wagon's edge.

I could kiss the caster for the perfectly timed interruption.

A beat passes with us squared off, and then Jarek breaks away. Without hesitation, he grips Ianca's waist and lifts her down. Far too fast for a woman so frail. It earns an admonished gasp from Gesine, who hops down to catch Ianca, as if she may collapse.

But Ianca merely laughs, an old woman's cackle that turns heads. "So many little nymphs running around." Hidden deep within her cowl, her cloudy, useless eyes lift to Jarek's face as if she can see it clearly. "*Weak* little nymphs."

"This way, Ianca." Gesine coaxes her toward Elisaf and the new wagon, saying something my ears can't catch.

Jarek watches them go.

"I think she called you weak," I mock whisper.

"We both know I am neither weak nor a nymph, and that she is mad."

Eden rushes toward us from the barn. I'm noticing that she always moves in a hurry as if Lady Danthrin were still following her with a switch.

Either way, it's another well-timed disruption, so I don't have to deal with Jarek's questions.

"Your Highness, we've packed your things. Can I help you with anything else as we prepare for travel? Some hot oats or fruit, perhaps? You haven't eaten, and you must be hungry."

"I could eat. But hold on a second. I need to talk to you, as soon as Jarek finds someone else to bother."

Eden glances up at the warrior but quickly averts her attention to the ground when she sees that he's studying her.

His lips twist. "Will I have the displeasure of riding with you today, *Your Highness*? Or will you be riding the king again?"

My cheeks burn. Does *everyone* know what happened in the bathhouse last night?

With a smirk of satisfaction, he marches toward his horse, not waiting for an answer.

I push aside my embarrassment. "Eden, did you tell the king that you want to come with me?"

"Yes. If I am adequate to serve Her Highness, that is." She punctuates that with a curtsy.

"Of course. You are amazing, Eden."

She beams.

I hope she's still beaming in ten minutes. "But there is something you need to know."

"Prepare to move out!" Jarek bellows.

The sun soaks the valley in morning light as the Legion mounts their horses. Rengard left with the fog and the Freywich mortals, minus Brawley, the sturdy twenty-year-old stable boy with an itch for adventure, and Eden, who I could not convince to leave regardless of how bleak a picture I painted. She's now busy familiarizing herself with the Bellcross mortals and our new inventory of supplies.

Zander moves swiftly toward his horse. He seems more motivated—or maybe rushed—since his friend departed, and I know that once he climbs into his saddle, getting a moment alone with him will be impossible.

I intercept him as he reaches the animal. "Hey."

He sighs as if he'd been expecting this encounter. "Good morning, Romeria."

Back to cool and aloof. But I see through his guise now. "What did Rengard need to tell you?"

"He has received word of poisonings north of us. The villages and towns are reporting many cases. It only makes sense that we're seeing its prevalence there, given where the Ybarisans are camped, but it will spread. Most land stewards have yet to hear of what has happened in Cirilea, but they must be warned. Rengard was up all night, dispatching messages."

"This is the uprising you were talking about."

"Yes, and it's escalating rapidly. Atticus has sent a contingent from Lyndel to quell it, and they will travel through the mountain pass, which is why we must make haste to avoid them. Rest stops will be brief, mainly for the benefit of the horses. We may not even pitch tents."

"How far is it to the caves?"

"Five days." Zander peers at the wagons. "Possibly longer. I'd like you to spend as much of the journey with Gesine and Ianca as possible. I fear time is not on our side, in more ways than one. The seer is fading fast."

"Yeah, I'm worried, too. You think we can learn something from her?"

"I do not pretend to know what to think anymore. About anything." His hazel eyes skate over my mouth, stirring heady memories of last night, of his hands, his lips, the weight of his body on top of mine.

His mouth quirks. "Careful with those thoughts of yours. They tend to cause me difficulties."

"And regrets?" I fight the urge to touch him ... anywhere, really.

Zander's attention drifts over the horde of waiting legionaries. "My only regret is that I had to leave you last night. And now." He meets my gaze just long enough to show me the sincerity in his words before he hoists his body onto his horse. "We need to move." He canters away.

I grit my teeth to keep the foolish grin from emerging.

Pan is waving me over to the forest-green wagon adorned with swirls of gold detail where his scrawny frame is crammed onto one side of the driver's bench. The emblem on his thumb sparkles every time he moves his hand. He didn't make a sound when Gesine emblazoned it into his flesh. In the end, the rush was unnecessary. The subject of Pan's fate never came up with Rengard, unless he and Zander spoke about it on their walk. But now he's marked with a symbol familiar to Mordain, though its meaning remains a mystery.

"I've never ridden in the front of a wagon before!" He gestures to the burly mortal driver who takes up most of the seat. "This is Bregen."

The man bows his head. "Your Highness."

I climb into the back of the windowless wagon, packed with animal hides and spare clothing, the smell of tanned leather pungent. Ianca is curled up in soft gray furs, her head propped on Gesine's lap as the caster strokes her forehead, much like a mother might console an ill child.

Tears roll down Gesine's cheeks. A rare display of emotion from the otherwise emotionless caster.

What must it be like to watch someone you love fade away like this? To have this immense healing power flowing through your veins and be powerless to stop death?

"Little nymphs. So many of them running around now," Ianca babbles, her eyes shuttering. "One spark, two sparks, a *thousand* sparks …" Within moments, she's drifted off, either naturally or more than likely with Gesine's help.

The wagon jolts forward and I half sit, half fall into my spot before shifting to get comfortable. "Why does she keep talking about nymphs?"

Gesine swipes her palm across her cheeks. "Because that is what courses through these Islorian immortals. The nymph affinity." She slides out from beneath Ianca, tucking a pillow under the seer's head. "The blood curse robs them of their natural elven connection to the world, but when they are conceived on Hudem—Wendeline explained how they produce offspring, did she not?"

"On the stone in the nymphaeum. With an audience."

"That would not be my preference either." She chuckles. "Nonetheless, these children are born with nymph power. A glimmer of it, the tiniest spark. *Much* weaker than the affinity their Ybarisan cousins possess."

That's why Ianca called Jarek weak. "Does that make them nymphs, then?"

"No. Well, not the nymphs as we believe we know them to be.

Those creatures were said to be powerful and diabolical, prone to inspiring chaos. So much so that the fates confined them behind that door."

"And now Malachi wants to let them out."

She bites her bottom lip. "What Malachi wants is all still speculation at this point. Come now, we have a long way to go, and I believe you owe me a great tale about Romy Watts of New York City."

"And you plucked it off her neck, just like that. In front of everyone."

"They were too busy watching the bride and groom's first dance." The twelve-carat diamond collar necklace, with a Tiffany's price tag of over $200,000, slipped off the mother-of-the-bride's neck like a snake uncoiling from a tree branch. "I stuck it in my pocket, grabbed a slice of cake, and walked out."

"Fascinating." Gesine's eyes twinkle with genuine intrigue. She's listened for hours as I downloaded twenty-one years' worth of tragedy and sorrow, of a girl struggling to climb out of the deep hole destiny tossed her into, only to be kicked back down. By the time Pan pops his head through the small window to announce that we're stopping for the night, I've described at least a dozen jewelry heists, and Gesine hasn't shared an ounce of judgment for my crimes.

Ianca hasn't stirred since we left the farm this morning, but now her lips move with low, unintelligible mutters.

"Don't worry. I'm here." Gesine smooths hair off the seer's forehead. "We're stopping for the night."

"I am growing weak," Ianca whispers.

"Surely a stew or porridge will help."

The seer's wrinkled, gnarled hand fumbles to grasp Gesine's. "So good to me. Always so good. Even with all the trouble I've caused."

I feel like I'm intruding on a private moment. "I'll go find Eden. She'll know what there is to eat." And hopefully, I'll also find another exchange with Zander. I haven't been able to get him out of my mind all day, and aside from the brief midday stop at a river, I haven't caught so much as a glimpse.

I push on the wagon door, and it creaks open.

The hilly landscape on our journey to Bellcross has given way to flat plains, fields of golden wheat and late corn swaying in the breeze. The sun has dipped past the horizon, and the air is noticeably chillier than last night. Elisaf said that would be the case as we move farther north.

Pan, Brawley, and a handful of legionaries lead horses to a nearby stream for watering. No one has started a fire, though, and the tents remain packed.

Eden's long, silky blond hair catches my eye. She's over by the makeshift corral.

With Jarek.

"Eden!"

She turns to meet my call. The grin she's wearing is broad and genuine, and likely not meant for me.

I jerk my head to beckon her, sparing a second to glare at Jarek.

She rushes over. "Yes, Your Highness? I was about to come ask what you'd like to eat, but did you need me for anything?"

"I wanted to check on you to see how you were doing. I haven't seen you all day."

"Oh, I'm well. The mortals from Bellcross are all so generous. Freida is originally from a village by Northmost. And Hettie is my age. She's lived in Bellcross her entire life and her keeper passed on recently. He was nearly *nine hundred* years old ..." Eden rambles on, glowing as she describes the tributaries traveling in the wagon with her.

And I can't help but smile as I listen quietly. We've only been away from Freywich for a few days, and already she seems different from that frightful girl sitting at the bottom of the stairs, waiting for a bell to ring.

"I was told we're not setting up tents, and that you will be sleeping in the wagon?"

That explains the lack of a real camp. "Zander wants to keep our stay short."

Jarek's deep laughter draws Eden's attention back to him. He's with Horik, their stances casual, like two regular men sharing an amusing tale.

"I didn't think you liked him."

"Who, Jarek?" She bites her bottom lip. "I've talked to him a few times since Freywich. He's much nicer than he looks. Sweet, even."

Jarek? Sweet? Alarm bells ring in my head. There's only one reason any woman would call him that. "Has he tried to feed off you?"

"No. I offered, but he said you have forbidden it."

My eyebrows pop. "You *offered*?"

Panic stirs across Eden's face. "I didn't think … I'm sorry, I did not realize I shouldn't …" She stammers, her face paling.

"Oh my God, no, Eden." I squeeze her forearm for reassurance. My reaction must be harsher than I intended. "You don't need to be afraid of me. I'm not angry." That damn Lady Danthrin. If I ever see her again, I might strangle her for what she's done to this girl. "You don't need to be anyone's tributary anymore. We're not going to force you to do that. Do you understand what I'm saying?"

She nods slowly, as if allowing that to sink in. "But I do not mind, Your Highness. Not for the warriors who keep us safe, like Jarek. They need their strength to protect us."

"Which is why Lord Rengard sent us some."

"Not enough," she counters. "And with this poison, it's dangerous for them to go looking. Why should the other mortals be required and not me?"

Because you've been through enough? But the truth is, they probably all have.

"I do not mind, honestly. It is something they need that I can provide." She says *they*, but her eyes wander to where Jarek unsaddles his horse.

I stifle my groan.

"They were preparing a platter of cheese, fruits, and bread for you when I left. Shall I bring it to the wagon when it is ready?"

"Please. The sooner the better for Ianca."

With a curtsy, Eden hurries away, stealing several sideways glances at the warrior.

I march over. "What are you doing?"

"Checking for any swelling or possible injury." Jarek smooths his palm along his horse's legs. "You can't ride a horse all day and then turn your back on it."

"I mean with Eden."

"I don't know what you're talking about."

"I saw you over here, laughing with her."

He pauses in his ministrations to give me an incredulous look. "I'm not permitted to laugh?"

"Not with her. I know your kind. I know what you're up to."

He stands, towering over me. His lips twist with thoughts he doesn't share.

"She offered herself to you."

"And I declined."

"Why?"

"Because you forbade it."

"No, that can't be why."

He snorts. "And why can't it?"

Because it would mean Jarek's not as horrible as I've made him out to be.

"Romeria?" Zander's voice grabs my attention. It looks like he was halfway to my wagon when he saw me here.

"Please tell me, then, who am I permitted to approach?" Jarek asks with mock innocence. "Since you seem to be the one dictating."

"You can feed off Pan." Satisfaction swells inside me as I stroll toward Zander, Jarek's gruff laughter following me most of the way.

"What was that about?" Zander's gaze is unreadable.

"Nothing much. Told him to stay away from Eden and then wished him dead. I didn't mean it, though."

He grunts. "That is an improvement."

"I guess?" I fight the urge to lean into Zander's broad chest, to inhale his woodsy scent. All I want to do is pick up where we left off last night. "Did we make good time today?"

"Adequate, but we will not stay long. Just enough to rest the horses, and then we will continue. Do not be surprised if your wagon is moving before daybreak."

Considering the bumpy road on the way here, I assume that won't be a restful sleep.

Zander's eyes wander over my face. "How was your time spent today?"

"Ianca slept the whole day, so Gesine and I talked."

"And did you learn anything?"

I frown. "Actually, no. It was mainly me doing all the talking and Gesine asking *a lot* of questions."

His lips purse in thought. "Abarrane has agreed to train you, but I would prefer you spend your time honing your affinities."

Dealing with Abarrane this morning was enough for one day. I'd like to hone *other* skills. "Where are you sleeping tonight?"

A crooked smile curls his lips. "Why do you ask?"

"No reason." On impulse, I step closer.

He doesn't back away, his lengthy, slow sigh kissing my cheek. "Who says I will sleep tonight?" A devilish twinkle glints in his eye. A dare, almost.

"You won't, if I have anything to do with it."

His chest lifts with a deep inhale, and then the playfulness evaporates. "We have much to plan. It has been decades since Elisaf and I were last in Venhorn. We're not sure what to expect, between the Ybarisans, the saplings, and even the mortals of Woodswich. Frankly, we are not sure what to expect between here and there either. I have sent Drakon and Iago ahead to scout our path in case of surprises, but we must strategize."

"So … king things again."

"As one does." He watches two legionaries lift a wine barrel out of the food wagon. "The others will likely find their rest on the ground around the wagons, so do not fear, you will be safe enough."

"I'm not worried." We're camped in the middle of a field. I hesitate. "This is nice. Being able to talk like this again."

"It is. But neither of us can forget our immediate priorities."

"I haven't." Though I'm realizing that nothing is *more* important to me than the looming male standing inches away.

My wagon door screeches open, and Gesine climbs down the steps with a stretch. She scans the camp, and upon spotting us rushes our way, her arms curled around her hunched body to ward off the chill. The smiles she offers to the nearby legionaries are returned, though stiff.

"They're warming up to her."

"They see her value. That does not mean they trust her." Zander watches her approach, and I can't help but feel his words are spoken for himself as much as the others.

"I did not appreciate how cozy the wagon was until now," Gesine announces with a shudder when she reaches us. "I suppose it helps that we're surrounded by skins." She dips her head in greeting. "Your Highness."

"Eden's bringing food."

"That is kind of her. And perhaps some of that wine I heard about. Ianca was always a big fan."

"I am sure the Legion will part with a mug or two." Zander chuckles. "Romeria was just telling me how she has been regaling you with tales of her exploits. Anything interesting?"

"Yes. I think so." Gesine glances around. "The more I consider it, the more I believe Romeria's talents lie in deception."

Zander barks out an unexpectedly loud laugh that turns a few heads. "I could have told you that without needing a day for conversation."

I throw a playful elbow toward his stomach. Before I pull away, he gives my arm a gentle squeeze.

Gesine's eyes glint with the exchange, but her expression smooths over in the next instant. "What I mean is, she may have been so successful in her previous life with"—she stalls —"*procuring* valuables by using her affinities to twist reality to her means, manipulating what people see."

"You can do that? I mean, *I* can do that? That's possible?"

"It would explain how you could unclasp a necklace from around a woman's neck in a room full of people and *not* garner notice. Or how you slipped that diamond ring off that girl's finger."

Korsakov's daughter. The heist that started it all.

Gesine kept probing for details—how many people were around, what were they doing while I was thieving—now I know why.

"What do you know of an ability such as this?" Zander asks, all hints of levity gone.

"The scribes document every caster who passes through the great halls of Mordain. Their affinities, their skills, their strengths. I have only ever heard of one such other, and it was long ago. She held affinities to both Aoife and Vin'nyla and it was said she could play tricks on minds, using air and water to bend light and control what people saw, but that was speculation. I don't really know *how* she did it, just as I can't wrap my head around the stone casters who build those passages within walls."

"I didn't know I was doing anything."

"But you felt it."

"Well, yeah, but … I assumed it was normal." That overwhelming rush of adrenaline, of nerves. An intoxicating mixture of thrill and fear.

"For someone with your power and your level of desperation, it would have been as simple as willing it to happen in the way you needed. If I am right, you will not have an issue replicating it. That is the thing with affinities. Once you use them a certain way, your muscle memory can recall them more readily. That man in the cave? If you should need to draw on your affinity to Vin'nyla to defend yourself like that again, you will find it easier next time."

Gesine said I used my affinity to air when I launched him into the stone. "Fantastic." I grimace and clench my fist, the feel of his snapping bones—like crushing a handful of potato chips—still fresh.

Zander's expression is pensive. "Romeria has this innate skill, and yet she was unable to lift my dagger from me the night she arrived."

"That is not a surprise. The ring was on her finger, quelling her caster affinities. And even if it wasn't, she was probably quite distraught and unfocused, given her reception."

"Fair enough."

"What will I be able to do with this skill?" I ask, my curiosity growing.

"That depends on your imagination. We should test it."

"Yes. I agree." Zander nods. "Let us not waste time."

"*Wow*. You both agree on something," I mock.

Zander's eyebrow arches. "Unless you'd rather I call Abarrane here with her blades."

"As fun as that sounds ..." The desire to stretch to my tiptoes and kiss Zander is overwhelming. I spin and head for the wagon before I lose that battle.

Zander's chuckles follow us.

"Am I mistaken, or has something shifted between you two?" Gesine whispers.

A faint smile curls my lips as I remember how little there was between us last night. "You're not mistaken."

She hums. "Good."

24
ZANDER

"Seven tributaries."

"Six. The female from Freywich is not an option."

The glare I get from Abarrane promises harsh words later. "*Six* tributaries for nineteen of us—twenty-one, if we include His Highness and Elisaf." She shakes her head. "Feedings are no more than once a week for now, but when we are deep within the range, each legionary will be allowed to take the vein once every second week, unless injured."

"Twice a month," Jarek echoes from his seat in the weapons wagon we've converted into a makeshift meeting room. His pursed lips reveal his doubt. "When we need to be at our strongest, fending off saplings and whatever other beasts lurk in there that the caster will surely draw out?"

He's not wrong about that concern, but it's not Gesine's affinities I'm worried about. She's nothing more than a firefly compared to the beacon that is Romeria. Any Nulling creature within range will find us.

"We cannot risk any of these mortals falling to illness because they are too weak," Abarrane counters.

"Perhaps it would be prudent to find more on our travels

north, then." Jarek's tone is calm and respectful, but there is an underlying challenge that says he knows he's right.

"Yes. More like that imbecile we're now saddled with?" she snaps.

I sit back and listen to them argue over the mortals as if they're nothing more than rations to be divvied up. This is at the very essence of our blood curse. Romeria would be horrified to listen.

"May I remind you that the reason I must hear that idiot prattle on incessantly is because *someone* saw a row of scantily clad women on a balcony and couldn't keep his fangs in or his pants on? Did you honestly think I would not put two and two together?" Abarrane shakes her head. "Only a fool would take that sort of risk."

Jarek smirks, her rebuke sliding off his arrogant shoulders without a hint of ruffling his ego. "It was ten minutes, and I assumed I was leaving Romeria with someone capable of controlling her brash impulses." His eyes cut to Elisaf. "It seems I was wrong."

I bite my tongue against the urge to answer for my friend and guard. According to Abarrane, I have a bad habit of defending Elisaf before he has a chance to defend himself. In this case, she is right. The Legion won't grant him the admiration he deserves if I'm constantly sheltering him.

Besides, he is more than capable of handling himself.

A small smile curls Elisaf's lips. "And after spending days on horseback with Her Highness, *I* assumed someone would be intelligent enough to see that there is no controlling Romeria. But it seems *I* was wrong."

Jarek's molars grind. He'll see that as a confrontation, hopefully not one he's stupid enough to act on because then I *will* step in, and it will be with the sharp point of my blade.

I temper my anger over their bickering. Yelling will achieve nothing. "I can attest to Elisaf's claim, but we are not here to discuss Romeria's stubbornness, and the idea of bringing *more* mortals with us , when we may struggle to keep those currently present alive, is pure folly. We need to move beyond Bellcross and consider what lies ahead." I tap on the map Rengard supplied, unfurled in the center of the wagon. "It is another five days to the caves. According to Rengard, an uprising is already upon us, having started months ago and growing steadily. Any one of the villages along this corridor could be a breeding ground for Ybaris's poison. For our sake, we must assume all of them are. Which means there is to be *no* feeding on anyone, no matter how tempting or innocent they appear. Make that *very* clear."

"Aye." Abarrane spears Jarek with a glare.

"Now … Norcaster is a day's travel from here." I point to the influential town at the mouth of the mountain corridor. "It may provide valuable insight about where the Ybarisans are and how they are distributing these vials. For all we know, Ybarisans are hiding there, aided by the mortals."

"That is more probable in Woodswich, where there is no elven oversight," Elisaf says.

"Likely, yes, but I will not discount that it has migrated south. We will camp a safe distance from Norcaster's wall and venture in to gather any information we can."

"It is best I bow out of that excursion. My presence might draw too much attention," Jarek says, earning Abarrane's chuckle. Clearly there was an altercation the last time he was there.

"That is fine. You will ensure Romeria is safe within the camp."

"Second-in-command, and I am relegated to guard duties?"

I match his glower. "You are protecting our future. I should think that a noble cause."

Jarek opens his mouth but decides against speaking his thoughts, answering with a firm nod instead.

"Is it wise to spend the extra time in Norcaster when we know Telor is marching through the eastern pass?" Elisaf draws a finger along the corridor that Lyndel's army will use, the only way through, short of going south around the mountain range. "Would it not be safer to push ahead to avoid a confrontation? He will not venture this way without at least five hundred men or more."

"He is coming with a thousand. We cannot afford a confrontation with them," I agree. "We must get to the mountains first and prepare for their arrival, because they *will* march north for us and the Ybarisans. I must find a way to reach Lord Telor and prove to him that I am not the conspirator Atticus has painted me to be."

Telor has always been a staunch supporter of my family, but he's also a leader I could sit with and discuss a future for Islor that did not allow lords like Adley to benefit from mortal suffering.

I just don't know if he'll listen to me anymore.

"You think you can gain control of the northern army," Jarek says slowly, as if putting pieces together.

"I must try." I've given this much thought since climbing on to my horse this morning. "Fighting against Telor would be foolish. We need to work to win back support now if I am to reclaim the throne."

"But we are heading into a territory with no escape, unless you mean to lead us into the rift."

Jarek does not mince words. I see what Abarrane means about him. "It is our best option." Our *only* option.

Jarek shakes his head. "And if it does not work? If you cannot convince Lord Telor to defy the seated king in favor of the fleeing one?"

"Then we make sure he knows what starting a war with me will feel like." I was a young child the day my father discovered I was not born like others, that the gift Hudem had granted me was far more potent. He warned me there was a time to flaunt the true might of a king and a time to guard it well, and this was a secret I needed to shield until the day revealing it would give my enemies pause.

Word of Freywich's fate would have reached Cirilea by now. How accurate the account provided to Atticus was—including how large the orchard Danthrin had gone out of his way to hide from the crown—remains to be seen. Regardless, anyone who has heard will know I am not some outcast mutt scurrying through the streets with his tail between his legs.

"When the time comes, let us hope our caster can help deliver that message." Abarrane's eyes meet mine, and I know she doesn't mean Gesine.

"The princess traveled here with five hundred Ybarisan soldiers. Many of them were not in Cirilea during the attack. There could be as many as two, three *hundred* enemy soldiers waiting in that valley. What happens when we find them?" Jarek's eyes narrow as he assesses me, waiting for an answer to a good question.

But I've already considered this. "The valley is large, and it could take weeks to find them. Our first priority will be a secure home base. Also, you forget that Romeria is Ybarisan and heir to the throne. Those are her men to command." Whether they'll listen is another story.

"I have *not* forgotten that."

I hear the words he doesn't speak: *Have you?*

"You may go now." Abarrane's dismissal is sharp.

Jarek leaves without another word, his doubt and mistrust lingering like a toxic cloud.

"Your Highness?" Elisaf asks.

I wave toward the door, granting him freedom from this cramped space. It's me Abarrane wants to chew a piece off. She's been waiting for her moment all day.

And I know what this is about.

She waits until the wagon's door clicks closed. "Lord Telor might be swayed to grant you his loyalty, but not with *her* on your arm."

"Romeria is not on my arm."

"Oh, I must be mistaken," she says with mock innocence. "Though last night she was certainly on your—"

"That is my business, and not up for discussion. That I am sitting in here and not secluded in a wagon with her"—where I would much prefer to be—"should mean something to you."

"Actions may speak louder than words, but words also carry meaning, and you swore to me that your heart would no longer dictate your decisions. And yet now we are stewards to one of these tainted mortals, and you are forbidding the use of another. Do not tell me she is not the one dictating those poor choices."

"They are choices, surely, but I do not see them as poor. The truth remains that we cannot win the throne back without her."

"So we are appeasing her, then? Is that your ploy? To help sway her toward our needs when the time comes?"

I could lie. I probably *should* lie. It would certainly appease Abarrane. "What I do with Romeria in private has no bearing on our path forward, and I will not explain myself to *anyone*." I deliver the warning with a sharp edge. "We must squash this uprising and isolate the poison before it causes irreparable harm to Islor." If it isn't already too late.

"As you command, Your Highness." Her teeth grit as she bites her tongue.

I sigh. "I have not lost my focus or my common sense, Abarrane."

"I hope not. Because all of Islor depends on it."

25
ROMERIA

"It's not going to work. I always waited until people's attention was divided. You're staring *right at me*."

"Perhaps. Or maybe it is because I know what you are doing. But let us try one more time." Gesine holds out her hand.

I drop my ring into her palm.

"Ianca?"

"Silly game," the seer mutters.

This silly game started when Gesine handed her the ring to see if she could sense anything of the spells Sofie cast over it. Ianca merely shook her head and mumbled something unintelligible about nymphs.

"I know. But we're trying to help Romeria." Gesine slips my ring onto Ianca's finger for the seventh time and then shifts in her seat to give me her peripheral vision. Her orb of light floats to the other side of the wagon, throwing her into the shadows. "There. Is this better?"

"No."

"Try anyway. Pretend Ianca is a wealthy socialite, you are at a ball, and Korsakov has hired you to steal her precious ring."

With a heavy sigh, I focus on the seer, her cloudy eyes staring at me, through me. My affinities are packed away in a tight ball in my chest. It took only seconds for me to enclose them this time. It felt like an achievement.

But with this, I'm failing miserably.

The familiar adrenaline flares as I reach forward and carefully slip the ring off Ianca's gnarled finger.

Gesine's shoulders sink.

All I can do is shrug. "I guess you're wrong about this skill set. Maybe people in my world are too easily distracted."

"I was so sure." Disappointment laces her voice, and I feel its weight. I was hoping she was right too. It would be a connection to my past life. Despite how I crumbled that cave, that I could have been one of these key casters without knowing still doesn't seem real. This would have been proof.

"Are we done now?" Ianca asks.

"Yes, we are finished for today."

"I need to lie down." She fumbles with her ring finger. "Where did it go?"

A beat passes as realization settles in. Gesine and I share a look.

"Did you not feel Romeria take the ring from you?"

"She took it?" She paws at her hand again as if to confirm it's not there. Another second passes, and then she lets out a raucous cackle. "Do it again, Other Romeria!"

I'd feel more confident in my abilities if my target wasn't a seer with no vision and a scattered mind, but even still, a wide grin stretches across my lips.

I slip the ring from Ianca's finger five more times without her notice before the novelty wears off and she demands rest. With a soft "good night" and a promise that we'll continue tomorrow, Gesine helps her under the skins and settles in next to her, curling a protective arm around the seer. The globe fades until nothing exists, casting the wagon in darkness.

I contemplate venturing out to find Zander, but it's silent outside, and I know his concerns about the Legion losing faith in him aren't overstated.

Pulling the soft gray pelt over my torso, I drift off replaying so many old memories through a new lens.

A key caster's lens.

It's still pitch-black when I'm jostled awake by hands groping my body, digging, searching.

I open my mouth to scream and brace myself to defend.

"Where is it, where is it, where is it …"

Ianca's reedy voice stalls my reaction.

I remain frozen as her poking hands fumble for my ring finger. Her fist clamps over it, squeezing hard enough to draw my wince.

"So much agony!" she wails into the darkness, on the verge of sobs. "Centuries of suffering by his will."

My heart hammers. "Who suffers?" I dare ask in a whisper.

"The key caster."

Me?

A second later, Gesine's light globe sheds light on the wagon's interior, just bright enough to allow shadows. Ianca's eyes are closed, her wrinkled thumb rubbing back and forth over the white stone of my ring. She's muttering under her breath, the words incomprehensible. She's speaking another language.

I seek out Gesine.

She gives an almost imperceptible headshake, then puts her finger to her lips.

"Tempt the fates, you get what you get. Tempt the fates, this is what you get." Ianca tsks. "What a poor, forlorn soul. Hanging in eternity, but only for a second. A cruel trick Malachi plays." Her breathing is ragged, wheezy. "But that's the only way his flaming-haired demon will come to him."

My scalp tingles with familiarity. My father said something similar, and I'm sure he was talking about Sofie.

Ianca's weathered face pinches as if pained. "Oh, he has found his skin and will prove a mighty and dreadful king. She will be his queen and have no choice in the matter. She doesn't see it yet, but *I* do."

I can't help myself. "Who will be his queen?"

Ianca's eyes open, revealing pale-silver irises that shine in the darkness. "Their laughter, it calls to you, doesn't it?"

I falter, unnerved and unsure if she's speaking to me. "Whose laughter?"

"You think you have choices, but you have none, child. None but one. I see it now, and it is so clear—"

The wagon door flies open with a noisy creak. Zander fills the entrance, his gaze dissecting the scene without saying a word.

"Such a powerful nymph." Ianca releases my hand, the moment already faded from her thoughts.

Though far from faded in mine, my pulse racing.

She struggles to get up. "If only Ailill had one."

"Had one what?" Zander frowns. "What does that mean? What does she mean?"

Gesine moves fast, guiding Ianca back to her bed. "Rest now. Go back to sleep."

"No, she should explain herself," Zander pushes.

"She cannot. That is plain to see," Gesine snaps.

Ianca answers with a chortle. "Powerful, *angry* nymph."

Gesine coaxes her to lie down, smoothing her hand over the seer's forehead. In moments, she drifts off, Gesine's mystery healing power effective.

Zander steps inside and pulls the door shut, demanding, "Shield." The wagon's ceiling is low, so he crouches, his severe gaze shifting between me to Gesine to Ianca's still form, before settling back on me. "Are you okay?"

"Yeah, I'm fine." I allow myself a calming breath, though Ianca's words have rattled me. "And here I thought this morning's wake-up was bad."

"I'm sorry, I did not notice her slip away until I woke to her speaking," Gesine says.

Zander smooths a comforting hand over my knee. "What happened? Did she say something important?"

"She was holding my ring as if she could read something from it. But she had it on her finger earlier and didn't see *anything*." I look to Gesine for an answer.

"Not at the time. I was dismayed, but something changed. She was obviously learning *something* from the caster's affinities tied to it."

"All I caught was nonsense. Did it mean anything to either of you?"

"There was much that wasn't clear." Gesine's eyes are locked on a spot on the wagon's floor, deep thought wrinkling her forehead. "'Eternity, but only for a second.' I have seen iterations of the same thing, and it has always meant one place. The Nulling. She was talking about someone who was trapped there for tempting Malachi."

"It has to be Sofie's husband." But I already guessed as much. "And the flaming-haired demon—I'm pretty sure that's Sofie."

"So Sofie tempted Malachi, and the price was her husband."

"Tempted him with what, though?"

"Whatever it was, it must not have worked out as planned, but that is always the case when you summon the fates." Gesine bites her lip. "'Centuries of suffering by his will.' That's what Ianca said."

"Yeah, the *key caster* suffers."

"You have surely suffered, but not for centuries." Realization fills Gesine's face with a soft gasp. "Of course. Malachi used one key caster to send another here."

"You mean, Sofie is also a key caster?"

"An immortal one, like you, Romeria."

My jaw hangs as I process this. Wendeline said I was the only one of my kind, as far as she knew, but that was in this world. "It would explain a lot. The odd way she spoke, as if she was from another era, the castle she lived in, and the comments about how long it's been since she's seen her husband, as if it had been decades." Or more.

"She must have summoned Malachi to grant her that immortality, so she could avoid the change. And why risk a fate's wrath, why choose to live an immortal life, if not for love? Which means her husband must have been immortal."

"His name was Elijah. *Is* Elijah?" I picture the still form lying in what was essentially an open stone coffin, surrounded by statues of the fates. An altar to summon the god who banished him.

Zander isn't often quiet, but now he says nothing as we try to make sense of Ianca's ramblings.

Gesine purses her lips, studying the sleeping woman. "Perhaps we will get more out of her another night."

I don't think I'll be able to sleep in the same wagon with them again after that, but I keep that thought to myself for now. There's a bigger issue. "She said I wouldn't have a choice. What did that mean? A choice about what?"

Gesine's gaze flitters to Zander. "I cannot be sure."

"I would not take much stock in it. She called me an angry nymph," he mutters wryly.

"That's because you were born on Hudem. You have their power in you. Right, Gesine?"

"That is correct, though none of you are actually nymphs."

"Still, there's a link to what she's saying. It's not complete nonsense." Like all those crazy things my father said over the years, about demons walking among us, can probably be tied back to some reality. I always discounted his words; I won't make that mistake again. "I think everything Ianca said until she opened her eyes was about Sofie, Elijah, and Malachi. We know Malachi wants me to open the nymphaeum door so he can rule, so he must want Sofie to be his queen." I falter. "But how would Sofie get here?"

"Through the Nulling," Gesine says matter-of-factly. "If

Malachi were to banish her there as he has her husband, they could enter this world through a tear. It's the only way."

"And it would only tear if I try to open the door."

"Try, or succeed. The Nulling will tear either way. It is a *gift* from the fates for anyone who wishes to release the nymphs from their boundaries. A snare to be triggered."

"We know that for sure?"

"I am quite certain, yes."

The pieces are slowly clicking together—noisily, disjointedly—but they are finding places that seem to fit. "What about Elijah? He's in the Nulling too. If Sofie is to become queen, would he become king?" A terrible one, according to Ianca.

"Malachi would not go to this effort for someone else's benefit."

"This is all speculation," Zander says, leveling Gesine with a glare.

My thoughts are moving too fast, though. "What if that's what Ianca means about not having a choice? I keep saying I'm not going to open it, but what if she's saying I'll *have* to?"

"That is one way to interpret her words," Gesine says.

"And what's the other way?" Because I don't see any but the version I spelled out.

"Everyone has a choice. *You* have a choice. And right now, that choice must be to focus your efforts on developing your skills, not on a seer's nonsense." Zander stands abruptly and heads for the exit. "It is time we move."

26
SOFIE

The ring felt heavier on her finger than usual. It had to be because each day that stretched on with no sign of progress grew longer. Nearly three centuries had come and gone, and now there was a second body lying next to the first, two souls trapped in a scheme of Malachi's making.

And Sofie was still waiting.

Waiting, and aching, and agonizing, praying that one day she would feel Elijah's arms again. Not as they were now, idle by his side, frozen in time, but wrapped around her in an affectionate embrace as they had been that last fateful night.

She stole a glance to where the Fate of Fire loomed. He was here almost daily now upon summoning. Sometimes she could forget what a foreboding, cruel power he was. Other times, with his horns twisting toward the crumbling ceiling, and the formidable male body he assumed while he stood within the sanctum, his gaze burning into her, it was all she could do not to tremble.

To think such a force was bound to exist in this world only within the confines of these pillars, this corporeal form evaporating into air the moment he attempted to venture beyond, seemed unfathomable. But she'd seen it happen with her own eyes.

It was a prison.

No wonder Malachi wanted free of it.

And in this other world—where Romeria survived, and these nymphs waited to be unleashed—he would be free.

And then so would Sofie and Elijah.

"Are we any closer?" She faltered over the question, always cautious of probing too much in case his frustration was high that day. If it was, she would usually bear the brunt of his anger.

Today, though, an optimistic aura swirled around him. "She is beginning to see the truth of her situation." His deep voice rumbled in the cavernous space. "How long before she follows through with the commitment she made to us, I cannot say."

Sofie scowled at the body beside her husband, though she supposed it wasn't charitable of her to hold such animosity toward the girl. She wasn't given a choice in any of this.

Then again, neither was Sofie.

"Can we not remove her?" Romeria's form was now an empty shell, preserved by whatever power remained within the jagged horn still protruding from her chest. What Sofie had done could not be undone. She would never wake in this body again.

"Pull the token from her body and watch her shrivel and rot?" Malachi's lips curved into a wicked smile. "I could, though I think seeing her—seeing them both—is a good reminder of what we have accomplished together. Do you not agree?" He gestured toward the stone coffin.

Sofie followed his direction.

And buckled with a gasp, pawing at the empty space where Elijah lay only seconds ago. "Where is he? What did you do with him?" she cried out. She had often wondered if this form she had protected and dressed and doted over for the past three centuries was an illusion, a mighty trick of the mind that had her believing the flesh beneath her fingers was real. If that was the case, it was one she welcomed, for if she could not look upon Elijah's face every day, she would go mad. "*Please*."

"As you wish, my love."

In the next instant, Elijah was back as if he had never left, Sofie's hand resting on his shoulder.

Her relief shook her knees. Another ploy by the cruel fate.

Malachi's beady eyes scoured the details of the four totems surrounding the sanctum altar. "Being here within the realm, my power flowing freely in whichever way I wish, always invigorates me."

Within these pillars was the only place he could channel his power in this world without using her as a conduit. Did he spend his time in other realms too? Answering summons from other desperate creatures such as herself? She never dared ask, nor did she consider not summoning him daily. The risk of earning his wrath was too great.

Sofie swallowed. "Once Romeria opens the nymphaeum, you will send me to the Nulling so Elijah and I can pass through, yes?" That was still the plan? From what Malachi had described in sparing detail, the Nulling served as a thruway of sorts between worlds. A space where creatures could be easily banished but not as easily released.

The stone floor of the vault shook beneath Malachi's footsteps as he rounded the coffin. He never concealed his earthly form with trivial fabrics and had come to expect the same of her. Which is why she always shed her clothes at the door to the vault and why now, upon seeing how his body was reacting in anticipation of hers, she climbed onto the altar without question.

"Do not worry. You two will be reunited." Malachi's hands were like vise grips as they settled onto her knees, prying them apart. "And you will be a queen."

27
ROMERIA

We've moved at a relentless pace all morning, having abandoned camp minutes after Zander left our wagon. There was nothing to do but stay buried within the animal pelts, bracing against the bumpy road, my mind consumed with deciphering Ianca's ramblings until Gesine coaxed me out of my dark thoughts. From there, I spent hours attempting to create a *simple* ball of water in my palm using my caster affinity to Aoife.

I couldn't manage so much as a drop.

By the time we stop for a break at midday, I am anxious to escape the confines of this wagon. I need back on a horse, ideally without a companion. Something I never thought I'd wish for.

The mountain range in the distance temporarily distracts me from my mission, the expanse of jagged, white-tipped peaks both mesmerizing and daunting as they ascend into a thick sheet of gray cloud. My feet stall in the middle of the bustle as I admire the view.

"Are you *trying* to get run over?" Abarrane steers her horse around me. "It's like you have never seen mountains before."

"I haven't." It's my first time seeing anything like this landscape in either world. But I'll have plenty of time to stare at them in the coming days and weeks.

"Eventually, you will wish you never laid eyes upon them." With that stark warning, she leads her horse away in a trot.

"Can't wait." I continue on my course, spotting Zander. He's where I hoped he'd be, and I march toward him now, my heart skipping beats with anticipation of being near him again.

He's mid conversation with Elisaf, but his gaze snags on me, and he can't seem to peel away as I get closer, the smile he's wearing secretive. "You seem intent on a specific purpose."

"I am." Two, actually, beyond seeing Zander's face again.

"Your Highness." Elisaf bows dramatically.

"My lord," I mock, earning his laughter as he walks away.

A curious frown touches Zander's brow as he watches his friend's retreating back. "What is that about?"

"An inside joke." That I don't want to waste my time explaining when I have more important things to discuss. "I have a theory about what Ianca said."

His eyes flip to the wagon, its door propped open. Gesine stands on the step, accepting bread and cheese from Eden. "That you came up with on your own or with aid?"

"On my own. Gesine was too busy trying to teach me how to form balls of water."

"And how did that go—"

"Terrible." I glance around to make sure we're alone. "Ianca said something about Malachi finding his skin. I couldn't make sense of it before, but then I thought about what Gesine told me, about how the fates can only take on physical forms within the boundaries of the sanctum's pillars. I think Malachi has plans to assume Elijah's body. Don't ask me how, but if he could do *this* to *me,* I'm sure he can figure out a way. Then he becomes king, and Sofie is his queen, whether she likes it or not." Ianca alluded to Sofie having no idea of Malachi's plans and no choice in accepting it.

How will Sofie react once she realizes Malachi never intends to truly release Elijah?

"That is … a theory," Zander says slowly. "But for now, let us focus on fact. And the fact is, you still have much to learn."

"You're right, I do." Which brings me to my second reason for marching over here. "I'm going to take this one." I stroke the nearby horse's flank. It's a sleek, chocolate-colored beast, one from Freywich, and it's already wearing a saddle.

"What do you mean, 'take it'?"

"I mean ride it."

"With whom?"

"Myself."

He opens his mouth—

"Remember how you said I needed to learn? That day, when we were going to the crown hunt?" *When you slipped your hands beneath my cloak to cop a feel?*

The corner of Zander's mouth curves. "I seem to recall something about that, yes. But we are moving at a brisk pace to reach Norcaster before that weather meets us. Now is probably not a good time for basic riding instruction."

"I think now is the perfect time." I throw my hands out toward the miles of flat ground, with no living soul in sight beyond our company. "There might not be a better time, based on what Abarrane said of the mountains."

He pauses, his lips pursed as if looking for any excuse to deny me. "It is important that you spend as much time as possible with Gesine and Ianca—"

"All she does is sleep." I drop my voice to add, "I keep wanting to check her pulse."

He sighs. "Yes, that concern has crossed my mind."

"I *need* a break from the wagon, and if the night of the attack taught us anything, I have a lot to learn about *everything*. Including how to ride a horse."

"I agree." Jarek strolls up to us, leading his white stallion by its reins. "I will ensure she remains in her saddle, Your Highness."

Zander's eyes narrow as if doubting Jarek's intentions. As am I. But I see the moment his doubt shifts to acceptance. "Very well.

Both you and Elisaf will ride at her flanks the entire journey. Should we fall under attack, your priority is getting her to the caster's side."

"Aye, Your Highness." Jarek offers a curt bow.

With one last glance at me, Zander strolls away.

I watch his back a moment before spinning to face off against the warrior. "What are you up to?"

"I'm greeting the horse." Jarek smooths a gentle hand over its snout. "You should do the same. It's only polite before you climb onto his back."

"No, I mean, why are you *offering* to protect me? You've always taken issue with it."

"I cannot blame you for wanting to avoid that seer. She makes everyone uncomfortable."

"Don't try to make me believe you care about my comfort." This is a guy who keeps throwing around his second-in-command status. Someone like that does not babysit.

"You are right. I don't particularly care about that." He seems to consider his answer. "Both the king and the commander believe you are vital to our success. The mortal Eden cannot stop singing your praises, and I'm certain Elisaf would eviscerate himself on his sword if you asked it of him."

My face scrunches at the image that sparks.

"Either they're all fools, or perhaps I am."

And *I* would be the fool if I didn't think he was trying to win my confidence for his gain. But sure, I'll play along. "Is that a rhetorical question, or should I answer? *Please*, can I answer?"

My stomach growls noisily, ruining my clever moment.

With a smirk, Jarek pulls two apples from his saddle, tossing them to me.

"Seriously, how many more of those do you have?"

"One's for you. One's for Eros."

"Who?"

"The horse you're determined to ride. It's best you make friends. Maybe he won't throw you off."

"Oh. Right." I tuck my apple into a pocket in my cloak and venture over to offer the fruit to the beast, holding it in my open palm. He leans in to sniff first before collecting it with a snuffle, his lips feathering across my skin, stirring my giggle. "I'd never ridden a horse before I came here."

Jarek's frown makes me realize my mistake.

"That I remember," I add, cursing myself for my mistake. *We're back to this game*. I'm so sick of it.

If Jarek thinks there is more to that, he doesn't let on.

"He's beautiful." I hadn't considered this horse much beyond knowing he was one of Freywich's, and he's been riderless since those two mortals left. Now, I study his slender head and near-black eyes as he chews.

"He's a rare breed from Kier. Fast and strong, with exceptional stamina. Even the concave shape of his neck is unique." Jarek strokes his mane. "Very few can be found in Islor."

"How did a lowly nobleman from Islor's west side end up with him, then?"

"Good question, but not important. What is crucial is that you both get used to each other before we start on this next stretch. Mount him." It sounds like a command he might give the Legion warriors.

After so many days of this, I hoist myself into the saddle without difficulty, collecting the reins as I've watched others do countless times.

"We're going to start slow." Jarek holds the harness and leads the horse around in a circle, his footfalls measured and steady, his deep voice even and conversational. "Keep a tight hold of the reins at all times but give them some slack for his benefit. Your posture is key. Shoulders back, sit up straight."

"I know all that already."

"As far as I'm concerned, you don't know anything." He glances back at me. "Do you want to learn or not?"

For the next half hour, Jarek walks me through various commands, tips, and warnings—how to use my legs and heels to signal directions, the right way to use the reins—and he does it with surprisingly minimal attitude. When the wagons roll again and our procession moves forward, my mind swims with new knowledge.

"Look at you." Elisaf sidles up next to me. "You're a natural."

"A natural pain in my arse," Jarek mutters, slipping into his usual abrasive demeanor. It doesn't bother me as much, though. I've seen another, less prickly side beneath all that leather and steel.

I hum as we move toward the mountains, feeling like I've accomplished *something* today. Leading a horse, I can wrap my head around.

Creating balls of water out of thin air and a seer who shares bad omens in the middle of the night is another story.

28
ZANDER

"Could she be right?"

Gesine studies the crop of firelight in the distance that marks Norcaster. A hub for the villages that speckle the flatlands between the east and western ridgelines of the Venhorn Mountains, a rustic town with a well-fortified wall and a lord who, according to Theon, talks as though he rules the north and has no use for a king.

"Yes."

Her frank answer catches me off guard. I scan the activity around us as the camp unfolds, ensuring we are not within earshot of anyone. "About what, exactly?"

"About *everything*. As the hidden texts from Shadowhelm alluded, the last time Aoife and Malachi walked among us, they did it by assuming the forms of kings and queens already on the throne. I see no reason why Malachi could not possess the physical form of one who walked out of the Nulling instead."

"And then take the throne as a commoner? An outsider? Would he not be better suited to claiming Atticus's form?" Or mine? A worry stirs inside. Would mine not be more appealing, given the power that courses through it? His power?

"Perhaps. But do not forget he will also have an army of Nulling creatures and a key caster as his bride."

I smooth my palm over my mouth to smother the groan. "Of course, there would be another key caster." One who is far more skilled than ours.

"Romeria will likely have a score to settle, after what Sofie did to her. But this Sofie has been through much. I wonder how she will handle coming this far to rescue her love from the Nulling, only to lose him to Malachi's aim for a throne?" Gesine ponders this out loud, but I sense she already has an opinion.

"Not well would be my guess." And an angry key caster is dangerous. "But you speak as though we are opening the nymphaeum door and unleashing this upon Islor, which is *not* the case. Unless you know something? Have you gained any more insight from your seer?"

Gesine's face pinches. "She does not remember any of what she said last night. She does not believe me that it even happened. But now you must see the value of a seer beyond simple ramblings. You see why I was so adamant about taking her from Bellcross."

What I have seen is that Ianca and Gesine were far more than friends. The gentle touches, the flinches of agony that Gesine can't hide every time she looks at or mentions the other woman. "Perhaps. Though dire warnings delivered in incoherent riddles hold as much risk as they do worth. I cannot have Romeria's head filled with these distractions."

She spent the afternoon two rows behind me, flanked by Jarek and Elisaf, her brow furrowed as she gripped her reins. Too many times I felt the urge to fall back and ride alongside her.

Abarrane's watchful gaze and words of caution kept me in place.

To think I am a king and others are dictating my actions.

"She is smart and already figuring things out on her own. Do you not think it wise to begin sharing the various possibilities for the future as they affect her?"

"Maybe." I've hated skirting questions, deceiving her. "But not yet. We need her attention on learning to wield her affinities, not on the many ways Malachi plans to bring us ruin."

"I agree, though I cannot promise what happened last night with Ianca will not happen again. You might wish to find Romeria her own sleeping quarters."

I scan the field where we've settled. "They will be pitching tents tonight, to shelter from the coming weather, so she can move to one of them." Ideally with me in it.

By the tiny smile that curls Gesine's lips, I suspect the caster is hoping for that. But to what benefit, I can't be sure. Is it to help keep us together, moving toward one goal—fulfilling this prophecy she is so adamant is true?

There's no use demanding an answer. I'm well-versed in Mordain's doublespeak. The answer she'll give me won't necessarily be the one I'm asking for. Still, the caster has proven herself reliable, helpful, and skilled. We've benefited greatly from having her here.

"Your Highness." Abarrane marches toward us, a sour expression twisting her face. For once, I don't think it has anything to do with Gesine's presence.

"Please keep Romeria focused on her affinities."

"Of course." Gesine takes that as her dismissal, rushing away before having to cross paths with the commander.

"No word from Iago and Drakon?" Of all the legionaries, they are the two Abarrane most often sends ahead to scout. Both are accomplished warriors but more importantly, they're personable. Sometimes a charmed tongue is more effective than a sharp blade.

"Do you see either of them here?"

I don't scold her for her harsh tone. My question was senseless. The two legionaries knew where to meet us and should have been waiting. "Perhaps they are simply caught up at the tavern."

"Then they would be idiots. I did not train them to be idiots," she snaps. "This has Isembert written all over it."

Again, I forgive her for her mood. She has taught every one of these warriors—many of them as children in my castle sparring square—and she has the same worries now that I have. Theon warned us of Isembert's suspicion and of the stories of travelers going missing. For the two legionaries to not return to us when they knew time is of the essence …

Abarrane is right to be agitated.

The ride to the wall is at least half an hour, and dusk is waning to darkness. The impending rain will follow closely after, making the trek bleak. "Let me get Elisaf."

"We may need Jarek's blade."

"No. The three of us are enough, and he will draw attention. Besides, I need him to stay with Romeria."

Abarrane's eyebrow lifts. "She will agree to stay here?"

One thing I've learned about Romeria is that she is probably already looking for an excuse to lurk in the shadows of that town. There is *no way* she will agree to stay behind.

But I'm not giving her a choice this time. It's too dangerous. "I will deal with Romeria. Tell your warriors only one fire and to keep it small. We shouldn't make our presence known."

29

ROMERIA

"Your Highness." Brawley reaches for my horse's bridle.

"No." Jarek hops out of his saddle and steps in to cut off the stable hand. "She wants to ride this horse, she can learn how to care for it too."

Brawley pales as he falters between the looming warrior and me. It's his job to handle the horses before and after a day's ride. It's all he knows how to do. "But … Your Highness?"

I wave him off. "It's fine. Zorya's waiting for your help."

The mortal can't get away fast enough, and Zorya is only too happy to hand him her reins.

Slowly, I climb down from Eros's back. My body is stiff from so many hours of focusing on my posture, but I refuse to whimper or complain or do anything that might hint at it.

Beside me, Elisaf smiles. "You did well today."

My pride swells. "I did, didn't I?" I rode the entire afternoon without losing control once.

"She was adequate," Jarek counters, "for someone keeping pace with overloaded supply wagons."

I snort. "You know what? From *you*, I will take that as a shining compliment."

"Take it how you want, as long as you learn how to handle your tack. Start here." Jarek walks me through the steps, using his horse as an example and waiting for me to follow with mine. When I'm forced to admit that I'm not strong enough to lift the heavy saddle without dragging it off the horse's back, he doesn't give me grief, his arms tensing as he hauls it away.

"You're not a bad teacher."

Jarek ignores my praise, handing me the reins. "Now you walk him to help cool him down." He whistles at Brawley, shifting on his feet nearby. The mortal dives for the tack while Jarek, Elisaf, and I leisurely lead our horses toward the small pond.

I point to the glow of lights in the distance. "Have either of you been there before?"

"Norcaster? Yes. Anyone traveling this way stops there." Elisaf strokes his horse's snout.

I copy the move, and Eros treats me to an affectionate nuzzle. "What's it like?"

"Smaller than you'd expect for such an important post in the north. Far more rustic than anything you've seen in Islor. The people are resilient and less refined. They've learned to survive much—both elven and mortal. The homes are simple and small and built for the harsh weather. The snow and wind that blows in off the range can be vicious on the coldest days. They have one tavern in the center of town where every traveler eventually lands, with room and board upstairs for a handsome fee, and a roaring fire to warm up next to with your mead or stew."

"Until a table of inebriated bastards picks a fight with you." Jarek jerks his chin at Horik in greeting.

"That has never happened to me there," Elisaf counters.

"I guess you don't look like much of a threat, because it has happened to me on *many* occasions there."

"Maybe you have a face people feel compelled to punch," I throw back.

The corners of his mouth curl. "I've heard that once or twice."

But Elisaf's words trigger a thought. "If every traveler goes through there, shouldn't we go in to see what we can find out about this poison? Maybe Ybarisans are around."

"Scouts have gone in to gather information. They will send more if needed."

That's right. I noticed Drakon has been gone for a couple days. It's impossible to miss when the burly redhead isn't here. He's so loud.

"And there is no 'we.'" Jarek chuckles. "After the stunt you pulled in Bellcross, I hazard the king won't allow you within a hundred leagues of any town or city for some time."

My anger flares. "I don't have a keeper, and no one tells me what to do anymore." I have been surviving on my own since I was fifteen, dealing with the murderous likes of Korsakov and his crew, and now I'm being told where I can and can't go? Me, who apparently has this incomparable power within, waiting to surge?

Who has no clue how to use said power, but that's beside the point. I have other skills.

"These mortals aren't like the ones you've met so far." Elisaf's tone is gentle by comparison. "They're brasher and bolder and tend to be more independent. In many ways, they coexist in a manner the king respects. But that does not mean they would not look for opportunities to gain power. That is the way of all. With the rebellion stirring, if they were to discover who you are and what your blood can do, they might use it to their advantage."

"They would bleed you dry, filling entire jars with the poison in your veins to use as a weapon," Jarek clarifies. "In case you were wondering what he is dancing around."

I chase away the mental image his words stir. "Except they won't figure out who I am."

"That's because you're not going anywhere near Norcaster. The king has charged me with your safety, and unlike *others* who put up with your games, I won't bend so easily. But I dare you to try. *Please*." The look Jarek gives me is one of wicked challenge.

Arguing with the bullheaded male is not worth it. And I have a better weapon. "That's fine. I'll talk to Zander about it. Oh, look, there he is now." My heart skips a beat at the sleek form that walks straight for us.

Jarek's molars grind with frustration as he marches away, earning my grin.

"Why must you antagonize him like that?"

"Because it's fun." I scratch Eros's snout and am gifted a head nudge against my cheek in answer as Zander arrives.

"You two seem taken with each other." He smiles, but I note how tight it is.

"Is something wrong?"

"Yes, I do not want a mad seer pouncing on you again. That will be yours for tonight." He points to the tent Bregen just finished putting up. Pan is lugging a metal bowl on a stand toward it, and Eden trails behind with a pile of furs. "Foul weather approaches. You should get comfortable in there now."

A tent to myself … "What about you? Where are you staying tonight?"

Zander's gaze drifts over my face, settling on my mouth. "There will be enough room for two."

The heat of that simple statement ignites my pulse. I remember hating when he could read it. Now? Seeing that little smile that touches his lips as he senses my excitement?

Elisaf clears his throat as if to remind us he's still here.

"Go on." He jerks his chin toward it. "I will be there as soon as I can."

It's a dismissal—he wants to speak to Elisaf—but I don't care because it's quickly turning miserable out here, and he's already made his promise to me for tonight.

I'm humming as I head for shelter.

"How is that, Your Highness?" Eden kneels before the brazier, rubbing her hands together. We lit it together, her teaching me how to stack the coal. Now it burns low, enough to fight the drop in temperature. Outside the shelter of this little tent, the wind blows in a biting cold.

"It's perfect. Thank you."

She beams with pride. "Do you need more bedding?"

I survey the silky soft furs beneath me. "I think I have enough." Whatever heat I need, I'll get when my body is pressed against Zander's.

A twinge of anxiousness pricks me. He said he'd be here as soon as possible, but it's been at least an hour. "Where are you sleeping tonight, Eden? Do you know?"

"They've set up a large tent for the mortals. It will be *far more* comfortable than sleeping in that cramped wagon. Or worse, out in the open like last night. I don't think I slept."

Did she hear Ianca's wails before Gesine set that shield? "Are you still happy you came with me?"

Her smile drops off, replaced by stark seriousness. "Oh yes! I'm not complaining! I would *never* wish to be anywhere else—"

I laugh. "Relax, Eden. It's okay, even if you want to complain. And trust me, I was crawling up the walls in my wagon earlier. That's why I ended up riding all afternoon."

"Yes, I imagine that would have been more pleasant." She giggles nervously. "Can I speak freely?"

"You don't have to ask me that."

"I do, but ..." She bites her lip as if testing her thoughts before uttering them. "You are like no other immortal I've ever met. Is it because you are Ybarisan?"

No, it's because I'm human. If only I could explain. "Maybe."

She shifts the hot coals with a set of iron tongs. "I'm happy traveling with you. I do look forward to being somewhere more ... permanent, but I was not lying when I said there was nowhere I would rather be than here, with you and the king."

"Who is not technically the king right now," I remind her.

"But he will be again. I have faith." Her firm nod says she truly believes that.

I want to believe it too. But what will happen to me then? I don't expect Islor will welcome me with open arms … ever. Will Zander defy them and marry me? Or will he keep what we have hidden?

How long can a king rule with a shadow queen?

The flap to my tent pulls open, and in barges Jarek, his tall, muscular frame filling the space. "The witch wants to speak to you outside."

"Now?" I make a point of shivering against the wave of brusque cold he let in. His clothes are still dry, so at least it doesn't look like it's raining yet. "Why?"

"How would I know? I'm not her messenger."

"But you kind of are."

His sigh is laced with irritation. "*Must* you have the last word every time?"

"Yeah?"

He shakes his head before dismissing me, his steely eyes shifting to Eden. "The stew is ready. Have you eaten?"

"No, not yet." She clears a sudden hoarseness from her throat and emphasizes her answer with a sharp headshake. But her cheeks are burning.

I stifle my groan, seeing where this is going. "Tell Gesine I'll be there in a minute."

"Tell her yourself," he mutters, and in the next breath, his voice softens. "I will ensure there is a bowl waiting for you."

"Thank you." Eden's hands stall with the tongs, her smile following him out of my tent. When she realizes I'm watching her, she stiffens and refocuses on her task.

"What is it about him you find attractive?" Yes, his face is enticing, as is his body—I can say so with confidence after that day I saw *all* of him in the river—but he's such an asshole. Then again, I would have said the same about Zander initially. And maybe if Zander wasn't in the picture, I might find Jarek appealing, too, in some twisted way.

But I'm a conniving thief, a practiced liar, a survivor.

Eden seems too pure for the likes of him.

Her mouth hangs open, faltering on her words as she searches for an answer she thinks I'd want to hear.

"No judgment. I'm curious what a nice girl like you finds attractive about a brutal warrior like him." The guy may have murdered those Freywich keepers on orders from Zander, but he enjoyed every second of the monstrous act.

She swallows hard. "His strength. His fearlessness." She bites her bottom lip. "His kindness, on the rare occasion he shows it."

Like just now, checking in to see if she'd eaten. Or to see her, period.

In a world where someone like Eden is preyed upon by unscrupulous keepers, of course she would be looking for a protective wing to take shelter under.

Maybe Eden is learning to be a survivor too.

As much as I want to steer her away from the warrior, there couldn't be a better immortal to take a special interest in her. He will kill for her … literally. And what right do I have to dictate who she cares for, who she allows to take her vein or lie in her bed? If I'm adamant that these mortals have the right to choose their paths, then I have to be willing to accept that this is what Eden wants for herself. Maybe that will change one day, when she grows confident and learns what real freedom feels like. But for now, still reeling from the nightmare that was Lord and Lady Danthrin, she's looking for safety. And Jarek can give her that.

"I'm not going to stop you, Eden. But don't forget what he is, and what you are, and what *exactly* he's looking for." And all the rules that govern what happens when her heart gets tangled.

She nods. "I am a mortal, and he is elven—"

"Not just elven. An elven warrior who enjoys killing and has had more women under him than you would *ever* want to know about."

Her cheeks flush. "I will not lose myself to a fantasy of what can never be. I know this. But I like that I can give him strength. That he needs me for it."

That he is vulnerable to her is what she's really saying.

Her, or any other mortal willing to give him their vein, but I don't point that out. "Know that you can say no at any time—to *any* of it."

She inhales deeply, and when she releases the lungs' worth of air, there's no missing the shake in the sound. Of relief or excitement, I can't be sure. "Thank you, Your Highness, for your understanding and kindness."

The jury's out on whether anyone can call sitting back and watching her make this mistake a kindness. But how else does anyone learn their most valuable life lessons?

"Go and eat before it gets cold."

Setting the tongs on the brazier, she scrambles to her feet and moves for the flap, but stalls. "I will bring you a bowl—"

"I'll get my own. I need to find out what Gesine wants first."

With a curtsy, she rushes out.

I tug on my cloak and venture into the night after her, squinting against the drizzle. The camp is quiet, most having ducked into the shelter of tents and wagons, save for the sentries who stand guard around the perimeter, their backs rigid and gazes keen.

My urge is to search for Zander—or Abarrane, who is never far from him—but the solitary figure standing nearby, facing the east, draws my attention.

"Jarek said you wanted to see me?"

Gesine peers from beneath the cowl of her cloak. "I wasn't sure if he would pass along that message."

"Not without complaint. Did you need something?"

"Yes." She gestures in front of her. "I need you to practice."

"Practice what?"

"Whatever you wish." She glances over her shoulder. "There is plenty to work with here, and no one to question anything. Remove your ring."

I slip off the chunky gold band and tuck it into my pocket. After a few breaths, the buzz dissipates, collecting within my chest.

"It has become easy to center yourself, hasn't it? Remember how it wasn't, not that long ago?" I can barely make out the shape of her features in the dark, but I hear the smile in her voice. "Soon, it will be as natural to you as breathing."

"If only everything else would be this easy to pick up."

"It will be. One day, it will be as if your instinct has figured out what this body of yours can do, and it will not forget how to find its way to that place again."

"I already brought down a cave. How do I do that again?" I joke.

"What did you feel when it happened?"

"Other than the man's bones crumbling in my palm?" I pull the cowl of my cloak to shelter my face. "Terror." The memory is still so fresh—of Pan sprawled on his knees, of the bandit hoisting the sword, vengeance twisting his face. "And rage."

"And what did you feel inside? What did that rush of air feel like?"

"Like that. Air. Or wind. A gust, rising up and out of me." Flowing through my limbs, shooting out to assault that man.

"That was you channeling Vin'nyla's element. They all come as surges of power, but each has its own signature and feels slightly different. Aminadav's is like a deep rumble—"

"I felt that too. Right after, when the ground was shaking and then the cave collapsed."

"See? And Aoife's is cool, like fresh water. I do not believe you have found that one yet. And I have never experienced Malachi's, but from what I have heard, a burst of searing heat will hit you."

"Makes sense. Fire."

"It does. Eventually, you will be able to beckon the one you need as easily as your brain tells your arm to lift or your mouth to open, and then you can wield it as a formidable weapon. But for now, you must teach your brain to recognize each one, and for that, we must figure out how best to coax them out of you."

"Okay?"

"Let us try something. Imagine your affinities are like individual threads, and they're all wound up, packed tightly into that hard ball in your chest, waiting for you to grab one and pull."

I picture a ball of colorful yarn sitting deep inside me. "All right?"

A glimmer sparks in her eyes, and suddenly the drizzle intensifies to a brief downpour before cutting off abruptly.

"You made it rain."

"I made it rain *more*. Your turn. Picture yourself pulling on the thread that represents water."

I try to follow her instructions. Nothing happens.

"Maybe we should try one you've already summoned." She points to a nearby tree, its leaves fluttering in the cold wind. Her eyes shimmer again, and the tree sways as if hit with a strong gust. "Your turn. Picture yourself yanking a thread of air and drawing it loose."

I do as asked but nothing happens. There isn't even a swell of adrenaline.

"It's a difficult concept to wrap your head around. Here, let us try something simpler. Hold up your hand in front of you."

I do, feeling silly.

"Now picture a flame igniting at the tip of your finger."

I remember Sofie doing that, making it dance from one to the next, up and down her hand, in a bid to make me believe her.

Again, nothing happens.

I sigh heavily, dropping my arm. "How have I been using these powers to steal diamonds when I had no idea I could, and now that I know about them, and can feel them inside me, I can't do *anything*!"

"Do not despair, Romeria." Gesine pats my shoulder. "Most of the battle is finding them, but they are in there, and we *will* learn how to unlock them."

"I hope you're right. Otherwise, Zander is going to be *really* disappointed."

Deep laughter sounds, drawing my focus back to camp. I

would much rather be in my tent with him than standing out here, the damp night soaking into my bones. *Where is he?*

"He left."

"What?"

"It is the king who you are looking for, yes? He left with Abarrane and Elisaf."

My mouth gapes. "*When*?"

"Soon after we arrived. They went to Norcaster to look for the missing scouts."

"The scouts are *missing*?" What the hell could have happened to Drakon?

I replay our brief conversation earlier, and it dawns on me that Zander knew when I sensed something was bothering him, and he smoothly distracted me with promises of a night with him.

The town is nothing more than a faint glow in the murkiness. "Who else did they take?"

"It was only the three of them. The mortals and supplies need protection. From what I have heard of these northern villages, they don't take kindly to strangers, and a group of warriors appearing would stir attention, especially if two have already sparked trouble."

I shake my head, my anger swelling. That's why he sent me to the tent. He was coming to get Elisaf, and he knew I would insist on going. But to sneak out without so much as a word? "If the scouts didn't come back, there's going to be a good reason for it. It could be a trap. And if something happens to Zander, then all this will be for nothing." Everything will fall apart. "That was stupid, to go into a place like that with only the three of them." Regardless of how powerful Zander is with a flame and how skilled Abarrane is with a sword.

The large tent in the center opens, and Jarek steps out, his arm slung across Eden's shoulders. She appears so small and frail as she huddles against him.

That didn't take long.

As if sensing me watching, Jarek's attention veers my way. I can't read his expression from here but seeing me observing doesn't falter his pace.

"Does he know they left?"

"Yes. Of course."

"And he was fine with it?" Maybe I'm overreacting.

"He is Abarrane's second, and he follows orders. His order is to protect you. It seems there are few the king trusts to do that properly."

Jarek and Eden duck inside another tent.

"Yeah, well, my protector seems preoccupied with something else for the moment," I mutter. Probably for more than a moment.

"He assumes you will not go anywhere."

"How could I? Sentries guard the entire camp." I mark four from this angle, and there are likely two more on the side I can't see.

"And an entire audience of spectators watched as you slipped a necklace off a woman's neck."

Her meaning sinks in. "Are you suggesting I try to sneak out of here?"

"Oh no, I would not dare go against the king's wishes by suggesting you do anything of the sort." She pauses. "But if anyone could manage to leave without notice, I imagine it would be you. And if you could not manage it, if the sentries caught you, I assume the punishment doled out by His Highness would be minimal."

Zander would be pissed, but it's not like I can't handle that. I'm schooled in angry Zander. He once ordered my execution, after all.

Now that Gesine has planted that seed, my mind whirls. Is it possible? Could I use these deceptive powers she insists I have, that I'm not entirely sold on, to walk out right under their noses? No, not walk out. Norcaster is too far. *Ride* out. Me and a thousand-pound horse, like a ghost.

Or a chameleon, blending into its surroundings.

Maybe Korsakov's pet name for me was more accurate than he could ever have imagined.

"Completely off topic, but I've been meaning to give you this." Gesine fishes into her cloak and pulls out the small burgundy satchel that keeps the dried mushrooms. "I think you can decide when you need them going forward."

Because I will need to mask the scent of my Ybarisan blood if I go into Norcaster.

She offers a second satchel as well. I know the feel of coins in my palm.

"I should retire to the wagon now. I bid you good night—"

"Wait! Seriously, Gesine ..." I falter over my question, lowering to a whisper. "You don't think it's too dangerous for me to go there alone? I mean, I can't even make it rain when it's already raining." How am I to protect myself?

She pauses as if to consider my question. "I think every choice you have had to make since the day your father went through the change has led you into danger. But they have also been the right ones, or at least the ones that guided you here, to this moment. And every decision you make going forward will be fraught with peril. But you will not thrive waiting for others to make your choices for you."

She smiles. "Also, your affinities, caster or elven, are only part of what makes you so special, but when you truly need them, they do not seem to fail you. Good night." Her gaze flitters around us, and then she whispers, "And good luck."

My pulse races as the caster vanishes into the forest-green wagon, pulling the door closed to remove herself from all culpability. She's right. Zander would threaten Abarrane's blade on her neck for even suggesting I sneak out.

What will he do to me if I succeed?

Frankly, I'm too angry at him for treating me like an idiot, sending me off to my tent in heady anticipation of a night with him when his plans included something vastly different. Beyond that he's put himself in danger by going without me, he didn't even give me a chance to go in and see what I could learn about *my blood*. It's as if he doesn't trust my abilities.

I'm the one who tracked down Gesine!

The tent Jarek and Eden tucked into sits quietly, its door flap secured. If I'm going to attempt anything, it has to be now.

A glow catches my attention. It's Pan—or rather, Pan's shining mark—as he scurries across the camp, his arms hugging his body against the cold.

I move toward him, hissing his name.

"Romy! Hey! I was wondering—"

I grab hold of his scrawny arm and yank him into my tent.

"Did I do somethin' wrong?" His eyes widen with panic.

"No. But I don't have much time, so I need you to shut up, listen, and answer my questions concisely, okay?"

"What does that word mean—"

"Shortest answer possible. Got it?"

He opens his mouth, but then firmly clamps it shut and nods.

"How did you get the poison? Was that story about the peddler giving it to you to repel immortals the truth?"

He falters.

"*Pan*." I glare at him, running out of patience, an invisible clock ticking in my ear.

"I got it from a friend of a friend."

I wait a beat. "Okay, I need a *little more* info than that. Who offered it to you? Why? Where were you?"

He swallows hard. "So, I was out back of the smithy's shop. It was two days after my ma died, and Oswald made me chop wood all day until my hands were covered in blisters. Merita, one of the ladies from the bakery down the street, came by with some bread. She was a good friend of my ma's, and she knew Oswald probably wouldn't feed me. We got to talkin' about how horrible he was and all the things he'd done to my family and me over the years, and how he shouldn't be able to have any more tributaries, but no one would stop him. So then Merita said *I* should stop him, that my ma would be proud of me for doin' it. So I said, 'How?'

And she told me about a guy named Colgan at the butcher and a poison he could give me." He shrugs. "I thought about it for a few days and then thought about my sister and my ma, and decided, yeah, Oswald needs to be stopped. So I went in and told this Colgan guy that Merita sent me, and he pulled out a small vial and told me to open my mouth."

"Just like that?"

"For a few coins that I got out of the river. People like tossin' money in for wishes."

"That's why you were at the river." Of course, someone would look for ways to make a profit. I can't blame them. They're taking a huge risk, an instant death sentence if they're caught. "They're mortals, Merita and Colgan."

He nods. "Probably long gone now, though, after the whole thing in the square."

If they have any common sense, yeah; otherwise they'll be executed. Zander *should* probably send word to Rengard with those names, anyway.

"You knew it was poison. They told you the truth about that."

"Yeah …" He scratches his head. "But I didn't know about the whole screamin' thing."

"And what were you planning on doing once Oswald fed on you?"

He shrugs. "Hightail it outta there and pray I didn't get caught."

This is how the Ybarisans are spreading the poison. Tyree said they were targeting anyone tired of losing family, and they're using mortals to focus on people who might not be the brightest but have been mistreated by their keepers.

The fact that at least some of these poison dealers are charging money for it might work to our advantage. I would venture a guess most of these mortals can't afford the price and might not have a wish river to steal from. It won't stop them forever—where there is a will, there is a way—but it could slow down the distribution.

If the poison made it to Bellcross, there's no way Norcaster isn't already full of it, along with plenty of valuable information someone like me could get.

There's no doubt in my mind anymore.

"Were you heading to the horses?"

"Yeah, I always check on 'em at night."

"How close is the guard?"

His boyish face furrows with deep thought. "Maybe forty paces?"

That's not *too* close. "Can you saddle a horse quickly and without notice? In the dark?"

A cocky grin stretches his mouth. "Standing on my head. Why?"

An idea forms, likely a stupid one. "I have to get into Norcaster tonight without the Legion knowing, and I need your help to do it."

His grin buckles into a wince. "Does the king know?"

I smile sweetly. "He'll find out soon enough. And Pan? Put on some gloves. You glow in the dark."

They can't see me.

I need to get to Norcaster.

A familiar adrenaline fires through me as I hurry across the camp, stealing a peek toward Jarek's tent. If there's one legionary whose eyes I won't be able to pull the proverbial wool over, it's him.

Thankfully, he's still preoccupied.

They can't see me.

I need to get to Norcaster.

Those words play over and over through my mind, my hood pulled over to conceal my face. Another layer of deception, though who knows if *any* of this will work. Aoife's ring is secure in my pocket, leaving my caster affinities free for wielding, and my hope clings to Gesine's claims that I can twist what people see, that I've done it many times already without realizing it.

So far, all sentries remain focused outward, into the dark.

Ahead, I can see faint movement beside Eros, the mop of curly brown hair hidden under a dark cloak. The leather saddle is already strapped to the horse's back. I allow myself a small smile of satisfaction as I move in. Pan keeps surprising me.

He sees me and grins, displaying a thumbs-up.

I press my finger to my lips to remind him and then mount Eros's back.

Pan climbs up behind me, his slight frame like that of a child as he curls his arms around my waist.

We need to get to Norcaster.

With a deep breath, I guide Eros forward, out of the camp, my pulse thrumming in my ears.

No one stops us.

No one shouts.

No one so much as glances our way.

Gesine was right, after all.

This intense rush, the swell of emotion inside my chest … It was never simply adrenaline—it was my caster affinities protecting me all along.

My confidence soars as we pick up speed. I hold on tight as Eros gallops across the vast expanse of darkness.

30
ZANDER

The Greasy Yak is as I remember it, right down to the stench of grimy bodies and sour ale, barmaids in revealing dresses offering more than pints, and a drunk fiddler in the corner playing a spirited tune. Even the charred beam above remains, where a candle once ignited a fire that was quickly doused. It's an unsightly mark, but the structure still holds, and in a town like Norcaster, that's all that matters.

While the rustic tavern may be the same, the cloying tension in the air is new. We felt it the moment we passed through the main gates, and it intensified when we reached the square and spotted the ten rotting corpses swinging from the gallows. Mortal corpses. It was a moment of relief for Abarrane, whose hand was already reaching for her pommel.

Beyond the bodies was a row of pillories, fifteen stocked with mortals, women and men stripped down and trembling in the cold rain.

My rage ignited, the urge to punish those who took it upon themselves to exact justice overwhelming. As the king of Islor, I would have demanded to speak to Isembert.

But I am here as nothing more than a weary traveler, seeking a warm, dry place and some company.

I could do nothing but walk past.

Walk past and be thankful Romeria is not here to witness this. Fates only know the scene she would create, and we are not here to cause trouble, at least not until our scouts are located.

"Somethin' wrong with the ale, sweetheart?"

I resist the urge to shift away from the ample, cream-colored breasts shoved in my face as Etta leans in to collect the empty glasses others at the banquet table left behind. "Savoring it."

"Hmm … you're one of those." She winks. "Where you from?"

"Northmost. Heading to Lyndel through the pass."

"I've met a few from Northmost." Her eyes rake over my face, keen interest showing. "None o' them locked like you."

Isembert may be cautious of travelers entering Norcaster's walls, but within *these* walls, they are only too happy to collect coin and dole out compliments to anyone paying.

I force a smile. She's an attractive and friendly mortal, and under very different circumstances—in a different time in my life—she may have piqued my curiosity for the night. But tonight, she's only useful to me for the information she can provide.

From across the room, Elisaf sips his pint and talks casually with the barkeep, a barrel-chested man with a mustache that curls down on either side. Abarrane parted ways with us outside and now lurks in the shadows, looking for her two warriors. It's for the best. She lacks a certain finesse.

"That is quite the body count in the square tonight."

"Isn't it, though? Third batch in as many weeks. Biggest one yet, but I heard there's more comin' tomorrow." She balances the edge of her tray in the crook of her hip. "I don't know what they were thinkin', poisonin' themselves like that. Where were they thinkin' on runnin' to after? Woodswich?" She snorts, as if the idea is preposterous.

"Is that what happened? They all killed their keepers?"

"The ones hangin' from the gallows, aye. No denyin' what they did. Those screams could be heard far beyond the wall, some claim." Etta shudders. "The guards caught most o' them before they could escape. Four from nearby villages, brought in on Isembert's orders."

"And the ones in the pillories?"

"Kin of the hanged. Wives and husbands. One daughter. It's assumed they've taken the poison, too, so Lord Isembert has demanded they be kept in the square until they confess."

Force them to confess, truthfully or not, and they're rewarded with execution. Deny the crimes and they die, anyway, in a much longer, more humiliating fashion, freezing and pissing all over themselves in public. This Lord Isembert could be right about their guilt, but he could just as easily be wrong.

I stifle my curse, wishing I had Gesine here to test them. But the bigger issue is that this is the third execution of this kind in this town, and it hasn't stopped these mortals. Either they're ingesting the poison by choice or are unaware. Both scenarios present concerns.

"These vials I keep hearing about ... are they plentiful in Norcaster?"

She shrugs. "They're around. It's probably not safe to take just any vein offered to you. O' course, you got nothin' to worry about from any of Guernet's girls. He treats us well." She juts her chin toward the barkeep. "And none of us are too keen on ending up in the square or takin' our chances in Woodswich. Though, we don't mind being stripped and bent over under the right circumstances." She winks again.

"I'll keep that in mind." It's been so long since I've been in these parts, I forgot how refreshing it is. These northern mortals are a sturdier, obstinate lot for the most part, and not weighed down by politics and class like elsewhere in Islor. "Anything else exciting happening lately? Interesting visitors passing through, rumors ..."

She frowns. "Not that I can think of ... Oh! There have been rumblings of a new king. Don't know if it's true. Not that it matters much around here. We'll never see the likes of royalty comin' this way. Too dainty for the hard life. Holler if ya need me, and I'll come runnin'." With an affectionate squeeze across my nape, she saunters off to flirt with the next table.

My hands clamp tightly over my stein.

If a town like Norcaster has already heard about Atticus, news is spreading faster than I anticipated. Atticus has been busy, securing his throne and spreading falsities. If he—

All thoughts and worries evaporate as I spot the last face I expected to see standing in the doorway of the Greasy Yak.

31
ROMERIA

I slow Eros to a canter as we approach Norcaster's wooden gate. It didn't look like much before, but up close, it is far more daunting, at least twenty-five feet high, the silhouettes of the archers manning it eerily still.

"Am I allowed to talk now?" Pan whispers.

"About what?"

"About how none of those legionaries noticed us leave?"

"We can talk about that later." Though I have no idea what I'll say. "Right now, I'm your keeper, and we're heading to Bellcross to see an aunt who has fallen ill."

"My aunt or yours?"

Maybe it would have been better to leave Pan behind, but it's too late now, and if I'm right, he'll prove useful. "Mine. Your gloves are on?" The last thing I need is for someone to notice his glowing mark.

He waves his covered hand in answer.

"Okay. Remember the plan and let me do all the talking."

A smaller gate built into the main one swings open. It's just tall enough to allow a person on horseback through, guarded by a stocky soldier gripping a sword.

"State your purpose!" he barks.

I push my hood back. "A bowl of stew in the tavern and a warm, dry bed for myself and my tributary, kind sir."

His beady eyes roam my features, and I catch the spark of interest in them, as expected. If I have to keep Princess Romeria's face, I may as well put it to good use. "Aye. It's a wet one tonight." Backing up, he waves us in.

We canter through town, taking in as much as we can. Elisaf wasn't exaggerating. The houses are all wooden and small—one to two rooms each—with thatched roofs and stone chimneys that expel smoky plumes, the scent of burning wood melding with the damp air.

Half the torches smolder, failing in their simple task, unable to withstand the rain. Others are sheltered by glass covers and offer enough light to guide our path through the narrow, empty streets.

"Which way to the tavern?" Pan asks.

It's in the center of town, according to Elisaf. I draw my hood again, feeling spies within the shadows, likely not people we want to meet. "This way."

"That has to be it." The carved sign for the Greasy Yak sits high on the building's face, illuminated by a single lantern on one side. It's the largest structure we've seen so far in Norcaster, three stories tall, with a balcony wrapped around the second floor and larger dormers adorning the third. It's the only place that seems alive with activity, windows glowing with candlelight, the faint hum of music and laughter drifting out into the night.

And it's in the center of town, directly across from the town square.

Where ten lifeless bodies dangle from ropes.

"Oh my God." I stare in horror at the evidence of an execution. But that's not the worst of it. Fifteen others are still alive and trapped in wooden structures that hold their hands and heads in place while forcing them to stand at an uncomfortable incline.

Pan curses. "Oswald put me in a pillory once, for taking cured meat while everyone was sleeping. People threw horse dung at me. Better than rocks, though."

Around these people's feet are rocks the size of baseballs.

"Wonder what they did to deserve that."

He shouldn't wonder. I don't wonder at all. "They took the poison." A drop of my blood. They didn't want to be fed on and abused anymore, so they made a stand, and now they're being punished. Not hung, though. At least not yet. Why? To make them suffer more?

A familiar surge rises from deep inside, stirred by the overwhelming wave of anger and despair. Gesine warned me about this. Digging into my pocket, I slip on my ring, squashing a potential eruption I won't be able to reverse.

It does nothing to calm my rage. "Why did they have to take their clothes?" As if the method isn't torturous enough, they have to humiliate them like that?

"No point wastin' good wool," Pan says matter-of-factly.

On people who are going to die here, he doesn't need to say.

"We can't leave them like that." The people hanging on the gallows are beyond saving, but the ones still alive suffer needlessly. I have to do *something*.

"Beg your pardon, but I think that guard with the big sword might say different. Unless you want to tell him who you are and see if he'd listen?"

I follow his gaze toward the man sheltered under a porch overhang, watching. And curse under my breath.

"I'm guessing you getting caught within five minutes of coming through the gates wouldn't be helpful to anyone."

A subtle reminder that I need to focus. Pan is right.

"We'll figure this out later." A stable on the left side keeps dozens of horses. I steer Eros there.

"That's His Highness's horse." Pan points to the black stallion Zander has been riding since Bellcross. "And those are the commander's and Elisaf's beside."

"No real names or titles here," I hiss, even though a thrill stirs in me as it does every time I know Zander is near.

"Right." He pauses. "Who are you going to be, then?"

I borrow Gesine's fake name. "Cordelia. And you're Dunn."

"Hey! I knew a Dunn once."

"Did he end up on the gallows for talking too much?" Because if this keeps up, Pan is going to blow our cover.

He presses his lips tight in response.

A stable boy comes around to greet us as we dismount, and I fish out some coin, silently thanking Gesine. She knew I would try to escape as soon as she planted that thought in my head. Why she was so willing to allow it—to even encourage it—I'll have to consider later.

Right now, I have work to do.

Despite my churning nerves, I push my hood back, lift my chin, and push through the heavy wooden door, Pan trailing after me.

Boisterous laughter and a fiddler's jig carries through saloon doors to our right. But ahead, a heavyset woman with rosy cheeks staffs the front desk. She looks up from her needlework to appraise me through round, wire-rimmed glasses perched on her nose. They have no lenses in them. "What can I do for yous tonight?" A gold cuff peeking beneath frizzy auburn hair marks her a mortal.

I channel my best Gesine impression of poise and civility. "We are in need of a warm meal and possibly a room for the night."

"I can help ya with the meal, but the inn is already brimming. Though there's a tavern full of patrons who may be willin' to share their bed with a pretty thing like you, if you play your cards right."

There's one patron in there who was supposed to be in my bed with me already.

"I will keep that in mind, thank you."

"Go on in, then, and find an empty spot." She jerks her chin to the right before shifting her focus back to her needlework. "One o' the girls will be with ya when she can."

She's speaking to me as if we're equals.

We are *equal*, I chastise myself. Maybe I've been playing the role of future queen for too long. Something tells me being royalty wouldn't make a difference to her. Still, it's refreshing, and the smile I'm wearing as I push through the swinging doors feels genuine.

A wall of stifling heat from the fire and the smell of sweat, smoke, and sour hops hits me, but I focus on the dingy tavern, a simple rectangular room with long, cafeteria-style tables and benches and a bar where metal steins line the counter as fast as the husky bartender can pour from the keg behind.

And it is packed with patrons, shouting and sloshing ale from their mugs as the fiddler on a wooden platform stomps his foot in time with his upbeat melody.

It's as if that horrifying scene outside doesn't exist, and those poor people aren't out there freezing and aching within their wooden traps while listening to the revelry.

That reminder dampens my spirits, but I can't think about them now. I scan the dimly lit room. The patrons are mostly male and the staff is mostly female, the waitresses' breasts spilling from low necklines of their dresses.

It became easy for me to mark the mortals from the elven in Cirilea, but here they're all dressed similarly, in leathers and furs, and rugged in appearance, with wild manes of hair, some with even wilder beards. No one is bowing and deferring to anyone, even though there are plenty of cuffs marking ears. Some, I note, are a dull silver patina as opposed to the typical gold.

"Um … Cordelia?" Pan hisses in my ear, nodding ahead of us.

Zander sits at the end of a table, cupping a copper mug between two hands.

Glaring at me.

He's trying to stay calm, but his nostrils flare—a sure sign he is fuming, wondering how the hell I got here.

My heart skitters as I set my jaw with stubbornness. I look forward to that argument later. Zander doesn't scare me anymore.

I scan the room. Elisaf is nearby, standing at the bar, chatting up the bartender. I don't see Abarrane. She's likely in an alleyway, torturing someone for information about Drakon and Iago. Either way, they've split up, which is a smart strategy.

Several curious heads have turned to regard me, leering men holding out hope for a female body under them tonight, willingly or not. Opportunists pondering what my belongings might be worth. I've been around enough of this type to know that for every saint in this room, there are five sinners, and I'm drawing too much attention by standing here.

Somewhere in a corner, by a wall, would be best. "Come on, this way." Pan trails me as I weave through the crowd to the end of a long table, the bottoms of our boots peeling away from the sticky wooden plank floor with each step. As contrary as this place is to Cirilea and its gilded towers and copper tubs, it feels more familiar to what I spent many years of my life surrounded by—the crooked crowd and the squalor.

Pan and I have just seated ourselves when two men farther down slide along their benches toward us. They might pass for twins—both as wide as they are tall—though the one next to Pan is decades older, only a few sparse hairs left on his head. Still, they're built like they could pull an oxcart.

"What's a pretty lass like you doin' showin' up here all alone?" The older one grins, exposing a mouth that's missing more teeth than it's kept. He's too rough-looking to be elven, yet he doesn't have an ear cuff to mark him as otherwise.

Poised and polite might have worked for the lady at the door, but it won't help me here. "Who says I'm alone?"

"He don't count." He throws a thumb at Pan, sloshing his beer across the lacquered wooden table. "So, you got an invisible mate?"

"Oh no, he's *very* visible." And watching from three rows over. Zander's not making a move, though. Either he's too angry that I showed up against his wishes, or he's giving me a long leash to see how badly I'll tangle myself up in it. "He's looking for accommodations. The inn seems to be full."

"Not gonna find much 'round here tonight." The man beside me leans closer, his hairy forearm brushing against me. He smells of raw onions and plaque, his breath so foul, I'm forced to shift away. "But I know a place not too far, where I'm stayin'. They could probably squeeze you in. And I'm free for a give and take, to the right female." He flicks at his ear, highlighting the missing cuff.

A mental image of Bexley and her Seacadorian captain hits me. That is the kind of "give and take" arrangement this guy is trying to sell me.

I meet Zander's gaze. The bastard is smiling into his mug. He must be able to read the disgust in my pulse from all the way over there. I can almost hear his mocking. *Let's see how you get out of this one.*

Elisaf has finally spotted me. His brow furrows as he watches this exchange unfold.

"As appealing as that offer is, I think I'll pass. My mate doesn't like to share."

"Your loss." The guy grumbles as he slides away, back the way he came.

I stifle my laugh, unable to manage any mortal speaking to me like that in Cirilea, or anywhere else.

The other man lingers. "Name's Fearghal."

"Hello, Fearghal." He's not someone I could fight off if I had to. I can't tell if he's going to be a problem yet. But I decide to use him to my advantage. "What do you know about those people out there?" I jerk my head toward the square. "What'd they do wrong?"

He glances around and then leans in. "I hear it's 'cause they took that poison."

I mock gasp. "I've heard about that. I wasn't sure if it was real or rumor."

"Oh, it's real, and it's got all your kind on edge, for good reason. Make sure you know the company you keep." He gives Pan a pointed look.

"Me?" Pan squeaks. "I could *never* do somethin' like that. She treats me better than anyone I've ever known, except maybe my ma. But even she used to smack me good sometimes for causin' her trouble. Ro"—he falters, catching himself with a wide-eyed flash of panic—"she cares about mortals."

Fearghal pats Pan's shoulder with a heavy hand. "Well, then you are luckier than all those poor sods outside. Between us, their keepers probably deserved it, the way things work around here." He chugs back a mouthful.

He's not concerned about offending me. I can use that to my advantage. "You're right, they probably did. And I doubt those people in the pillories deserve what's happening to them."

A spark of something stirs in his eyes. "Where you from?"

"Bellcross."

His lips purse. He doesn't believe me.

"Originally Salt Bay, though."

The doubt softens. "That's quite a ways from here."

"Ever been?"

"Nah. Never been past Norcaster. No reason to."

"It's nice in the south." I hold my breath, hoping he doesn't press further.

"People been sayin' they're all up in arms over these Ybarisans the king let across the rift."

"They've caused a lot of problems for a lot of people."

"Some say that. Then some say the Ybarisans are tryin' to help the mortals." He shrugs. "That's not me sayin' it, but it's some people."

"Some mortals."

"Aye. Ones who want freedom like I have." He flicks his naked earlobe. "These people, living 'round here?" He waves a finger around the room. "'Course they have it a bit better than those in the south. From what I've heard, anyway. But they'd still rather not have keepers to deal with, and a lot of 'em have been talkin'. There's been a lot of talk."

"About what?"

He shrugs, his eyes cutting to me, then away. "Things."

About being rid of their keepers, living for themselves. I know what he's hinting at, but I can't push too hard or he'll get cagey. I switch gears. "I've heard these Ybarisans are cruel."

"They ain't so bad." He pauses. "From what I heard, anyway. I wouldn't know." He slurps his ale.

"So, you're from Norcaster?"

"Nah." He wipes his mouth with the back of his hand. "Just down to get some supplies before I head back up to Woodswich. Ever heard of it?"

This explains the lack of a cuff. "Mortals live without keepers up there, right?"

"Been there all my life. Me and my wife, Norel, and our flock of chickens and goats. Never came down here until I turned into an old, ugly bugger. Nobody bothers me."

I lean in, layering on a healthy dose of giddy innocence to stroke this fool's ego. "What's it like there? Are the rumors true?"

"Depends what you've heard."

"Let's see ..." I pretend to pick my thoughts. He's exactly what I was hoping to find here—someone who will divulge anything I want to know whether he realizes it or not.

I'm almost certain he's met Princess Romeria's soldiers.

I can't believe my luck.

A commotion stirs, turning heads toward the doorway, where Jarek has strolled in, all leather, blades, and hard lines.

My body tenses. An angry Jarek, I am terrified of.

He locates me in seconds, and the murderous look on his face only adds to my apprehension.

Like in Bellcross's square, people fall back as he cuts through the crowd, as if they can sense the fury radiating off the warrior, and they know he'll walk through them. Or maybe it's his size that inspires them to move. He's a full head taller than most.

Whatever is about to happen, it isn't going to be pleasant for me. Still, I plaster on an adoring smile and wave him over. "There he is!"

Fearghal watches Jarek approach with a note of concern. "*That's* your mate?"

"Yes. Isn't he handsome? Hey, honey, did you find us a room for the night?" I call out, the words dripping with sweetness.

Jarek falters, caught off guard, but he recuperates quickly, his gray gaze landing on our companion. "Leave. Now."

"Nice talkin' to ya." Fearghal collects his beer and shifts back to join his friend, adding a few feet for good measure.

I stifle my curse, keeping up appearances. "See, now that's why you always get into fights when you come here. You're not nice."

Jarek replaces the man who was beside me, swinging his leg over the bench to straddle it. His leathers are soaked from the rain, as are his braids. He didn't even pause to throw on a cloak before hopping on his horse and racing here. "What *the fuck* do you think you are doing?" he hisses.

"I *was* getting valuable information from Fearghal who's from Woodswich and has met Ybarisans, but then you had to ruin it. By the way, thanks for the riding lessons. Couldn't have done it without you." A small part of me feels guilty. Abarrane may punish him for this when she finds out.

"We're leaving. *Now.*" His calloused hand curls around my elbow.

"I'm already here, and I'm not going anywhere without Zander. Also ..." I warn in a whisper, "Have you ever seen the kind of scene I can cause? I promise, it won't be subtle."

After a moment's pause, Jarek releases me, his teeth grinding.

I drum my fingers against the table. "Now, where's the waitress? I could use a beer."

Jarek's attention swings to Pan. "And *you*. Wait until the commander gets hold of you for helping with this scheme."

Pan's face pales.

"Leave him alone. He was only doing what I told him to."

"That won't protect him." Jarek surveys the tavern, his eyes landing first on Zander, then on Elisaf, who is watching with a smug expression. "I wondered why you would change your mind about Eden. I should have known it was for nefarious reasons, given who you are."

"I'd love to take credit for that level of scheming, but that was coincidental." I drop my voice. "I changed my mind *before* I found out that Zander came here looking for missing scouts, something *you* neglected to mention."

"Why would I mention something you don't need to know?"

I snort. "Either way, it worked to my advantage. And aren't you supposed to be in a good mood after, *you know* ..."

"After Loth barged into the tent to inform me that your horse was gone, and so were you, and no one could explain how?" He glares at me. "And when I interrogated the witch—"

"You did what?" I snap, my blasé act vanishing. "Gesine had nothing to do with it. Your guards weren't doing their jobs."

A young, dimple-cheeked barmaid interrupts us. "A round to start?"

"Please. Just two, though." I cast a thumb toward Jarek. "He can't handle his ale."

Her curious blue eyes flitter over Jarek before shifting to Pan, who can't seem to peel his gaze off her cleavage. He looks two seconds away from needing a napkin to wipe drool off his chin. "Aren't you a cute one." She reaches out to stroke his cheek before strolling away, her hips swinging.

Pan tracks her steps the entire way.

I give him a swift kick under the table. "Hey, *Dunn*, didn't you have something you needed to check on?"

He snaps back to attention, his cheeks flushed. "Huh? Oh, yeah." He pats his pocket where several coins are tucked.

"Be smart and safe. You hear me?"

With an impish grin, he trots away, out through the saloon door.

"What kind of mischief is that idiot up to now?" Jarek mutters.

"He's going to get information that a mortal servant will be able to find far easier than I can, especially with you breathing down my neck."

Jarek snorts. "He'll get nothing that Abarrane can't find, and he will get himself killed for it."

My focus veers back to our previous conversation. "If you harmed Gesine in any way, I promise, you will pay for it."

"The witch is fine." A grim smile touches his lips. "And how will I pay? Will you splash me with water?"

"Looks like someone already did."

The fiddler ends his tune and announces a short break to "water the grass and fetch a fresh pint," leaving us with a steady hum of drunken conversations.

The waitress swoops in with our ales.

"Since he's gone … Cheers." I slide Pan's mug over and clank mine against it before taking a sip. It's sour and hoppy, and stronger than I'm used to. "Try not to get too sloppy drunk tonight."

"You really are a pain in my arse." Jarek sighs before collecting his and sucking back a mouthful. "Have you seen Abarrane?"

I shake my head.

"She's likely scouring the cellars and dungeons. Fates help everyone if Drakon and Iago do not walk out of here tonight." His focus shifts to more important things, at least, than how I escaped.

"You saw the people in the square?"

"Aye. And I imagine we'll see many more before our journey ends." I can't tell whether the thought of that bothers him like it does me.

A curvy blond waitress shoves her cleavage inches from Zander's face while she checks his mug of ale. The move is shamefully overt and pathetic, yet Zander doesn't shift away, flinch, or indicate that he isn't enjoying the fleshy display.

My stomach tightens. She's wearing a cuff on her ear, marking her a mortal, though I assumed as much. All the servers here are marked, their dresses designed to offer more than an enticing look. They're advertising easy access to generous veins, and she's trying to tempt him.

Zander's been to Norcaster before. Did he take the bait last time?

"Don't be an idiot," Jarek scolds.

"Huh?"

"He abandoned his crown and kingdom *for you*. I do not think there is another female in this entire realm you need fear will ever be able to compete with you for his attention." Jarek's gaze dips to the waitress's cleavage. "As remarkable as *those* may be."

Is my jealousy *that* obvious?

Jarek's words are oddly comforting, though.

Still, Zander could appear to appreciate *those* a little less …

On impulse, I channel my elven affinity toward the fresh mug of beer as she's setting it down.

It splashes into Zander's lap, and he stiffens, telling me I've hit my mark.

"There. That should cool him down," I murmur around a sip, satisfied.

The waitress apologizes profusely, but Zander's eyes fly to mine, his head cocked in question.

I shrug.

The grin I get in return is dark and wicked and promises retribution. I'm going to pay for this—for all of it—later.

I can't wait.

"Can you try not to keep up the entire camp this time?"

My cheeks burn as I grasp Jarek's meaning. "We weren't *that* loud."

He smirks. "*He* wasn't."

I push aside my embarrassment. "Aw, it's okay." I reach up to toy with the thick rope of braided hair draped over his shoulder. The sides are growing in, covering his scalp in soft fuzz. "One day, if you try *really* hard, you'll please someone that much too."

The muscles in his jaw tighten, but humor glints in those eyes as he works his way through a suitable—surely biting—retort.

I'm saved from hearing it by the four guards who file in through the swinging doors.

Followed by another four.

And another four.

32
ROMERIA

Jarek curses and shifts in his seat to face the wall, stretching his arm across the table in front of me. To anyone else, he looks like he's getting closer, but I know he's trying to hide his presence. Given his size, it's almost laughable.

"Who did you piss off? I'm guessing the one in the front?" The male is dressed in finer leather and a fur capelet that is too heavy for these temperatures, even in this damp weather. Elven, definitely, and he must be important in this rabble. He's earning plenty of looks as he strolls toward the bar to share quiet words with the barkeep. Even Fearghal and his revolting companion seem apprehensive as they quietly watch the newcomers weave through the crowd.

"That is Lord Isembert. Norcaster and all its surrounding villages, aside from Woodswich, answer to him. He thinks his balls are the biggest in all of Venhorn. Maybe they are, but they hang far too low for his own good."

I cringe at the crude visual. "So you've met him before?"

"I've met him." Jarek uses his proximity to me to steal a glance over his shoulder, the tip of his nose skating across my cheek.

"The last time I was here, his men picked a fight and didn't like losing. He swore he'd have me executed if I ever came back."

"And yet *here you are*."

"Thanks to you."

"And you're not afraid?"

"Of what, dying? No. If it is my time, then so be it. But I will not do so for an unworthy cause."

I'm close enough to pick out blue-silver flecks within Jarek's otherwise steel-gray eyes. I see his conviction in them. Is he saying I'm unworthy?

Or that I *am* worthy?

It is impossible to read him.

Jarek shifts away after a beat to face the wall again. "What are they doing now?"

I take a long sip of my beer while surveying the twelve men. "Three have sat at the table next to Zander's. The others are fanning out around him."

"They've marked him."

"What does that mean?"

"It means they have questions, and they are going to demand answers." He seeks out Elisaf, who gives a subtle nod. He sees what's happening too.

Instead of sitting on the bench, Isembert settles on a table, giving me a profile view of the prominent bump in his nose and broad forehead.

"Maybe he won't remember you." Though something to distract this lord from his keen focus on Zander would be ideal.

"I killed four of his men. He'll remember me." Jarek's gaze is razor sharp as he watches from within the cover of an amorous partner. Frankly, he could sit on my lap and I wouldn't care right now. All I care about is the situation Zander has found himself in.

A hush falls over the room as people's curiosity—or trepidation—swells.

Zander isn't blind to what's happening. He sits with his hands folded in front of him, waiting, as the fire in the hearth rages. *Kindling for his affinity should he need it,* I remind myself. Though, in a tavern made of wood, we're basically in a tinderbox.

"Here you go, sweetheart." The waitress sets a fresh mug of ale in front of Zander to replace the one I dumped in his lap.

"Thank you." His attention is locked on Isembert.

She glances at the lord.

The next moment happens in a blink, my eyes barely catching the glint of silver on her thumb before she's dragging something across Zander's neck.

He reacts instantly and with incredible speed, seizing her wrist and pulling it away.

But it's too late.

My stomach drops as I recognize the merth luster, as the trickle of blood appears, and realize what she's done—immobilized Zander's affinity.

One of the men behind him—a guard—has moved in to press the tip of his sword against Zander's jugular, freezing him in place.

On instinct, I move to stand.

"*No.*" Jarek's arm loops around my waist before I've shifted an inch. "Do not do *anything* to draw attention to yourself. We need to see how this plays out." His free hand settles on the dagger at his side, waiting.

Zander remains still as the men strip him of his weapons, his gaze locked on the lord, unreadable.

Where the inside of the Greasy Yak was once boisterous, now every cleared throat echoes through the space. Behind the bar, the waitress sobs as she cradles her wrist. She was likely given no choice but to comply with the lord's instructions, yet I can't muster pity for her.

"Norcaster has had more than its fair share of strangers filtering through its gate as of late," Isembert announces in a baritone, the slight accent making his words sound harsh. He's educated, though, more refined than the ox twins and probably most people here. "You are yet another. A well-armed one, at that."

Zander's face is a picture of ease, despite the blood trickling down his neck and the blade against his throat. "I did not realize that Norcaster had sealed its gates to weary travelers who wish to protect themselves."

"Is that all you are? A weary traveler? With your companion at the bar, playing stranger and asking questions?" He nods toward Elisaf. "And the female warrior you came through the gate with tonight." Isembert scans the tavern, and Jarek ducks his head, but I doubt the lord is focusing on anyone. He's simply making his point. "Where is she?"

"Humping someone in an alleyway, if she's lucky."

Nervous chuckles float around the room.

Isembert smiles, but it's not genuine. "One can't be too careful lately, with these Ybarisans out peddling poison to kill our kind."

Zander's eyebrow arches. "Are you pegging me as Ybarisan?"

"Are you?"

"While I have been called a *sweetheart* from time to time"—his eyes cut to the treacherous waitress—"I do not believe they were referring to the scent of my blood. A Ybarisan, I most certainly am not."

Isembert's lips twist. "What is your name, weary traveler?"

"Zander." A slow, mischievous smile touches his lips, and I know he's decided before he says it out loud. "But you may call me King."

Whispers flare. Even the guard holding Zander at sword point wavers, his blade shifting away a few inches.

"Fuck." Jarek heaves a sigh. "This is going to get ugly."

Isembert's hand flies up. "Silence!"

Quiet falls.

"*King* Zander." If the lord is at all surprised, he hides it well. "What brings us the *honor* of your appearance?" He sneers, not a hint of deference. "Could it be that you are fleeing the kingdom you lost after bedding that Ybarisan whore and betraying your people?"

"See?" Jarek whispers. "Big, fucking balls."

I'm going to enjoy crushing them. My ring burns against my finger, and I take deep breaths to calm myself before I turn every mug of ale into a flying weapon.

A muscle twitches in Zander's jaw, the only sign that the lord's words bother him.

"The people within these mountains lead simple lives, in relative peace, and may not be current with the political circus of the south. Let me spend a moment enlightening them, for I receive regular news, and the latest is disturbing, to say the least." Isembert stands and begins pacing around the tavern. "Those Ybarisan monsters you've heard rumors of, skulking through villages, intent on destroying Islor with their poison? They were invited to cross the rift by *this male*"—he jabs a finger toward Zander—"and his family. The Ybarisan princess they swore would bring peace and prosperity to our realm? She has brought war and ruin, the poison that bleeds into Islor the very blood from her veins. It is said just one drop will kill any elven."

A chorus of gasps sounds. They may have heard about the poison, but clearly they haven't heard all the details.

"And even after she killed King Eachann and Queen Esma—his parents!—*still* he promised her the throne next to him, with all its wealth and power. What kind of king does that? Unless he is aligned with her in thought. Unless he has already betrayed his people."

On instinct, I spin my ring until the stone is hidden and hope the lord doesn't notice me. Even those bandits could see value in it.

Isembert's boots scuff across the hardwood as he approaches this side of the room, slowing next to Elisaf, as if taunting him. "Now they flee together, the disgraced King Zander and his poisonous princess, heading north to collect her soldiers and continue what they started. That is why he is here now. Those mortals who hang from the gallows?" He casts a wayward hand toward the square. "They do so because of *him*. The keepers who were so violently murdered may as well have been by *his* hand. His, and the realm of Ybaris."

Isembert is mere feet from us. Any second, he's going to see Jarek.

"Are you finished yet? Should I clap now or wait?" Zander says, bored.

Isembert spins, turning his attention back to him. "Where is your darling queen now?"

Zander stares at the lord, his expression blank.

"Do you not have *anything* to say for your misdeeds? Will you not defend yourself at all?"

The corners of Zander's mouth curl. His signature arrogant smile. "I am a king. I do not explain myself to *anyone*, especially not petty, self-declared lords who have been permitted to play in the sandbox for far too long."

A mixture of shock and satisfaction flourishes across countless faces. I imagine they've never heard anyone speak to their lord like that, self-declared or not.

Rage morphs Isembert's features. This can't end well.

I want to scream at Zander to stop antagonizing him. He has no weapons and can't tap into his affinity. He's going to get himself killed.

I focus on my breathing as my panic stirs again.

But Jarek has weapons, as does Elisaf.

I have weapons. A sharp merth dagger that cuts through flesh and affinities that have saved us from dire situations more than once. But it's not my elven affinity that will help us here.

I toy with my ring and the idea of slipping it off, hoping for the best.

But if they harm Zander, I'm liable to bring down this entire tavern over our heads, and how will that help us?

Two hairy-knuckled fists drop onto the table in front of us. One of the men who came in with Isembert, a beast with broad shoulders and a spiked mace dangling from his shoulder, glares at Jarek. "My lord? This one is with the Legion."

It's a few seconds before Isembert peels his focus from Zander. "Ah, the great and terrible Jarek. I should have known this skulking king didn't enter Norcaster alone. Can I assume that female warrior wandering the streets is also with the Legion? She must be looking for the two others who were here last night, asking questions."

"Where are they?" Jarek demands to know.

"Rethinking their allegiances by now, I would imagine." His claim suggests something wicked.

Jarek's teeth grind in my ear.

Isembert edges closer toward us. "I thought I was clear about what would happen the next time you stepped foot within my walls."

"You were." Jarek remains calm as he sets his mug down. "Will it be this imbecile delivering your judgment? Because it didn't work out well for him last time either."

The man snaps his meaty fingers. Three others close in, drawing blades that glint in the firelight.

Jarek raises a finger. "Hold that thought. You." Turning to me, he offers a flat smile. "This was fun, but time to find another lap to warm." Giving me a gentle but firm shove off the bench—away from the battle about to erupt—Jarek stands and draws a sword and dagger. The ring of steel shivers through the alehouse.

Elisaf follows suit.

Oh my God. They're going to start swinging blades in the middle of a tavern *full* of people. The bar fights I witnessed in my old life seem like a nursery school spat.

And there is still a sword pressed against Zander's throat.

The waitresses scramble to hide behind the bar. They've likely had to clean up more than one pool of blood from this floor in the past. Several patrons quietly filter out the door while others brandish their weapons—for protection, or an excuse to use them.

I do the only thing I can think of: edge toward the wall and draw my dagger.

A palpable tension pulses as time stands still, muscles corded and senses riveted, everyone waiting for the first twitch, the first command, the first reason to swing. Anyone watching must be able to see each beat of my heart pulsing in my throat.

And then a bloodcurdling scream peals through the paralyzed room.

It's coming from above us, in one of the inn's rooms, and there is no mistaking what it means. I've heard it far too many times now.

The distraction is what Zander needed, and he doesn't waste it, spinning out of his seat to disarm the man holding him at sword point before cutting him down with his own blade. In seconds, he's slayed two more men and is moving in on a fourth, wielding a sword in each hand.

Elisaf and Jarek fight off opponents in their respective corners, Jarek standing on the table, swinging his blades so fast I can't follow either of them as he cleaves into flesh. The hairy-knuckled beast lies facedown on the tavern floor, nothing more than a bloody obstacle to trip over.

The sounds that have exploded in the tavern are deafening, of clashing steel and battle screams and moans of agony. It's enough to make me grip my dagger and press my back against the wall as I watch my three companions slice, stab, and twist away from rival attacks.

The ox twins have shifted into a corner and are still downing ale, watching the battle unfold, their swords inert on the table in front of them.

Maybe they're smarter than I gave them credit for.

Suddenly, a hand clamps over my wrist and tugs at me. On instinct, I swing my dagger toward the assailant, only to register that it's Pan a split second before I stab him.

He yelps and jumps back, holding up his hands in surrender.

"This way!" He jerks his head toward a hidden door in the corner. Of course he's found it. He's as resourceful as I was in my old life.

I falter, scanning the tavern again. It's nothing but a flurry of blades, the skilled swordsmen easily cutting down drunken opponents caught up in the moment.

Zander catches my attention. "Go! Now!" he shouts, pointing toward the door, a second before one of Isembert's men charges him. He barely lifts his sword in time to block the attack, and then he's checking to see where I am again. "Get out of here!" he roars.

I'm risking his life by standing here.

"Go." I shove Pan toward the concealed exit.

He leads me down a narrow hall surely meant for servants, hopping over crates and spare pillows strewn across the path, before pushing through another door. We spill out near the stable yard.

The cold rain against my face is a welcome relief.

As is the sight of Abarrane, Eros's reins in her grip. "Leave *now*," she growls, not wasting time with her usual threats of bodily harm.

"They need you inside!" She's alone, which means she hasn't found Drakon or Iago yet. "Isembert knows where the scouts are, and he's in there." I jerk my head toward the tavern.

Her eyes flare with determination. Shoving the reins into Pan's hand, she draws her sword and disappears through the door.

"I thought she was gonna kill me for sure." Pan leans over to brace his hands on his knees, catching his breath. "Scariest moment of my life. Even scarier than when Oswald had me on that fountain. Scarier than when those guys dragged us into the woods …"

I dismiss Pan's prattles and peer up into the soulless sky, squinting against the rain. The screaming from the inn room has stopped, replaced by the sounds of a brutal battle.

I hope Zander and Elisaf are fine. And even Jarek. But I can't do anything for them.

I draw my hood over my head and tuck my ring in my pocket. "Stay here."

Pan's protests fade as I move away from the Greasy Yak, my boots splashing through puddles. People leak out of the door in a panic, some holding wounds, others in hysterics, yet others with their heads down, intent on escaping the chaos to the safety of their hovels.

It's the perfect time.

It's the only time.

I embrace the swell of adrenaline buzzing in my core as I stalk toward the square. The guard watching over the prisoners runs past me and into the tavern's fray, not so much as glancing my way. *No one* looks at me, the lone hooded figure walking toward the condemned mortals. Even they don't hint at noticing me.

I am a ghost.

That certainty brings with it a wave of confidence.

The female on the end—a young woman of maybe twenty—sobs quietly, but otherwise no one makes a sound, trembling in the cold. A few are slumped, their knees buckled. I'm not sure they're alive. The pungent smell of urine and vomit curls my nostrils, the rain unable to wash it away.

How long have these people been here?

It's so dark, and the trigger to open these contraptions so I can release these people is not obvious—

"You have to pull the peg out."

I jump at Pan's voice suddenly behind me. "I told you to stay over there!"

"And the commander told you to leave. Looks like neither of us is a good listener." He grabs the wooden dowel and wrenches it until it slides out.

Pan was watching me the entire time I walked over here. It makes sense; it's like that night with Gesine and the ring. I couldn't hide what she knew was happening.

I will have to remember that little loophole.

The prisoners begin shifting, their heads turning toward us.

The spell my affinity wove must be broken, but I don't have time to worry about that now. "Let's get them out of here."

Grabbing one end of the stocks, Pan heaves. "It's kinda heavy," he grits out.

I dive in, and together we hoist the top piece high enough for the girl to squirm out. Quickly, I unfasten my cloak and throw it over her as Pan works on the next peg.

One by one, we free the prisoners. A few break off in a stumbling run, weak and disoriented, but most help, catching those who can't stand on their own anymore.

We've released the last, a man who staggers off in the opposite direction of the tavern, when shouts call out. A moment later, my ears catch a distinctive hiss I've come to know all too well.

The fleeing man drops, an arrow protruding from his back.

"Stop! All of you!"

At the guard's command, the other prisoners panic and scatter. They're picked off one by one, three of them hit by arrows in mere seconds.

If this keeps up, there will be none left to save. I need to do something.

You will be limited only by the boundaries of your imagination.

And the only thing I can imagine right now is retaliation.

I used the rain before to stop a charging nethertaur. Now I welcome the surge of power deep inside and allow my mind's eye to see the drops shifting direction and gaining speed, merging, forging into the arrows aimed at these people.

When they hit their mark, they are as hard and sharp as metal slicing through flesh.

Grim satisfaction washes over me as the two guards felling these prisoners collapse.

But more men are coming, rushing toward us, all wielding swords. The closest has his sights on the girl wearing my cloak, cowering next to a woman.

The power surge rises faster this time, as if answering my need, and fills me with a euphoric burst of energy similar to the night I saved Pan. I throw out my hand, and the rushing soldier catapults backward, crashing into a thatched house.

Another soldier runs toward us.

And another.

I stop them, too, sending them soaring.

Victory buoys me. Gesine was right. Channeling Vin'nyla's affinity is becoming easier with each assault.

A fourth soldier, I send colliding into the gallows. The heavy post cracks with his bones, groaning until it finally splinters. The hanging bodies drop to the ground, no longer on display.

Pan gapes at me.

More soldiers approach, too many for me to stop one by one. Eventually, one will slip through.

I need help. I need Zander.

But he's still inside. I can't rely on anyone but myself right now.

What I need is a barrier, something that will stop the enemy in their tracks, but the mortal prisoners are still spread out. "Closer. I need you closer to me!" I scream.

They tremble as they rush in.

There's only one defense I can think of, and the moment the idea forms in my mind, a searing surge floods my core.

Flames explode around us.

33
ZANDER

Abarrane pauses to spit a mouthful of blood onto the floor and wipe her face against her sleeve, before pushing her blade farther into a kneeling Isembert's shoulder. "Where are they?"

He manages a weak laugh through his pained grimace. "By now? Dead, or wishing they were."

With a cry of rage, she heaves her sword out of his flesh, steps back, and swings her blade.

"No!" I roar, but it's too late.

Isembert's body crumples to the floor, his head rolling under a chair.

"Fates," Jarek mutters, rubbing away blood that splattered his cheek.

"Keeping him alive was a waste of time. He was not going to tell me anything." Abarrane stoops to collect the severed head by the hair. She holds the gruesome sight up in the light. "But his soldiers will, or *they* will wish they were dead by the time I am finished with them."

"If there are any left to question." I look around at the carnage within the tavern. Bodies everywhere. The eleven men who came with Isembert, plus a dozen or so who were looking to ingratiate themselves with their lord by joining the battle, several drunken fools who thought themselves warriors, and a barmaid who didn't appreciate seeing one of her regulars cut down.

"I need to find Romeria—"

"She is on her way back to camp with the imbecile. I made sure of it." Abarrane's focus settles on the two men who accosted Romeria earlier, still sitting at their table, drinking their ale.

"Polite questions will do."

"Aye." She moves for them, Isembert's head dangling from her grip.

While I would love to interrogate Jarek on exactly how Romeria escaped his watch in the first place, those questions will have to wait.

The mortal who cut me—Etta—is behind the bar, trembling, her flirtatious smile long gone. When she sees me approaching, she shifts behind her keeper. Her pulse sings of terror and guilt. "I'm sorry, my lord … I mean, Your Highness … Lord Isembert demands we inform him whenever there be any stranger in here, askin' questions, 'specially 'bout the poison. He didn't give me no choice. Said he'd harm my boys if I didn't comply." Tears pour down her cheeks. "Please don't kill me. I'm all they have left."

"I'm not going to kill you." If anything, Etta proved a good reminder that even in an area such as Norcaster, the right—or wrong—nobility can play puppeteer to anyone. "What do you know about the two legionaries who are missing? I assume they came here last night?"

She peeks up at the keeper, who nudges her forward, nodding.

"They were here, yeah. Real late. Got into a game o' draughts with a few regulars. The one left for some fresh air and didn't come back. So then the other one, the big, red-haired fella, went lookin' for him, and that's the last I saw of 'em. Honest."

"Do you have any idea where Isembert could be holding them? A cellar or tomb …"

"I'm sorry." Her head shakes. "If I knew, I would tell ya. I swear."

"I believe you."

She hesitates. "Are you truly the king?"

I smile despite myself. "Some would disagree, but I did sit on a throne not long ago." Though it feels like ages now.

She swallows. "You're kinder than I expected."

"I try to be."

"I'm sorry, 'bout the thing." She draws a line on her neck, mimicking where and how she cut me.

"It will heal."

"Would ya look at that." The barkeep's eyes widen at something beyond me. "That's some fire on a night like this."

My head snaps to the window.

That is an *impossible* fire for a night like this. At least, impossible through regular means.

Jarek and Elisaf chase after me as we rush out the tavern door. The square has been transformed with bodies, blood, and a ring of fire, the flames easily reaching eight feet in the air. High enough to shield the people inside from the waiting soldiers.

They're the mortals who were trapped in the pillories.

"Fates." Jarek stares dumbstruck at the display of power. "How are you doing that?" His gaze cuts to my neck, as if to confirm for himself that the slice the barmaid inflicted is still oozing. Of course he would assume it's me. I *should* be the only one capable.

In doorways and windows, sheltering beneath wagons, the people of Norcaster watch with a mixture of fascination and horror. Exact truths can likely still be obscured from townsfolk, but after this, there will be no hiding Romeria from the people who matter.

And maybe that's the way this tide must turn for us to move forward.

A form stands in the inferno's center, her eyes blazing with a silver-white light.

There you are.

Finally.

"I am not the one doing that. Come. She needs our help."

34
ROMERIA

Now I understand what Gesine meant by threads.

Because I am clinging to this scorching-hot thread of Malachi's affinity like a mountain climber clings to a ledge after losing her footing. My knees threaten to buckle from the strain, but if I relent, if I let these flames dwindle before Zander and the others dispatch the circling enemy, they will move in and cut us down.

And so I hang on as my body trembles, and I watch as flames reflect off blades as bodies drop, one by one.

"It's okay. Romy! You can stop now!" Pan's shout is a distant echo in my ear. "They're all dead!"

With a groan of relief, I let go.

And crumple.

Pan catches me before I hit the ground. "I got you," he grunts, sliding his head and shoulders under my arm to prop me onto my feet as best he can.

My senses are distorted, wobbly, like I'm underwater. An overwhelming wave of nausea hits, and I lean sideways to heave the ale I drank earlier.

"King? King!" Pan's struggling to support my dead weight. "Help!"

Seconds later, I'm shuffled into different arms. Stronger arms.

"Romeria! Can you hear me?"

"Gesine," I mumble. This is how Gesine feels after expending all her power. Now I understand.

"Elisaf. Get the caster!"

"No." I don't need a caster. I need rest. But the prisoners … they need her.

Using every bit of strength I can scrape together, I lift my head. They're still there, huddled and in shock. Three who were shot with arrows writhe on the ground. "Help them. Save them."

With that, I succumb to the darkness.

I wake in a room, buried beneath wool blankets. Sunlight streams through a dormer window, cracked open to allow a cool, crisp morning breeze. My pillow prickles against my skin, its stuffing of bird feathers poking through the linen sham.

Gesine's chair creaks as she stands, moving for a metal pitcher. "They had some last-minute vacancies in the inn above the tavern, so they could accommodate us."

"I'll bet they did," I croak. How many guests never made it to their rooms last night? How many bodies did they have to clean up? "Please tell me that's not ale you're pouring."

She laughs. "I think you'll do better with water for now."

My clothes hang near the hearth where a small fire burns.

"Borrowed from one of the barmaids," Gesine explains when she sees me peering down at the modest nightgown someone changed me into while I was unconscious.

I struggle to sit up. Every muscle aches.

"The discomfort will ease soon," Gesine promises, slipping the mug into my grasp. "A few more hours, and you will feel like yourself again."

"I can't feel my affinities." The tiny, hard ball normally in my chest is nonexistent, the buzz so faint it's barely noticeable.

"They do not run on an unlimited tap. You burned through them last night, and they need time to replenish. As you grow stronger and use your affinities more often, you will draw upon more before you empty. You have not reached your full potential yet. Far from it."

The cool liquid is a balm for my parched throat. "I know what you mean about the threads now."

"You felt it."

"Yeah. With the fire." I take another sip. "Where's Ianca?"

"Outside in her wagon. She stayed at camp last night, but the company came in this morning. Zorya is watching over her now. She is too weak to step out, and it is best she not attract attention. There is enough on us at the moment." Gesine wanders over to peer out the window. "From what I hear, that was some display last night."

"Yeah, I'm not sure how I did it. I mean, I couldn't before, with you, right?"

"I have a theory." Her lips twist. "Every time you have managed to wield your power, you have done so because you were protecting others. The water shield that night? The beast tearing through a camp? The cave you collapsed? Whether elven or caster affinity, you've channeled to save lives."

"So you knew I would be able to, if something bad enough happened here that I needed them."

"I hoped."

I smooth my thumb over my ring finger.

Only to realize it's naked. Panic explodes as I search my memory. The last time I was wearing it … "That girl! The one I gave my cloak to—"

"She returned the cloak, along with your ring that was in the pocket." Gesine points to the bedside table where the chunky gold band sits, the dull white stone staring at me.

I heave a sigh of relief. To think I once likened that piece of jewelry to a bubblegum-machine prize? Who could ever imagine the power it holds? "How are the prisoners?"

"I healed three mortals shot by arrows, as well as those who had been left in the pillories. Some were in poor health. I doubt they would have survived the night had you not freed them." She pauses. "Nine have tainted blood. Four took the poison willingly, while the others had no idea. Their spouses must have slipped it into their drinks."

I curse. It's one thing to take it voluntarily but another to be given no option. How many more times will that happen? "Have you told Zander?"

"I have."

"And?"

"He gave them a choice: execution by King Atticus's will, or life with a mark, by his."

Zander offered what I would have asked him to. "And what did they say?"

"They all chose life."

"Of course they did. Because they want to live." But they're willing to die for their freedom and the freedom of their loved ones.

"He's offered the same to anyone in Norcaster who comes forward voluntarily, rather than kill their keeper and run. But I do not pretend to know how he thinks he will protect them from those same keepers after we leave."

It's simple. "We can't leave them behind. We have to bring them north with us."

"That is a conversation for the two of you. He has already declared it unsafe for mortals where we are going."

"Have they found Drakon and Iago yet?"

She shakes her head. "I fear any who might have had answers have left them on the tavern floor with their blood."

"If anyone can find out, it'll be Abarrane." She'll drag the words off their tongues.

"She is certainly on a mission to try." Gesine moves for the door. "The king asked that I fetch him when you stirred. There is a basin with lukewarm water and a few supplies I scrounged for you to wash with."

"Thank you, Gesine."

"He was here with you for much of the night."

"Is he angry that I snuck out?"

She pauses. "Perhaps. But all I noticed is how very much in love he is."

That brings a soft smile to my lips.

With that, she ducks out quietly.

I spend a few minutes washing up with the toiletries provided, smiling at the salt-and-mint paste. The first time I found a similar paste and linen cloth in my bathing room at the castle, I assumed it was an exfoliant. Corrin mocked me for days about rubbing toothpaste on my cheeks.

I wonder how she's doing, how they're all doing, with a usurper king and that vile creature about to take the queen's throne.

Zander walks through my door unannounced as I've finished rinsing my mouth.

Warmth blooms in my chest.

"How are you feeling?" he asks.

"A little shaky, but fine for the most part." My energy is quickly returning. Even faster now, with each potent heartbeat the sight of him stirs.

He pushes the door shut, his gaze drifting over my gauzy linen gown. His clothes are still marked with the blood and grime of last night's battle, but he's washed his hands and face at least. Not that I care. The last time I saw him, a ring of men with swords was trying to kill him.

I'm so relieved to see him alive.

A heady tension builds in this little room as my fingers itch to touch him, as much for comfort as this exploding physical urge.

His throat bobs with a hard swallow. "We have much to discuss."

"So much." But now, I can only think of how much I need him.

I refuse to think of anything else. My body thrums with anticipation. "Later." With impatient fingers, I unfasten the buttons at the collar of my nightgown and push it off my shoulders. It slides soundlessly to the worn wood floor, fanning around my feet.

Zander's eyes flare, dragging over the length of my naked body as he sheds weapons and clothes with surprising speed. He stalks toward me with an intensity bordering on predatory. Our bodies collide, nothing left between us but raw desire and the heat of bare skin.

His mouth closes over mine as if he's been waiting an eternity to kiss me. Strong arms wrap around my frame, one hand slipping over the small of my back, the other, weaving through my hair at my nape.

"Are you angry with me?" I whisper against his lips.

"Angry? No. I am thoroughly impressed." The warmth of his powerful body sinks into me as he pulls me close, until every inch of our bodies touch, from our toes to our foreheads. "You never cease to amaze me with the way you always fight for the vulnerable, the weak. How can I be angry when I am consumed with admiration?" He hesitates, his breath grazing my cheek. "Are you angry with me—"

"Yes." I punctuate that with a soft bite against his bottom lip, drawing a growl from deep inside his chest.

"Let me make it up to you, then."

I revel in the feel of his face now buried in my neck, his tongue tracing along my skin with gentle sweeps. It's such a disparity to his grip on my hips—tight but short of painful—as he guides us backward to the narrow table against the wall.

His biceps tense beneath my palms as he hoists me onto its surface.

"What's wrong? The bed not good enough for you?" I tease.

"We'll end up there, eventually." He pushes my thighs apart, his fingers grazing over sensitive flesh.

I don't care where he takes me as long as it's soon, I silently admit, admiring his hard length as I adjust my position to invite him in.

But he leans in instead, his lips catching my nipple, wetting it before his teeth graze it.

I arch my back to give him better access, letting my head fall against the wall with a moan, reveling in the various sensations.

"You never worry that I'm going to take your vein, do you," he purrs before sucking.

"I would hope you're not that stupid."

His chuckle vibrates in my chest. "If anyone could make me that stupid, I dare say it would be you."

I crack an eyelid. "Do I need to worry?"

"No." He drops to his knees in front of me, pressing a kiss to my navel before shifting farther down. "But know that I would die happy, despite my screams."

"Do you ever wish you could?" I don't have to elaborate.

His eyes are pools of heated gold when he peers up at me. "Yes."

My stomach flutters with his candor. "You've never shown me your teeth. Like, *really* shown them to me."

"Because I hate them. I hate everything they stand for, everything they make me." He presses a kiss against my inner thigh.

I knew this already. But I love everything that makes him who he is. "Show me now."

He swallows. "*Now* would be a very"—he presses another kiss against my inner thigh—"very"—and another, higher—"dangerous time to do that." He leans in but pauses, his breath skating over my sensitive flesh for three long beats, just long enough to melt my core, aching with need, before he closes the distance with his skilled tongue.

A whimper escapes me.

It takes only minutes of watching him before my hips are rolling and I'm grabbing a fistful of his golden-brown hair to pull him closer, desperate for my release. Conscious of the open window and the milling people outside—and Jarek's taunting—I bite my bottom lip to keep the noise to a minimum as I unravel for him.

Zander climbs to his feet. "You're trying to be quiet with me." His voice holds an accusatory tone.

I reach down between us to give him a stroke. "I don't feel like being teased by the Legion later."

"Is that so?" He claims my mouth with a wild kiss, his tongue diving in deep, uninhibited strokes as he sinks into me. The primal sound that escapes him can't be mistaken for anything else and surely carried outside these walls.

Pulling himself out slowly, he pauses at my entrance and presses his forehead against mine. He holds my gaze without flinching. "*Let* them hear it. I don't care if they hear it."

He sinks in again, fully seated this time, my body stretching around him. His grip on my hips tightens. "Let them know how desperate I am for you, how you haunt my every waking thought."

I roll my hips, coaxing him to keep going.

He responds with a hard thrust, but then stalls again, a somber expression taking over his face. "Whether it was a curse of fates or prophecy that brought us together, I no longer care, and I will not allow anything or anyone to keep us from each other again." His brow tightens. "If that is what you want."

My heart swells with his display of vulnerability. "I can't live in this world if it's not with you by my side."

"Then that is where I will be. Always." He responds with a kiss that bleeds promise as he sinks into me again.

I cling to his straining arms and whisper his name over and over as his thrusts turn hard and merciless, his guttural moans overt and raw.

Eventually, he wins, dragging my cries out of me.

By the time I feel him pulsating deep inside, all of Norcaster must be listening.

"How long did this take Gesine to heal?" I trace the silver line across Zander's neck where the waitress cut him.

"Not long. Maybe ten minutes? Another scar for my collection."

"You bled a lot for such a tiny scratch."

"It was actually quite deep." His gaze is on the sloped ceiling above us as we lie together in bed, my body nestled against his side. Despite the cool air, he hasn't drawn the wool blankets over himself, and I appreciate the view. He's a sculpture of perfection, lazing in the afterglow of our intimacy—two rounds of it.

I know. My rage flares. "Have you found the woman who did it?"

"I have. That was her gown you stripped off earlier. She was kind enough to offer it when I carried you in, soaked."

"How generous." My molars grind. "It doesn't seem her style, though. My breasts weren't hanging out. It needs fewer buttons for that."

He laughs. "Good linen is hard to come by, especially up here. Do not ruin it in your anger."

"She could have killed you."

His laughter falls off with a sigh that lifts his bare chest. "I will admit, she caught me off guard. It will not happen again." He pauses. "Just as I will never attempt to shelter you by keeping you away."

"You mean like sending me off to the tent, excited, and then jumping on a horse and riding into danger?" My hand skates over his chest, his abdomen, moving downward. "Forcing me to sneak out to find you?"

"You were excited? About what?" he asks with mock innocence.

I grip his length, a touch tighter than I usually would, and his stomach muscles spasm.

"I am finally beginning to see that I cannot keep you out of trouble. Despite my every effort, you will find a way to step deep into it."

"I think I did well last night." I tell him what I learned from Pan about the true source of the poison.

"So the Ybarisans have allied with mortals."

"And they're targeting mortals with terrible keepers and nothing to lose."

"To start with. It won't remain like that. Especially not as the elven retaliate. That was the third execution in Norcaster. It might make some of these mortals think twice, but not enough. How long before these gallows and pillories become permanent fixtures in every square in every corner of Islor?"

Which brings me to those prisoners. "The people we saved last night, the mortals you had Gesine mark? We can't leave them here. You know that."

He sighs, as if he's had this conversation too many times. Or maybe he's dwelled on it too long himself. "What kind of new life can I give these people? What hope? I am a king without a castle or even a home. We are scurrying to Venhorn's caves because, sadly, that is the safest place for us in Islor, but it is only temporary, and between the saplings and whatever Nulling beasts may still lurk, it will be fraught with danger. How can I bring these mortals there?"

"It could be the safest place for them. It's not the humans the saplings want, and if they're marked, they can't be fed on or turned."

He pauses, as if considering, but then shakes his head. "We will see."

I snort. "That's what my parents used to say when they meant no."

He turns to study my face. "You haven't told me much about your parents."

"That's a long story for another day." When we have the luxury of time. Right now, we have more important things to discuss. "What about Jarek? What are we going to tell him about last night? Did he figure it out?" I made those water arrows using my elven affinity, which is no secret, but the blasts of wind that crushed bones and the ring of fire so hot it singed the ends of my hair are not so easily explained. I know he witnessed the latter. He was fighting outside it.

And then there's still the question of how Pan and I left the camp on horseback right out from under the legionaries' noses. Jarek won't let that go so easily either.

"The truth."

My eyebrows pop. "How much truth?"

"As much as makes sense to share. It is too late for less, anyway. At first, he thought the ring of fire was my doing, but eventually, he saw your eyes."

"Did they glow?" I picture Gesine, standing at the helm of that little fishing boat with her radiant emerald irises as she propelled us forward on a violent wind.

He chuckles. "I would say so."

"What color? Blue?"

"No. More a silver. Almost like merth. They were brilliant in the night. There was no missing them. I told him what you are, but the details surrounding the how and why have not been passed along."

"So he knows I'm a key caster."

"Yes."

"Is he angry? Afraid?" Abarrane was afraid when she first learned the truth.

"I do not think he is capable of fear. But I imagine we will feel the bitterness of his temper for some time yet. He is arrogant and prideful, and as Abarrane's chosen second, he does not feel she should be keeping secrets like this from him." Zander rolls onto his side to face me, his fingertip tracing my cheek. "I have been so focused on protecting you at all costs that I didn't properly weigh the option of being honest. I have not given Jarek the benefit of the truth, even though he has given me no reason to suspect his loyalty. He has followed us this far. If he is to keep following, he must understand all that is at risk. We do not have a choice."

"What about Pan? Do we tell him too?"

Zander snorts. "He will follow you over a cliff, truth or not. We may need to muzzle him so every stranger from here to Fernhoth doesn't learn the truth before we get to safety. But Jarek … you will need to let him in and win him over. I cannot do that for you, and you need him in your corner if you want the Legion there without fail. There is an odd pecking order among them. Abarrane leads them without question, but Jarek can sway their hearts. They respect him."

"I was making progress with him before this." Even with sneaking out of camp.

"Yes, I noticed how much *progress* you two were making with each other last night," he murmurs wryly.

"You mean when he was trying to use me as a human shield to hide from Isembert? It was like a rhinoceros standing behind a lamppost."

"I do not know what this rhinoceros is, but that is not what I saw. I would have believed you two planned to leave together, up to one of the inn's rooms."

I roll my eyes. "So we can play a game of who can bury their dagger deepest into the other? Please, that was all a cover. He likes sweet and innocent mortals, something I am not." I lost anything that resembled innocence years ago.

"Good, because I would have to kill him otherwise."

I laugh, even as I revel in what he's revealing. "Is the king of Islor *jealous*?"

"Do not be absurd." But his lazy smirk says he knows he is.

"Should we talk about what *I* saw? How was that beer in your lap, by the way?"

"Effective." He chuckles. "A nice touch. I am glad you are using your skills for mature and laudable purposes."

I give his chest a playful pinch. "I think I made up for it later."

"I would have to agree." His smile falls with a hard swallow. "I fear that what we are seeing here is only a taste of what is ahead for Islor. If that is the case, I will need you beside me and ready to fight, every step of the way."

I smooth a hand over his heart, my palm absorbing the warmth. "You already have me by your side. You know that. And if Gesine is right, maybe we can end this curse together, before there's too much more fighting." Maybe I can still unravel everything Princess Romeria has done to Zander, his family, and his people. Or at least mend it.

I press my lips against his, stealing a tender kiss that he matches. But when I pull away, his brow is tight. "What's wrong?"

He hesitates. "I am not certain that I want her to be right."

"Why not?" Realization slips along my spine like a cold trickle of water. "What *aren't* you telling me?"

His eyes meet mine and I see an apology there. "Gesine thinks the only way to end this blood curse may be to open the nymphaeum door."

35
ROMERIA

I listen with a mixture of shock, hurt, and anger as Zander explains all that Gesine divulged to him in Gully's Pass, all that they both have been keeping from me—about the nymphaeum's original purpose, this secret book found in Shadowhelm that confirmed Malachi had succeeded in ruling these lands once before.

"But we can't open that door." My brain combs through everything I know of the risk. "That would mean opening the Nulling and releasing an army of whatever terrible creatures are waiting in there. Nobody wants that." It's why they've been executing key casters for the past two thousand years.

Nobody … except Malachi and Sofie.

"*I* certainly do not want that. And there are too many unknowns and no guarantees to consider it an option. The nymphs may not wish to help us. Or they might, but at a terrible cost. You might not even survive opening the door, and I could not bear losing you like that. Perhaps that makes me an unfit king. So be it, but the risk is too great." He strokes my cheek with the soft pad of his thumb, his eyes shining with sincerity. "When she first told me, I did not know what to do with that information, how to process it. But you needed to focus on learning as much as possible about what you are, so we can take back the throne. That is why I did not tell you."

I don't miss the "we" in that statement.

"What about this Stonekeep place? Do you think there's any truth to what Gesine said about that?" If there is, it sounds like the nymphs would *help* Islor.

Zander chuckles, but it lacks mirth. "I have stood before it more than once, and I have no faith that there is aid for us there. It is an engraving on a mountain wall that has existed for thousands of years, surrounded by deadlands. Nothing more. We cannot rely on prophecy to help us. And do not mention any of this to the others. They will fear it, and they will think I am entertaining Mordain's guidance."

I sigh. Still keeping secrets. "But what if opening this door *is* the only way?" What if we need the nymphs' help?

"No. We will find another way to stop this poison from destroying all that Islor is." His jaw sets with determination.

But mine sets with worry.

Zander offers me a tentative smile over his shoulder as he leads me down the narrow stairs of the inn.

A guilty gesture.

His reasoning was sound—commendable, even—but still … How could he keep something like this from me? He and Gesine, conspiring since Gully's Pass while burying me in the dark. Shrugging off my questions, steering me away from the truth, even when I was trying to piece together Ianca's gibberish.

Not so much gibberish after all.

Zander might not want to admit it, but what if Gesine is right and there is no other way to rid them of this blood curse? What if I must do the very thing I've sworn I never would? What is a bigger risk to Islor—the poison slowly tearing it apart, or Malachi and his Nulling army?

Either way, it feels like I'm the one dooming these people.

The same woman from last night is perched on her stool at the bottom of the steps. When she looks up and sees us descending, she offers, "Can't say we've e'er had a king stay here before. Or a queen, for that matter." No salutations, no bows. Either she didn't have a teacher like Corrin to berate her into learning proper etiquette, or more than likely, she doesn't care for custom.

Her eyes flip to me, filled with a new hint of caution. "I see you found yourself a room after all."

"I guess I played my cards right."

She pauses a beat and then snorts. Her frizzy hair sways with her curt chin jerk toward the tavern doors. "There's some oats and links waitin' if you're hungry."

"You're *open*?"

She stares at me like I'm an idiot. "People need to eat."

"Right. Of course."

"Thank you." Zander leads me away, his hand on the small of my back. "They're an interesting lot up here." If he's bothered by her lack of etiquette, he doesn't let on, though something tells me he might appreciate it.

The Greasy Yak is quiet this morning. About a third of the tables are occupied by people digging into a hot breakfast, and in a few cases, a morning ale. One group of weathered patrons looks like they might have been here last night and never left.

It's surprisingly clean, considering the body count it boasted only hours ago. The corpses have all been cleared out—to where, I'd rather not know—and three gangly teenage boys are on their knees, scrubbing the floor with a bucket of soapy water and wire-bristle brushes.

Maybe it's because I know what happened, but the smell of death clings to the air, overpowering the melding scent of ale and sizzling pork.

And everyone is staring at me.

Or it could be Zander they're gawking at. I'm sure word of the king's arrival has spread to every nook of Norcaster by now.

Or it could be *both* of us drawing attention because it's quiet enough that a rather noisy activity from two floors up might have carried. My cheeks burn at the thought.

From a far corner, a willowy young woman offers me a tentative wave.

I frown. Do I know her…

It's the sobbing girl from the pillory. I scan the faces around her. They're all here. Dressed and healthy, though visibly nervous, several of them stealing frequent glances at the intersecting crescent moons marked on their hands.

"Their keepers were poisoned, and many of them have tainted blood. No one will take them in. Elisaf told them to come here until we can decide what to do with them," Zander says, answering my unasked question.

"We already know what to do with them." I offer the girl a small smile.

"Why do I suspect you have dug your heels in on this matter?"

"Because you're more than a good lay? And by lay, I mean you're good at—"

"I understand." He flashes an exasperated look, but the corners of his mouth curve.

Two legionaries linger nearby, waiting. It's obvious they want to speak to Zander.

"I will bring you something to eat." He ushers me in the other direction, where Gesine, Abarrane, Jarek, and Elisaf sit. "You can be angry with me if it makes you feel better, but do not take it out on Gesine. She had no choice."

"I thought we all have a choice," I mutter, heading for the table, my stomach tense at the sight of Jarek. The truth is, I'm not really angry with Zander. Annoyed, yes. But I think it's disappointment that overwhelms me. I'd convinced myself that this prophecy was true. I wanted it to be true.

But now I appreciate Zander's warnings about Mordain and casters, and the half-truths they deliver that may as well be blatant lies. If Gesine had told us from the beginning that I needed to open the nymphaeum door to end this blood curse, we might never have left Cirilea together.

"... not understand how two legionaries have utterly vanished from this town, and *no one* can tell us *anything*." Abarrane punctuates her anger by stabbing her sausage link with a fork. "It does not make sense."

"You beheaded the one with the answers. *That* did not make sense either." Jarek stirs a heaping spoonful of honey into a mug of tea. It seems so out of character for a warrior whose diet has consisted solely of roasted meat, apples, and young women up until now.

I bite my tongue against the urge to make a joke—Abarrane's liable to spear me for finding humor in anything—and take the seat at the end across from Gesine. "What about Isembert's servants? Do they know anything?"

"His tributaries, I found in a cellar like pigeons, wallowing in their filth, kept there so they could not poison themselves and kill him. If they knew something, they would have sung the moment I unlocked the door."

"What about a wife? Did he have one?"

"A wife and several mistresses. They welcomed his cock but not his secrets." She sneers. "Fools, all of them. Even *you* have more sense than that." She gets up and marches out the door.

"I *think* that was meant as a compliment?" I say to no one in particular.

Elisaf watches her go. "She would have handled this better had she found her men hanging from the gallows. It is this in-between she struggles with most."

"She doesn't like feeling helpless. None of us do." Jarek's focus drifts out the window. He hasn't made eye contact with me yet, which is not normal. He's usually thrown in at least one barbed insult by now.

Is Zander right and it's his pride over being kept in the dark that has him so angry? Just as *I* am unhappy with being kept in the dark about something that undoubtedly involves me?

Or is Jarek plotting to kill me in the name of Islor?

"Here. It looks mildly edible." Zander sets a bowl of oats in front of me.

"Thank you." This may be the first time the king of Islor has ever served me. "Has anyone seen Pan?"

"He was here, looking for you. Abarrane scared him away." Gesine adjusts her cloak to cover her gold collar before displaying a polite smile at the older couple who gawks from several tables over.

"Good. I was worried he might have run off after last night."

"He is not going anywhere. He knows the safest place is with us." Zander takes Abarrane's spot, plucking the sausage link off her abandoned plate.

"And what of the other mortals?" Elisaf asks.

"Perhaps we can convince the barkeep to take some in to work here for room and board. He seems decent."

"The barkeep whose servant did *that* to you?" I point to his neck.

"They will all be dead by the end of the week, along with the barkeep, if he attempts to help them," Jarek's tone is deadpan, factual. "Either by Isembert's replacement, the keepers who wait for our departure so they can cleanse their town, or Lyndel's army who will hunt them down when they sweep through. All you've done by marking them is set clear targets."

Zander sighs with resignation. "Would it have been wiser to leave them unmarked so more of our kind would die?"

"Do not ask me what I think would be *wise* because I doubt you will like the answer."

"You can't kill them. They haven't hurt anyone," I hiss. *Yet.*

A vein in Jarek's forehead throbs, but when he speaks, it's to Zander, as if I'm not here. "Even the most principled of these keepers will eventually realize that protecting these mortals is far more trouble than it's worth. All that was done to save them will be for naught the moment we turn our backs, and they will die with their pretty little marks on their hands. A mark that will become a symbol of certain death soon enough."

"He's right." And maybe he'll help convince Zander of my reasoning. "They don't have Atticus's protection, and fear is overshadowing compassion or reason. Look how easily Isembert strolled in here last night and took over. People like this barkeep mean well, but they won't burn their lives to the ground for these mortals. We *have* to bring them with us."

Jarek scowls. "*That* is not what I said."

"I don't hear you offering any other solutions."

"We already have enough mortals to protect. They likely won't survive in those caves," Elisaf says more gently.

"They *definitely* won't survive here, so give them a choice. Who knows? They might surprise you."

"*More* surprises?" Jarek spears me with a steely look. "I think I've had enough."

"Enough with the bickering. You two sound like children." Zander pinches the bridge of his nose. "Romeria, eat before it gets cold."

I dig into the gritty slop, pausing long enough to mumble, "He started it." *Now* I sound like a child.

Gesine pushes my bowl forward. "It will help restore your power faster."

My power is already returning, to my great relief. I intentionally left my ring off so I would feel when that persistent buzz returned. Ironic, really, that I was so quick to avoid feeling these affinities before, when I didn't know what to do with them. But when I woke this morning and sensed the emptiness, I felt as if I'd lost something vital.

"And where are we going again?" Jarek's eyes flicker to me. "Oh right, north, where there is a small army of *Ybarisans* waiting for us."

"We've discussed this already." Zander's voice is crisp. He may be expecting Jarek's unruliness, but that doesn't mean he welcomes it.

"And yet new, rather important details have emerged since."

"Your point, legionary?"

But I see his point. "He thinks I'm leading you into a trap."

"Is that so?" Zander rests his elbows on the table and levels Jarek with a challenging look.

The warrior matches it for three long beats before standing. "The commander has permitted me to stay behind and hunt for the trail to Drakon and Iago."

Zander's jaw tenses. "We need your skilled blade on the journey north."

"You seem to be well-equipped to defend yourself. I will rejoin once I find them."

Zander could defy Abarrane's order, but I know he'd rather not do it openly, not when things are so volatile already. "Good luck."

"Aye." Jarek takes off, as if he can't get away fast enough.

As much as he wants to find his fellow legionaries, something tells me this has as much to do with getting far away from me. That realization stirs a strange and unexpected frustration. As much as I hated Jarek at the start, he was growing on me. I felt safer with him around. Zander was safer with him around.

Now we're back to him wishing me dead.

Worse, a small, niggling prick in my conscience says I should have insisted we tell him everything. He has a right to feel betrayed.

Approaching boot steps announce Zorya seconds before she stops at our table. "Witch."

"Is something the matter?" Worry mars Gesine's face as she peers up at the warrior. "Is it Ianca?"

"Still alive. Babbling in another language. She sleeps more than a dormant nethertaur." Zorya shifts her one eye to Zander. "We have gathered them all outside, Your Highness."

"How many are there?"

"Many."

"Fates." Zander smooths a hand over his mouth as we take in the crowd of mortals standing in the square.

Young men and women.

Children.

There must be fifty total. The Legion circles, weapons drawn, but their blades aren't meant for them. The warriors are facing off against the indignant spectators watching from beyond, many armed with weapons of their own.

"Who are they?" I ask.

"Tributaries we found locked in cellars when we were looking for Iago and Drakon."

"There are children here." A rush of adrenaline stirs inside me. I focus on my breathing before my emotions take over.

"Yes. Their keepers insisted they were protecting them for the future, though we've heard claims that suggest otherwise." Zander glares at the immortals beyond the ring. They look like wolves, circling and eager to pick off prey. "They're declaring they have the right to protect themselves by *Isembert's* law."

"And Atticus's, too, I would wager," Elisaf mutters. "As soon as we leave, they'll tuck them back into their cages."

This is what Zander predicted would happen, and it's all because blood from this body I inhabit—*my* body now—is being dispersed in vials.

Jarek paces along a fence line, his sword casually twirling within his grasp. An arrogant taunt for those along the perimeter, or an itch to trade blows? Is it the kill he enjoys, or does he thrill in delivering harsh punishment to those who deserve it?

Either way, it has the desired effect. The keepers near him have shifted back.

"Those came on their own, Your Highness." Brynn points to a smaller group of sixteen mortals. Three families, by the look of it. "They are asking to receive their mark from the king."

"Have they all taken the poison?" Zander asks, looking to Gesine.

"I cannot know until I check each of them, but I imagine they have and are now responding to your offer."

I study a little girl hugging a stuffed animal to her chest, her mother with a protective hand on her shoulder. It reminds me of Gracen and her kids. "It won't matter if they haven't, now that they've come here." Their keepers will have them killed either way.

"Romeria is right. There is no going back for them now." Pity fills Gesine's face.

"They should have run. Now they may as well slip nooses around their children's necks." Zorya throws a casual hand toward the gallows. "Why would they be so stupid?"

Last night, all I could see—all I focused on—were the people within the contraptions and how to get them out. Now I see the elaborate construction of Norcaster's death square for what it is: a staging platform, the long, wooden beams that provide ample space for mortals to hang. More than functional—a performance to provoke fear.

One side has collapsed, splintered in the battle.

I did that.

I remember now.

A perfect blackened circle surrounds the pillories where I huddled with and protected the victims. I did that, too, with merely a thought, and then Zander and the legionaries defended them.

How long after we leave will one of these circling vultures name themselves the new Isembert and have those gallows repaired?

How long before more families swing from the ropes or die a slow death within their entrapment?

These people need us.

"They're not stupid. They're desperate. They want a chance for a new life, and they're hopeful a *king* can give it to them."

Cords of muscle in Zander's neck tense. "You've made your point, Romeria."

"Good. So you agree with me."

"You do not know what you are suggesting."

"I know how to survive, and these people won't survive without you." I think of the nobility standing in Cirilea's court, of touring the gardens as if all is right in the world, and it makes me shudder that they are the ones making the decisions for these people; they are tasked with solving problems. "Islor needs to start seeing what kind of king you are and what you stand for, not the lies Atticus is spreading. Look at all these people, Zander. *Really* look at them, and imagine where Islor will be in six months, a year, five years, when fear takes over like it's already taking over here."

His hazel eyes drift among the group of solemn faces, stalling on the children.

"If you believe in choice, then let these people choose to follow you while they still can."

Zander sighs. "You are right. You are always right."

"I know."

He makes a sound, not quite laughter. The mood is far too heavy for that. With a deep breath, he steps forward, holding up a hand for silence.

The crowd quiets instantly.

"I am Zander, the true king of Islor, and regardless of what you have heard, or what you will hear in the coming weeks and months, I have no wish to destroy Islor. In fact, I am desperately trying to save it." His baritone voice carries over the crowd, much like it did that fated day in the arena. "Most of you have likely heard about the poison that tears Islor apart from the inside out."

A few gazes dart to me. What must this look like, for those who know the truth of its source? We can't worry about that now, though.

"But there has been another poison flowing within Islor long before this one, and it has been seeping into our way of life for far too long. I have never hidden my vision for the future of the realm from the court. In fact, I have spoken about it at length, to the great discomfort of those who fear change. It is one reason I am standing here now instead of in Cirilea. But my vision holds true. I wish for an Islor where mortals and elven coexist as equals in peace, where there are no keepers, where mortals are not property, where there is prosperity for all."

A buzz swells over the crowd as gasps and whispers meld, from shock to hope to anger.

I watch the keepers closely as Zander's words sink in. Wives lean into husbands, and husbands lean into their wives, lips flapping with outrage. I can imagine the things they're saying.

It's impossible.

It's not right.

He means to kill us.

"It's a good thing you ain't the king no more, then!" a man shouts, and several others echo it. The noise stirs courage, and a small crowd moves in toward the male legionary blocking their passage.

He'll cut a handful down within a breath, but how many will eek through? How many more keepers will this show of bravery inspire? And how many innocent lives will be lost to collateral damage? It'll be a slaughter no matter what.

Panic swells inside me, and with it, a fiery heat, one I recognize from last night. On instinct, I reach deep within, and it surges. My affinities are becoming familiar, accessible. Like opening a cupboard door and finding my options waiting for me to grasp.

And what better time to test them.

With a steady gaze on the broken gallows, I reach for that strength, and in my mind's eye, see the wood burst in flames.

The blaze that ignites sends nearby spectators stumbling and scattering.

I shift my attention to the pillories next and torch them as well.

"Now you're showing off," Zander mutters.

"Jealous?"

The corner of his mouth twitches. "Yes."

"Do not burn yourself out needlessly," Gesine warns, but her lips wobble, like she's hiding a grin.

The memory of my knees buckling and stomach heaving last night makes me release my hold. The flames die instantly but continue eating away at the blackened wood. Soon it will be good for nothing but a bonfire.

My impulse served the desired effect. No one is threatening to attack anymore. Now they're all staring at me, even the legionaries who may have heard whispers of last night but didn't witness it. Surely they're all wondering what I am, with my glowing silver-white eyes.

But Zander pulls everyone's attention back quickly. "An army is on its way from Lyndel. I expect it will be brutal and merciless in its hunt for both the vials of poison and any tainted mortals. The Legion and I will not be here when it arrives, and any mortal who wishes to accompany us north is welcome. I cannot promise you an easy path, but I can promise it will not be one where you live in a cage and must die to be free."

The mortals shift on their feet, stealing wary glances at one another. I see their silent war waging inside, of doubt, of fear, of hope.

I've been there.

I again swallow my nerves and step forward. "I understand what it is like to feel alone and helpless. I know what it's like to be unsure if you're better off staying in the terrible situation you know, or leaping into another, possibly scarier one ahead." My voice carries through the eerily silent square. "But I can promise you, if you stay, they *will* put you back in the cages you were pulled from today, and you may never be free again because this poison won't disappear. It's already making its way deeper into Islor. It's reached as far as Salt Bay in the south and Hawkrest in the east. If you want to build a new life, come with us."

I look to one of the mothers, her arms curled protectively

around two young boys in front of her. "You will never have your children taken away from you again. You will never be forced to give what you don't want again." I feel Zander's eyes on my profile, but I keep trained on these people, who seem to be listening. "And you will have a king who fights for an Islor that values you for more than the blood coursing through your veins." On impulse, I reach out, weaving my fingers between his. "And *despite* the blood coursing through your veins."

At the tied hands of the Ybarisan daughter of Aoife and the Islorian son of Malachi.

I can hear Gesine chanting her prophecies inside my head.

Zander squeezes my hand before lifting it to his mouth. It's the first open gesture of affection since Cirilea. "If you choose to accompany us, your obligation to your keepers is over." Objections rise, but Zander raises his voice to speak over them. "You will be under my protection, and any who feel justified in interfering with the departure of those under my protection"—he swings his hard gaze toward the horde of sour-faced keepers—"will not see the sun set on this day. I promise you."

With that threat laid bare, he turns to Brynn. "Release those who would prefer to stay. We will not force anyone. But for those who wish to come, have two legionaries accompany them to their homes to collect whatever clothing and belongings may be useful on this trek. And should their keepers so much as utter a threat, show them the sharp end of your blade with haste. We don't have time to spare."

"With pleasure, Your Highness." She spins on her heel.

"Gesine, test that group and mark them as required." The demanding, calm king has returned.

She dips her head. "Your Highness."

"We will need more horses and wagons, more supplies." He searches the square as if taking stock of what is available.

"I'll bet Isembert has a few," I offer. "And I'd say he owes us after last night's stress."

"I've always despised pilfering, especially now that I'm taking their literal lifeblood with me."

"We are at war," Elisaf reminds him.

"Why does that not make me feel better about it?"

"Romy!" Pan's familiar chirpy voice from behind me lightens my mood.

Until I see his split lip and swollen right eye. "What happened to you?" Blood drips down his chin.

"A lot. So, funny story. I ran into Fearghal. Remember him from last night?" He gestures next to him.

So preoccupied with Pan's battered face, I hadn't noticed the man from Woodswich standing next to him. I offer a tight smile and get a gap-toothed grin in return.

"We got to talkin' about things. You know, Woodswich and the Ybarisans, and the poison. Oh, look what I found!" He pulls a small glass vial from his pocket.

Zander, who was listening with a hint of a smirk, now sticks his hand out, all amusement gone. "Give it here."

Pan drops it into his palm. "It's like the one Colgan had."

Zander holds it up into the daylight. "And the one we found on your lady maid, Romeria."

"It's tiny."

"Yes, now you can appreciate how easily it can be hidden. Pan, how did you come across this?"

"It wasn't too hard, not with the coins Romy gave me." Pan wipes away the blood from his chin. His gloves are off and the mark on his hand glows.

"But what happened to your face?" I press.

"Oh, right. So, I was tellin' Fearghal how you're the Ybarisan princess, but you're not evil. You're the nicest person I've ever met, and you saved me from Oswald stickin' me with his dagger—"

"You have to speed it up, Pan." The square is controlled chaos with tributaries being ushered into the tavern. Now is not the time for a lengthy tale.

"Yeah, okay. I told him how I came here with you to look for the two legionaries who went missing and how no one's been able to find so much as a hair. And then Fearghal said he had a gut feeling and that maybe we should go and talk to that *other guy* from last night. So we looked around until we found him and asked some questions he didn't want to answer. That's how I earned this"—he points to his injured face—"but we got it out of him."

"Got *what* out of him?"

"Where the scouts went."

Zander's focus shifts from the vial to the toothless mortal. "You know where they are?"

"Aye. Sort of." Fearghal shrugs. "They're on their way to the saplings."

36
ROMERIA

All I can think about as Abarrane crouches in front of the man, her face inches from his, is how foul his breath must be after a night of drinking and sleeping, given how rancid it was when he propositioned me last night.

Pan and Fearghal rooted him out in this animal stable, surrounded by musty hay and horseshit, sleeping off the copious ale. Even half unconscious and hungover, he came up swinging, delivering several solid blows before Fearghal pinned him down and Pan hog-tied him.

This must be where he was thinking of squeezing me in for his little "give-and-take" deal. The thought stirs the urge to lose my porridge.

"Where would they be by now?" Abarrane hisses.

"I dunno."

"Wrong answer." The tip of her dagger digs into his chin, blood welling where the skin splits.

He grimaces. "I saw 'em leavin' before dawn yesterday with a wagon and other supplies to take north. That's at least a day of traveling? They probably would have handed off their cargo by now."

"Where?"

"Hard to say. There's a couple different meet spots. The saplings watch for signals. They always find 'em."

"Flann here's been on those runs before, so he knows at least one of those meet spots."

The man glares at Fearghal. "What are ya doin'? Shut your big mouth!"

"How many mortals are transporting them?" Zander asks.

With another sneer at his bar mate, Flann says, "Three, likely. I ran into two of 'em in town the other day, but they usually travel in threes. Any time Isembert's got one of yous from down south to get rid of, he calls them. If you're missing people, he's behind this."

"Unfortunately, corpses don't speak. If you do not want to become one, you better keep telling us what we want to know." Abarrane releases her grip on his hair and stands. "So Isembert sends immortal travelers to the saplings, and in return, the saplings leave Norcaster alone. Clever. How long has he been conspiring with them?"

Zander's nostrils flare. "For as long as elven have been going missing in these parts, I would wager. It's how he's remained in power for so long."

Holding power by sacrificing his own kind. Except he didn't see them as his own kind. They were from the south and bowed to the king. Enemies, as far as he was concerned.

"This does not make sense." Jarek shakes his head. "I've seen Drakon fight a nethertaur on his own. How would three mortals best him?"

"Maybe your guys had too much mead."

Abarrane grabs a fistful of Flann's hair again, wrenching his head back. "They could drown in a vat of it, and they would still fight off your friends."

"Dunno what to tell ya, then. Maybe they had help," Flann manages through a pained wince. "I heard 'em talkin' about the Ybarisans once."

"That makes even less sense." She shoves his face into the dirt.

He's throwing out any bit of information he can, hoping for a reprieve from Abarrane's abuse.

I have questions, and so far Fearghal has been the gold mine I'd pegged him for. "How many Ybarisans are left up there?"

He scratches his chin. "Hard to say. No one's gone lookin' for exactly where they are, and they mostly keep to themselves, but from what I've heard, I'd guess at least two hundred."

I share a look with Zander. He's thinking the same. Two hundred elven soldiers. That could either be a huge aid or a huge problem, depending on how willing they are to abandon their previous orders and follow new ones. "And how many vials of this poison?"

"Dunno." Fearghal hesitates. "But most from Woodswich have taken it. Includin' Flann here."

"You bastard—"

Abarrane kicks the hog-tied man in the gut, earning a grunt.

I don't feel sorry for him, though. He was trying to lure me in to kill me.

"I questioned you both last night, and you had nothing to say. Why the change of heart?" Abarrane's attention has swung to Fearghal, her hand on the hilt of her dagger.

"Aye. I wasn't too eager to get involved with any of yous. You're a vicious lot," he admits. "But Pan's my kind, and he swears on his life by her"—he looks at me—"and she saved a lot of lives. People who didn't deserve to be in pillories. I don't like seein' my kind hang or be kept in cages 'cause they want to live like I do. That's not right." He looks to Zander. "And if you spoke truth back there, it seems like you don't think so neither. We need a king like you for change."

Zander's chin drops, his focus diverted to the barn floor. I know what he's thinking. They *had* a king like him, but he never had a chance, not the second Princess Romeria crossed the rift.

"We've likely gotten all we will from this lout. I will follow the road north to see if I can find any clues." Jarek makes to move.

"No." The single word from Zander's mouth freezes him. "I

need every warrior. *These people* need every warrior. And we do not know what we're facing. If you go out alone, you could end up shackled like the others."

Jarek looks to Abarrane. For a different answer? For an argument?

Her face is unreadable. "As the king orders."

After a lengthy pause, Jarek offers a curt "Commander," and then strolls out, his posture stiff.

Abarrane's sharp gaze drags over Flann, as if considering how she'd like to carve him up. "At least we know where to look now."

"Thanks to Pan," I remind her. Maybe she'll stop threatening the poor guy now.

"I figured I'd help in whatever way I can," he chirps.

"You *did* help, in a big way." I smile. "Why don't you go ask Gesine to heal you?"

His mouth falls open. "You think she can do that?"

I chuckle, remembering the arrow embedded between Zorya's ribs. "Yes, Pan. She can fix a black eye." Then again, I would be wise to remember that it wasn't too long ago I was in awe of Wendeline as she erased my cuts and bruises.

Zander's rapt focus is on Fearghal. He's searching for any signs of deception. "You two were at the tavern together. How did you know he would have information about our scouts?"

Fearghal's gaze narrows on the hamstrung lout. "Aye, we're both from Woodswich, and we've traveled together the odd time, but we're not the same, Flann and me. I don't look for opportunities like he does. But I keep my ears open enough that I know he's made friends in bad places."

I know what Fearghal means. Opportunities that might benefit him, even if it involves stealing, raping, killing. People who look for opportunities like that tend to befriend others of the same ilk. Korsakov made it a point to know every unsavory human within a fifty-mile radius.

"If you wouldn't be mindin', I'd like to travel back north with yous," Fearghal says. "Somethin' tells me I don't want to be a mortal in Norcaster in the comin' days."

After a moment, Zander nods.

"What do you want me to do with this sack?" Abarrane hoofs Flann with her toe.

"Keep him tied up. We still need him."

"You know he tried to get me to feed from him, back when he thought I was one of you. He's going out of his way to bait and kill Islorian immortals."

Zander's teeth clench. "Have Gesine mark his forehead."

The sun is high when our company is ready to leave Norcaster.

"Make sure the path is clear."

"Aye, Your Highness." Abarrane swings herself onto her horse and moves for the gate.

Zander observes the growing collection of wagons and horses. "How many in total?"

"Eighty-six new mortals. Twelve children," Elisaf confirms. Of the fifty mortals found in cellars, forty-two are leaving with us. The other eight decided they could not abandon their keepers or were too afraid of what lay ahead. They vanished quickly. No one is likely to see them again. The rest are made up of those who came for a mark and those who heard Zander's offer of protection and abandoned their keepers.

Eighty-six new mortals, on top of those from Bellcross, and only seventeen legionaries left. The ratio is far from ideal, but I set my chin with determination. We're doing the right thing.

Zander worries his lip. "Do we have enough food? Skins? Clothing?"

"We gathered what we could. Emptied Isembert's coffers."

"I do not enjoy pilfering," he mutters, and Elisaf and I share a look. It's the third time he's said those exact words this morning.

"You don't think Lyndel's army will clean them out when they come through? We may as well get first dibs," I say, trying to ease his conscience.

"I do not know what these *first dibs* are, but I'm sure you are right. As usual."

"Do not fill her head with that," Elisaf teases, earning my gentle elbow.

With a soft chuckle, Zander's eyes drift behind me. "What did you mark these mortals with, High Priestess? They all bear the crescent emblem, but some do not glow."

I turn to find Gesine approaching.

"Yes, Your Highness. I thought it would be wise to ease my workload and lessen the risk that one of them may be tainted without their knowledge, so I improvised. Should any of them become contaminated in the future, the mark will illuminate."

"Clever."

"I thought so." She smiles, though it's tight. "Romeria, Ianca has asked to speak with you."

"Me? Really?" She's never seemed lucid enough to beckon me.

"To be more precise, to Other Romeria. You must ride in the wagon with us." She heads back to it, assuming I'll follow.

Eros is already saddled and standing beside Zander's horse. I was looking forward to riding out of this fucking hellscape and into the scenic mountains next to him.

"Go. Switch out at our first rest. It is for the best, in case someone is foolish enough to aim an arrow." Zander skims the milling spectators. Only two keepers attempted to stop their caged tributaries from leaving with us. Their spouses are likely preparing burial spots right now.

"As long as you don't take off to find these saplings without me, or something else equally dumb."

"I think I've learned my lesson in that regard." Zander leans down to press his lips against mine. It's a tender kiss, and yet desire for so much more flares in the pit of my stomach. "Later," he whispers, capping it off with a peck against my nose before shifting away. "For now, see Ianca."

I weave through the wagons already loaded with the women and children. Other mortals have found horses to ride. Some are on foot, shifting nervously as they steal glances around, as if expecting to be yanked from the line.

All offer me bows as I pass.

And all the legionaries seem intent on avoiding eye contact. They don't acknowledge me. I want to think it's because their attention is rapt on the external threat, but this gut feeling says otherwise. Is it by their own volition or inspired by Jarek's bitterness?

"Your Highness!" Eden scurries up to me, her arms loaded with a heap of clothing. "Pan told me about last night."

What did he tell her, I wonder, because Zander warned him to keep what he saw to himself. People will find out, but we don't need to broadcast it, especially when I'm still far too inexperienced to defend myself.

"How are you, Eden?" I haven't seen her since Jarek led her into that tent.

She lifts her arms. "I have things to mend to keep me busy."

I hesitate. "And how was last night with Jarek?"

"Oh." She flushes. "Fine."

"Did you … did he …" How do I ask? Do I have a right to ask? Is it any of my business?

Eden clues in to my meaning and shakes her head. "No, we talked. That's all."

My eyebrows arch. "*Talked*?" Jarek talked? "About what? How to kill people?"

"No!" She giggles as if I'm joking. "About our childhoods, our parents."

"*Really*?" Jarek had a willing and beautiful mortal in a tent and told tales of dear mommy and daddy? "I can't see it."

As if his ears were burning, the warrior and his white stallion trot toward us.

Eden smiles at him as he approaches. "I told you he can be sweet."

His horse is heading straight for me, forcing me to step back or risk getting run over. I tell myself it's coincidence, but Jarek's half turn to check over his shoulder, to see us in his peripherals, tells me he knew what he was doing. "Yeah, I see what you mean."

"Ready!" he hollers, his intense focus swinging to those still lingering in the square, watching the spectacle, probably holding their breaths until we're gone. The legionaries mount their horses and shift to form a perimeter around our expansive caravan, their swords drawn and senses vigilant.

"I should go. Do you need anything?"

"No. See you at the first rest."

Pan is already perched next to Bregen in the driver's seat, and his new best friend Fearghal sits on a horse. I assume he'll be riding alongside us for the journey.

"Is it true you got a seer and a caster in there?" Fearghal's eyes are wide with genuine awe.

"Maybe." I still don't trust the Woodswich mortal—as much as I'm beginning to like him—but I smile like I do. If he is planning on trying something, it's better if he drops his guard first.

Climbing back into the wagon, the air stale and pungent, feels like a punishment after being out of it for so long. But when I see Ianca, lying beneath the furs, the skin hanging off her face as if there's nothing for it to cling to anymore, I understand why I've been summoned.

Gesine nods, confirming it.

Ianca's time in this world is almost over, and they both know it.

The seer's vacant, clouded eyes stare at the wagon's ceiling. "Come closer, child."

With caution—I never know what to expect—I edge in and sit on the bench across from her.

"You can hear them, can't you?"

"Who?"

"The nymphs."

I assume she's talking about the Islorian immortals. "I can."

"They await your arrival."

"My arrival where?"

But she doesn't answer, working her mouth as if struggling to pull words.

"Ianca, here is water." Gesine moves in with a mug, reaching to tilt her head.

But Ianca waves her off. "Islor must fall before it can rise, and the queen of two moons shall reign as none other before her."

Queen of two moons? "Do you mean of Islor?" Or Ybaris? Or *all* of it?

"You must bleed for them to bow. That is the only way."

I frown at Gesine, but she shakes her head.

"You should have let the warrior slit my throat while I was sleeping. She wanted to do it, you know." Ianca shuts her eyes.

"Zorya?" Gesine flinches. "Fates, no. You know I would never allow that."

"There are no fates where I am going, but I will know silence again soon enough."

Another shout sounds outside, and then our wagon jerks forward.

Ianca begins rambling in another language.

"What is she saying now?"

Gesine shakes her head. "It is not a language she or I know."

And yet Ianca seems to be speaking it fluently. Finally, her thin, parched lips still and she falls quiet, and I assume she has drifted off through all the dips and bumps along the pockmarked road.

Or worse.

I hesitate. "Is she ..."

"Not yet. I can still sense whatever dribs of her life remain." Gesine blinks back tears. "But it wavers now, fading fast."

I study the sleeping seer. "What did she used to look like?"

That question brings a sad smile to Gesine's lips. "Hair like spun gold and eyes like the water of the Endless Sea—dark and blue and bottomless. Beautiful. But it was her humor that I loved most. A kind humor, never at the expense of others." She wipes away a tear. "It is unfathomable how quickly this happened."

"How long were you two together?"

"We were friends first. And then we were relegated to the same room. Ianca used to keep me up half the night talking. It was not until a few years later that we became *more*. We made a silly pact to go through the change together, though that is beyond our control. I knew I would have to watch her go through this alone."

How painful that must be.

And how terrifying, witnessing the grim details of what's yet in store for her.

A lump swells in my throat with the thought that I will lose Gesine to this change one day, too, and that day may not be far from now. Even if I don't wholly trust the caster, I like her, and I've come to rely on her as more than a teacher. She's become a friend and confidante.

"What do you think she meant, what she said about me bleeding for them to bow? Who is going to bow? The Islorians? The Ybarisans?"

"I do not know, but I hope it becomes clear soon. I need *something* to become clear soon. This cannot all be for naught …" Gesine's voice trails, her brow pinching. "I think … she may be—"

Ianca starts with a gasp, her hand flying out to grasp my wrist with surprising strength. "Ulysede," she whispers, and then, just as quickly, her grip slackens, her hand falling to hang limp.

Gesine dips her head and whispers something I can't make out and then louder, declares, "*Now* she is gone."

"I'm *so* sorry."

With silent tears flowing freely down her cheeks, she draws a wool blanket over Ianca's face. "She is at peace, and we do not have time for sorrow." Taking a deep breath, she steels her jaw and lifts her hand in the air, palm up. A ball of water appears. "You must practice now, so you are ready for whatever is to come."

37
ROMERIA

The wagon stops as I'm marveling at the flame dancing along my fingers, skipping from one tip to the next.

Marveling, while trying to shed the disquiet of having a corpse nearby.

We've been at this for hours, Gesine helping coax my caster affinities out of hiding as they seem to do when I'm not under direct threat. We've had some success, at least with my link to Malachi. I have yet to find so much as a drop of water. What that means, I can't imagine. Gesine swears the fates can't cut anyone off from the affinities they're born with.

But I've tried my hardest to keep her mind busy on training me, and in return she has kept her composure with surprising skill.

The tiny window behind the driver's bench slides open, and Pan's face pokes in. His mouth hangs open. "How're you doin' that?"

"Magic." I grin. "Why are we stopped?"

"There's a town up ahead. The king wants you both up front with him."

"Why?"

"Dunno, but there's a lot of smoke."

Gesine and I share a look.

"That sounds like trouble." But why would Zander want me in the thick of it, then?

"Trouble, yes. But also fresh air."

We climb out of the wagon, Gesine on my heels, as eager to escape our little box as I am.

I shudder against the chill as I survey our new surroundings. We're in a dense swath of lofty trees a hundred—maybe more—feet tall. While I know those formidable mountains have embraced us into their fold by now, the view of them is blocked.

"I believe they call them Blackwoods." Gesine's eyes follow mine, taking in the sturdy ashen-colored trunks and evergreen canopies that allow in only dappled light. Their roots crawl along the ground, creating gnarly bulges that no wagon could pass over. The path we're on must have been carved out over the centuries.

Our long convoy has stalled, curious heads poking out of wagons while the legionaries' acute concentration remains outward, on every twig snap and animal call.

A mortal girl of no more than five peeks out from a gap within the wagon boards. I wink at her, hoping the simple act offers some reassurance when I have no idea why we're stopped. It must have something to do with the fifteen-foot wooden wall ahead, blocking our passage. Beyond it, multiple streams of smoke curl into the sky.

"That's Kamstead, the last of what they call *civilized* villages before things get *real* wild." From atop his horse, Fearghal escorts us to the front of the line where Zander waits, holding Eros's reins for me.

"What's going on?" I collect them, and despite the somber mood, my stomach flutters as Zander slides his thumb across my palm. The simple touch feels like a reminder of this morning and a promise for later.

"I do not know yet, but that is far too much smoke for simply expelling a draft."

I hoist myself into my saddle.

"Thank you." Gesine settles onto the back of Elisaf's horse. In the daylight, there is no hiding the sorrow wilting her features.

Zander looks to me, his unspoken question hanging in the air, and I offer a subtle nod.

His shoulders sink. "I am sorry for your loss, High Priestess."

She swallows hard, her eyes watering. "What do we know of this village?"

Zander looks to Fearghal.

"Like I was sayin', it's called Kamstead. Maybe sixty livin' there. Used to be all mortals, but then Isembert decided he wanted his kind here to collect a tithe on the trade that comes through. It's the one main road between north and south. Rumor has it Isembert promised 'em he had a deal to protect 'em from the saplin's and that they'd get a cut of the coin."

It's not so much rumor as fact. "What are these elven like? Anything like Isembert?" Self-proclaimed lords who don't deserve the stations they've climbed to?

He shrugs. "Maybe fifteen of 'em. I don't care much for any of 'em for what they are, but the times I've been here, the lot seemed reasonable enough. None of 'em like anyone from the south, but that's most of the north. The village is built around the road, and they control passage through either side with their gates. Sometimes they can be thorny about who they let through." He peers over his shoulder at the long line of mortals and legionaries. "Not sure they'll take kindly to this."

"Would they have let the Ybarisans through?" I ask.

"Aye. The wall ain't *that* strong. When a line of soldiers shows up, you open the gate."

Zander studies the wooden barrier. Four archers watch from the ramparts. A minute ago, there was only one. "Are they fighters?"

"You won't see 'em throwing down their swords in easy surrender, that's for sure. They've been gettin' some saplin's lately, from what I heard last time I came through, even with Isembert's deal."

A deal that I hope the next leader of Norcaster doesn't honor.

"Is there a way around the village?" Elisaf asks.

"I mean, you could squeeze a horse through the thicket, but not one of those." He points toward the line of wagons.

Zander's lips press together. "Then we will go through. A shield, if you will?"

"Your Highness." Gesine's eyes flare with a vibrant emerald luster.

"Fearghal, you know these people?"

"Aye, one or two."

"Then you come with us." He nods toward our small group of five.

Abarrane leads us toward the wall, her sword still tucked in its sheath.

I inhale, and my nose curls. "What is that?" A pungent stench of smoldering, wet wood and something else—vaguely like beef or pork, only sweeter and yet with a metallic component.

"Burning flesh," Elisaf answers.

My stomach drops. No wonder Zander seems so apprehensive.

We're twenty feet away when a man with an arrow aimed at Zander yells, "Who are you?"

"I am the king of Islor. Lower your weapons."

He falters before stiffening again. "There ain't no king in these parts."

"And yet here I stand."

"Not as easy as it was in Freywich," Elisaf murmurs under his breath.

"Lower your weapons and open the gate." Zander sounds bored and unbothered, but I know better than to believe the act.

The soldier lets his arrow fly in response. It sails toward us, only to bounce off thin air and drop to the ground.

The archers exchange bewildered looks.

"Perhaps you can reason with them?" Zander looks to Fearghal.

Fearghal nods and then bellows, "Elsten, you in there?"

No one answers.

"Elsten, if you're in there, open the gate! They just wanna pass through. They're not gonna cause you no trouble, but I promise, you don't wanna pick a fight with this lot."

After a long pause, a man yells, "Go around!"

Fearghal snorts. "There *ain't* no goin' around! We got wagons!"

"They are hiding something they do not wish us to see." That sharp edge in Zander's voice creeps in. "Open the gate, or we will open it for you."

The archers don't move.

"Why must people test my patience today?" Zander turns to me. "Remember how you took down that cave?"

"Yeah?" How could I forget?

"Can you do the same thing now, to that?" He gestures toward the thick timbers, bound and braced with cord and pegs and sturdy crossbeams.

"I can try." My well of elemental power is flowing again, waiting to be unleashed. This is why he wanted me up here. "But we don't know what's waiting for us on the other side."

"I will take care of that. You focus on that gate."

"Right." There's fire beyond, and where there's fire, he has his affinity.

Taking a deep breath, I reach for the thread that brings forth air.

But it doesn't answer my call.

"Remember who you are protecting, Romeria." Gesine's glowing gaze is on the archers who shift nervously. "These people behind us. The little girl in the wagon. The king. If you do not take that gate down, they will sit in these deep woods until nightfall and nothing good can come of it. They will *not* be safe. At this moment, that gate is the *only* thing keeping them from safety. It *must* come down."

I know what she's doing—drawing out these instincts she

claims drive my ability to channel more easily—and it's working. Her words stir my anxiety.

I reach for that thread again. This time it unspools and lengthens, the energy radiating until it surges to my fingertips, my body vibrating. I throw my hand out, and the force of the affinity launches forward.

The gate explodes as if hit by a wrecking ball, sending archers flying and logs scattering like twigs in the wind.

A thrill swirls inside me, even as I pray I haven't caused anyone irreparable harm.

Abarrane and Elisaf draw their swords, bracing for the potential rush of villagers.

But no one charges out.

"Jarek! Zorya!" Abarrane hollers.

Two sets of hooves pound on the dirt road as the legionaries close in.

"You and Gesine, stay on your horses no matter what. Gesine, protect her," Zander warns.

We move in past the destroyed wall, the village eerily quiet other than a few coughs from the shadows.

"Fates," Elijah whispers. "What happened here?"

"A massacre." Zander hops off his horse. The others, save for Gesine and me, follow.

Grimy faces peep from small windows of tiny huts. Women and children, mainly, while the men stand at the doors, brandishing rusty swords and daggers as if to declare they will fight to the death for those inside.

And along the street in front of us, piles of bodies are heaped over stacks of wood, burning.

I press my cloak against my nose to cover the stench of charred flesh, my stomach roiling, threatening to spill.

Abarrane walks a slow circle around one of the bonfires, the tip of her blade dragging through the dirt. "Who are they?" she asks no one in particular.

Silence answers, the villagers' anxious gazes shifting, some stalling on Gesine and the gold that peeks out beneath her cloak. Even up here in the remotest part of Islor, at least a few must have heard the fabled tales of the collared casters.

Fearghal crouches for a closer look at one of the faces piled on the bonfire, not yet scorched. The head isn't attached to a body. "I reco'nize him. That's Corbett. He was a leader, you might say." He scans the other piles. "That's another one. Looks like all the elven are dead."

The villagers killed the immortals … It dawns on me. Of course. "They poisoned them all."

"And now they're burning the evidence in the center of their village." Abarrane snorts. "Imbeciles."

The men near her adjust their grips on their swords as if anticipating she'll pounce on them any second.

"Now we know what they were hiding," Zander mutters.

There's no way these villagers would have heard that Isembert is dead and therefore not likely to come here and punish them.

Fearghal looks to a brawny man gripping a mace with two hands. "What did ya do, Elsten?"

The man—Elsten—sets his jaw. "What we needed to do. What the Ybarisans told us to do."

Zander moves in, making them adjust their stances. "And what did they tell you to do?"

Elsten stiffens his posture. "When the elven bastards start screamin', cut their throats to dull the sound until they bleed out or the poison finishes 'em off."

"You did all this in one night?" I cringe at the gruesome piles. Fearghal had said there were fifteen elven here, out of sixty villagers. Many of these men wear soiled bandages on their arms and legs, across their foreheads. They must have battled. Not all the elven died so easily.

His face is stony as he considers me, like he's deciding if he wants to answer. "They fed on us *every* night. We'd had enough."

"This type of killing would have taken planning, coordination." Jarek's footfalls are slow, measured, and ominous as he paces.

"They been trading our kids to the saplin's!" a woman cries out from the shadows.

"Is that true?" Zander asks, his eyes on Elsten.

The mortal swallows hard. "The saplings never bothered us before, but lately, they been showing up, demanding a vein. Corbett didn't like bein' someone's regular meal, so he pulled a few of our children out of bed one night, turned 'em into your kind, and handed 'em over to the saplings to buy them a few months. Gave 'em something to live off in whatever hole they crawl into durin' the day. Doubt they're still alive."

Zander curses. "And what did the other keepers do about this?"

"A few o' them were angry with Corbett, but in the end, they didn't do nothing, didn't punish him at all. Said that's the way things are, livin' up here. That's our risk. Not theirs. *Ours*. So when the Ybarisans showed up with those little glass bottles and told us the keepers would never be able to do that again if we listened to 'em … we listened."

Of course they did.

I would have too.

Zander absorbs this as he studies the burning corpses. "How many Ybarisans have come through here?"

"The whole lot of them at first, when they were headin' north with their supplies. But then a few would come south, and the keepers started shutting the gates on 'em. Didn't like 'em coming through."

"And what was your arrangement with them?" Zander uses a conversational tone rather than accusatory, the usual cold edge when he's questioning those who have wronged him absent. It's smart; we need information.

Still, the man balks.

"We'll get the answers from you one way or another, so you

may as well tell him what he wants to know." Jarek weaves through the men, towering over them.

Another speaks up, a wiry man with a scruffy face. "We helped 'em get those vials out."

"How?"

"We'd meet 'em in the eastern woods, past the summer crops. They would give us the vials, and we would take 'em with us on our trade routes. Find others who were sick of Islor's ways to pass 'em along to."

"And where have those trade routes led since the Ybarisans arrived?"

"*Everywhere*. Bellcross, Lyndel, Cirilea ..."

I think of that massive ten-day fair, all those people from all over Islor, coming in to sell their keepers' wares.

The poison was already all around us.

And now it must be making its way across Islor, tucked into wagons and pockets as disgruntled mortals head home.

"How many of those vials has this village moved?" Zander's voice has turned gruff. He must have come to the same conclusion.

The man scratches his head. "I don't think anyone ever kept count. A lot. Hundreds? Maybe more?"

Not enough to pollute every mortal's blood, but enough to cause hysteria.

"What other instructions did they give you?" Zander asks.

"They told us to wait until Hudem to take the drops."

"But you didn't."

"Nah. Like Elsten said, we'd had enough."

"I'd bet all my chickens in my coop that Flann was helpin' move some of it. He's back and forth all the time, cartin' skins and the like. And those fellas that got your men would have no trouble collectin' coin from Isembert in one hand while passin' out this poison to stick it to the elven usin' the other. There's a lot of folks comin' in and out for trade this time of year." Fearghal shakes his head at these villagers. "So, you got your dream of bein' a real Woodswich now, huh? Except it's through cold-blooded murder!"

I can't tell if Fearghal is going along with our way of thinking, or if he honestly finds what these mortals have done appalling.

Elsten sets his jaw. "None of them did anything to stop Corbett. You think they wouldn't do the same if it came to them or us for those saplin's?"

To that, Fearghal can only shrug. He knows as well as I do that Elsten has a point.

"What is your judgment, Your Highness?" Jarek asks, nodding to the sky. The sun is hinting at its descent.

Zander studies it for a long moment. "The village will open the northern gate and allow our company to pass without interference. If *any* so much as raises a sword, I will burn every inch of this village, with everyone in it." The bonfires flare to three times their height to emphasize his point.

Gasps sound and the villagers back away. They have no idea what their king is capable of.

Zander mounts his horse. "Should the Ybarisans come this way again, let them know their princess is in the north and looking for them."

Ten minutes later, the last legionary is passing the northern gates behind our wagons, and Eros canters alongside Zander's black stallion, our pace separating us from the others by a few horse lengths.

Zander's mood is as dark as a brewing storm.

"What made you let them go?" I ask gently.

Zander falters, as if searching for a suitable answer. "I fear Islor's entire fabric is unraveling before our eyes. I cannot see anymore where the line is between right and wrong. If we unleash harsh punishment upon the keepers for their abusive ways, should we not also deliver it to those mortals who plan and enact nothing short of murder?"

"Which would be those people back there."

"Yes. Passing judgment and conviction should be easy in this case, and yet I find my blade heavy and my words lost. These mortals felt desperate and betrayed by the rule of Islor. By *me*, for allowing this to happen to their children, to their kin. The crown has abandoned them for the past hundred years, permitting those like Danthrin and Isembert to gain power and influence. And while not all these immortals were outright cruel to them, it only takes some to breed this kind of hatred. In the mortals' eyes, I am their enemy, and the Ybarisans, their saviors."

He shakes his head. "These people see only what surrounds them in this tiny town in this mountain range. It's all that matters. It is their whole world. They cannot see the cascading effect of their actions toward the cataclysmic ruin of Islor."

"It doesn't make it okay."

"No, it does not. But this wildfire of anger and loathing will burn to every corner as my kind reacts from fear and inflicts more pain, cruelty, and injustice. I fear it is too late already. Too late to do anything to stop the momentum of what is to come." His shoulders sag. "Regardless, I have a caravan of mortals who have not yet committed murder, and I do not feel like adding to the massacre today. Nor do I have time, if we are to get to a safe place before nightfall.

"But Kamstead will not escape punishment. This village, and all others around here, will have an army passing through soon enough, and when the soldiers go to feed and begin to scream, what do you think that army will do?"

"They'll slaughter them all." It won't be worth keeping them alive.

Zander's expression is grim. "One way or another, these mortals will pay their dues. But we cannot lose our focus."

"What that guy back there said about waiting until Hudem… why would the Ybarisans tell them to do that?"

"Because it is customary on Hudem that *all* immortals feed. Hiding the poison until then is the wiser plan."

"It gives them more time to disperse it through the trade channels without raising alarms." I see what he means.

"It is fortunate, in a way, that some mortals have not waited. But who is to say how many *are*? The next Hudem may see far more murders than the last."

Something Ianca said the first day we met in Bellcross stirs in my mind then.

When the second moon falls asleep and the sun awakes, all will suffer for what they have done.

Could that be what she meant? Was she seeing the aftermath of a massacre?

I've never seen Zander this crestfallen yet. My heart feels like a lead weight, watching it. "Stop for a second?"

He slows his horse to a standstill.

"Halt!" a legionary yells, and a cacophony of creaks sound as the long line of wagons stalls behind us.

I hop off Eros, leaving his reins dangling for someone to collect. I don't care who.

Zander watches as I use the stirrups to hoist myself into his saddle behind him.

I mold my body flush against his and curl my arms around his torso.

He half turns, peering at me over his shoulder, our faces inches apart. "It has been awhile."

Since the morning after we ran from Cirilea, heading to Gully's Pass, to be exact.

"I thought you preferred riding alone?"

"Not today," I whisper, my hands smoothing over his chest, both for distraction and for comfort. "We'll figure it out together, I promise."

His brow pinches. "Fearghal? How far to that clearing?"

"About ten leagues." The mortal squints up at the sky through the looming trees. "We should just make it."

"We're a bit out in the open here, aren't we?" We emerged from the thicket of trees and into this expanse of sparse grass and boulders as the sun was scraping across the western mountain ridge. The legionaries and mortals moved quickly to build a suitable camp before darkness fell, erecting tents inside the circle of wagons and stacking piles of foraged wood as tall as me at the four corners of our campground. To mark a perimeter, Elisaf explained, for the creatures deterred by fire.

When I asked him which creatures he meant, he quickly found a task that needed urgent completion.

"That is the intention." Zander studies the landscape alongside me. The surrounding wall of forest is at least half a mile in every direction, and beyond, jagged mountains loom, no longer a distant view. "We expect to attract attention tonight. This way, we will see them coming from any angle."

"The saplings?"

"This is where Flann said they met them once."

"Why do I feel like bait?"

"They have no use for you. But we are bait no matter where we go. At least this way, we control the situation."

I inhale deeply. The air here is thinner, suggesting a higher altitude, and it reminds me of an approaching winter—cool and dry. Sleeping outside tonight isn't appealing, but I doubt anyone will sleep. "I hate this."

"So do I, but we have little choice if we want to find Drakon and Iago alive." His gaze drifts over my outfit. "There are warmer clothes in the supplies Theon sent us. You should find some."

"I will." People began pulling on layers as we moved farther into Venhorn's wild landscape. Now, many don fur vests. With the sun behind the mountain walls, the temperature drops degrees by the minute.

Beyond the invisible border of our camp, near a crop of stones, two mortals gently lower Ianca's wrapped body into a hole. Gesine stands nearby, her head bowed as if in prayer. "I should pay my respects."

"I will join you shortly. We must start these fires."

"Need a spark?" I hold up a finger, and a small flame appears on its tip. It has become so easy to beckon on a whim, now that I know what to look for inside. "I'm like a Zippo."

"You say strange things." Zander leans in to press a close-mouthed kiss against my lips. His dark mood hasn't lifted, and I know he's still dwelling on the horrors of Kamstead and the doom it may foreshadow for Islor.

While I can't fix that dilemma, I can offer him a temporary distraction. "I can *do* strange things too"—I nip his bottom lip—"if you're nice to me later."

The corner of his mouth curves. "That is intriguing."

I feel the tiniest tug on my affinity.

All four pits ignite.

Darkness has arrived as Gesine and I walk back from Ianca's grave toward the raging firepits, no doubt visible from any point in this basin. Gesine is still solemn, but her aura is lighter—more settled—than earlier in the day.

"Zander told me about Stonekeep."

"He did?" She hums softly. "And what did he tell you? Allow me to guess. He said it was complete folly and we will find nothing there but disappointment?"

"Something like that, yeah."

"An Islorian king who has no use for prophecy. I suppose that shouldn't surprise me." A tiny, knowing smile touches her lips. "He is rather stubborn in that regard, but that will soon change."

"You really believe there's something there that will help Islor?"

Her green eyes flash. "Help? No. I believe there is something there that will *save* Islor."

"Ybarisan!" Abarrane hollers, marching across the camp, a lengthy wooden stick in each hand.

I curse under my breath. The last thing I'm in the mood for is her saltiness. "What do you need?" I ask with forced patience.

She tosses one stick at me without warning.

I fumble but manage to catch it.

"The king wants me to train you."

"Okay …" I search for Zander and find him talking to Fearghal. "Right now?"

"Yes." Without warning, Abarrane launches herself at me, slamming the wooden sword out of my hand with hers before her foot lands square against my chest. I tumble backward and land flat on my back, struggling to inhale, my chest feeling like it's caved in.

"Are you done already?" she taunts.

I focus on the smattering of stars as I wait for my breath to return and the pain to subside. Finally, I'm left with only a dull ache and my staggering rage.

"That's not *training*, Abarrane!" I pull myself up to a sitting position with a curse. The well of power inside gurgles with anticipation, as if begging to be unleashed on her.

"But it is. Training is teaching." She crouches beside me, the perpetual hostility in her eyes missing. "I am teaching you that you are still weak and vulnerable, and I am teaching my warriors that whatever else you may be, you are flesh and blood and can be killed." Her gaze flickers to Zander, paused in his conversation and watching this unfold, before shifting back to me. "But that you can be one of us."

Several of the legionaries loiter, Jarek among them. Is that what they want to do? Kill me?

Or is Abarrane saying this is part of the process to win them over?

"Fine, but can we do without the roundhouse kicks?"

Abarrane's lips twist as she considers this. "I will handle you like one of the weak, little elven children from Cirilea."

"It's all I ask." I heave myself to my feet with a wince.

Gesine lingers nearby. "If you are going to do this, I suggest you wear your ring." Her voice carries that edge of warning.

I fish the gold band from my pocket and slip it on. It severs my link to my affinities instantly, leaving me feeling empty and exposed.

Abarrane twirls her wooden sword stick with ease. "You think a piece of jewelry will protect her, witch?"

Gesine stares coolly at her. "No, I am trying to protect all of you."

38
ZANDER

The first primal scream reverberates across the mountain range as the sliver of moon passes the peak ahead of us. The few mortals still absorbing warmth from the fire before they retire to their tents search around in a panic. Being from Norcaster, they wouldn't be familiar with these wild sounds.

Fearghal waves it off. "It's a golbikc. Noisy creatures, but they probably won't bother us."

"*Probably*?" someone echoes with trepidation.

"Have I mentioned how much I *hate* these mountains?" Elisaf picks off a chunk of venison from his share of tonight's dinner.

"Not much has changed." The air is still sharp, the scenery still splendid, and the nightly worry that one may be woken from their slumber by something trying to feed off them ever present.

He lowers his voice. "We have two powerful casters with us. You *do* remember the kinds of beasts they might entice, right?"

"I *do*." I throw a sharp look his way, a warning. "And that is why the fires will burn all night. The Legion is prepared, and there is no reason to cause more alarm over something that *might* happen." Romeria is already apprehensive enough about the saplings.

Elisaf nods, understanding. "Could you ever have foreseen us running here for refuge?"

"Not in a thousand years. Nor would I believe I would trust a caster." *Again*.

Gesine sits huddled under skins on the steps of the wagon she occupied with the seer, her blank stare shifting between the dark nothingness and to where Abarrane and Romeria trade slow-moving parries with wooden swords.

"What do you think of her?" I ask.

"Which her?"

I smirk. "I already know what you think of Romeria." If there is anyone Elisaf would betray me for, it is her. But his comment is a glaring reminder. "I suppose I *should* begin seeing her as a caster as well."

"Everyone else is. And you know whose lead they will follow in that regard." Elisaf studies the form beyond the safety of our camp, perched on the crop of stones near Ianca's final resting spot, his unbound hair reaching halfway down his back.

"I respect his counsel and need his sword, but I cannot decide if he will be our greatest ally or our worst enemy."

"Perhaps both."

I watch one of the infected mortals Romeria rescued from the pillories leave the fire and walk slowly toward the tents, his cautious gaze on Brynn. These mortals don't trust the legionaries who are ready to defend them with their lives. I suppose I can't blame them. As far as they're concerned, all our kind is capable of is taking.

Their blood.

Their kin.

Their choice.

Their freedom.

The mark on the mortal's hand glows like a firefly in the dark, blinking in and out with his stride. Did he *honestly* not know his wife had tainted him, or is that the story he will carry to his grave?

I study the vial of Romeria's blood that Pan procured with coin in Norcaster. "To have *that* much poison collected … she must have been sitting for weeks as they bled her," I think out loud. What must have been going through Princess Romeria's mind as she allowed it? How does one have *that* much hatred in their heart for a people they have never met?

Maybe the very existence of my kind deserves it.

"It was not a hasty plan on her or Neilina's part," Elisaf agrees. "Neither was sending half their army to these mountains under cover to exploit the north's trade routes and their animosity."

"Even if Romeria had died during the attack, Ybaris still would have succeeded in tearing apart Islor." *Is* succeeding at it.

He pauses. "But how would they have known this weakness? How would they have known how fragile your rule is in these parts?"

It's obvious. "Someone has been feeding them valuable information. That is the only explanation. To what end, though, I am still unsure."

"To end your rule of Islor, or to end Islor itself."

"Yes, that is growing more apparent. The more we learn, the more I feel certain we are preparing to fight a battle that is already lost." I keep thinking about Kamstead. "And what would make these saplings become *so* brazen, breaking a beneficial arrangement with Isembert that keeps them fed without risk, demanding the veins of immortals and then accepting turned children in place?"

"Desperation … hunger …" Elisaf throws out ideas.

"Or another alliance that benefits them more."

"With the Ybarisans," he gives voice to my thoughts.

That sapling who tried to take Annika knew Romeria. They were familiar with each other. A connection exists there, though I haven't yet deciphered what it could be.

A high-pitched screech echoes through the valley.

"A hag. Now *that's* somethin' to run from," Fearghal announces with far too much zeal.

39
ROMERIA

Taking a deep breath, I trudge beyond the invisible border of the camp, my nerves on edge as much from the frequent and hair-raising screams that echo through the wilderness as the brooding warrior perched on the rocks ahead. Zorya redid his braids earlier, but only half of them, leaving the other half of his ash-brown hair cascading down his back.

"What do you want?" Jarek snaps, not even turning around.

"How did you know—"

"Your footfalls." He pauses. "And your blood stinks."

I snort as I settle on the boulder beside him, noting how the distant campfire shimmers in the blade he grasps. "No, it doesn't. I have another day before the morels start fading." And even when they do, I know the smell of my blood entices him. Entices *all* of them, no matter how they feel about me. "Which direction do you think they'll come from?"

"The trees."

"We're surrounded by trees."

"Then my answer is logical. Why are you here, Romeria? To pester me? Or to tell me more lies?"

"I never lied to you."

"You never told me the truth."

"Seeing how you're reacting, can you blame me?" I shift to get more comfortable, wincing at the ache in my thigh where Abarrane chopped me with her wooden stick. Gesine offered to heal the bruising, but the commander scoffed at the idea, insisting I should learn to heal like the warriors I'm trying to impress. "Zander and Abarrane were worried you'd kill me if you knew."

"I haven't killed you yet, have I?" he asks, deadpan.

"Should I thank you for that?"

"It would be the courteous thing to do."

My head falls back with an unexpected laugh, but it's what I needed to crack into this stifling tension between us. "Thank you for *not* killing me."

"Yet."

"*Yet*," I correct. "Can I ask that you resist the urge?"

"What do you think I've been doing since the moment I met you?" The faintest hint of amusement touches his voice now.

I cling to it. "I don't believe that. At first, yeah, but not anymore. I think you were starting to like me. Or at least tolerate me." I feel Jarek's gaze on my profile, but I keep mine focused on the darkness ahead. "I talked to Eden."

Silence is the only answer I get.

"Why do you make yourself out to be a perpetual prick when you can actually be decent and principled?"

"A perpetual prick. I like that."

I lock my arm against the impulse to elbow his side. We may be talking, but that doesn't mean he won't turn on me like a rabid dog might snap at its owner. "She's been through a lot. I'm worried that anyone who shows her even an inch of kindness will get *whatever* they want from her."

"And you assume I would take advantage of her, like a predator homes in on its prey."

"Well … *yes*."

A harsh screech cuts through the night.

I shudder. "What was that?"

"A wild cat. It's a mating call." He pauses. "Not all that different from the sounds you were making this morning—"

"Shut up." This time I *do* elbow him. At least he's joking with me now.

A slightly more comfortable silence falls over us.

"Thank you, by the way, for last night. I don't know what would have happened if you hadn't chased me down." And that is the simple truth. Would Zander and Elisaf have been able to fight their way out without Jarek's strength and skill?

My ring is still on my finger. I slide it off and secure it in my cloak pocket, welcoming the vibrant pulse.

It's like a second heartbeat to me now.

"What is so special about that ring?" Jarek asks after a moment.

"Zander gave it to me."

"And yet another lie. Are they practiced, or do they just slide off that slippery tongue of yours?"

"It's not a lie! He gave it to me!"

"I think it is more than that, though. The night of the attack outside Bellcross, you did not want to leave without it. Why?"

How do I explain without getting into the convoluted and frankly preposterous journey I've taken to get here? "Because it helps me, but mostly it protects others."

"From whom?"

From me, apparently. "It's a very long story, and not one I trust you with yet."

Jarek snorts. "That is an odd word for *you* to wield."

"Maybe." The truth is, I learned distrust long ago, a master of duplicity by the time I arrived here.

"How can any of us *ever* trust you? You are Mordain."

"No, I'm not."

"Then what are you?"

Maybe Zander's right, and it's time to start letting him in. Letting them all in. "At heart, I'm human. It's how I was born and raised. But this body is elven, and the affinities tied to it are caster, and I'm only just learning how to use them."

"Princess Romeria was raised in Argon as an immortal heir to the Ybarisan throne."

"She was."

He inhales deeply, as if breathing in my admission, my choice of words not lost on him. "Is this something Mordain did?"

I shake my head. "They don't even know I exist." Yet. "This was all Queen Neilina, who forced Ianca to summon Aoife—"

He curses and slides off the rock. "I don't think I want to hear any more."

"That's fine, but at least let me say this." I pause to make sure he isn't marching away from me. "I didn't ask for any of it. I didn't *want any* of it. I was living my life when I got pulled in, but now I'm stuck here, and all I want to do is help these people and fix what's happening in Islor. And as much as you or Atticus may think killing me is the answer, it's not. It's already too late for that, and I can help, I *know* I can." I just don't know how yet.

My candid words are met with silence.

"Jarek?"

"They're here."

My pulse races. "Where?" I squint into the darkness but can't see anything.

Until I can.

Ten stealthy dark forms move forward in a line. I can barely make them out, save for the glowing silver ropes that dangle at their sides.

"What are those?" I ask, but I think I already know because I've seen rope like that—at the bottom of a river, wrapped around Annika.

"That is raw merth." Jarek curses. "Where the fuck did they get it? And so much of it?"

It clicks. "From the Ybarisans." Of course. Ybaris is the only place it grows.

And every last one of these deadly legionaries will buckle under its crippling effects.

"Get back behind the line," Jarek growls, sliding out a second blade from the sheath at his hip.

"Come with me!" I beg. "You can't fight them all off if they have merth!"

"Not with you here, I can't. Go!" he roars, stalking forward into the night, his blades at the ready.

"Romeria!" Zander bellows.

A second later, panicked shouts rise from the other side of camp.

40
ROMERIA

My lungs burn as I cross the invisible border. The camp has erupted in chaos, legionaries running to meet attackers from all sides while shouting at the mortals to remain hidden within the protection of the wagons.

"Stay here!" Zander orders and charges out before I can respond. Flames ignite along the camp's perimeter, forming six-foot walls of fire that connect at the bonfires in each corner, keeping the mortals and me inside and everyone else out.

Beyond the fire lines, countless steel clangs and shouts sound, but I can't see anything.

"Romeria!" Gesine, still in her beige dress, scales up the side of our wagon.

I scramble to follow, and together we survey the scene from our new vantage point.

My terror swells. Is this what they were expecting?

The flaming walls create a box of protection around the camp similar to the circle I used in Norcaster, while its glow casts a wide expanse of light, allowing us to see far beyond.

We watch as the Legion fights the enemy, blades and bodies moving with expert strokes and lightning-quick reflexes.

The saplings all have stark white hair.

The one who threw Annika into the river had the same. I couldn't make out his face then, despite the brilliant moonlight shining from above. But I can see their faces now, and I understand what Elisaf meant when he said they couldn't be mistaken for anything else. They look like the elven, but unappealing versions, their foreheads bulging, brows prominent, cheeks sunken in.

"Why are there so many?" At least three for every one of our warriors, and they're all around us.

"We cannot let them overpower us at any cost."

If it were blade against blade, I wouldn't be so worried, but already, several legionaries lay motionless on the ground, the silver cords curled around their limbs, rendering them immobile. And suffering. Like a thousand razor blades slicing across skin, Annika had said.

"Are the saplings immune to the merth?"

"Essentially, yes." Gesine's irises begin to glow as she draws on her affinities. "We must aid our warriors however we can."

I call on my affinities, and they answer instantly, stretching into my fingertips, waiting.

Zorya battles two males, a blade in each of her hands, matching every blow with ferocious strikes, driving them away before they can get too close. The recent loss of an eye seemingly has not affected her skill. One sapling lunges, and she spins out of his reach before snapping back and deflecting the other's sword. A quick maneuver gives her a window to drop to her knee and ram her blade into her second opponent's stomach. He buckles, and after tearing her sword out, she steps into position for another lethal swing.

The other sapling takes the split-second opportunity and loops the merth cord around Zorya's neck. She slumps, her blade falling from her grip to lay next to her.

My reaction is spontaneous. The burst of air I throw toward the male requires no thought, no planning. It slams into him and he soars backward to collide with the sapling Brynn is fighting. Both sprawl to the ground.

Brynn doesn't waste a moment. With a battle cry, she drives her blade into one chest before yanking it out and swinging her sword toward the neck of the one rising to his feet.

I flinch as the sapling's head sails through the air, landing some distance away.

"Brynn!" I scream.

Her head snaps toward me, bewilderment on her face.

I point to Zorya.

With a nod, she charges toward her fallen comrade, stumbling as she reaches her side.

"It's the merth. Even being near it for too long can weaken them." We watch Brynn draw a dagger. She uses the blade to drag the merth away, flinging it into the fire.

Zorya is on her feet almost instantly.

And my shoulders sag.

But there's little relief to be had as I survey the scene. Plenty of saplings have been cut down, but more than a few legionaries have already fallen to merth cords. The ones who haven't yet don't have a second to spare, swarmed as they fight, trying to fend off saplings and their vicious bindings.

This is what the saplings had planned, though. They won't kill the legionaries. They want to paralyze them so they can drag them to their caves and shackle them for their blood supply. It's probably how they—or their mortal counterparts—trapped Iago and Drakon.

"We have to help them."

Gesine shoots a fireball toward a sapling that's just taken down a legionary. "Is that not what we're doing?"

"It's not enough!"

"It is difficult, in such close combat." She pauses, searches for another opening to strike.

An arrow glides over the flaming perimeter to sink into a

sapling's back. Loth finishes him off with a swing of his sword, cleaving into his neck.

The arrow came from within our camp. "Who was that?" I search and find Fearghal teetering on one of Norcaster's rickety wagons, a bow in his grip.

He pauses long enough to offer a toothy grin. "We don't eat if we can't use one of these."

He's not the only one taking position on a wagon. Several other mortals have followed suit, clutching bows they must have scavenged from the weapons wagon. How many of them have aim as good as Fearghal's, though?

I get an answer a moment later, as one fires an arrow aimed at a sapling, and it grazes Horik's shoulder.

"Don't take the shot unless you're clear!" I bellow. The last thing we need is to shoot our own warriors.

But that's not our only worry. The fire boundary around the camp is wavering, the flames already half their prior height and shrinking.

I panic as I scour the field for Zander, fearing the worst, but he's still on his feet, back-to-back with Elisaf, meeting each blade strike.

"He cannot continue fighting them *and* stoke this fire," Gesine warns. "It is impossible. They need to end this quickly."

But they're far from success. Too many legionaries have fallen and not enough saplings have. Abarrane has lost her sword, but so has her opponent. They're trading a flurry of punches and kicks, but she's wobbling, her footing not as assured as usual. It has to be on account of the glowing cord the sapling has tucked within his sleeve. How long before even she is overpowered?

My attention veers beyond her to the crop of rocks I left when I raced back. "Where is he? Where is Jarek?" From this vantage point and with the fire burning, I can see all around the camp.

But I can't see the fierce warrior *anywhere*.

My stomach sinks with cold fear.

Two more legionaries fall, the saplings using their merth cords like lassos to incapacitate them.

We are going to lose.

And the fire wall is waning.

There's an opening, and Gesine sends a fire bolt toward a sapling. He screams as his entire body ignites, drawing the other saplings' notice.

"On the wagon!" one of them yells.

Seconds later, arrows sail toward us. Fearghal and another mortal are hit. Fearghal tumbles off with a howl.

Gesine throws a shield up around the wagons, blocking a second volley. "You *must* attack! Use your fear!"

I know I have to, but I can't blast them without risk of hitting the remaining legionaries. I frantically search for other ideas.

The pond.

I may not be able to create water, but I can manipulate it into something deadly.

I let the adrenaline surge inside me and merge with all my fear and anger as I conjure a picture of an octopus with clawed tentacles reaching out from the water's surface. A split second later, my vision comes to life, latching onto a nearby sapling's limbs, clamping down tight.

I grit my teeth as I coax the water beast to pull. The sapling's screams cut off as his body parts fly in various directions.

Gesine's expression is a mix of shock, amazement, and horror, but when she sees me watching her, my stomach lurching at what I animated, she urges, "Again!"

I catch and tear apart two more saplings before they smarten up and move out of reach. I let my octopus dissolve quietly into the pond.

"Romeria!" Gesine shouts, pointing toward another corner where a sapling has hopped over the weakened fire line.

He cuts down a brave mortal with a single sweep of his sword before charging for the next. His path is clear. He's coming for us.

My rage surges. I hit him with a blast of air that sends him flying into the firepit, his horrendous screams making me shudder, but I refocus as another sapling crosses the line.

And another.

They've officially breached the camp. We can't fight them all off.

"Zander!" I shriek.

He's charging for a sapling when I call him. His head snaps toward me, and upon seeing the situation, he abandons his chase and races in, Elisaf in close pursuit.

All over the grass, legionaries lie motionless, paralyzed by silver cord. Even Abarrane has succumbed. But within the camp's boundaries, saplings stream in from all sides.

"I have to free them. I'm the only one who can." They need Gesine up here, fighting.

"Be careful. And remember, the longer they are bound, the longer it will take them to recuperate." She drops the shield and begins blasting again as I scramble down.

Pan struggles to drag Fearghal out of harm's way, the bulky man groaning in pain.

I lend my strength, and together we tuck him under a wagon. "Hang in there, and Gesine will fix it for you."

"Aye. Not the way I pictured goin'."

"Pan, I need your help. Come with me now."

Together we leap over the dwindling fire border, now merely a charred line with glowing embers. Sprinting from one legionary to the next, we yank away the merth cords.

One by one, the legionaries stir with gasps before fumbling for their swords and staggering to their feet.

Pan frees Abarrane before I can, and when I reach her, she's up and seething.

"They're in the camp!" I point toward it. "Zander is there."

With an enraged battle cry, she charges toward them.

"Have you seen Jarek?"

Pan shakes his head, and I curse.

He must have fallen where he met that line of saplings. I squint, but it's too far away and I can't see anything.

"What do I do with these?" Pan holds up a bunch of merth cords.

"Burn them in the pit and then go hide under a wagon! Do not get yourself killed!" I don't wait, rushing off in the direction of Ianca's burial site, my pulse hammering as I stumble and veer around rocks and blueberry bushes.

Three bodies lie facedown in the grass, but none are Jarek, their hair a signature stark white.

I keep moving farther away from camp, the darkness swallowing me whole, wishing I had Gesine's floating orb. But I have my own light source, I remember. I call on my affinity and ignite a bush, followed by another, and another. They create a path forward, leading me along a trail of sapling corpses.

Finally, I spot Jarek twenty feet away, lying next to a sapling, his double-edged sword buried in the sapling's chest.

A silver cord is wrapped around Jarek's neck. It looks like the sapling made a last-ditch effort to subdue him as the warrior cleaved into him.

I rush over, and snatching the merth away, I toss it at a flaming bush.

I'm breathless as I wait for him to stir.

But he doesn't move.

"Jarek … Jarek!"

A thin moan slips from his lips, but no words.

Something's wrong. My frantic hands fumble over his body, discovering the hilt of a dagger that blends in with his leather, sticking out of his broad chest. I don't have to see the metal to know it's a merth blade.

"Gesine!" I shriek into the night, my voice cracking with dread.

She jerks in my direction, and seconds later she's clambering off the wagon. I watch with horror as she swerves to avoid a sapling's blade a second before Abarrane chops into its side.

All around the camp, it looks like the tide is turning, the sapling numbers shrinking as the Legion hacks and carves and maims with vengeance.

Gesine rushes past the bonfire, heading toward us.

I ignite a few more bushes to help her find her way. "Okay, she's coming. Help is coming. Stay alive until she gets here, you *big dummy*." My words are laced with emotion. "Why didn't you listen to me!"

I swear the corner of Jarek's mouth twitches.

Gesine's breath is ragged as she reaches us, Zander on her heels.

I scramble aside to give her room. "You can fix this, right?"

She hovers her hands over the wound. "This is a merth blade, Romeria—"

"But you can fix it?" I plead.

Her brow wrinkles. "I will do what I can, but it will need all my power and then some." She spares me a doubtful look before settling in. With a deep breath and a pause, as if counting down, she wrenches the blade from Jarek's chest, earning his gasp. She tosses it away and clamps both hands over the wound, her eyelids shuttering.

I can do nothing but wait.

Zander pulls me to my feet. "Are you okay?"

I peer down at my hands, slick with Jarek's blood. "Fearghal was shot."

"It did not hit a major artery, so he should survive. Others were not so lucky."

"It looks like we're winning, though?"

He peers back at the camp, to where Abarrane has pinned one of the last saplings to the ground but hasn't slaughtered him yet. "What you did, Romeria, going out there to free all the fallen legionaries—"

"What Pan and I did," I correct him.

He smiles. "What you *and Pan* did … it is the reason we will survive. And when we interrogate one of these saplings and find out where Iago and—"

A deafening screech rattles my eardrums, cutting off all conversation, all thought.

Every hair on my body stands on end. "What was that?" Whatever it was, it was close.

"Nothing good." Zander squints into the darkness, searching, his sword in his grip. Using the burning bushes, he ignites a line of flame that crawls along the grass, reaching outward, granting more light.

A dark form with four glowing red eyes watches us from the shadows no more than fifty yards away.

"*What is that*?" I hiss.

When it realizes it's been spotted, it unfolds its body, quadrupling in size, revealing two serpentine-like heads lined with barbed spikes down both necks and a tail twice the length of its massive body.

"A grif. It's a type of wyvern, a creature from the Nulling. It's very rare." Zander curses. "I cannot believe it has found us already."

A Nulling creature. "It's here because of me, isn't it?" Like the nethertaur, it was drawn to my affinities.

"It does not matter why it is here. You cannot fight this, Romeria."

"And *you* can?" It's easily five times the size of the last beast.

Zander's line of flame flares as it skitters along the ground toward the beast, forcing it backward, away from us. "I can try. Return to camp."

But ... "I'm *not* leaving Gesine." She kneels in front of Jarek, vulnerable as she battles to save his life. And I already know I'm no safer at camp than I am out here. That nethertaur ripped through tents, skewering people, in its bid to find me. This grif will hunt me down anywhere, and it'll maim or kill anything in its path. Everyone is safer with me staying where I am.

Legionaries rush to our aid, sprinting past us and into the

danger zone. I don't know if *all* of them together can stop something this size.

"Fine. But once it charges, it is impossible to stop. Do not do anything to attract its attention." Zander moves in, his steps calculated.

On impulse, I fumble for my dagger. It's useless, and yet it brings comfort as I grip it tightly and hover over Gesine. Jarek's face is still and ashen. "How is he?"

I get no response, but I tell myself it means nothing; she never breaks her concentration while in the midst of healing.

The flames encircle the grif, leaving the beast little room to maneuver, a reality it seems aware of as it shifts from clawed foot to clawed foot, its growing agitation visible.

Zander has steered its attention in another direction, away from Gesine and me. "*Ready*!" he bellows, a battle call to those waiting in the wings, their blades drawn.

A moment later, the circle of fire bursts and the flames rise to crawl over the grif's body. With an earsplitting screech, it charges through the fire, barreling toward Zander. Shouts sound, and he and the others scatter from its pounding feet, only to loop around and dive in.

It roars as first one blade, then another, pierces its scaly flesh—quick jabs before the legionaries steal away, rolling and jumping to avoid its snapping jaws. Not all of them are fast enough, though. The grif wields its tail as a mighty weapon, sweeping it sideways to slam into one of the males, sending him sailing through the air. Another, it impales with the barbed tip. The legionary screams as it tosses him around, the force no doubt tearing apart his insides.

By the time Zander hits it with blasts of fire and it shakes off its prey, the legionary's body shows no signs of life.

The grif backs away, out of reach of swords and fire. It lingers, as if calculating its next move.

"Flanks!" Abarrane screams. The group splits to attack from the sides. But with two heads to track their efforts and that vicious tail, sneaking up proves impossible, and they scatter backward again.

It stomps a foot in challenge.

Zander hits it with another blast of fire, and this time when it charges forward, it does so with surprising speed that I don't think Zander anticipated.

My heart is in my throat as he leaps out of reach seconds before the grif's teeth clamp over his head. At my fingertips, my powers pulse, ready to be unleashed on this thing should it succeed in catching him.

The grif pauses, lifting one of its snouts into the air before swinging in my direction.

My stomach drops.

It can smell me. Or Gesine.

Maybe both.

Either way, it came for us, and now it knows where we are.

Elisaf uses that moment's distraction to rush in with a mighty cleave against its neck. Any other creature would surely have lost its head to a sword swing like that, but it does little except anger the grif. With a shrill screech, the beast lunges, and one of its gaping maws latches onto Elisaf's thigh.

I hear the bones crunch from here.

"No!" My legs move of their own accord, the power source inside me bursting at the seams.

"Romeria, get back!" Zander shouts, but I ignore him. I can't stand by and watch.

The grif has Elisaf gripped between his teeth, shaking him around like a dog with a toy, while the snapping jaws of its second head fends off Abarrane's approach.

I slam a blast of air into its chest.

It rears back with a roar, releasing Elisaf, who falls limp to the ground.

The terror that I've lost my closest friend grips me as I hit the beast's chest with another blast, and another, forcing it back farther each time.

Zander rushes to my side, his breath labored.

"How do we kill this thing?" My voice bleeds with desperation.

"I do not know that we can. I've only ever seen one in my lifetime, during the rift war. That one was winged."

"Some of them *fly*?" I stare at the beast in horror. As if it wasn't bad enough as it is.

"Right out of the rift. It killed dozens of us before five casters from Ybaris's side managed to take it down. It was the only time we were on the same side during that fight."

Five? I may be powerful, but I'm only one and I'm still learning. I check over my shoulder to where Gesine works on Jarek. She hasn't given up yet. That must bode well for him, but it's no help to us. We need her knowledge, if not her power. "We have to keep it busy until she's done."

The grif sniffs the air again, first with one head and then the other, but it doesn't charge yet, not like the nethertaur did.

"It knows what you are. It can smell the power in your body, and it is wary."

"A lot of good that'll do us." My heart constricts at the sight of Elisaf lying there. He still isn't moving.

"You cannot help him right now."

One of the legionaries fires an arrow at the grif's head, striking it in the eye.

It snarls in protest, clawing at the embedded object. A second arrow sails into one of its mouths. A third misses its mark, bouncing off its scales. But the beast has had enough of being a target. It advances on the legionaries with renewed energy.

I hit it with a blast of air, but it doesn't even break its stride.

"Spread out!" Zander hollers a second before its jaws snap at Zorya. She dodges and swings back, thrusting a dagger into its side before pivoting out of reach, only to stumble. She rolls at the last instant, narrowly avoiding the crushing weight of its paw.

Abarrane leaps in to stab at its neck, distracting it until Zorya can clamber to her feet and get away.

"We can stab it all night, and it won't make a difference. This thing will keep attacking and eventually, it will catch us," Zander says grimly.

"What other choice do we have?"

He looks to Gesine. "None."

"Can you keep it busy until she's finished with Jarek?"

"We can try. Stay out of its range, Romeria. Please." He moves in again, sending fire bugs crawling over the grif's scaly body to draw its attention away from the Legion and back to him.

And I run to Elisaf, skidding to my knees to cradle his head.

The flesh in his leg is shredded down to splintered bones, the metallic tinge of blood so thick it coats my tongue. The main artery in his leg has been serrated by that beast's teeth, and blood pours freely. He'll bleed out long before his elven body can mend itself, and Gesine can't help speed things along. She already has one dire case.

"Have I told you … how much … I hate … these mountains?" he manages through gritted teeth.

Tears stream down my cheeks. "No, you are *not* allowed to go anywhere. Do you understand?"

"You are … the best thing … that has happened … to Zander …" He swallows. "Protect him."

"That's what you're for, so stay with me. Gesine will fix you." Except he's fading fast, and Gesine likely won't have anything left to give him.

If *I* can do anything to help, I have to try, and it has to be now.

On instinct, I hover my hands over his thigh, silently begging for my powers to help me.

A thread lashes out. Something cool and comforting, urging me to reach for it, to grab on and pull.

I do, and it unravels instantly, surging upward.

I realize what this is: my connection to Aoife, the one caster affinity that has eluded me completely thus far. The one I need to heal.

I have no idea what I'm doing, but nothing to lose. I don't

waste another second, channeling it into Elisaf, visualizing his bones sturdy and his flesh whole, rippling with muscle as he dances around the Cirilean sparring court, a competent adversary for Zander.

Elisaf sighs as my affinity cocoons his broken body and eases his pain. It quickly spreads, countless tendrils like tiny knitting needles, weaving fibers back together and staunching the flow of blood.

I'm doing it.

I'm putting my friend back together.

My heart sings with joy as I lose myself in this task, coaxing the magic to work faster. Of all the gifts and tricks I've learned so far, I would trade them *all* for this one ability, here and now.

"Zander!"

The ring of desperation in Abarrane's screech splits my concentration and my hold on the healing thread. My attention snaps toward the battle. Zander is sprawled on his back, and the giant spear on the end of the grif's tail aims down with a mighty thrust.

He's not going to escape it this time.

"*No*!" The word tears from my throat.

A surge of power like nothing I've ever felt shatters inside me.

41

ZANDER

I leap out of the way, but not fast enough.

The grif's tail catches my shoulder, sending my sword flying one way and my body another. I crash into the ground, the impact like colliding with a stone wall. I struggle to regain my focus.

"Zander!" Abarrane's shriek is the only warning I have before I see the deadly spear driving toward my chest.

Nothing can protect me now—not my elven make, not my noble blood, and surely not Malachi's fire in my veins.

A shrill scream rattles my eardrums a split second before a brilliant white light blinds me from witnessing my impending doom.

Intense heat scorches my skin.

42
ROMERIA

"Romeria … Romeria!"

I regain consciousness with a slap across the cheek. Abarrane hovers over me, scowling, only her face is lined with worry rather than anger or annoyance.

My head swims in that underwater sensation again, the one that means I've drained my power. I struggle to lean up onto my elbow, my arm wobbly.

The first person I see is Elisaf. He's propped up with Zorya's help, his tawny skin still tinged with an ashen pallor.

But he's alive. I didn't fix all of him, but maybe I fixed enough.

"Zander …," My speech is garbled.

"He's there. See?" Abarrane points to the figure walking toward me, slightly hobbled, his arm tucked into his side.

Behind him, the beast lies in a smoldering heap, its scaly flesh charred. "What happened?" I ask, but I don't have the energy to wait for an answer.

I float away to the sound of Abarrane's laughter.

When I stir again, I'm in a wagon and early dawn glimpses through the tiny driver's window, cracked open for fresh air or light, or both.

My cheeks are chilled, but animal furs and a solid body wedged against my back keep me warm. I recognize the sweet woodsy scent even before I roll over to find Zander next to me.

"Good morning." He presses his lips against mine in a slow, intimate kiss that awakens my senses. "How are you feeling?"

"Tired," I croak, my throat raw. Not a hint of that second heartbeat lingers in my chest, my affinities drained. "What happened last night?"

He curls an arm around me, pulling me tight. "One moment, I was watching the grif's tail spike coming straight for me, and the next, I couldn't see anything at all. There was a blinding light and a wave of heat so hot, I thought my skin was burning." He frowns as if he's recalling the moments but isn't sure of the truth. "And then the grif was dead, and I was unharmed. Other than my shoulder"—he rolls it—"which has healed already."

Healed. That word … "I was with Elisaf … I was trying to fix his leg, and then I heard Abarrane scream your name, and I knew that thing was going to kill you."

"It would have tore me apart from the inside out like it did Darragh."

I grimace at the gruesome image he conjures.

"But you destroyed it with whatever you channeled."

What *did* I channel? I've wielded all four affinities now, and none felt like that. I wonder what Gesine might know of it.

Gesine.

Jarek.

I'm suddenly wide awake. "Was she able to save him? Jarek. Is he going to be okay?" I hold my breath, dreading the answer in case it's not the one I want.

"Gesine still needs to finish repairing the damage, but he will survive."

Tension slides from my body. I can't explain this feeling, but something deep inside senses I will need Jarek by my side. "And what about Elisaf? I didn't know what I was doing, but I think it was working?"

"You stemmed the blood loss and repaired enough of the damage to tide him over until Gesine could tend to him. He is alive because of you." Zander strokes hair off my face. "We are *all* alive because of you. And everyone is grateful." He leans in to press a kiss against the hollow of my throat.

"It's a nice change from what everyone's *usually* saying about me."

He chuckles, his breath tickling my skin. "I imagine so."

A dark thought strikes me, rousing my fear. What are the chances another grif will find me?" "They won't be grateful if they have to keep doing this.

He pulls away, revealing a somber expression. "They are rare, but I cannot say for certain how long before another surfaces. In any case, we should reach the caves in two or three days, and they cannot follow us in there. They won't fit through the entrance."

"Suddenly these caves don't seem so bad."

He chuckles. "They are quite comfortable, from what I remember. Spacious."

"As comfortable as a queen's quarters in the castle?" I wonder if Saoirse has already moved in.

"More comfortable than this wagon." His tongue traces a line over my collarbone.

"It's growing on me." Especially now, with Zander here. I close my eyes as his teeth playfully scrape against my skin. There was once a time, so long ago now, that he did the same for a very different reason. I whisper, "Show them to me?" I don't have to elaborate.

He freezes.

"*Please*?"

"Why would you want to see the part of me I abhor so much?"

"Because it *is* a part of you, and I want to know *every* part of you, inside and out, good and … otherwise." I hesitate. "We have a long life together ahead of us, don't we?" Or have I misread that?

I swallow my doubt and wait for him to deny me again, to find some excuse about why it's not safe. When he pulls back and the two white, needlelike fangs are already elongated, awaiting my inspection, I'm taken aback for a few seconds.

They're nothing like the daaknar's frothing yellow fangs. These are delicate—not two inches long, widening closer to his gums, but only marginally, and gleaming white—even though the ends will draw blood with a simple touch.

"Does it hurt when they come out?" I remember him wincing the night I saw him feeding on that tributary in his bedchamber.

He shakes his head, studying me closely. Maybe he expects fear or disgust, but all I feel is curiosity.

I reach up and slide my finger along the inside of one, avoiding the razor-sharp tip.

A sigh slips from him, and when I meet his eyes again, they've gone molten.

"That feels good?"

"Yes," he admits softly.

I touch the other one, earning another sound, this one deep within his throat.

"*How* good?" On impulse, I reach down and smooth my hand over the front of his pants. He's impossibly hard. Did touching his fangs cause that? Are they for more than feeding?

No wonder the act so often ends with sex.

Does Zander feel an impulse every time he slides these teeth into a woman's neck? Will he, from now on? If I spend any time thinking about it, I might get angry and jealous, but I remind myself that I can't be angry about that; it's not his fault. It's how Malachi designed his kind.

All I can ask is that he doesn't act on that need.

Unless it's with me.

I lean in and ever so carefully drag the tip of my tongue along that same inside edge.

His fangs vanish with his snarl, and in the next instant, he's on top of me. "Do not torment me like that." He punctuates his words with a thrust that goes nowhere, our clothes an effective barrier. Rarely are we ever dressed when we're in bed together. It adds a layer of heady anticipation now.

"Is *that* what you think I was doing? Tormenting you?" I work my hands between us and push against his stomach until he lifts himself high enough that I can reach the strings of his breeches. My fingers fumble as I hastily unfasten them, exposing the velvety soft skin beneath. It's only been a day since we were alone like this, and yet it feels like an eternity. I curl my hand around his hard length, drawing a desperate moan from his lips as I stroke him.

"Please."

"I like it when the king begs, I tease, reaching for his pants, intent on pushing them down for easier access.

A bloodcurdling scream stalls my hands and terror slows my heartbeat.

Oh my God.

Not again.

"It's okay. It's just one of the saplings."

"*Just*?"

"Abarrane has been questioning them all night about Iago and Drakon's whereabouts." His gaze flips to the little window. "And now the sun is coming up."

Which means the sapling is burning alive under it.

Another scream pierces the silence.

"It should be over soon."

While I have no love for those creatures who came here, intent on stealing the Legion away, I cannot tolerate torture, especially not this form of it.

My hands fall from Zander's pants.

With a groan, Zander settles beside me again, accepting that the mood is effectively ruined.

As the long train of wagons and horses heads north, my focus grazes over the seven unmarked graves by the crop of stones. I couldn't save everyone last night. Two legionaries are buried on either side of Ianca, along with four mortals. I didn't know any of them, and yet watching those who did quietly weep stirs a lump in my throat.

"You did that." Saddled in his horse next to mine, Zander nods toward the carnage in the open field. "You did what none of us could."

The grif rests where it fell, where wild animals will pick at its corpse until it's too rotten even for them. It's more horrific in the daylight, a small mountain of charred, scaly meat. The trails of inky blood that still ooze, leaking into the surrounding soil, will keep anything from growing in that spot for years to come, according to Gesine.

Yes, I did that.

But I take in the scorched earth around it—the vast expanse of blackened grass, the scattered boulders once nestled together, the few spindly trees that thrived but now lay like broken twigs—and I remind myself that I also did *that.* I saw Zander seconds away from death, and my worst fears exploded inside me. I couldn't control what I unleashed. I could have caught Zander in that blast, or any of the legionaries. Or *all* of them.

How I didn't is beyond me.

Now I know what Gesine means about my emotions causing destruction.

The thought of it makes me shudder.

Next to the beast are all the dead saplings, including the burned body of the one Abarrane couldn't break for information about Drakon and Iago's location. As the sun crested the mountain ridge, the Legion stood and silently watched its rays cook him. They watched while I hid in the wagon, plugging my ears against his screams.

The other sapling is bound and stuffed in the wagon with Flann, away from the daylight, so Abarrane can continue her questioning tonight. I hope she pulls something from him because I can't stomach another morning like today.

A white stallion appears beside me, slowing to match Eros's canter. Fresh swirls of blood decorate its sides.

"We have no need to man our spits anymore. Just ask the Ybarisan to roast our meat for us!" Jarek bellows. He's pale and moving stiffly, but otherwise, he seems in good spirits. If he needs more repairs, he'll have to wait. Gesine is with Elisaf in a wagon, finishing what I started on his leg.

The legionaries answer with a chorus of cheers and laughter.

"Perhaps not so crispy, though." Jarek smirks, but neither his tone nor his demeanor carry that same sharp edge he normally wields for me.

No one would be the wiser that he nearly died last night.

Would have died, Gesine promised, had I not gone searching for him when I did.

But I know.

And he knows.

And when our eyes meet, something silent passes between us that I don't fully understand but makes me think I have nothing to worry about from the fierce warrior anymore.

He trots ahead to Abarrane's side.

"*That* is Stonekeep." Zander regards the sheer wall of rock that soars high into the sky. Its symmetrical shape reminds me of a cathedral's facade, stretching up to a peak. But that's all it is—a giant rock wall. Nothing else surrounds it but more mountains.

This is the place Gesine is so desperate to reach? The place she believes will save Islor?

We traveled through the lush forest for two days before the looming trees began thinning, turning sparse and twiggy, and then vanished altogether. Now our caravan is crossing an expanse of arid, cracked soil, hard rock, and frigid air, the wind trying its hardest to cut through the leather and fur layers I found laid out for me the morning after the grif attack.

No wonder Zander was hesitant to tell the others about the caster's push to stop here. There is *nothing* for us here.

Riding with Elisaf, Gesine is quiet, her expression blank as we plod along. If she is apprehensive that this prophecy she clings to is about to prove false, she doesn't reveal it.

I bite my tongue because adding my doubt to the mix doesn't help, especially when we've come this far. Not without challenges, though. Yesterday, we lost a wagon, its axle splintering on the rough terrain. The mortals occupying it shifted to other wagons and horses, though some have no choice but to walk. Two more wagons crack and squeal with each turn of their wheels, a sign that they're ready to follow suit.

We can't continue this trek much longer.

"We *must* veer east if we are to reach shelter by nightfall," Abarrane announces.

I check the sun's position. No more Nulling creatures have visited our camp—thank God—but how many times will we be so lucky, especially as we move closer toward the rift? "Where are these caves?"

"Another few hours that way." Zander points past the wall to where the snow-capped mountains dip into a crevice of green before stealing a glance toward Gesine. "We should head straight there so we can settle, and perhaps venture back in a few days' time when we have rested—"

"No." The word comes hard and fast from Gesine's lips. With a breath, her typical serene demeanor is back. "We do not know what lies ahead or behind us, how far the Islorian army truly is, or how close the Ybarisans are. We do not know what else may surprise us out here." She doesn't have to mention the grif—it's still on our minds. "Each new day brings danger. A few days may change the course of everything, and there is something Romeria *must* see here, today."

Zander's lips purse. We're down to fifteen legionaries, and they've been keeping them close rather than sending out scouts. Gesine's not wrong; we really don't have a good grasp of what waits for us ahead.

"What is the witch talking about?" Jarek demands. "What must Romeria see in these deadlands?"

I stifle my sigh. I warned Zander that he should tell the others. "There's something at Stonekeep that Gesine feels is vital to Islor." I hesitate. "It has to do with a prophecy."

"*Prophecy*?" Abarrane hisses. "We are following Mordain's nonsense now?"

"No, we're trusting someone who has done nothing but help us so far," I snap. "We will leave the wagons here and ride ahead with a few warriors. They could use a rest, anyway."

Zander glances back at the mortals who follow us blindly, as if to confirm my claim. The ones on foot are hobbling. "If it helps Gesine see the error in relying on prophecy once and for all, then so be it. Let us go now."

Her sharp green eyes settle on the stone wall, still at least a mile away. "There is something there for us. I know it."

Eros weaves around the boulders, his footing cautious on the loose stone as our group of seven closes in. Abarrane, Zorya, and Jarek scan meticulously, as if expecting an assault.

But my attention is on the massive wall in front of us. As vast as it seemed from a distance, it's taller than even the skyscrapers that grace New York City's skyline.

And it's plastered in familiar carvings.

"It's like the stone in the nymphaeum." It bears the strange swirling alphabet no one seems able to read, only that wall of carving resembled a door in its shape. The carvings here have no apparent rhyme or reason as they crawl up the flat side of the mountain.

"What is known as Stonekeep existed before the casters. The assumption has always been that it was created by the nymphs, though we have no written trace of its origin."

"You've never seen this before."

"Only in illustrations. To see it in reality …." Her awe-filled words drift as she tips her head back to regard it.

"We are here, as you requested, High Priestess. I do not see anything that I have not seen before. So tell us, since I assume you are still withholding vital information, what is so special about this wall of carved rock that you have us following the guidance of seers?" Zander's horse shifts on its feet, its impatience mirroring that of its rider's.

Gesine slides from Elisaf's saddle and strolls over. She reaches forward and presses a tentative hand against the stone, closing her eyes. "Romeria, come."

I dismount and follow her over.

"What do you sense?" There's urgency in her question. She so badly wishes for an answer other than "nothing," to prove herself and the casters right.

The same impulse I felt in the nymphaeum stirs in me now, and instead of pressing my palm against the stone as Gesine does, I run my fingertip along one of the engraved curls.

Faint laughter stirs in my ears. "Did you hear that?"

"Hear what?" Abarrane snaps, her head swiveling, searching for a threat.

I've heard it before, that day in the nymphaeum with Annika. At the time, I dismissed it as Saoirse and her flock.

I slide a fingertip over the engraving again, and the infectious giggles multiply.

You can hear them, can't you?

Ianca kept asking, kept saying it, and I didn't understand —until now.

Realization rolls over me, a conflicting wave of excitement and fear. "The nymphs. I can hear the nymphs."

But *how* can I hear them?

And what does that mean?

"What are they saying?" Gesine whispers, as if afraid to disrupt them.

"Nothing. They're laughing." At me? With me?

"According to the texts in Shadowhelm, they did not communicate using our methods."

"Are you saying they're trying to talk to me?"

Zander hops off his horse and strolls over to mimic my finger trail but shakes his head. "I can't hear anything."

I slowly trace the swirling lines, following them along the massive wall. "They're getting louder, and there's more of them."

"Keep going. They may be leading you somewhere." Gesine follows beside me, wringing her hands. This is what she'd hoped for, I realize.

To what end, though?

Did she understand what Ianca meant all along?

The chorus grows, the sounds pulling my smile despite my apprehension. It reminds me of a classroom of preschoolers, laughing hysterically at a joke.

Until they cut off abruptly.

The eerie silence echoes in my ears.

"What's wrong?" Gesine presses.

I shake my head, straining to listen. "I think I hear … music?" A soft, haunting melody, the chords drawn out. So contrary to the elation a moment ago.

"What is this?" Gesine peers closely at where I paused when the laughter stopped. Within the carvings on the wall is a small open space. "It looks to be the shape of a hand, does it not?"

"It does." Tentatively, I fit mine within it and then pull back with a hiss as the jagged edge of stone scrapes across my skin, drawing blood.

Laughter coils in my ears and resonates, tugging at my core where my affinities thrum with anticipation.

"'You must bleed for them to bow. That is the only way.'" Gesine echoes Ianca's final words, shaking her head. "Fates, she knew. She saw this." She looks to me. "What is it telling you to do?"

The pieces are clicking together, and with them, a euphoric sense of accomplishment. Something deep inside prods, comforts, promises me this is the only path forward.

Gritting my teeth, I fit my hand back into the space, pushing farther. The soft music spikes as the stone thorns dig into my flesh. My affinities flare. I can only follow instinct now as I pull on the threads reaching out for me—all four affinities—allowing them to unravel and flow outward. I watch with a mixture of fascination and fear as a trail of my blood races along the carved lines, fanning out over the design.

"What is happening?" Zander's face pales as he follows the trail. "That is too much blood."

Gesine backs up to take in a better view. "Perhaps, but I fear it is too late to stop it now."

"What have you done, witch?" Jarek draws his sword, rage contorting his face as he narrows in on the caster.

"Nothing but ensure prophecy comes to pass." Gesine's green eyes glow as she arms herself with her affinities. "This is what must be."

As if in answer to her declaration, the ground rumbles, distracting Jarek from whatever he was planning. A deafening crack sounds and our horses rear, nearly throwing off their skilled riders.

The sheer rock wall splits, the center sliding backward into itself, releasing my hand from its fanged grip.

A city opens beyond.

43
ZANDER

"What is this place?" I whisper to no one in particular as we lead our horses through two open portcullises. The tunnel chiseled from the mountain is perhaps fifty paces deep, and on the other side, cobblestone streets fan out in various directions, each lined with elaborate stone buildings, their windows adorned with bursts of summer flowers. Lush trees mark corners next to park benches. It's as manicured as my castle grounds.

And none of it makes sense.

"Our future, I think." Gesine's eyes are wide with genuine shock as she takes in the same sights. "This must be what the seers have seen. The nymphs' token."

"They left us a *city*?"

"A haven."

"A haven for whom?" Abarrane's sword is in her nimble grip, her stance rigid. "We have no idea what else lives in here."

It is eerily empty, not a living being in sight. Not a bird, not a squirrel.

Not one of us.

Jarek scans the buildings, a weapon in each hand as if expecting a Nulling creature to materialize at any moment.

But an odd calm, one I cannot explain, has settled over me since passing through the gates.

"Is it me, or is it warm here?" Romeria tugs at her cloak collar as she guides Eros around in a slow circle, taking in the ghost city.

It's definitely warmer. Too warm for our leathers and furs, but my bigger concern is the blood dripping freely from Romeria's hand. A demand that Gesine heal her is on the tip of my tongue when Romeria gasps, her focus on something behind us.

We all whip around as one, as if anticipating an attack.

There, carved into the stone above the gate, are two crescent moons, intersected. The symbol no one can explain beyond seer visions, the mark Gesine has been emblazoning on mortals' hands.

"Ulysede," Romeria whispers, as if some great secret has dawned on her. A knowing look passes between her and the caster. "This is Ulysede. *This* is what Ianca was talking about. A place."

"Ianca knew about this city and you did not think to tell us?" I snap, my accusation aimed at the caster.

But she shakes her head, appearing as baffled as I feel. "I do not know what she knew or saw in her last days, but she said the word Ulysede." Gesine reaches toward Romeria's shredded hand. "Let me heal that for you."

While they dismount so Gesine can tend to Romeria's wounds, the legionaries close in on Elisaf and me.

"How many thousands of years has this city been hiding behind that wall, and we have been none the wiser?" Jarek studies the countless windows around us.

Hiding.

Or waiting for us.

Not *us*, I accept, my gaze falling on Romeria as she stares, mesmerized by how prophecy seems to be unfolding.

Prophecy. The caster was right all along.

"I dislike this place," Zorya mutters. "It feels off. What do we know of the nymphs, anyway?"

Nothing good. They cause chaos and barter in lives, and yet now they seem to have offered a lifeline to us when we needed it most?

"What are your orders for the Legion, Your Highness?" Abarrane asks. She so rarely asks for my opinion before giving her own, it throws me off. She is as rattled by this place as I am.

I look up to clear blue skies. We should be standing within the mountain. Another oddity. Regardless, leaving this place for the caves makes little sense until we know more. "Secure one of these buildings and settle the mortals before nightfall. Bring the weapons and whatever supplies are necessary."

"And what of the city? When do we secure that?" Jarek's knuckles are white around the pommels of his blades.

Secure it.

Explore it.

Will we ever understand it?

"Now. At least a portion of it. Jarek, you will come with us to see where this road leads." A city like this *must* have a castle.

Abarrane shakes her head. "Is it wise to venture out with so little protection?"

"We are not without protection. Far from it," Jarek answers before I can, his focus on Romeria.

"He is right," I agree. "And if this Ulysede is to be our end, then so be it."

"Very well. With me, warrior." Abarrane and Zorya dismount and sprint to the nearest building, drawing a second blade each while Jarek investigates the levers at the gate.

Elisaf edges closer to me.

"Do not tell me you are afraid of a little exploration?" I tease to hide my trepidation. But Elisaf knows me too well for that to work.

"No, that is not it." He studies me closely. "Do you not feel it?"

"Feel what?"

Hope flashes in his brown eyes. "The absence of hunger."

44
ROMERIA

I halt Eros next to Zander. "Is this place real?"

"If it is not, we are all sharing the same hallucination." He's equally mesmerized by the cobblestone bridge that stretches over a river, the water's surface like blue glass. On the other end, two mammoth stone statues of winged, humanlike forms face each other, creating an archway. But beyond is the real shock, the road leading to a castle of white walls and royal blue spires, with stone-bridge walkways high in the sky, connecting the many towers.

"It will grow dark soon. Should we turn back?" Jarek's suspicious gaze is on the violet sky and the merging shadows.

Instead of answering, Zander looks toward me, waiting.

He's letting me decide.

"Not yet." I can't say how long the five of us have been exploring this hidden and vacant city, but the thought of turning back for the safety of numbers has never entered my mind. As unsettling as Ulysede leaves me, I don't feel the same foreboding that Jarek seems to. He's right, though. It'll be dark soon.

"Some light?" I gesture toward the lanterns that line the bridge and present a small flame on my fingertip.

With a smirk, Zander draws from the spark with a slight tug.

The city ignites with light, thousands of lanterns twinkling in every direction.

"Impressive."

But he shakes his head. "That was not me."

My scalp prickles. *If not Zander* ... who else here could do that?

"Whatever connection to the nymphs that has maintained this city all these millennia must be responding to your power," Gesine offers, though her forehead wrinkles with uncertainty.

"So?" I nod toward the castle. "Shouldn't we check it out?"

We lead the pack over the bridge, an energy buzzing in Zander. I sensed it as soon as we passed through the gate—he's on edge and yet excited. Hopeful.

And why shouldn't he be?

This morning, he was a fleeing king without a kingdom.

Now one waits for him to claim it.

"What are those?" Elisaf points to the winged creatures as we ride beneath them.

"The nymphs, based on one depiction the seers have seen."

"*One* depiction?" His eyes narrow. "And what would the other depictions look like?"

Gesine studies the pointed ears and spiked shoulders. "Not quite as friendly."

"She calls this friendly," Jarek mutters, urging his horse up the path.

"It's as if they built it yesterday." Zander smooths a fingertip across a bust to test for dust. It comes back clean.

Our footsteps echo as we stroll through the castle's great hall, past a grand water fountain with another pair of the winged creatures at its center, through elegant room after elegant room, their ceilings painted in murals that will surely tell of Ulysede's history, when we have time to study them.

"I believe that is a library." Elisaf points to a room with floor-to-ceiling shelves stacked with books.

"The knowledge that must wait within those walls." Gesine's path veers toward it.

"You may spend the balance of your days buried in books if you so choose, *after* we find the throne room." Zander eyes the caster. He didn't trust her wholly before, but he trusts her even less now.

"Of course, Your Highness." She swerves to rejoin us.

The throne room isn't so much a room, we discover, pushing through a set of grand doors to find ourselves outside. Trees with weeping branches and gnarly roots shelter the area, and vines bursting with tiny rose blossoms crawl across the castle's exterior, their floral perfume heady in the air. It's wild and unkempt and screams of age—so contrary to the rest of Ulysede.

And in the center is a pavilion of black stone. Thorny rose vines and ivy cling to the four carved pillars, each representing a fate. Beyond, the throne sits.

"I will check the perimeter." Jarek stalks toward dark corners, blades in hands, searching for threats.

"Your Highness." Elisaf nods upward.

We all follow his direction to see the two moons hanging in the sky. Both are crescents, though the lower, brighter one is approaching full.

"How are we seeing the blood moon when it is not Hudem?" Zander asks what is surely on everyone's mind.

Gesine shrugs, unable to offer a suggestion as she moves for the sanctum.

"This reminds me of the nymphaeum." There is no wall at the back closing off the area, but the statues of the fates are nearly identical in size and design, and a simple stone block sits in the center. Above is a similar circular opening in the pavilion's roof. I'll bet the full blood moon's light shines down over this altar like the one in Cirilea.

"Does that altar have engravings on it like this?" Gesine drags her finger along the stone's surface.

Zander shakes his head. "That altar is smooth."

I slide my finger over a letter. No childish laughter responds. "This isn't like the writing on the nymphaeum door." Or the wall outside.

Gesine cocks her head to study it closer. "I have seen this alphabet before, in the tome we discovered in Shadowhelm."

"Can you read it?" Zander asks.

"It will require effort, as I am not as proficient as some of Mordain's scribe sisters, but I might be capable. Give me a moment to try."

I wander to the dais while Gesine tries to decipher the script. There's only one throne, assembled from polished metals and stark-white branches and vines, its back soaring at least ten feet high. More of the same language scrawls along its jagged top rail.

"Odd to have it located here, is it not?" Zander has followed me over and now peers around us. "There is nowhere convenient for a gathering."

"This is *all* odd, if you ask me."

On the forest-green velvet seat is a crown that looks more like a weapon, its bony silver spikes like a skeletal hand.

And it's waiting.

"Care to claim your throne, Your Highness?" I gesture dramatically.

Zander smirks as he closes in, collecting the crown, studying it. His amusement fades, replaced by a somber expression. "I already have a throne, whether or not Atticus agrees. But this city beyond reach for millennia has opened on a whim for you, Romeria. It is as if it was expecting you all this time."

"It has been." Gesine's nervous excitement radiates off her as she climbs the steps from the sanctum. "Nymph power forged Ulysede tens of thousands of years ago, a place of refuge within this world. When they saw they had earned the fates' wrath, the nymphs froze and sealed this city, only to open again when the queen for all arrives."

My heart races. "'The queen for all'? It says that?"

"It does. Do you understand what this means?" Gesine rushes her words. "The prophecy is real, and you are at its heart."

"Which prophecy?" She has described so many.

"I think they are all connected."

"Part of a greater puzzle." A dazed look fills Zander's face. He has denied the legitimacy of these seers' visions the entire journey here. Is he happy to be wrong?

I point to the cursive along the top of the throne. "What does that say?"

Gesine's brow furrows as she interprets it. "'She who wears the crown will reign over all.' That is you, Romeria. Of that, there is no doubt."

"As I said …" Zander gently sets the spiked ornamentation on my head.

And then he does something that stalls my breath.

He drops to one knee.

The others follow. Even Jarek has reappeared and sheathed his swords to bow.

A strange, numbness washes over me. This is all happening too fast. Only months ago, I was a thief-for-hire, sent here to steal a stone. Now, I'm being handed a kingdom.

"But I don't want to be a queen."

Zander chuckles as he peers up at me. "And that is precisely why you must be one."

I reach up, tentatively stroking a finger over a sharp edge. It pricks me, drawing blood.

Childlike laughter and music curl in my ears.

"I promised you a queen's quarters, did I not?"

From my balcony, I turn to find Zander leaning against the door frame, arms folded across his broad chest. "You did."

"Does it meet your standards?" he asks with mock concern.

My gaze drifts over the spacious suite, from the murals painted on the vaulted ceilings to the grand stone fireplace to the double doors that lead into a luxurious bedroom of rich, dark fabrics. Beyond is a closet full of silk gowns and a bath chamber of copper and glass where hot water flows with a simple flick of my wrist on the knob.

"It's adequate." My new rooms are twice the size of those in Cirilea. The entire place glows with candlelight and smells of jasmine, though I haven't found a single bloom yet.

He smirks as he strolls in, his footfalls hollow against the polished marble floors.

"Have you found your king's quarters yet?"

"It's likely a dirty dungeon in the bowels of the castle. I don't believe the nymphs have any use for me." His eyes graze the enormous bed waiting for us to fill it.

"Did Jarek or Elisaf find anything interesting out there?" They left to secure the castle nearly an hour ago.

"Interesting or worrisome ... I suppose we will see which soon enough. Jarek has returned with Eden. The mortals are safely inside, and the gates are secure. The Legion will remain vigilant for threats. We will decide what to do with everyone after a night's rest."

"Abarrane?"

"She is outside at the wagons where she can properly question the sapling without the worry of disturbing anyone."

I shudder. If Abarrane has given thought to that, she must intend something especially gruesome. "Is she safe out there?"

"Loth and Horik are with her, and they can reach the first gate should they need to."

"The Ybarisans will look for me, if the message you left at Kamstead reaches them."

"Eventually," he agrees, his eyes drifting from my

unadorned head to the side table where I've left my thorny crown. "But they will not get past those gates if we do not wish them to."

"Gesine?" I ask, but I already know the answer.

"In the library, taking stock of all those rare books. Many are written in that same language. I imagine the knowledge within those pages will satisfy her curiosity until the day she dies." He leans against the balcony rail, peering out over the city landscape. "I know she has been an invaluable guide for you, but she still is and will always be Mordain. Do not be surprised when she suggests notifying her scribe sisters of this place and of you, a key caster queen, anointed by the nymphs."

"We can't keep Ulysede secret forever." What will the guild say when they learn of me?

He sighs. "No, I suppose not."

From our perch at the top of the tallest castle tower, we have a bird's-eye view of the secret city behind the mountain wall. Thousands of tiny flames twinkle in the silent night, marking streets lined with empty houses waiting for residents, shops waiting for visitors, cafés waiting for the smell of baked bread to waft from their windows. Beyond where the lights cut off is only darkness. I'm curious what I'll discover there tomorrow, in the light of day. The other side of this mountain wall, or something else unexpected?

"It seems too good to be true." What dark secrets does Ulysede keep from us? From me, its chosen queen, according to prophecy?

"I know the feeling." Zander's posture remains rigid.

"Why? You think there's something wrong?"

"Within these walls? Nothing, which is concerning for a cynic such as myself. I struggle to believe that the nymphs have afforded us a haven so grand without plans of exacting a hefty toll." He hesitates. "I did not want to mention it earlier in case it was only temporary, but my craving for mortal blood is gone."

"What do you mean, *gone*?"

"I no longer feel it. Neither does Elisaf nor the others." His gaze drags over my neck. "I can smell your Ybarisan blood, but it does not stir the same pull as before."

My heart pounds. "Does that mean the curse has ended?"

"Within Ulysede? Perhaps."

I smooth my palm across his forearm as a thrill courses through my veins. "This is what we've wanted all along, right?" An end to his need for blood.

"It is." He bites his bottom lip. "But what about Islor? The people out there will still suffer."

"So, we bring them here. Look at all these houses, waiting to be filled."

He chuckles. "This city can house thousands, yes. Tens of thousands, even. But it is nowhere near big enough for *everyone*. Not even close. I fear we have solved our problems, but Islor's will only worsen. And what kind of king would I be if I abandoned them all to it?"

Not the king he was born to be.

Not the person I love.

But … "What are you saying?" Panic stirs. "You're not going to leave me here alone, are you?

"You are not alone. You have eighty-nine mortals to rule. That is a nice, small number for a new queen. I believe Jarek would make an exemplary commander and would accept the position."

"I don't want *any* of this if you're not here." I'll leave it all—and the crown—right where I found it.

He reaches out to collect my hand, pressing his lips to the back of it. "I do not wish to, but I must help my people and my realm. If I do not, then I do not deserve to be called king. But the nymphs have given us a gift and we would be foolish to dismiss it so hastily. You must reign here." His eyes linger on the blood moon crescent. "And I have much to do outside these walls before I can ever hope to enjoy peace within them."

"You're right. You can't just turn your back on your people." I slink my arms around his waist. "So tonight, we enjoy this moment. Tomorrow, we figure out how to save Islor *together*."

45
ATTICUS

"What news from Bellcross?"

Boaz offers a curt headshake. "Nothing yet."

"Nothing short of treason, Your Highness." Adley picks at a loose thread on his silk jacket. "My contacts put the traitors in the city three weeks ago. That is plenty of time for Lord Rengard to send a message."

My teeth grind as I pace around the war room table.

Adley's contacts.

I'm fucking tired of hearing about Adley's contacts.

But not as tired as I am of hearing Adley.

I knew Zander would go to Theon and that Theon would help rather than betray him. But now what? The Lord of Bellcross is beloved in the west. Punish him and my enemies will reproduce like rabbits overnight.

I make a point of putting my back to Adley when I ask, "And Lord Telor?"

"They are sweeping through the northern villages. Zander has come and gone with the Ybarisan traitor and her caster."

"To what outcome? Tell me it wasn't as bad as Freywich." I will admit, news of that slaughter surprised me. I didn't think

Zander had it in him to murder all those keepers and make a spectacle of it.

"Worse, I fear. They killed many soldiers, beheaded the Lord of Norcaster, and pillaged their supplies. Dozens of mortals and winter stores were taken before they continued. He and that caster of Neilina's unleashed their power on the town square."

"Leave it to Zander to get tangled up with another caster after the last one betrayed him so thoroughly." I study the map. "And they're heading north? We know this?"

"It is what we've heard and what makes sense. She will be looking for her Ybarisan army, if she hasn't already found them."

I can't imagine what good Romeria thinks a few hundred or her soldiers will be against thousands of mine. Then again, they're gifted in ways mine are not, and their elven affinities may prove dangerous.

"It is only a matter of time before we find them. They cannot go anywhere. They will be trapped."

I study the map on the table. "Which is why this move makes little sense. Zander's not stupid." Though he *is* desperate, and more familiar with Venhorn's caves than any of us.

"The exiled king turned on his crown and his realm for that treacherous spider," Boaz says gruffly. "How he lost his way so utterly, I cannot fathom."

I can. I escorted that same treacherous spider south from the rift, her charm weaving an alluring spell that so utterly blinded me, I would have done anything she asked of me by the time we reached Cirilea.

I'm not proud of what I coveted.

I'm even less proud of what I took.

But my brother is still caught in her web, with no hope of extricating himself, which is why I had to save him from himself the day of the tournament.

"Might I suggest, it would be a valiant campaign for you as the new king to ride to Venhorn with a contingent and face off against him?" Adley says. "After the wedding, of course."

"Oh, *of course*." I feign a frown. *After* next week's wedding, so Saoirse is firmly entrenched on the throne should something untoward happen to me.

To Boaz, I ask, "And what of the poison?"

"Reports continue to come in daily. Too many to read, Your Highness. It is spreading."

And I do not know how to stop it.

A knock sounds at the door.

"Come in," I bark, welcoming the interruption.

The guard opens it with a bow.

Annika sweeps in, her lengthy blond curls tied at her nape. "You summoned me?" She poorly hides her contempt for me beneath a shining veneer.

"Yes." I wave a dismissive hand at the others. "Leave us."

Only when the door closes behind Adley's back do I allow a breath of relief.

"What's wrong? You don't like the feel of his slippery tongue sliding in and out of your ear?" she mocks. "I'm sure his daughter's will be *so much* more pleasant."

Annika has not been shy with her opinion of my betrothal since I announced it. I can't tell if she's so vehemently opposed to it on principle, or if her ego can't bear the idea of bowing to Saoirse. "I'm trying to save Islor."

"You think uniting with Kettling will save Islor?" She laughs, but it is without mirth. "That will only tear it apart faster."

"That alone won't save Islor, you are right." I hesitate because I know she will hate this even more than she hates her future sister-in-law. "Which is why I've decided you will marry Tyree."

Her face drains of color. "Are you insane?" she hisses.

"No. Actually, I am quite sane, unlike the last king."

"I can't marry him. His blood is toxic!"

"Then don't feed off him. I know that'll be challenging for you, but you can resist."

She swallows, searching for an angle out of this. "What about the prince from Skatrana? I'm betrothed to him."

Now it's my turn to laugh. "The human? For one, you can't get to Skatrana to marry him, and that marriage is no longer advantageous to Islor. What we need is an open path to Ybaris." Now more than ever.

"Neilina will never agree to this."

"You let me worry about what Neilina will allow." She's lost both children and her husband—though I doubt she cares about the latter, seeing as it was her order, and possibly her hand, that drove the merth blade through his heart.

"Marry him, and then what? You cannot be foolish enough to release him from his cell."

"It will be a long time before he walks freely," I admit.

"And do not *dare* suggest I consummate this farce," she scoffs.

"He is not *that* bad, is he? I've even heard some call him handsome."

Her face twists with disgust.

"We are all required to do things that are not necessarily pleasant in the name of Islor." The thought of my lips touching Saoirse's—let alone other parts of her—makes me shudder.

Another knock sounds.

It's never ending. "Enter."

Boaz strolls in.

"And if I do not agree with this, will you have your henchman kill me as he tried to kill our brother?" Annika scowls at the captain of the king's guard.

I sigh. When I discovered Boaz had given the order to fire arrows at a boat carrying Zander, I nearly executed him on the spot. But I need people around me I can trust, and they are too far and too few at the moment. "What is it, Boaz?"

"I apologize for the interruption, but this arrived, and I thought you should see it right away." He hands me a letter.

I frown at the seal—black with silver speckles. "I don't recognize this name … Ulysede. Where is that? Near Udrel?"

"I have never heard of this place before, Your Highness, which is why I brought it straight here."

I tear open the seal.

FATE & FLAME, BOOK 3

The Fate and Flame series will continue with Book Three. Follow K.A. Tucker on social media or subscribe to her newsletter to receive details when available.

ACKNOWLEDGMENTS

Every time I start a book, I have an idea of where it will go, but it usually veers off course somewhere along the line. This one took a sharp right, surprising me in the best way. The more I dig into this world, the more I love writing in it.

A book doesn't produce itself (even if the writer has been hiding in her office, avoiding messages, and binging on coffee and fraktels for four months straight to hit her deadline) and I have a few people I'd like to thank.

Jenn Sommersby, thank you for your editing prowess as you wade through all my eyes and gazes and tones. I feel fortunate to have found you all those years ago. Never leave me.

Chanpreet Singh, thank you for your scrupulous peepers. You are a delight.

Hang Le, you are a true talent. I can't wait to see what we cook up next.

Nina Grinstead and the VPR team, thank you for your enthusiasm and expertise.

Stacey Donaghy of Donaghy Literary Group, thank you for championing my career and getting this series into the hands of foreign readers.

To Amélie, Tami, and Sarah, for helping with my Facebook reader group.

My family, thank you for keeping me afloat.

ABOUT THE AUTHOR

K.A. Tucker writes captivating stories with an edge.

She is the internationally bestselling author of the Ten Tiny Breaths, Burying Water and The Simple Wild series, He Will Be My Ruin, Until It Fades, Keep Her Safe, Be the Girl, and Say You Still Love Me. Her books have been featured in national publications including USA Today, Globe & Mail, Suspense Magazine, Publisher's Weekly, Oprah Mag, and First for Women.

K.A. Tucker currently resides in a quaint town outside of Toronto.

Learn more about K.A. Tucker and her books at katuckerbooks.com

Printed in Great Britain
by Amazon

83500147R00267